The Knowing

Al Bates

Blue Star Productions

THE KNOWING
A Blue Star Productions
Publication

No part of this book may be reproduced or transmitted without written permission from the publisher.

This is a work of fiction. The characters, names, incidents, dialogue and plot are a product of the author's imagination.

ISBN 1-881542-26-2
Copyright © 1996 by Al Bates
First Printing: July 1996

Published by Blue Star Productions
A Division of Book World, Inc.
9666 E Riggs Rd #194
Sun Lakes AZ 84\5248
Ph/Fax: 602.895.7995
E-Mail: BDebolt@aol.com

THE KNOWING

Chapter One:
The Find

MYRA WAS WORKING AT home the day the call came in.

A late October cold front had come through the day before dropping the morning temperatures into the low fifties. She and John had celebrated the end of another long hot Texas summer by cuddling in the cool covers before he left for the Center.

Resisting turning on the central heat, she had bundled in a comfortable pair of faded sweats and socks and nestled into her cozy work habitat — a pile of big soft pillows against the king-sized headboard, laptop on a serving tray across her legs, and photos, news clippings, cassette recorder and research notes scattered all around her.

It was a feel-good day, cool, bright and sunny. A day she would search for an excuse to be doing something outside. She'd used up all those days. There was nowhere she had to be but right where she was, writing. She'd put off her feature article on the budgetary wastes in the space industry hoping she'd find an explosive angle to tie a rumored scandal to one of the candidates in a lackluster congressional election. She was facing a weekend deadline on the *Chronicle's* voting pullout section and she had no verified proof that would make her story the least bit interesting. She stared out the patio window for long pauses, searching the brightly colored leaves of a pistachio tree for the right words. What was it about pistachios, Chinese tallows, or whatever they were called, that made them the only trees in South Texas to flash colors that bright? There could be a story there.

When the phone rang she let it go three times while she finished putting down a sudden inspiration.

"Yeah," she snapped before realizing she wasn't in her *Chronicle* office. "Well, yes, this is John Sherman's number . . . yes, the UFO investigator," she said, cautiously. "Who's this? Roland Barrett? Oh, yes, the rancher. West Columbia. Yes, I do remember. This is Myra Bennett. Yes, the newspaper lady with the cameras. No, John's not here right now. He's over at the Center. What's happened? The little aliens get another cow?"

Memory of the ranch incident flashed through Myra's mind . . .

She, John and another Clear Lake UFO Club member, Bryan Hayfield, had met rancher Roland Barrett through a West Columbia veterinarian almost a year ago when one of Roland's cows had been mysteriously mutilated. His cattle ranch was ten to fifteen miles the other side of West Columbia. In the Barrett's north forty, standing over the bloodless bovine carcass with its tongue, eyes, ears and particular sex organs surgically removed, John told Roland and his wife, Ethel, what they were up against; the facts. Myra snapped off some photos.

"No, it's not some satanic cult or some kind of strange beast you never heard of," John had told Barrett. "It's just these little aliens in their space craft. That's why you don't see any footprints, stomped grass, or mess around the body. They capture the animal in a paralytic blue beam, lift it up into their craft, do their business and then drop what they don't need right back where you found it."

"Say what?" Roland gasped, pushing his sweat-stained Stetson back off his forehead. "Aliens? Ya mean, things flyin' around in space?" He looked at Ethel, they had seen such things on TV, but never really believed it. Science fiction. Could it be true, and those little creatures had butchered his cow?

"That's right." John said. "Skinny little gray beings about four-and-a-half feet tall, with big heads and big black shiny eyes. We've never actually seen them do it, but there are eyewitness reports that back up everything I just told you. See those incisions? They're done with hi-tech lasers. No one on Earth has portable equipment that can do that. And, as horrible as it may sound, they do all that while the poor animal's still alive."

"Oh, my God!" Ethel gagged behind a hand over her nose. "Why on Earth would they do such a thing?"

"For food," John shrugged. Strands of his flaxen hair fell across his sweaty brow. "They grind up all the innards with the blood and smear the mixture on their bodies. Their skin inhales it, then excretes it."

"I've been in the cattle business a long time," Roland said, "and I ain't never seen anything like this. Never even heard of such a thing. Little space people stealin' cows."

"What on Earth's gonna happen next?" Ethel gasped.

"Where're these little people from?" Roland asked, squinting in the bright sunlight. "Mars?"

"Mars. The Moon." John said. "Stop-offs. But this particular group's home planet is Zeta Reticuli," John said. "A planet in a star system some fifteen, sixteen light years from here." He knew the Barretts had no idea about stars and planets and space time. No need getting into any details.

"That's why we call 'em, Zetas," Bryan added.

"Hmmm," Roland mused, shaking his head. "That sounds like a long trip. I guess they gotta eat somewhere. I don't mind givin' a stranger a meal, but I don't take to anybody stealin' from me."

"I don't think you'd want to welcome these strangers," Bryan said.

Myra took more pictures.

"Does the government know about this?" Roland asked.

"Yes, sorry to say, they do," John nodded. "But they'll deny it. They're afraid of them. They know they don't have the technology to stop them. So, the Zetas take what they want — more than a thousand head a year."

John had chosen not to tell the Barretts about the highly secretive meeting in the early fifties between the Sirian/Zetas, MJ-12 and President Eisenhower at Edwards AFB, where a treaty was agreed upon, whereas, the Zetas were given rights to unlimited human abductions and cattle mutilations in exchange for three flyable space craft. Under the circumstances, that would have been too much for the Barretts to handle. There wasn't anything left to do but document the kill. John left them with one of his UFO Club cards and asked them to call if they ever had another visit from the aliens.

. . . Myra listened now as rancher Barrett told her his latest story, stuttering and stumbling with excitement. "No," she gasped, remembering and picturing Roland's rugged old face, his freckled lips quivering in excitement. "Are you sure? Did you touch it? Well, don't. God, please, don't. What size was it?" The laptop's cursor blinked impatiently. Her mind raced. She couldn't think of what to say. She had to talk to John. She removed the tray and computer from over her legs and sat on the edge of the bed. Her heart rate jumped ten beats with the adrenalin charge.

"Look, Mr. Barrett, I don't know what to tell you," she stammered. "Don't do anything. Don't call anyone else. Don't say anything, okay? Look, let me call John, he'll know what to do. Just give me your number and I'll have him call you as soon as he can." She pulled the computer toward her and typed his phone number into her text. "Look, don't do anything, don't say anything," she repeated. "Stay right where you are, by the phone. John's going to call you right back. Who else knows?"

Just he and his wife, Ethel. "Okay. Y'all stay right there. John's gonna call you right back. Bye."

She hung up, closed her eyes, sank back in the pillows and took several deep breaths to calm herself. "Thank you, Father," she whispered prayerfully. She sat up, wrote Barrett's number down, clicked off the computer, shoved the tray away and punched in John's office number.

John answered.

"Hon, our world just did a flip-flop. Drop everything and get home as fast as you can."

JOHN SHERMAN WAS a project engineer for McDonnell-Douglas Corporation at NASA. He had been there for twenty-five years, through Gemini, Apollo and now the Shuttle and Space Station. Enough seniority for no one to question his calmly hanging up a phone, taking his coat and briefcase and leaving. Sometimes he would tell a secretary where he was going, a sudden meeting, or something. This time he was thinking of only one thing . . . go.

He couldn't imagine what the emergency could be. The only thing they never spoke of on his office phone was anything to do with UFO business. If it was that, she'd just ask him to call her from another phone, never, *get home fast*.

The ten-minute trip from his office to his townhouse's back door took him eight this time.

When he came through the door his inquisitive eyes met the excitement in Myra's. She leaned against the breakfast bar waving a note paper and grinning, about to burst with the news.

"Roland Barrett," she gushed. "Remember him? The rancher the other side of West Columbia?"

He took the note paper and saw Roland's name and number. "Roland Barrett?" he muttered to himself, then, "Yes, yes, the mutilation." He frowned, puzzled at her grin and shrugged. "What? The Zetas take another cow?"

"He found a space craft sitting on his ranch this morning," she said, as calmly as she could around her broad grin.

"What?" he gasped incredulously.

"A space craft! An alien space craft! Can you believe it?"

"Are you — is he sure?"

"He described it to me over the phone," she said and threw her arms around him. "It's a shiny little saucer all in one piece, he said. Not a scratch or dent on it. Just sitting there, big as you please."

"Are you kidding?"

"Would I kid about this, hon? It's Christmas come early! Call him. He's waiting. He doesn't know what to do."

John took her note to the phone and punched in the number. Listening to the rings he watched her slide onto a barstool and literally glow with anticipation. He had never seen her shiver from excited anxiety.

"He say how big it was?" he asked.

"About twenty, twenty-five feet across," she said.

Roland answered.

"Mr. Barrett," John said in his jovial, business voice. "Myra tells me you have something for us. You did? That's hard to believe, but . . . That's great! Yes, I see. No, she told me some, but not all of it. Yes, go ahead. I'm listening."

Myra grinned, watching John's excitement grow as he listened to the story Roland told her earlier. She went to the coffee pot and motioned if he wanted a cup. He nodded. She poured two cups and handed him one.

He sipped while he heard how Roland had been out in his lower pastures early that morning looking for some missing cows that must have gotten lost in that storm the other night when the front came through. He had been riding his horse along the edge of a gully, about a mile or two from the house, to see if maybe some heifers had gotten down in the mud and water and couldn't get out. He hadn't been hunting too long when he saw the sun reflecting off a strange object. Bright as a mirror. Couldn't miss it. He went over to take a look, and lo and behold, it was one of those space ships. "It was sitting down in the middle of some scrub oaks, like maybe someone was trying to hide it, or it could've landed in there, but it would've had to come straight down, 'cause it was sorta caught in the trees."

"Look, Mr. Barrett," John interrupted. "Have you seen anyone on your road this morning? Military vehicles, trucks? Going up and down, like they're looking for something? Any military helicopters flying low over your pastures?"

He said he hadn't.

"Good. That's good," John sighed. "Okay, look, if anyone shows up at your door, tell them you don't know anything, haven't seen anything. We're on our way down." He looked at the clock. "Give us about an hour. One o'clock. Okay? Fine. Yes. Thank you. We'll see you then. Oh, wait. Tell me again how to get there. Yes. Uh huh. Okay. Right. We will. Thank you. Bye."

He hung up and grabbed Myra, almost spilling her coffee. They hugged and he swung her around as he yelped and laughed.

"Yes! Yes! Yes!" he shouted. "We've got one! We've got one!" They laughed. "Oh, baby do you know what this means? It's great! We've got 'em! No one's gonna deny it now! What a beautiful day!"

"Come on." he said. "Get changed. We have to hurry. They might be on to it already."

"Can I go like this?"

They scurried for the bedroom. "No. Jeans, boots. It's probably ankle deep in mud. Bushes and woods, remember?"

In the bedroom he grabbed the phone again. "We gotta call Bryan," he said. "He needs to see this." He punched in Bryan's number and glanced at her work scattered on the bed. She had already stripped out of her warm-ups and was searching for an old sweater and jeans. "Bryan!" he said after Bryan answered. "Take an early and long lunch. Myra and I'll meet you out front in twenty minutes. We've got something to show you. No. Can't say. Tell you when we see you."

A PSYCHIATRIST, BRYAN Mayfield's job at NASA consisted mostly of testing astronauts, crew members and other personnel. He and fellow psychiatrist, Marsha Adams, also handled some of the personal problems of anyone on the NASA payroll. Bryan had been at NASA for about nine years and a member of the Clear Lake UFO Club from the first time he had heard about it from John, who was its founder.

John and Myra pulled up in front of Bryan's building in her Jag sedan. Folding his six-four frame into the back seat, Bryan noticed their casual dress and Myra busy loading her cameras.

"What is this?" Bryan asked, bewildered by their excitement. "What're you doing and where're we going?"

"Bryan, you won't believe this," Myra grinned excitedly. "You remember the cattle mutilation on that ranch outside of West Columbia about a year ago? Rancher's name was Barrett, Roland Barrett?"

Bryan recalled the incident, easily. "Yes. What about it?"

John headed out of the Center and west on NASA Road 1.

"While looking for some strays this morning," Myra said, slowly and dramatically. "Mr. Barrett came across an alien space craft hidden in some trees on his ranch."

Bryan's jaw dropped as he stared at her. He glanced

at John's verifying nod and grin. "You're kidding!" he gasped.

Holding her wide grin, she shook her head.

"You're not kidding."

She giggled. "Are you ready for this? We're on our way to see it. Can you handle that?"

Bryan tossed his jacket, loosened his tie and whooped. "Yahooo! This is unbelievable!"

"No, no, no," Myra laughed. "It's incredible!"

"I don't wanna believe it until I see it," Bryan cautioned.

"Yes, we know," Myra grinned. "But isn't it wonderful to imagine? How good can luck be?"

WHEREVER HE FELT safe to do so, John shattered the speed limits across FM 528, around Alvin on Texas 35, cut off at FM 1462 to Rosharon and on toward Texas 36.

"He said no one's been around," John said. "If it came in last night, they're bound to have seen it. I don't see how it could have gotten through Cheyenne Mountain, and surely not Pine Gap." They knew both government installations to be top secret Norad radar stations with highly sensitive grids that covered the entire earth. Any size solid object, coming in or going out, would be picked up on their radar scopes. "And, if it's possible we've beat them to it, I think we should take it ourselves."

"How? Take it where?" Bryan asked.

"I don't know. Do it like they do. Truck it."

"How? We don't have the organization," Bryan pointed out. "A shuttle craft would be too big to hide."

"He said it wasn't but about twenty feet across. We can do it."

"Where'll we hide it?"

"I don't know. We'll find a place. Think!"

"Yes. Start thinking," Myra urged. "A place away

from everything, everyone. Big. Deserted.''

"A warehouse?" Bryan mused. "No. Too many people around.''

"An abandoned hangar.''

"You know of any out in the middle of nowhere?''

"Frank might know one," Bryan suggested. Frank Mason was a charter pilot and a member of the Club. "An abandoned airport?''

"No. Too obvious. How about an old abandoned barn?''

"Yes. Something like that.''

"We might be getting ahead of ourselves," John said. "Let's wait until we see the ship first.''

COMING DOWN HIGHWAY 36 they took a right at West Columbia and headed out Highway 35 toward Old Ocean. Between Old Ocean and Van Vleck, John slowed as they searched the road's north side for the Barrett ranch entrance.

"I don't know, it might be just a coincidence," John said, "But we had the same weather conditions right before the crash at Socorro and the crippled ship up in Dayton. Stormy, lightning, rain. This could be a crashed ship.''

"Did he say it was crashed — smashed?" Bryan asked.

"No," Myra said to the road ahead. "He said it didn't have a dent, or a scratch, as far as he could see.''

"It could still be a crash," Bryan said. "Ever heard of any aliens parking their ship for any great length of time?''

"Slow down," Myra said. "I think that's it.'' She pointed ahead. John had recognized the arched entrance gate before she pointed and was slowing to make the turn.

They crossed the drainage ditch's culvert bridge and rattled across the cattle guard to the gate. The rail fence came up to two brick columns supporting a metal archway with a circled B in its center. Like Roland had said, you couldn't miss it.

An old pickup with railing stakes was parked at the side door of the house. An old house up on blocks and a wide porch running around two sides. A saddled bay with white stockings stood under one of the five tall, spreading oaks that shaded the house and tool sheds with its browning leaves. Several peacocks and a line of ducks scurried from the drive as they pulled up to the front porch. Before they could get out Roland and his wife popped out the front door.

"Hi, Roland," John said, coming around the car and shaking Roland's hand as he came down the steps.

Roland smiled. "Sure glad to see ya." His old Stetson was cocked to one side exposing thinning red hair graying above his ears and the edge of his hard tan.

"You remember Myra and Bryan," John said. They shook hands.

"Yes, yes. How ya'll doin'? Ya'll 'member Ethel." He nodded at his wife. She stepped down a step, shyly brushing her hands on her apron and shook their hands.

"Well, is the craft still here?" John asked.

"Yep," Roland said with a quick glance toward the side of the house. "Far as I know. Hadn't seen it fly off or come out this way. 'Spose it's still down there in the trees." He started off around the house and they followed. Myra reached into the car and grabbed her cameras. "Might as well go take a look," he said. Ducks and peacocks scattered in front of them.

"Haven't seen any unusual activity around?" John asked.

"Nope," Roland shook his head.

"Strange," John mused, glancing at Bryan and Myra.

"Don't reckon you'll be able to drive your car down there. I was on my horse when I seen it. There's still about two foot a water in the gully, but you can see where it was up to the top yesterday. I got some horses and saddles. You folks ride?'' He glanced at their apprehensive shrugs.

"Well, I don't know," John said. "Is it too far to walk?"

"Probably over 'couple a miles. I don't wanna do it," he said. "Tell ya what. I got a big tractor. Let's go down to the barn and see what we can rig up."

They headed for the big barns.

"Just you and Ethel out here?" John asked.

"Yep. Don't have any ranch hands right now. Don't really need any. Already took most a the herd to market. I can find me some Mexican hands when I need 'em."

ROLAND BACKED HIS big tractor out of the lean-to shed and hooked it to a hay wagon. He threw a couple of hay bales on the front end of the wagon and covered them with a fairly clean canvas tarp. They climbed aboard and the makeshift tram chugged off toward the north forty. A smelly black exhaust swirled above and away in a alight breeze.

Not far into the pasture trip they saw what a difficult time they would have had walking. The tractor's big treads were already clogged with the thick black mud. Roland kept the big diesel in pulling gear most of the way. What standing water he couldn't go around he splashed right through. He ran over low brush and crunched fallen limbs into the ground. Small groups of cattle chewed their cud and stared quizzically. Roland whistled and hollered at them like he knew them by name. The tractor noise kept the conversation down to a minimum, but after about twenty minutes Roland was saying something and pointing to a ridge up ahead. They heard a "right over there," and their anticipation quickened their pulse. Myra snapped a few shots.

The top of the ridge dropped in front of them and they

saw a part of the ship through the trees. Roland pointed it out but he didn't have to. The shiny space craft sparkled in the afternoon sun. The sight was magnificent, bringing a shiver of excitement that raised the fine hairs on their necks. After all the years of hoping and praying for such a moment, they couldn't find the words to describe it.

"Is it true?" Bryan grinned. "Don't pinch me if I'm dreaming."

"No dream," John smiled. "It's really true."

Still unable to believe they were the first to the ship, they scoured the area and searched the sky.

"Isn't she beautiful?" Myra said and tried capturing the moment in as many pictures as she could. She jumped from the wagon and walked along the ridge snapping pictures.

"That's incredible," Bryan sighed. "Think of the distance that thing has traveled. The technology. What a jewel!"

As Roland had said, the ship was in a stand of scrub oak near the top of the far side of a gully running with two feet of muddy water. How'd it get in there? Not a broken limb, not even scraped bark. How in the world would they get a ship that size out of such an impossible situation?

"Can we get across?" John asked.

"Tractor can't. Too slippery," Roland said. "Horse could. Ya could wade if'n ya didn't mind gettin' wet and muddy. There's a place right down there apiece that's not too steep."

John called to Myra. She snapped a picture and came back.

"Ya'll go ahead," Roland said. "I'll wait right here."

John and Bryan started down the ridge toward the ford.

"Where're we going?" Myra asked, shouldering a camera strap.

"We're going to wade across," Bryan said.

"You might want to take off your boots and roll up

your pants,'' John said. ''It's gonna be cold.''

They made their way to the less steep place in the gully, took off their shoes and boots and rolled up their pants. After carefully easing down the embankment, they waded across the gully and up the other side.

They crept up to the ship as if they expected a door to fly open and would be zapped by a beam or something. Crows cackled in a tree close by and water rippled in the gully.

''That thing's probably hot,'' Bryan said. ''We should've brought a geiger counter.''

''Too late now,'' John said. ''We'll just have to take our chances.''

The ship was wedged between three scrub oaks and about eye level below the ridge. Myra snapped more pictures as they moved within a few yards. John and Bryan had their palms extended flat as if they expected to feel rays of heat.

''How do you think it got in there?'' Bryan said.

John shrugged. ''Doesn't figure,'' he said. They could see that none of the trees' branches were broken or burnt. ''Strange. Whoever put it there didn't want it easily seen, or moved.''

The craft was round and smooth as a burnished pot. About twenty feet in diameter at its widest point, rounded to the bottom and to its high domed top. It had no landing gear nor visible windows. They could see no rivets, construction seams, or means of entry.

John edged around the closest oak and cautiously extended his hand. He didn't feel any heat and he touched it. It felt cool in the shade and warm where the sun hit it. Myra snapped pictures of him touching the ship.

Comfortable with the assumption they could safely approach the ship all three began a closer examination, John and Bryan feeling their hands along its sides and Myra taking their picture.

"It's closed up tight," Bryan said. "There's no indication of any openings whatsoever."

"Not even a window," John said from the other side. "What d'ya make of it?"

"Not a Zeta ship," John said. "At least it's not anything like the ones we saw at Groom Lake."

"What then?" Bryan asked. "Whose?"

"Shuttle craft of some kind," John said. "Maybe carrying anywhere from one to ten beings, depending on their size. It's been here long enough for its fuel and power source to cool. Its exterior seems strong and resilient enough to withstand an impact without showing a mark of any kind." He applied pressure underneath and the ship rocked slightly. "And it seems light."

"Think we can move her?"

John backed away and surveyed the situation. He nodded. "We'll have to take out that tree." He pointed to the tree at the top of the ridge.

"We'll need some help. I don't know if we'll be able to get any heavy equipment in here, but I think we can do it."

"Don't you two see something strange here?" Myra said. "It's wedged in those trees as if the trees grew up around it. There're no skid marks or broken bushes."

"Maybe it went in sideways and settled like that," John said.

"What if they're still in there? Couldn't get the door open because of the trees?" Myra said. "What if they suddenly decide to take off again?"

"They would've already, if they could," John said.

The three stepped back and studied these possibilities.

"What if their friends come looking for them?" Bryan added.

"A lot of ifs." John stepped up to the ship and knocked on its side. He waited, listened. Nothing. He knocked again, louder and longer. After a short, silent wait, he stepped back and shrugged. "I don't like it being out here. Someone could report it to the wrong people. The military could already be looking for it. A flyover could spot it. I say, let's get it under cover and then we can see what's inside.''

Suddenly, a rustling in the tree above caught their attention. Looking up, they saw branches of leaves brushing from side to side, as if something was moving quickly. A big thick limb had broken off and was crashing toward them, leaves and twigs flying all around. They jumped aside as the heavy limb hit the ground, bounced and settled in the tall grass. And as they looked at it, the dark limb took the slick shape of a snake and slithered off under the ship and into the pastures.

"Geesh! What was that?'' Myra gasped.

"Snake,'' John said. "Big one. Must have been four feet or more.''

"In a tree? What kind of snake climbs trees?''

"Looked like a king snake,'' Bryan said. "They'll do that, climb trees. Maybe whoever owns this ship put it there to stand guard. The Zetas maybe. We know they're reptilian.'' Bryan chuckled at his reference.

"I've seen Zeta ships,'' John said, giving the ship another once over. "This isn't a Zeta ship.''

"No? Then whose?'' Myra asked.

"God only knows.''

THEY CROSSED BACK OVER the gully and told Roland their plans to move the ship. He agreed, saying he'd help any way he could. John asked if there was a dry, less steep place to cross the gully with a heavy truck. Roland said not on his ranch.

John and Bryan took the tarp from the hay bales, waded back across the gully and covered the ship the best they could. While doing this they fashioned a mental plan to get the ship out of the trees and across the gully.

"See that tall oak beyond the ship?'' John pointed it

out to Roland. "Do you have enough cable to stretch from about half way up that tree, above the ship, across the gully and to about the same height on that oak over here?"

Roland studied the distance. "That's about fifty, sixty yards," he figured. "Yep. Probably could find that much."

"What about a block tackle, a heavy pulley and some heavy rope?"

John's plan formed in Roland's head and he smiled. "Ya gonna lift her up and pulley her across the gully?"

"And drop her on a flat bed truck under this tree," John smiled, confidently.

Roland grinned a squint and nodded. "Yep. Think I got just what you'll need."

"A snake fell outta one of those trees," Myra said. "Did you see it?"

"Yep," Roland frowned. "King snake. Name's Arthur. See him 'round all the time. Friendly. Keeps the place shed of pesky rodents. Likes to climb trees." Roland smiled. "Can scare the pee outta the way he gets down."

ANXIETY AND EXCITEMENT made for a hectic, mind-probing trip back toward Clear Lake. Getting the ship off the ranch seemed easy enough; they'd rent a big tractor and trailer. Their biggest problem was where to hide a ship that size while they explored its technology. It was easy for the secret government, MJ-12, to hide their's. They had mountain caves and underground bunkers. East Texas was flat, open country. And, even if they could, they didn't have time to dig any caves.

"You remember the Henley case, about twenty-five years ago?" Myra said. "Where these guys killed some young boys and buried their bodies in a storage shed? No one ever expected a thing. They got away with it for years."

"That was a little boat storage shed," Bryan pointed out.   "Storage shed. *Big* storage shed," Myra mused.

"Think. What business do we have around here that has
big storage sheds? An oil field storage shed! I've seen
them. They work a field until it goes dry, then abandon the
sheds. I know. I wasn't married to the oil business all
those years for nothing. There's an old dry field just this
side of Alvin," she added. "Let's stop by and have a
look."

Next order of business was to select at least two more
loyal, tight-lipped members of the Club who could contrib-
ute some expertise to the task of exploring the ship's
technology and the possibility of eventually flying it. All
three agreed that one of them should be their close friend,
Frank Mason, the retired airline pilot, who had flown John
and Myra to Nevada and had taken the tour of Groom Lake
with them. Frank had actually been inside one of the alien
crafts and had hands-on telepathic instructions from one of
the little Gray Zeta robots. The other, they finally decided,
should be Boyd Holstead, a NASA structural engineer, who
knew the working parts of every rocket and space craft
from the early Mercury capsules to the Shuttles.

Who should know and who shouldn't? The fewer who
knew, the better their secret. Myra and John lived together
with no family. Bryan was twice divorced and was between
girlfriends at the moment. Frank and Boyd were married,
but their wives and families were not members of the Club
and could care less about joining. Out of over a hundred
signed, dues-paying Club members there were probably less
than a dozen couple memberships. The others were single
or had partners who didn't share their interest in any
extraterrestrial elements. Most of these wives and husbands
viewed their partners eccentric hobby as swapouts — "He
has his UFOs and I have my bingo, or my church group, or
my gambling, or whatever," and, "She can have that as
long as I can have my huntin', fishin' and TV ballgames."
Frank and Boyd's wives fit the first category. It would be
nice if they could tell the rest of the Club members; they all
had believed just as hard in the truth that someday they'd

find an answer. But the security risk was too great. So, it was settled, just the five.

COMING UP HIGHWAY 35 west of Alvin they searched the open fields on both sides of the highway for signs of the abandoned oil field road.

"It'll probably have a triangular gate across it," Myra said, to help. "You'll probably see some idle horsehead pumps."

A few miles after she said it, they spotted an iron pipe gate, a rutted shell road and the rusted pumps standing above the tall grass. John backed the Jag, turned into the road, gunned it through the high weeds around the gate and back onto the road beyond. They passed horsehead pumps — some pumping, most not. John dodged potholes and standing puddles. Eventually, the shell road became just two worn dirt and oil paths. They bounced and twisted, the Jag a speedboat in a sea of weeds, in places the rag weeds beside the old path were six-feet tall. Soon their search began to seem futile. They were looking for a wide place to turn around when they topped a little rise and wound through a stand of oak and pistachio and there it was — a big, barn-size, rusting tin; oil field tool shed. Exactly what they wanted.

John pulled the Jag off the path onto a weed-covered strip of oil encrusted shell in front of the building. Anxiously, they got out and began their inspection. From outside, it seemed the right size, about seventy by a hundred feet and maybe fifteen feet to its roof. Its shell and oil apron went around one side to two tall, wide-sliding doors. They pecked through cracks in its siding.

"Could we find anything better, or what?" John asked.

"Needs a lot of work," Bryan said.

"So," Myra said. "We can do it."

They searched the area in all directions. "Not a soul, or house, in sight for miles. Isolated. Perfect," John observed.

Signs on the building said it was owned by the South Texas Oil Tool Company. Myra wrote down their fading emergency number.

By five o'clock they were back at the Center letting Bryan off at his car. John and Myra left after saying they would call Frank and Boyd and set a meeting at their townhouse around eight.

"THIS IS UNBELIEVABLE!" Boyd gasped. He and Frank were carefully studying each print from Myra's cameras. She had taken the rolls by a one-hour photo place. The operators only check to see if its a good print and if there's any nude or porno stuff. After weeks and weeks of amateur photos they go blind to other subject matter. When she paid, all that the manager said was, "Thanks. Come again." She was relieved she didn't have to lie.

"What a break, he called you before he called the Sheriff!" Frank said.

"Pure luck," Myra said. "He had John's card. He matched the picture on the card to the craft."

"What kind of ship is it?" Frank asked, holding a picture to the light. "It doesn't look like any of the Zeta's we saw."

"It isn't," John said. "It has to be anyone else's but the Zeta's."

"Really? Why?"

"Just the fact MJ-12 wasn't right on top of it," John shrugged. "That ship must've time-traveled. That's the only way it could have gotten through the Norad grid and between those trees. Zetas don't travel the time portals."

"No bodies," Boyd said, flipping through pictures.

"No bodies. But we don't know what's inside."

"No door?"

"Not even the slightest slit."

"Aliens can walk through walls," Bryan said. "Problem is, we'll need to find the door."

"That's true," Boyd nodded. "For sure."

"Okay, here's the deal," John said. "We take the day off tomorrow. Is that a problem for anyone?" They glanced at each other. Boyd and Frank shook their heads. "Good. I've reserved a rig and trailer for tomorrow morning. Boyd, you still have a valid truck license?" Boyd nodded. "You and Frank pick up the truck first thing. Be sure they also give you the large tarp and wide load signs I ordered. Either of you have a chain saw?" Boyd nodded. "Bring it. Bryan and I will be waiting for you on the 528 side of the Mall. I've requested a motorcycle escort from the DPS. He's to meet us at the ranch entrance at four. We have to have the ship on the truck and covered by at least three. Myra is going to contact the tool company in the morning and make arrangements to rent the shed. If everything goes as planned she should have the keys and the shed open by the time we arrive with the ship."

"That's cutting it pretty close," Frank said.

"I know," John sighed. "But we leave that ship in the open too long and we lose it. We have to go for it and hope everything falls into place. We're used to tight schedules and team work. Everyone does their part and it gets done.

"None of this gets out. It's the five of us and that's it. No one else, under any circumstances. Anyone have a problem with that?"

Bryan and Boyd shook their heads.

"Loretta's always wanted to see one of those things," Frank said. "After I told her what we saw at Groom Lake she's just never believed me."

"Sorry, she'll have to wait," John said. "If and when we get her to fly, everyone's going to see it."

Frank grinned. "Yeah? Where're we going to fly her?"

"Someplace where we'll get the most coverage," John said. "We're open for ideas."

"How about the half-time of the next outdoor Super Bowl?" Boyd said, the sports fan that he was.

It had possibilities — national TV audience. "I like it," Myra said. "When will that be? Next January?"

"No. Next one's in Detroit. I believe the next one outdoors is in Miami."

"Okay," John said. "That's something to shoot for."

"Can we keep it hidden that long?"

"Don't know." John shrugged. "I'm praying it stays hidden until tomorrow."

THEIR DAY STARTED EARLY and everything was going like clockwork. From John's car in the Mall parking lot, John and Bryan saw the bright yellow heavy-duty, cab-over with eight-wheel trailer coming over the freeway overpass and up 528. They pulled out in front and led it on toward West Columbia. It was 8:25, a partly cloudy day with warming south winds. The cold snap had faded.

They rumbled through the ranch's front gate at 9:35. Roland and Ethel were waiting. They were surprised and amazed at seeing such a big truck, but it added a note of seriousness to their operation. John introduced them to Boyd and Frank outside the idling rig. Roland had stake railings on his hay wagon and it was loaded and ready to go with all the equipment John had asked for. Roland said he didn't know if the ground was dry enough to handle such a heavy truck, but just in case he would take them around another way; it was longer, but they'd have a better chance of not getting stuck.

With no time to waste and anxious for their task, John and Bryan hopped onto the hay wagon behind Roland climbing onto his tractor. Boyd and Frank hustled back into the truck and roared after Roland chugging away around the barns and into the higher pastures. Their diesel stacks trailed a smelly black cloud.

They made it to the gully in good time with the truck only having trouble in a couple of puddles. John directed Boyd where to park the trailer under the oak tree in line with the covered craft across the gully. Water still stood a soaking foot in the gully. Climbing out of the cab, Frank and Boyd got their first reality look at the prize under the tarp. It was 10:20.

By the numbers John went through his plan to move the craft from the trees, across the gully and onto the trailer. It seemed simple enough but a lot of hard work. Grabbing the chain saws and gas cans from the truck, they piled onto the hay wagon and Roland drove down the gully to the ford and crossed. The big tractor wheels rooster-tailed thick, muddy waters that rose to the wagon's bottom.

Boyd and Frank went to work with their saws removing the tree on the side of the craft closest to the gully. Behind them, Roland helped John and Bryan climb the tall oak and attach one end of the heavy cable. Suddenly, roaring saws and cracking limbs shattered the pastoral solitude. A flock of crows leaped from a nearby pasture, flew high and circled into a leafless cottonwood where they gathered on the branched bleachers.

It was almost noon before the cable was attached and the trees cleared. Next they unrolled the cable and ran the free end through the pulley above the block and tackle. By the time they got the cable end across the gully, all were breathing heavy, but still moving with plenty of determination. No one dared to be first to mention a break.

Climbing the tree and attaching the cable took a lot out of Bryan. He remembered tree climbing being much easier when he was younger. He hadn't realized he was so out of shape. Boyd volunteered to climb the second tree with John's help while Bryan and Frank fashioned a rope sling beneath and around the ship.

Boyd threaded the cable through a high fork in the tree, around a limb and lowered the end to be attached to Roland's tractor. When that was finished Roland started the tractor and pulled the cable taut. The pulley went up with the cable lifting the tackle block above the craft.

Now it was time for the hard part. Roland stayed with

his tractor while the others gathered around the craft and attached the sling to the block hook. Then with two of them working the block chains and two guiding the craft with the guy ropes, they began lifting it out of the trees. The ship went up, up and up, bumping and scraping trunks and limbs until it swung free above the remaining scrub oak. They gave the block chains a few tugs for good measure and locked them in.

Pulling the ship like a balloon float in a parade, they carefully made their way down the gully embankment and through the water. The ship cleared the top of the oak and wobbled over the gully.

Their plan was working. The ship moved slowly along the swaying cable. Roland's tractor dug in and held cable and ship tight as possible. Across the foot of water in the gully they climbed the other side, holding the lines and watching the ship above them. A beautiful sight but they didn't have time to stop and marvel at their dream coming true.

Puffing, panting and near exhaustion they finally had the craft over the trailer. Boyd unlocked the block chains and they slowly let the craft down. A few pulls on the guide ropes and the ship settled onto the center of the trailer. They breathed a sigh of relief and collapsed. John checked his watch. It was a little after two. Grinning through dirty, sweaty faces, they slapped high five congratulations, blisters and sore muscles be danged, and rewarded themselves with a short break.

Roland went to get his wagon while they lashed the ship to the trailer and loosely covered it with the tarp. The ship hung about six feet over each side.

"Anyone asks," Boyd said, "what'll we say's under there?"

"Say what the military always says," John grinned. "It's an experimental craft. Top secret stuff. We all have NASA I.D."

Roland left his cable attached to the other tree, saying

he'd get one of this ranch hands to take it down someday. No need putting themselves out climbing anymore trees. They threw the rest of the equipment into his wagon and the strange pasture caravan headed slowly and wearily back toward the ranch house.

At the back of the barns Roland furnished them with some stakes for the trailer so they could disguise the top shape of the ship when the tarp was tied tight around it. He threw in several bales of hay to steady and hide the ship's underside.

The truck rolled up to the side of the house, ready to go, at 3:30. Ethel popped out the side door and invited them in for sandwiches and ice tea. Working so intensely, they hadn't realized how dirty and hungry they were. Washing up and a snack breather sounded good.

Showing them to the bathrooms, Ethel told John that Myra had called and said to tell him the shed was rented.

"You have another way out to the front road?" John asked after cleaning up. "We'll never get the truck and ship through your entrance gate." He pulled out a chair at a table set with platters of sliced roast beef, bread, tomatoes, onions, lettuce, mayo, mustard and big glasses of ice filled tea.

"Shore," Roland said, slapping a table knife of mayo on a slice of bread. His thin hair was matted down in neatly combed strands. "There's a 'quipment gate other side of the barns. No trouble." He forked a couple slices of roast beef. Bryan and Boyd straggled in from the bathroom. "You fellers have a seat," he pointed with his fork, "and dig in. We don't wait on anyone 'round here."

"Ouuh! This looks real good, Mrs. Barrett," Boyd said. "I don't know when I've seen such a spread. I'm an old farm boy myself."

"Well, we have plenty," she smiled. "Ya'll just help yourselves. If I can get you somethin' else, just you say."

Frank came in and pulled out a chair and sat. They all smelled of Lifebouy soap. It seemed to fit with the thin lace curtains and the hundred-year-old furniture.

"We're used to feedin' ranch hands 'round here,"
Ethel said. "Ya'll look like you've put in a good days
work." She smiled proudly, as if preparing big meals was
her life's work. She wiped her hands on an apron. "Can I
get you anythin' else?"

"Oh, no ma'am," Boyd said. "This's plenty."

"Well now, if you don't see it, just ask. We got some
peach cobbler and vaniller ice cream when you get through
with that."

"What're ya figurin' on doin with that thing now?"
Roland asked."

"We're taking it back to Clear Lake," John said.
"We're gonna open it up, get inside, see what makes it
tick. Then we're going to see if we can fly it. Show it off
to the public. Make the government admit they've been
denying their involvement with these little beings. Maybe
we can get them to pay you and the other ranchers for the
cows they've been taking."

"You won't mind if we tell them we found it on your
ranch, would you?" Bryan asked.

"I don't know," Roland said after a sip of tea. "I'll
have to give that some thought. I don't want any trouble
from the government.

"Where ya figurin' on flyin' it?" he added, about to
take another bite. "Now, *that* Ethel and I might wanna
see."

"We haven't decided yet," John said. "But I'm sure
we'll draw a crowd wherever it is, and you and Ethel will
be the first ones we invite."

"Maybe you can see it on TV," Boyd smiled.

"Have to figure out how to fly it first," Frank said.

Roland nodded. "Well, I'm shore you fellers can do
it," he said around chewing. "Ya put in a good week's
work already. Me, I'll stick to ranchin'. Much easier on
old bones."

"But there is something you and Ethel have to do for

us," John said. He glanced at Ethel standing in the kitchen door. Roland stopped chewing. "You must not tell anyone about this, you understand? If anyone comes here asking about seeing a space craft, even if they say they're government people, just tell them you don't know anything, you never saw anything. Okay?"

Roland swallowed and nodded. "We won't get in any trouble will we?"

John shook his head. "No. But you will if you tell them you saw something and didn't call them." He was thinking of the many people who had disappeared after telling government agents about their encounters with alien craft and the beings.

"What'll they do?" Roland frowned.

"Oh, they have places they put people who see things they aren't supposed to see," John said.

"Where's that? Prison?"

"They have camps in New Mexico, Nevada."

Roland slowly shook his head and glanced at a concerned Ethel. "Never cared much for either a those places." He took another big bite of his sandwich and seemed to study a question as he chewed. Finally, he swallowed and chased it with a sip of tea and asked, "What about those stinky little aliens that stole my cow? You think they'll be back and be mad someone stole their space ship?"

John glanced at the others and they repressed a smile. "You won't have to worry about them," John said. "That ship on the truck's not one of theirs."

A QUARTER AFTER FOUR they were sitting on the front porch finishing another refill of tea when the DPS trooper came down the road, saw their truck and circled his Harley through the front gate. The law, in a shiny helmet, dark glasses, leather jacket, striped riding pants and boots, rolled suspiciously up to the truck. He swung off his bike and stripped his gloves as John led the others down the porch steps.

"Afternoon, officer," John smiled. His reflection in the officer's dark glasses returned a distorted image.

"Afternoon," he responded, coolly, tucking his gloves. He pulled papers from inside his jacket. Unfolding and glancing at them he looked back at John. "You John Sherman?"

"Yes. That's me. You're in the right place."

They shook hands. He looked at the trailer. "This the load?"

Is there another truck? "Yes. This is it."

"That's a wide load." That's what the signs said on the front and back.

"Yes, it is."

"What is it?" He swaggered toward an inspection of the load.

John followed. "It's an experimental craft," he said. "We were flying it out of Ellington and this is where it came down. This is what's left of it."

"That where you're taking it?"

"No. We have a small hangar this side of Alvin," John said. "Between Rosharon and Alvin. We'll take it up 36 to FM 1462 and then straight across. About thirty-five miles. We want to stay out of the traffic. Take about an hour an a half, at the most." He watched the trooper look under the tarp and pull at the ropes.

The trooper walked all the way around the trailer and back, pulling ropes, looking under the tarp and eyeballing the overhang. Having never seen a UFO close up before, and since they didn't exist anyway, he took them at their word, that he would be escorting the wreckage of a experimental craft.

"You know you're right at the limit on that overhang," the officer said, as he approached John.

"Yes, we know," John said, relieved at possibly passing a legal inspection.

The trooper surveyed the group. "Who's your driver?"

"I am," Boyd said.

The trooper held out his hand. "License."

Boyd whipped out of his billfold, selected the right card and handed it to him. The trooper held it in front of his dark glasses for a long moment then handed it back. "You'll have to keep your right wheels on the edge of the road." Boyd nodded. He smoothed the order out flat and handed it to John. "Sign right there," he said, taking a pen from his pocket and pointing at a line. John signed and handed it back. The trooper ripped off John's copy and folded the original back into his jacket. "Okay, let's go," he said, strutting to his cycle. "Follow me."

AFTER SAYING THEIR THANKS and good-byes to the Barretts, John and Boyd climbed into the truck and Bryan and Frank into John's car. Roland led the way around by the barns and the pens and opened the wide cattle gates. The trooper was waiting on the road with his emergency lights already spinning. Roland watched them straighten out and head back up the road. They waved and he closed the gates.

Except for some strong looks from passing motorists, the trip across FM 1462 to the cut-off was fast and uneventful. They watched the ship ride the trailer from all angles. When they lifted it from its resting place in the trees all of them had commented on how light it was for it's size. Whatever the metal of its construction, it was extremely resilient and light. Boyd said later, on the stretches of open road where they made good time, the ship seemed to add some lift to the trailer. The trooper waved good-bye at the old oil field road turn-off and sped off without the slightest interest in the rest of their trip. It was 5:30. The pipe gate was open which meant Myra had the keys and would be waiting at the shed. They rumbled on over the open fields, crushing the high grasses with the huge truck and feeling good about their day's work, sore muscles and all. They had escaped with the prize of their lives, without a hitch.

From the top of the ridge Myra saw them coming a mile off. Never one to miss a great picture, she snapped away with her camera. She had cut a wide path in the weeds around the building and had both doors open. When the truck roared over the ridge and came around the curve she was grinning as big as you please. They were a beautiful sight to behold and a moment to capture.

John wheeled his car around the truck, jumped out with a whoop, grabbed her up and swung her around. The others were right behind him and the five danced, slapping high fives as their scoring celebration flowed into the open shed.

In the fading light seeping through the wall cracks they could see that it was more than perfect. The doors were wide enough and plenty tall enough. Some rusting junk and pieces of pipe lay scattered in the corners, but that was fine, it could be moved. There were some leftover work benches they could put to use and skylights along both sides of the roof that would come in handy. Myra said the light company had scheduled to connect the power the next day. All that was left to do was introduce the ship to its new home on Earth.

Boyd circled the building with the truck, trampling a path through the weeds, and set the trailer to be backed through the doors. After several tries, and with plenty of directions, the trailer fit at a slight angle with room to spare. After seeing the ship inside they decided it would be too much trouble to remove it from the trailer, so they set the trailer's knees and blocks and unhooked the cab.

In the twilight, they stood in the open doors and assessed their good fortune. There was still much to do. The building had to be sealed from the inside and air conditioners brought in. Lights had to be set up, the right tools needed to be acquired and they would probably need reflecting heat suits. John said he would order a dozen from the same company NASA got theirs. And they had to do all that without letting anyone know what they were do-

ing. Each swore to the code of silence for the success of
their venture. In the tradition of the government, NASA
and all science projects, they felt their top secret should
have a name. Myra came up with the perfect code name.
What could be better than the first explorer's ship of
October be named the *Nina*.

DURING THE DAYS THEREAFTER they spent
as much as possible of their spare time at the storage shed.
They set up work schedules. A week passed before they
had the building secure enough to unwrap the ship. The
bare interior walls were sealed with half inch plywood and
painted black. Two air conditioning units were set in
opposite walls. Large workshop florescent units were hung
around the ship and over the work benches. John brought
in a geiger counter and found the ship to be leaking
radiation, but not enough to be harmful over short periods
of exposure. They kept their distance until the heat suits
arrived and they made a rule that the suits should be worn
at all times when working within ten feet of the ship. Since
their first priority was to get into the ship, they always wore
their suits.

John had DANGER/KEEP OUT signs painted for the
exterior; NO TRESPASSING. DANGER-RADIATION. BY
ORDER OF THE U.S. NAVY AND THE ATOMIC
ENERGY COMMISSION. They were copies of the signs
he, Myra and Frank had seen around Groom Lake.

Weeks passed, then a month and they hadn't found a
way into the ship. They hadn't even found a hint of a
crack. Thanksgiving and Christmas came and went. A
Super Bowl slipped by and still the puzzle hadn't been
solved. They were beginning to think that maybe there
wasn't a way in. Boyd rented a portable metal x-ray and
went over the entire ship with no positive results. The ship
was diagrammed with detailed drawings and each of them
worried their brains to come up with a solution. They se-

creted their drawings to their day jobs and studied them during breaks, or, sometimes, when they felt a sudden revelation. During times in the shed, they probed every inch, pushing, kicking, hammering the ship's outer skin. Nothing did the trick. The ship remained as tight as when they found it. Frustrated, they could almost feel its designers laughing from some far-off planet.

Finally, two weeks after a late Easter, on a rainy Sunday afternoon while they were all in the shed worrying over more calculations, a loud clap of thunder shook the whole building. A bolt of lightning had hit a tree not more than ten yards from the shed. Sparks flew from their fuse boxes. All were thrown, sprawling flat on the floor. Heavy metal pipes clanked, rolling from their storage places. Stunned, coughing in the dark, acrid haze of blown electrical power, they crawled, calling names, searching contact. All were okay, probably saved by their heat suits. Boyd began an inquiry about the whereabouts of the tool boxes and the flashlights therein. But as they began a groping search, two slivers of light streamed across them from the ship. Shocked, amazed, they stopped and stared into the spreading light. As if God had suddenly decided it was time for answered prayers, a door was opening in the ship's side. Bright light beamed around a door folding out and down into a ramp. The momentous event was accompanied by a distant thunder clap and a crescendo of heavy rain beating the tin roof. They stood, transfixed, squinting, incredulously, into the bright interior of the ship, ever so thankful for this appointed miracle.

Holding their breath, they waited for something, or someone, to step out. Nothing. No aliens. Just an eerie silence.

They glanced at each other, realizing what had happened; it was the lightning charge that had touched something they hadn't, or couldn't. Quickly, John found and grabbed the geiger counter and all five cautiously followed him toward the ramp. The geiger counter clicked wildly as they stole slowly up the ramp and then warily, reverently, stepped into the ship.

Inside, the ship seemed larger than its outside. Strange, as if of a different space. Its interior was trimmed in a golden glitter. A giant chair was molded into the center of a multi-leveled floor. A console of panels circled in front of the chair, and what appeared to be storage panels covered the curved wall behind the chair. A high, wide area above the panels, which appeared to be viewing screens, circled the entire ship. John set the wildly clicking geiger counter on the floor behind the chair.

Astounded, mesmerized by the other worldliness of the workmanship and the ship's simple complexities they wandered along the console and panels. Their gloved hands gently brushed across the switches, buttons and levers. What great civilization, so far advanced in technology, had created such a magnificent ship? Panel markings were classic symbols, hieroglyphic, or cuneiform, challenging in their designed simplicity. The ship was a hi-tech vessel of past, present and future; encapsulated timelessness.

John eased into the giant chair, Goldilock testing. His feet dangled and he leaned his shoulders to touch its back. He glanced at the others, breathlessly watching. "The big guys," he said. "Could be the Nordics."

"So. Where are they?" Bryan asked, glancing around. It was obvious there were no other compartments within the ship.

John slipped out of the chair, studying its design. "They could be anywhere. Pure Nordics, the Nefilim, have the power of teleporting, traveling time portals. Which could explain how this ship got through the Norad grid. We've got us a real find. What you see here is a classic time machine. A true chariot of the gods; our forefathers; our creators. They're back."

If they were awestruck before, this revelation added an even greater magnificence to the ship's omnipresence. Without realizing it, all five had taken a step backwards, toward the door.

"The gods?" Bryan asked.

"This is awesome!" Myra gasped.

"Eerie," Bryan said. His short hairs stood up as his nerves sent a shiver. "Maybe we'd better . . . "

"Yes. I think so," Myra said, anxiously, initiating their retreat. "We can talk about this outside. You never know, lighting could strike again and close that door."

They eased down the ramp and stood in the shaft of light staring back into the ship.

"Damn!" Boyd blurted. "A time machine! Think what we can do with this baby!"

"A Pleiadian ship, a Sirian ship, that's one thing," John said. "If this is a Nefilim ship, this is something else. No one just finds one of these sitting around. Where is he, she, or they, and what are they doing here, out of the portals?"

"Right," Bryan sighed. "I know these guys. Never saw their ship. But there has to be some sort of *miraculous mission* for the Nefilim to risk a physical contact with us and the Zetas."

Myra said. "Hope they don't get mad 'cause we stole their ship."

"Better hope they don't come after it," Bryan warned.

Chapter Two:
The Date

NO IMMEDIATE CONSEQUENCES ENSUED during the next few weeks. They were more comfortable going in and out of the ship and became bolder by the day. Boyd had fashioned two metal wedges for the door's sides to, hopefully, help prevent its closing tightly and unexpectedly. They reasoned the wedges themselves wouldn't prevent the door closing if it wanted to, but felt somewhat safer — and everyone stayed out of the ship during thunderstorms.

Most of their time in the ship consisted of exercises in pushing buttons and pulling switches in calculated sequences to find a way they might start the ship's power source. Eventually, having exhausted their random choices, they concluded their last method, which should possibly have been their first, was to decipher the panel markings.

All agreed with John that if the ship be of Annunaki or Nefilim design, then the panel symbols would be of the ancient Babylonian, Sumerian, or Assyrian language. The Annunaki were a group of giant space travelers from the wandering Tenth Planet, Nebiru, orbiting through Earth's solar family, between Mars and Jupiter every thirty-six hundred Earth years. They paid a visit to Earth some 500,000 years ago and set up their first colony north of the Persian Gulf. The Annunaki were recorded as Gods and

Creators of *Homo sapiens* in the Assyrian/Hittite Bible. The only mention of them in today's Bible is in Genesis as the Nefilim (Hebrew for *giant*) "the giants who came down from Heaven." The true history of Nebiru and its blond, blue-eyed giant inhabitants was unceremoniously eliminated from biblical writings by religious leaders around 325 AD, but more recently, in the seventies, restored to its proper place in Zecharia Sitchin's, *Earth Chronicles*. John and Bryan considered Sitchin a genius. His ability at deciphering ancient Assyrian/Sumerian text was renown among the true archaeologists of the day. John copied the panel ship's markings and sent them off to Dr. Sitchin with the explanation that they were from a crashed ship in South America. Since all sightings and crashes outside of the United States are reported regularly and ignored by the local media, this request by a U.S. UFO investigator would not seem unusual, nor would it draw any direct attention upon their covert venture.

In the meantime, while awaiting Dr. Sitchin's answers, they continued to explore the ship's mysteries on a limited schedule. It was during this time that Myra came up with another candidate in her fortuitous search at helping Bryan find a compatible companion, one who she felt matched up with his physical, mental and spiritual desires. Myra was familiar with his peculiarities when it came to women and was sure this single lady had all the qualities to pass his most stringent tests. Her name was Susan Sullivan, a high school English/Lit teacher Myra met in a creative writing workshop at the University of Houston Clear Lake.

"She's about my height, strawberry blond, blue eyes. A real smart, fun, beautiful lady," Myra said, late that night as they left the shed. John locked up as Bryan and Myra paused between their cars. "I've read some of her poetry. She's good. Writes about spiritual things. I think you'll like her," she added. "As a matter of fact, I'll go so far as to bet she'll even like you."

Bryan grinned in the sweep of Frank and Boyd's headlights as they drove away. "Single?" he asked.

"Divorced. Couple of years, I think. Maybe longer."

"Kids?"

"Hasn't mentioned any."

"Age?"

"Early forties, I'd guess."

"She have any interest in UFOs? Aliens? Space business?"

"Didn't get into that," Myra shrugged. "I figured if she passed on everything else, you could find that out yourself, and I know you will. She seems open-minded. Has a Master's, so I figured the IQ level's there."

"What'd you tell her about me?"

"That you were the smartest, best looking bachelor in all of Clear Lake, with killer blue eyes."

Bryan grinned. "Bull."

"Okay. That you were the most obstinate, cross-eyed, bowlegged hermit this side of the Pecos," Myra laughed. "Come on, Bryan, it's just a look-see date. No obligations. Okay?"

Bryan thought about it; a waste of time probably, but he had nothing else going. Single, triple-leveled women didn't come along everyday. "Okay," he shrugged. "We'll give it a shot."

"Great!" Myra beamed. "How about tomorrow night after our workshop?"

"Fine."

BRYAN AND JOHN MET SUSAN and Myra outside a local coffee shop around ten o'clock. Myra was right about his first requirement; Susan definitely met his physical desires. He knew this theory, that, spiritually, everyone is programmed for a certain physical attractiveness from lifetime to lifetime. The animal instinct was a given; if it wasn't there in the beginning, forget the rest.

Their smiling, eye contact didn't waver through the handshake, so maybe the attractiveness test had passed on an equal level. Myra was delighted. She nudged John and winked as they were led to a table.

Susan taught at Clear Lake High School. Shana, Bryan's ex-stepdaughter had been in her class. Besides her Master's in English she had a minor in History. She was athletic: tennis and jogging. Bryan, too. She was politically inclined and voiced conservative opinions. They had read many of the same books and liked the same movies. This was too good to be true. Bryan had suspicions that Myra might have coached her beforehand. She was married for sixteen years, single for eight and her son, Steve, did data processing for a company in Houston.

"You from Clear Lake? Houston?" Bryan asked.

"No," Susan nodded. "A small town in South Louisiana no one's ever heard of."

"There's no town in Louisiana smaller than Iota."

Susan was surprised. "You know Iota?"

"I spent half of my childhood in Iota," Bryan grinned. "I had an aunt who lived there, taught third grade at the school."

She gasped, "Your aunt was Mrs. Letz? I can't believe this? Where're you from?"

"Monroe. Did you know my cousin, Suzanne?"

"Yes. She was ahead of me, but I knew her. This is amazing."

There's no way Myra could have coached her on this. Bryan grinned. "The Rice Festival Queen."

"Yes." Susan shook her head, incredulously. "She was a pretty girl."

"Still is."

"Where is she now?"

"It's been a long time," Bryan said. "Some little town in Mississippi. Starts with a D, I think."

They couldn't get over the coincidence factor; definitely a positive boost to their meeting. They had more than a little in common. They reminisced, almost to the exclusion of Myra and John. They knew many of the same people from those days, played in the same areas, swam in the same rice canals and might have even passed close to each other during that time without the slightest awareness of their consequential futures. Meetings such as this had happened in their lives before, people from their past suddenly reappearing for some unexplainable reasons, and now one with romantic revelations they needed to explore.

Bryan was interested, hopeful, at least, this relationship had a better than good chance. He grinned and shrugged at Myra's inquiring glance as they left.

When Bryan walked Susan to her car, they set a movie date and maybe a late dinner for the following Wednesday evening. Even their choice of the movie they wanted to see said something about their similar tastes.

"I'M SORRY," SHE SNIFFED, dabbing her eyes with a tissue as they left the cineplex. "I can't help it."

Bryan grinned. "It's okay." He noticed a few other women from their theater wiping at moist eyes.

"I'm such a romantic. It was so sad, didn't you think?"

"A two-tissue ending," he said. "They did a good job pulling us in. I don't think there's anyone who can't relate to a failed love affair. It relates to our feminine sides. Most of the men were choked up, but they wouldn't be seen crying. Our society teaches men not to recognize that side of our egos. It was what Hollywood calls 'a woman's movie'."

"Oooo. I think I brought out the analysis," she sniffed and smiled.

"Sorry," he grinned. "You're the romantic, I'm the realist. Sometimes that's a good combination. Creates a balance."

"Well, I wanted him to take her with him."

"They only knew each other for, what, five days? I believe he was right in recognizing the relationship's limitations."

"You probably would have rather seen the space movie," she said, taking hold of his arm as they were passing the marquee posters.

"No. Like I said, I had seen it."

"Being in the space business, I suppose you see all of those kinds?"

"No way," he grinned. "Just the better ones."

"Did it have those monster aliens, killing and eating everyone? Yuck!" she grimmaced. "I can't watch those."

"Uh huh." He put his arm around her back and leaned close. "Lots of blood and gore."

"You like horror movies?"

He chuckled. "No. I see them strictly for the technical stuff, the special effects. It's amazing how much Hollywood doesn't know about what's out there. They have to add the monsters because the truth's not that exciting."

"You mean, there're no monsters out there?"

They reached his car and he unlocked her side. "Tell you the truth, we've never seen one." She slid in and he closed her door.

"They would've told us if there were, wouldn't they?" she asked, as he ducked into his side behind the wheel.

"No, they wouldn't have," he sighed. "There's a rule against it." He started the engine and backed out.

"A rule?" she asked, surprised. "You're kidding? What kind of rule?"

"One with a big penalty. They don't want us shaking up anyone's imagined reality. The real stuff's too scary."

He grinned, winked and added. "You know, the Orson Wells syndrome, Halloween, 1939, Mars Invasion?"

"That was before my time." She eyed him suspiciously, leaned back in her seat and pondered another question as they headed toward Galveston Bay.

She asked, "Do you read science fiction?"

"Not a lot. A book here and there. A story in *Omni* now and then. Some of it's pretty way out."

"Myra says John does. It's where he gets some of his best ideas. Technical things."

Bryan shrugged. "Yeah, I guess," he muttered. "You?" he asked, glancing at her. Her features were quite sensual in the soft street lights. "Read science fiction?"

"H.G. Wells' *The Time Machine*. It's one of my class assignments. He's one of the most imaginative, creative writers."

Bryan laughed. "Now there's a story that wasn't science fiction to begin with." He studied her reaction. "Oh, it's written like fiction, all right, but believe it or not, the part about time travel, the future, is fact."

"Fact? Time travel? How?"

"Ever hear of Nikola Tesla? *The Philadelphia Experiment?*"

"No."

"Tesla was an electro-physicist from around the turn of the century. Came over from Yugoslavia in the 1890s. A real genius. Worked for Edison, Westinghouse and J.P. Morgan before going out on his own. He created most of the electronic miracles we have today. One of his first labs was in New York's Waldorf Astoria penthouse. H.G. Wells used to stay at the Waldorf when he came to the States. He and Tesla became good friends. They swapped stories over late evening dinners. Tesla told Wells he had been working on a capsule in which he could do time travel. He showed Wells his plans and told him how objects could be surrounded by an electromagnetic field and moved in time. He even told Wells he received most all of his incredible ideas from 'beings from off this planet', is the way Tesla put it. Alien beings in time machine space craft. The time machine plans were from these aliens. Wells had himself a fantastic idea for a science fiction story and Tesla continued with his work, and by the early 1930s, at the University of Chicago, he did, successfully, transport objects in time, moving them back and forth."

"Are you kidding me? That's true?"

"It's true. It really happened."

"It's fact? How do you know? Where'd you get all that?"

"From researching the books and talking to the people who were involved," he said, proudly. "Would it surprise you to know that our government's been doing time travel since WWII?"

She studied his manner, "Yes. That's too incredible."

"Nicola Tesla was involved and his alien friends," Bryan went on. "During WWI, Roosevelt was the Secretary of the Navy and Tesla was his right hand man, creating a lot of the naval technology that helped win the war. The Rodgers antenna and the Tesla coil were a couple of them. Roosevelt heard about Tesla's success in Chicago and when Roosevelt became President in '33, he asked Tesla if he would work on an experiment that would make Navy ships radar invisible.

"Tesla said he would, so Roosevelt set him up in a couple of buildings on the Princeton University campus in The Institute of Advanced Studies. Tesla brought in all of his genius buddies to work on the project; Albert Einstein, David Hilbert, John Von Neumman, T. Townsend Brown, Gustav LeBon and James and Edward Cameron, among others. The operation was called the Rainbow Project. Roosevelt gave them a battleship and two tenders to work with."

He looked at her. She studied him, intensely, over-whelmed. "I'm sorry." he smiled. "When I get started on this I go on and on, not realizing that maybe there are those who don't want to know about all these things." He turned off onto the road leading to Fishbone's, one of the best seafood restaurants on the Galveston Bay channel.

"It's a little difficult to keep up with, but I'm trying," she said. "I must say, it's a bit unbelievable."

"There's an awful lot more," Bryan grinned. "Maybe you'd rather not hear."

"No, no, keep going," she said. "I want to hear it all. It's some history I haven't heard about, and you've obviously put in a great deal of research. So, what happened?"

"Well, they put their coils, the Tesla coils, around the battleship, the RF generators and transmitter tower on deck and their power sources on the tenders, ran lines to the big ship and turned it on. The battleship went radar invisible and then disappeared, slipped into a different time. They turned the power off and the big ship came back.

"It worked, but Roosevelt told them he only wanted radar invisibility. If the ships were completely invisible they'd be running into each other. So, they went back to work and did finally get the ship to hold on radar invisibility.

"But now, Roosevelt said they had to have all the equipment on one ship and a crew aboard. He gave them a DE, a Destroyer Escort, the *U.S.S. Eldridge,* and a volunteer crew of twenty-one for the final test. This was now 1942 and WWII was well underway and Roosevelt was pushing them for some positive results.

"Tesla knew the experiment was going to have problems with a crew aboard, and he resigned from the project. They moved the project to Philadelphia Harbor and John Von Neumman took over. And shortly after that, January '43, Tesla died.

"Von Neumman went ahead with the project, without Tesla's input from the aliens, and eventually ran into the problems Tesla had expected. He almost got some men killed. Finally in the summer of '43, Roosevelt gave them a deadline to get the job done or he was going to cancel it.

"So they got the equipment and the crew of twenty-one, plus the Cameron brothers to run the equipment, aboard the *Eldridge* on the morning of August, 12, 1943, and flipped the switch."

He pulled into Fishbone's parking lot. "Well, the *Eldridge* went radar invisible, as it was meant to, for about five minutes and then disappeared. Gone. And, finally, after about four hours, it came back, right to the same spot."

He got out, went around and opened her door.

"This is true? It sounds like science fiction," she said.

"True story,," Bryan said, locking and closing the door. "A company in England made a movie of the incident. It came out in '84 and was in the theaters two weeks before the government went to court, got an injunction and stopped its showing. They saw that the movie showed too much of what really happened and they didn't want the public to know any part of their big secret. But by '84 the secret government had the public in such denial that they thought the story, like you, was science fiction. So, when they got no static from the public, they let the movie company release it on video. It's called, *The Philadelphia Experiment,* and now anyone can see it on TV, or rent it at any video store." He laughed. "It's listed as Science Fiction."

"The Philadelphia Experiment? I want to remember that," she said. "So, the ship came back, then what?"

"When Von Neumman and his team finally got aboard the *Eldridge,* they found two sailors embedded in the ship's deck, one sailor with his arm embedded in a steel bulkhead and the other sailors above deck glowing, as if on fire, and floating in and out of reality; appear, disappear, reappear. They also found a dazed Edward Cameron and all of the power equipment smashed."

A maitre d' with an armload of menus met them inside the front door and showed them to a table for two in the

room with the windowed walls overlooking the channel and
the bay. She took their drink order and left.

They studied the menus. "Don't forget where you
were," she said. "I want to hear the rest of the story."

Fishbone's had all the seafood restaurant trappings;
corked fish net bunting strung on weathered walls, sea
shells and starfish, paintings and photos of sailing ships,
rusty nautical paraphernalia, lantern lamps, and a huge
aquarium that could accommodate several sea bass and a
small octopus. But what made Fishbone's romantic was its
multi-leveled, glassed dining rooms and wood decks that
faced the channel and the fishing boats tied up beneath its
high piers. At night the lights in and around the markets
shimmered on the channel waters, and by day tall boats and
yachts motoring to the bay from the lake marinas passed
within a few yards of Fishbone's.

"How about the large seafood platter?" she said,
closing her menu and setting it aside.

"Sounds good." he said and placed his menu atop
hers.

"I love this place," she said to their reflections in the
window and the boats moored in the channel. "It's been
a while since I was here last."

"Yeah, me too. A year, maybe," he said. "You can
hardly get in here on weekends."

Their waiter arrived with a bottle of chardonnay,
poured, then asked if they were ready to order. They did
and he left.

Bryan lifted his glass in a toast. "Here's to more and
better love." Susan grinned and winked. They clinked
glasses and sipped.

"Okay," she said, folding her arms and leaning toward
him. "Let's hear some more of the story."

"Let's see, where was I?"

"They just went aboard the ship and found everything
gone crazy. Did those sailors embedded in the ship die?"

"I don't know. I think they tried to save them."

"How did they get embedded in the ship?"

"They didn't know then, but they found out later."

"Okay. Go on."

"Well, when Von Neumman found Edward Cameron he wanted to know what had gone wrong. Edward told him when they turned the equipment on that it took on a power surge and everything went crazy. He and James ran up on deck, saw what was happening and jumped overboard. But they didn't fall into the water; they fell into space, a time tunnel of some kind. And fell into a fenced compound somewhere. They were captured by some guards and taken into an underground compound where they met John Von Neumman, and he was forty years older. It was 1983, and they were on Montauk, Long Island, and in the Phoenix Project. Von Neumman told Edward that he was still involved with time travel but he had much better equipment in '83. He also told them that one of the three space ships James had seen over the *Eldridge* the day before the experiment was pulled through the time tunnel with them and its alien crew was causing a big problem.

"The Montauk Von Neumman knew what had happened since he had already been through the whole thing. He told Edward and James that they had to go back through the tunnel and smash the equipment on the *Eldridge* to stop the ship from ripping a bigger hole in the hyperspace. He sent them back, they smashed the equipment, and the *Eldridge* returned to its place in the reality of a '43 Philadelphia Harbor. Edward told the 1943 Von Neumman that James had made a deal with the 1983 Von Neumman that he would return to '83 to help with and experiment, and he had."

Susan fell back into her chair. "That's incredible!" she gasped. "What else? Did they ever find out what had gone wrong?"

"Yes, they did. But that was several years later, at Los

Alamos.''

Their waiter returned with a large platter covered with boiled shrimp, oysters on shells, crab claws and morsels of fried fish and clams. He set a tray of sauces by the platter, asked if there was anything else and left.

"Okay. Los Alamos," she said, dipping a shrimp in a sauce. "This is really getting interesting."

"Well," Bryan began, dipping a morsel of fish, "Edward told them they had won the war with the atomic bomb. But Roosevelt decided to give them one last chance with the ship. They replaced their broken equipment on the *Eldridge* and tried it again, but without a crew. Same thing; the *Eldridge* went radar invisible, then disappeared. But this time it was back in fifteen minutes. They had reports, later, that the *Eldridge* was seen in Norfork Harbor during those fifteen minutes. Afterwards, when they went aboard, they found their equipment smashed, the same way. Who did it? They didn't know, couldn't figure. Anyway, Roosevelt canceled the project, buried the records and sent Von Neumman and his team to Los Alamos to help finish the A-Bomb.''

"At Los Alamo, Von Neumman and Oppenheimer didn't get along, but they finished the A-Bomb on time. The war was won, and they began work on the bigger H-Bomb. But while they were working on that, something else happened; an alien space craft crashed just outside of Socorro, New Mexico the summer of '47. The government covered it up and had the Army transport the wreckage, its crew, four dead, one live alien to Los Alamo.

"President Truman commissioned twelve men, among some of the country's top scientists, doctors and military leaders, to go to Los Alamo and find out if we were looking at an alien invasion. In the inner circle the group was known as Majestic 12, or MJ-12; they had Above Top Secret clearance and were to report only to the President.

"Von Neumman, his team of physicists and the other

atomic physicists already there were in on the secret examination. They had a live alien. He was a Gray Zeta and they eventually found that he was a biochemical robot, a clone. He had this unusual ability of walking through walls, so they had to make a special lead-lined room to keep him in. They kept him at Los Alamos for a year and a half.''

"Hold it. Back up here,'' Susan said. ''You mean to tell me, our government had a live alien and his crashed space ship at Los Alamos in 1947, and they never told us?'' She took a sip of wine. She was intrigued and trying hard to assimilate the facts. His story sounded believable, or was it his true blue eyes.

"Oh, yes,'' he assured her. "Greatest secret of this century. The little alien, they called him EBE-11 Extraterrestrial Biological Entity One, told John Von Neumman what he'd done wrong with the *Eldridge*. Tesla had designed a zero time reference generator for the ship as he had for all the other objects he'd sent into time. The generator was to bring the ship back to that space in time that it had left. It worked for the ship and all of the crew who were below deck. Every sailor above deck needed his own zero time reference. Each didn't have, so when they returned to that time they were in a different space, a different reality.''

"Zero time reference?'' she frowned. "Explain.''

"Well, the way I understand it,'' he said, "Einstein, Tesla and Hilbert had figured, don't ask me how, that in the cosmology of the universe, Earth has a zero time reference to everything in space/time. And everything that comes into being on Earth has its own reference point. When anything on Earth is moved into a different time, it has to be returned to that exact spot. All airplanes, space craft have these zero time generators. As long as all the passengers stay inside the craft, about all they'll suffer is jet lag. We go through all that with the astronauts. It's even worse with the weightless factor thrown in.

"EBE-1 told them that they, the Gray Zetas, had caused the power surge with a connecting time loop to the Phoenix Project. Remember the three space craft over the *Eldridge?* The government had been set up. The Grays knew that the Phoenix Project, still messing with the time tunnel at Montauk, would turn on their power at nine a.m. August 12, 1983 and, they had to get the Rainbow Project to turn theirs on at exactly the same time in 1943. The power surge pulled the *Eldridge* into the tunnel and ripped a forty-year hole in the hyperspace. It's what they needed to get into this time, since they had lost their ability to time travel as the result of an atomic winter after a Great War on their planet in Rigel, some eight hundred light years away."

She had a dazed look.

"I'm sorry," he said, "it's too much. Everything relates to something else. It's a long story. Gets pretty complicated. Maybe we should talk about something else."

"No. It's okay," she said. "It just takes some time to digest. You've been talking, and you haven't eaten. Here, I want you to eat some of this. It's very delicious."

He speared a morsel from the platter and studied her face in the light. "You're a very pretty lady," he smiled.

"Thank you," she blinked, shyly. "And you're a very handsome man and very . . . faceted."

"EBE-1 LIVED AT LOS ALAMOS for a year and a half," Bryan said, after a sip of wine. After bringing their bottle and glasses to an outside table on a deck overlooking the channel and bay, Susan had asked him what had happened to the little alien at Los Alamos. "They assigned an Air Force Captain to live with him day and night, be his buddy, get to know him. The two got to be as close as brothers.

"Eventually, in their interrogation, and the slow response to their questions, and the fact that they knew he was a robot, they realized they were talking to his controllers, somewhere out there in space, in another dimension. The big guys, so to speak. And when they did autopsies on his dead buddies they found that the relay system was in a mind control implant in their big brains. The implants were tied into their craft's onboard computers.

"You have a computer?"

"Yes."

"Did you know that John Von Neumman, the father of the electronic computer, took the first transistor off the onboard computers of that alien crashed ship? He sold 'his creation' to some big corporations, and so began miniaturization, and the great electronic and computer industry we have today."

Incredulously, she stared at him. "You mean, all this technology we have today, started with a crashed alien craft at Los Alamos?"

Bryan nodded. "Actually, it started with the aliens giving Tesla and his team all their miraculous ideas."

A light sea breeze rustled through the canopies above the tables. Lights from the piers and boats along both sides of the channel made strange rippling reflections in the choppy black waters. Boats rocked, their pulleys clanked against swaying masts, their hulls squeaked and bumped against tight moorings. Mullets jumped in the middle of the channel and a tern squawked at another over the Bay.

"Anyway," he went on. "They realized when Von Neumman took the ship's computers apart they sort of lost contact with the big guys. But they were intrigued with the idea of mind control implants and cloning and got into a whole mess of experiments on some military units during the Korean War and later on a few in the Viet Nam War. And even today their mind control implants are still going on, but that's another story; back to EBE-1.

"After about six months EBE-1 got to feeling sickly. They called in their expert doctors and their diagnosis was, that since he had blood that resembled the sap of a plant, what he probably needed was more light. So they set up a schedule for setting him out in the sun everyday, and he got better.

"But then, after about a year he began to get sick again. They didn't know what to do for him this time. They finally decided to send out a distress signal into the universe, Project Sigma, it was called, hoping the big guys would pick it up And come to EBE-1's rescue.

"Steven Spielberg made a movie about this incident. It was called, *E.T.* E.T. call home, remember?"

"Yes, I saw it," Susan recalled. "I loved that movie. It was so beautiful."

"Yes, E.T. was very loveable," Bryan went on. "But in the movie E.T. went home; in real life no one came to his rescue. EBE-1 died. His Air Force Captain buddy, who was the kid in the movie, Elliot, was devastated, he'd gotten to know him as a brother. They didn't find out until a year or so later that what had killed EBE-1 was air pollution."

Susan shook her head and sipped her wine. "Incredible."

"What they didn't know was that the big guys had picked up on their message, and in the summer of '52 they buzzed the White House. Then they sent a message through Sigma that they wanted a meeting. MJ-12 jumped at the opportunity of possibly getting more technology and the meeting was set for Edwards AFB in late November, after the elections.

"The President, a couple of Cabinet members and all the military MJ-12 members met the big guy aliens; EBE-1's creators, the taller, big nose, reptilian Zetas. Together they made a deal, sort of a treaty: the Zetas would give MJ-12 three flyable space craft, atomic fuel element 115, and advanced technology in exchange for their right to abduct, implant mind controls and harvest bovine parts at will under the cover of government denials."

"The President, Cabinet members, and military leaders were involved in this treaty?" she frowned, incredulously. "And no one was ever the wiser?"

"A couple Cabinet members," Bryan said. "The Military was being offered power and technology to control the world for a few cows and a few people's lives. They couldn't say no.

"MJ-12's bartered space ships were delivered to Groom Lake Test Site in Nevada where an underground storage facility was built in the mountains. In the beginning they had been funding these covert activities from ten billion in gold that they had stolen from Europe during WW II. But with this increased expansion, that soon ran out, so to keep Congress from knowing, they began to fund their 'black budget' projects from padded defense contracts and their vast-dealings in the drug market."

"Drug dealing! Our government?"

"Surprised? MJ-12, NSA, CIA, the Mafia, the United States is the world's biggest drug cartel. The reason behind the Viet Nam War was to protect the Laos/Cambodian heroin business. By the mid '80s they were buying eighteen hundred tons of heroin a year and selling it on the open market. When President Kennedy wanted to bring the troops home from Viet Nam and give his sagging polls a boost, MJ-12 told him no, they couldn't afford to lose those poppy fields to the commies. Kennedy told MJ-12 to get their act together, because he was going to tell the public the whole truth, be a hero and win the election. MJ-12 knew they couldn't let him do that; they had a deal with the Zetas. So MJ-12 put a contract with the Mob and CIA to have him eliminated."

She looked stunned. "Well, I always knew it wasn't just Oswald. Any fool could see that," she said. "It was the drugs and the alien treaty?"

Bryan nodded. "Oswald was, as he said, a patsy. And, as it turned out, so was everyone else.

"Tell you something funny," he went on. "When the Mob Dons got the contract on JFK, they felt it was too big a hit. They needed an okay from the Illuminati. The head of the Illuminati was Aristotle Onassis. When they called that summer, Jackie and her sister, Lee, were vacationing on Onassis's boat. Onassis had already become enamored with Jackie's beauty and charm, and then this opportunity to make her available, he was all too happy to okay the hit, even offered the services of his best assassins."

"Incredible!" Susan shook her head. "How do you know all this?"

"Most of it we put together from papers released through the Freedom of Information Act."

"We? Whose we?"

"The UFO Club. MUFON," he said, cautiously. "Mutual UFO Network. It's an organization that was created for all those seeking the truth of who and why aliens beings are interacting with Earth and why our government is denying their involvement."

"And, I take it, you're a member of this organization?"

He smiled. "Yes."

"And Myra and John?"

For a moment he thought about whether he had the right to involve John and Myra. "Yes," he said, and then for qualification. "We have over a hundred members in the Clear Lake area, hundreds of thousands world wide. We're not alone in our beliefs and efforts."

"I've never thought about it," she said and sipped her; wine. "I mean, I've heard stories, rumors, gossip, and in the back of my mind I've always felt, as with many things, the government wasn't being totally honest with us. I mean, the assassination. Anyone could see there was more to it than Oswald. But the troop pullout, I just don't want to believe our elected leaders are into buying and selling drugs. That's just a little hard for an honest, tax-paying American to take.''

"Not elected," Bryan injected. "MJ-12 was appointed. The government meant well in the beginning, they were just . . . taken in. But even before that, religious leaders were taken in by their denial of our ancestral history. And they too, in the beginning meant well; at least they had their reasons. But if they'd been honest with us, we could all see the mess we're in now. We would all know who we are, and what's going on. All of our problems today relate to the simple fact, we don't know who we are. We don't know our history, our ancestors.

"In my practice, before I signed on at NASA, I began to realize my patients' problems were much deeper than what we had been taught — about the mind, brain, ego, superego, the id — all that surface stuff. At the time, there was some revolutionary research being done in past lives and reincarnation. Fascinating things were being revealed; solid proof that most everyone brought their past lives' problems forward, one lifetime to the next, through our spiritual being.

"You know what I mean by spiritual being, our spiritual energy?''

Susan nodded. "Yes, I think so. I believe there's something there. I'm not sure I know that much about it.''

"Bodies die, spirits don't, they just keep going, life to life. So, there has to be a beginning to spirit energy somewhere in time. And if our energy travels through all of time, then our spiritual self must know all of our history, all the way back to its creation, and forward through all of its life problems. This thought got me started. If I was to help anyone I had to know the basis of their problems. And as it turned out, my search for the birth of spiritual self led to universal life, alien beings and how they got here, space craft, UFOs.''

"You're going to tell me now, that these aliens are related somehow to our spiritual self and God?"

Bryan shrugged. "Not if you don't want to hear it."

Susan thought about it. "I find all of this so amazing, so mind-boggling," she said. "I might as well hear the rest." She shivered and rubbed her arms.

"You cold?"

"A bit."

"Come on," Bryan said, standing and taking her hand. "I'll tell you the rest on the way home."

"I HADN'T REALIZED it was so late," Susan said, as they came out of Fishbone's. "But the company's been so wonderful I'd forgotten tomorrow's a school day."

"I shouldn't have gotten started," he said. "The story's so long and I didn't give you a chance to talk. I wanted to get to know you."

"No, no, no. It's okay. I'm glad you did. And I want to hear all of it, that is, if it's not too long."

"It is. Maybe I shouldn't. This part gets into religions, and I don't even know which one you profess to."

"I grew up Southern Baptist in Catholic surroundings," she laughed. "Right now, I'm open to just about anything."

"It could get rather long and complicated. We're talking about millions and millions of years."

"Surely, there's a short version for us non-initiated."

He was still thinking about where to start as he started the engine and headed out of the lot. "Okay," he began. "I'll start with Rigel 4. Rigel is a double blue-white star on the edge of the Orion Belt about 800 light years away, in the Lyran Constellation. Rigel 4 is the fourth planet from the Rigel star. We're Sol. 3, the third planet from our star, Sol. Rigel 4's inhabitants, Rigelians, were tall, blond, Nordic types who migrated there from other constellations closer to the universe's center. There were gazillions of years of planet hopping before Rigel, but I'll leave it at that.

"As time would have it, after several hundred thousands of years, a major confrontation arose between two factions of the Rigelians. It became a serious split and began to heat up, as it had with their ancestors on other planets before this one. We're talking, both sides with extremely powerful atomic weapons. A contingent of good guy Rigelians, sensing the coming conflict, commandeered a fleet of space ships and split to the safety of a planet in the Procyon star system.

"The Great War on Rigel was so fierce and horrendous that the planet's environment was completely destroyed. The survivors moved underground and lived there for hundreds of years. They mutated in the absence of air, water and light. They lost their abilities to procreate and began cloning to survive. The results were short skinny bodies with big heads, large black almond shaped eyes and some tiny holes for a nose and a tiny slit for a mouth, exactly like the little EBE-1 at Los Alamos.

"When these mutants finally felt it was safe to resurface again, they realized their devastated planet was no longer inhabitable. They picked up and moved to a new home, a planet in the star system Vega. From there they began a search for their escaped Rigelian brothers. They were a dying race and needed to integrate and regain their lost genetical heritage; their physical stature; their powers through spiritual energy and their ability to procreate.

"They eventually found their Blond brothers in Procyon and again a conflict erupted. The mutated brothers killed and captured some of the Blonds, but a lot of them escaped, again, to a planet in the Sirius trinary star system, which is about nine light years away. See the progression? They're getting closer.

"With their Blond prisoners, the mutants set out in search of the escaped blonds. But they went in the wrong direction, ending up in the Zeta Reticuli Star System. Hence, where they got their name - Zetas.

"The Zetas heard their blond brothers were in the Sirius area and eventually confronted them there where another horrendous atomic war broke out. Again, some of the blonds escaped to a passing comet/planet, Marduk, that orbits around Sirius and through our sun's solar system, between Mars and Jupiter, every 3600 years."

"This sounds like the plot to some science fiction, Star Wars movie," Susan said.

Bryan grinned. "Yes, it does. But, just as all of us have a spiritual heritage, so do science fiction writers. It might be that through their keen imaginations they're Able to see the truth a lot quicker than those in denial."

"Is that where you remembered it?"

"Well, yes," he shrugged, answering, cautiously. "And with the help of a very enlightening incident. When you get to know me better, I'll tell you about it. But most of my verifications came from non-fiction books. One set, *The Earth Chronicles,* by Zecharia Sitchin; six books that decipher the ancient Sumerian, Assyrian, Babylonian and Hittite texts and replace some of our Creators' history that was eliminated from the Bible."

"Eliminated from the Bible?" she frowned. "Like what?"

"That our Creators, the Annunaki came here in space ships from the tenth planet in our solar system."

"Tenth planet?" Susan said, tentatively.

"Marduk," Bryan said. "The Blonds' planet.

"Marduk? Our Creators, the Blonds, came here from another planet in our solar system? This is incredible! I know I keep saying that, but it is. I was taught that God was our Father and Creator in Heaven. And Jesus was his son."

"In a way, that's true," Bryan said. "God, the Creator of the Universe, in the beginning created all living creatures on all of the planets. Some evolved into the Blonds, and

the Zetas from the Blonds. These displaced Blonds, from
their wandering planet, splashed down on Earth in the
Persian Gulf over 500,000 years ago, went ashore and set
up their first colony between the Tigris and Euphrates
Rivers, where Iraq is today. The only mention of it in
today's Bible is in Genesis, 'the giants who came down
from Heaven.' The Hebrew word for the Blond giant Gods,
was *Nefilim.* They were between seven and eight
feet tall. Our ancestors were the Nefilim Blonds from
Marduk and their history of how and why they created us
was eliminated from the Bible's original text by a religious
mentality at the Council of Nicea in 325 A.D.''

Bryan parked in front of Susan's patio home. "So,
you see, the Blonds' and Zetas' conflict has progressed to
Earth. And is today the most important issue behind all
turmoil in the lives of homo sapiens.''

Getting out, he went around and opened her door. "All
our problems; society's conspiracies, political and religious,
and our emotional confusions, are directly related to this
conflict between the Blonds and Zetas that began millions
of years ago,'' Bryan said, as they strolled to her front
door.

"This has been a most interesting evening,'' she said.
"I've enjoyed it immensely, even though my head seems to
be spinning.'' She unlocked her door. "Those books, *The
Earth Chronicles?* I can get them at any of the big book
stores?''

"You might have to order them. They're under different titles, but all by Zecharia Sitchin. I can let you borrow
my copies if you can't find them.'' They embraced. "I
want to see you again,'' Bryan said.

"And I want to hear some more of the story.''

"And I want to hear about you,'' Bryan said. "I'm
going to be tied up for a few days with this next Shuttle
launch, but I'll call you.''

"It'll give me time to find those books. Thank you,
for an enjoyable evening.''

Chapter Three:
The Meeting

DESPITE THE LATE HOUR he had gotten to bed, Bryan woke early the next morning. He lay in bed, his mind churning with thoughts of Susan, a review of what he said, what she said and what they hadn't said. And, most of all, her reactions to his truth. She seemed open and receptive, but he wasn't ready to pass judgment on her acceptance, just yet. She was, physically, very pretty and quite desirable; a personal entrapment well experienced in tough lessons of past relationships and two divorces. There was just no way to force a balance in others' mental and spiritual levels.

Thoughts of the day's coming events began to filter between those aroused by his dreamy dissertation with Susan. Rehearsals for the meeting he was scheduled to have in a few hours with the Program Directors to discuss the progress with their new designs for the Space Station's Gravity Simulator began to take on a new feel. An aggressiveness he had long subdued crept into his intentions. He recognized his time to take action. A plan began to take shape. He jumped from bed, his mind quickly structuring timed steps. The meeting wasn't until ten; plenty of time. He hurried through his routine of dressing, grabbing a bite of breakfast and was on his way.

Driving down Space Center Boulevard he suddenly thought of Marsha. An obstacle, Marsha Adams was head psychiatrist at NASA and very meticulous in her methods

of putting together a presentation. She wouldn't like any
sudden changes. She would kill him, for sure. He sat at
the Nasa Road 1 light staring blankly through the passing
traffic and out over Clear Lake. What to do?

No way around it; he wouldn't tell her. The light
changed and he turned right. It was early, she wouldn't be
in yet, and he could put it together without her knowing.
He sped the short distance to the Space Center entrance, a
wave to the gate guard, past Space Center Rocket Park and
into his building's parking lot.

Inside, he hurried to the second floor, down the
hallway and through the glassed entrance. A couple of
secretaries, Gail and Lisa, were at their desks in front of a
wall list of special occupants:

FLIGHT SURGEONS
Michael J. Graham, MD PHD
Wade R. Rosenberg, MD
Philip P. Somer, MD
Jacqueline S. Hart, MD

FLIGHT PHYSIOLOGISTS
Edward B. Hasler, MD
Susan W. Gilbert, MD

FLIGHT PSYCHIATRISTS
Marsha C. Adams, PhD
Bryan K. Mayfield, PhD

FLIGHT TRAINERS
Lawrence J. Horn
Dianne S. Baker

Gail smiled. "'Morning, Bryan."
He paused at her desk. "Mornin'. Marsha in, yet?"
Gail glanced at Marsha's closed door and shook her

head. "No. Haven't seen her."

Bryan relaxed and smiled. "No calls," I he said, hurrying on into his office and closing the door.

Space memorabilia was scattered everywhere, on the walls, tables, desk and book shelves. Stand-outs were, an astronaut's soiled glove with attaching ring from a Gemini suit, a navy blue flight cap with a scrambled egg bill and COMMANDER in gold lettering above an Apollo II patch on its crown, a shiny metal canister with a NASA label, several models of old and new space craft, rows of flight patches, and photos, signed and framed, of suited astronauts alone and in groups. His office was not unlike any of the others who worked closely with the men and women who tested their combined efforts in space flight. They were his friends. They were astronauts because he had qualified their applications and they had gone on to prove him right. Happy and sad, these were the daily reminders of the tough space industry.

Behind his desk he began pulling folders from file drawers. He opened selected folders, spreading their contents, charts and diagrams, across his desk. Moving with focused intent, he sorted charts with diagrams and then into special groups. He was elated; the patterns fit exactly what he had suspected all along.

He went to an electronics cabinet that held his TV, VCRs, stereo and recording equipment. Opening cabinet doors, he began pulling out video tapes, checking their labels, and selectively stacking the ones he wanted. Selecting a new tape, he shoved it in the bottom VCR, then the top tape from his stack into the top VCR. He settled into his chair and arranged his selected group of charts and diagrams across his desk in front of him. Taking the TV remotes in each hand he clicked the top VCR to PLAY.

Foggy pictures of suited and helmeted silhouettes glowing with rainbow auras rolled onto the screen. Each stamped with a date, time and astronauts' names; Captain,

Commander, Colonel, Specialist, so and so. The dates covered flights for the past thirty years. Bryan checked each astronaut with his, or her, charts. Fast forward. Reverse. Stop. Record. Fast forward. Stop. Record. Reverse. Stop. Record. Again and again, checking his clock before and after inserting a tape from the dwindling stack. He was making good time.

The expected knock on his door came at precisely the gauged minute. He glanced at his clock and stopped taping. He ejected both tapes, satisfied he had more than enough evidence.

"Coming!" he called, shuffling the pile of charts back into their folders.

The door opened and Marsha Adams stood watching him. She lugged her briefcase and balanced rolled blue-prints under an arm.

"You ready?" she inquired, puzzled at his activity.

"Yes, just a minute," he gasped, without slowing down. He grabbed his new tape from his VCR. "Just let me get this, and I'll be right with you." Gathering up his folders, he quickly tossed them into his briefcase along with the new tape.

Marsha's curiosity mounted, watching his every move. In all of her sixty years, twenty five at NASA, she had never known anyone who could manage to incite so much controversy over so many subjects as Bryan. She knew him to be talented, subtle and astute. And she had a keen sense of knowing when his wheels were turning. She was suspicious this was one of those times.

"What's that?" she snapped, nodding at the contents in the briefcase.

"This? Just some backup." He smiled, closing his briefcases. "New outfit? Nice."

"Backup? What backup? We don't need any backup."

"I do." He snapped its latches and grabbed its handle.

"I have everything we need right here," Marsha assured

him.

"Grant me this, okay?"

She frowned as he came toward her. He noticed she had just a slight touch of makeup and a new hair style.

"Here. Let me take those." He took her rolled blueprints.

Ed Hasler and Dianne Baker, the other half of their Gravity Simulator presentation team, met them in the reception area and they were on their way.

IT WAS A SHORT WALK to the building where the conference was to be held. They strolled two-by-two along the walkways. Bryan fell back with Ed and listened to Marsha and Dianne's chatter that centered around the progressing countdown at the Cape. All but Dianne bemoaned some duty Mission Control over the weekend if the Shuttle got off as scheduled.

"We've got the catamaran packed and ready," she said. "I'll be thinking of you guys every time a wave washes over me."

"Yeah, sure, Dianne," Ed hissed. "Gimme a break."

Ed came to NASA right out of the NFL as one of the best sports physiologists in the country. He was a sports doctor who lived in a marina apartment over on the south side of the lake with an ex-astronaut.

And he was gay. How a gay had gotten past Marsha's and Bryan's rigorous testing and thorough background checking was still a puzzlement to both.

Bryan had talked privately with Ed, who was indeed a willing sharer, about why someone could be aroused by one particular physical body and turned off by all others.

Ed had no conclusions, but he had offered an opinion from direct observance. "In the sense of spiritual love," he said, "there is a divine intensity in the mental and spiritual that overrides the physical desires. But, when it comes down to the sexual desires, you just have to make do the best you can.''

Bryan's short stint at delving into the homosexual mind had not changed his own conclusions, that somehow every soul is already programmed, before each life, to find and love, in some manner, those other souls also similarly programmed, no matter what their physical form. Mystery solved? Maybe not.

Bryan had read in the *Earth Chronicles* that when the Nefilim decided to create an earthly slave force to work their gold mines they had experimented with many combinations of their sperm with the eggs of female animals they had found already here. Their genetic labs had produced a variety of half man-half/half-whatever before they clicked with a suitable hybrid from the egg of a female ape. Not quite satisfied with the resulting *homo sapiens* they began to screw around with the genes and the DNA chromosomes; xx-y, yy-x, xx-yy, xy-xx, etc. It could be, he figured, that a string of this whole mess of different mind, different body got its start way back then. It was something he had thought of often; hide the history, hide the origins.

In his periphery, Bryan caught a magnificent white sea gull floating thermals against a clear, azure blue sky, its motionless wings weaving a glide path down toward the little man-made lake between the buildings. It seemed to do a wing dip over the burned and rusting Mercury capsule, Freedom 7, an aging monument to the first space flight, sitting on its dolly at the building's front steps. Before entering the front doors, he saw the bird sail to a running stop at the lake's edge. The resident ducks flapped their wings at its intrusion and shoved off into the water, chattering and flicking their tails as they paddled.

AS PLANNED, the little group was a few minutes early. They found Kent Deerwood and Doug Farrell already there. Everyone smiled and shook hands with cordial greetings. Kent Deerwood was a veteran Marine fighter pilot from the plains of the Oklahoma panhandle. He was tough and highly perceptive. He knew the mechanics of flight and he had friends in high places. Doug Farrell was one of Rockwell's best design engineers with an experienced background in the Shuttle productions.

Marsha went to work setting the table for her presentation, placing folders of reports in front of four chairs opposing theirs. With Bryan and Ed's help she unrolled blueprints, back-rolled and flattened them on the table, pinning their, corners with available heavy ash trays, paperweights now that NASA was smoke free. She took her video and shoved it into the VCR portion of a TV atop a roll-away stand, and Dianne helped her position the setup at the end of the table. At that angle, the large model of the latest Space Station would be blocking the screen. Bryan moved it to an empty pedestal in a grouping of other space craft models. He peered into the open, working model of the Shuttle and counted the tiny astronaut dolls. Seven. All present and accounted for, all at their positions in frozen animation, all performing some task that seemed never to be completed. He remembered, a month after the Shuttle model had been placed in that room, two of its tiny astronauts vanished, disappeared, gone, jumped ship, sucked off into space, or a souvenir for some monstrous being. They were never found. Eventually, after a proper and lengthy search, reserves from the backup team were ordered to duty. The crew complete, the Toyland Space Ship continued its mission through motionless time.

Bryan glanced up at the framed portraits of famous faces on the guardian wall behind the models; Presidents John F. Kennedy and Lyndon B. Johnson, Governor John Connally, Senators Garth and Yarbrough, and a grouping of the First Seven. Their steady and determined glare dared Bryan to doubt their purpose. Their eyes seemed to follow him back to his seat.

Marsha was practicing with the TV remote when the last two, Program Director Dean Radford and Budget Coordinator Stan Miller strolled through the door, greeting and shaking hands as they made their way to their seats.

"Morning, ladies, gentlemen," a smiling Dean Radford growled, his voice coarse from his years of smoking. "Marsha, Bryan, Ed, Dianne. Good to see you. You're looking fine."

Dean Radford glanced at the material on the table and the TV cart parked nearby. "Well, looks like we're ready to go," he said, pulling out his chair. "Let's see what you have."

Everyone grabbed a chair. Radford adjusted his glasses and opened a report in front of him. The others followed suit with their folders. The administrators flipped through their pages, glancing quickly at what they seemed to recognize and absorb with no difficulty.

Radford closed and shoved his report folder aside, moved a couple of ashtrays and quickly leafed through the blueprints. He nodded, occasionally, then returned to the top page. He slid the papers down the table to his delegation. "It looks good. Impressive." He removed his glasses and swept the four across from him with a reassuring smile. "Good idea. Nice plan. Let's hope it works." He leaned back and addressed Marsha. "Let's take a look at the video."

"Yes, sir," Marsha said, sliding her chair back. She stood and clicked the TV on with the remote. "We've put together about twenty minutes of the Gravity mockup, Black Box and exercise harness in animated graphics and KC-135 zero gravity demos."

Radford pulled a cigarette pack from his pocket. "Anyone mind?" he asked, bumping one halfway out.

"This is a smoke free area," Ed said.

"I'm down to two in the morning," Radford said to his pack. "This is the second one." The TV came on as he pulled the cigarette from the pack with his lips. He fumbled for his lighter, snapped a flame and drew a painful, then relaxing puff. He shielded Ed's glare by leaning on the cigarette holding hand.

Pictures of jump-suited astronauts floating weightlessly inside the KC-135 mode flicked on the screen. Radford grabbed an ash tray and the blueprints' corners rolled up.

Marsha narrated. "This is the new configuration on the Black Box." The video was of an astronaut strapping himself into the exercise harness and pulling an oversized black helmet over his head. "The viewing screens inside the old version have been re-designed to a wrap-around." The TV pictures showed animated cutaway and exploded computer graphics of the helmet.

"These are those new virtual reality screens?" Deerwood asked.

"Yes. And each astronaut programs his or her personal videos, their own realities. Things from their daily lives."

"I would've loved to have trained with one of those in my day." Deerwood added. Ex-test pilot/ex-astronaut, an inner ear problem had denied him his Apollo mission.

"We've had a great deal of success in stabilization with this visualization system," Marsha commented, proudly, as the pictures flipped by.

Bryan's attention was suddenly distracted by the glaring whiteness of a sea gull sailing by the window beyond the TV. He glanced at the others. No one else seemed to have notice.

After reviewing some of the virtual reality scenes, the pictures switched back to an astronaut exercising within the harnessed weights and pulleys. He finished the required program, unlocked himself and floated free in the dead-fall enclosure.

The next pictures were of the centrifuge wheel; four man-sized, open cocoon like pods attached at the center, forming a wheel that took up a full cross-section of the KC-

135. A Black Box helmet covered each pod's head section at the center of the wheel. Three astronauts floated into the picture. One, Dianne, they recognized. She smiled at the camera and all in the room couldn't help smiling back.

"Looking good, Dianne!" Miller said.

A young finance wizard from Harvard, he escaped conviction in a failed savings and loan scandal mostly because he was the nephew of a congressman. He found his way to NASA because he knew a lot about spending other people's money and making them feel good about it. He fit right in with the space program.

On the TV, Dianne and another astronaut were being strapped into opposite pods of the wheel. All at the table had seen the functional operation of the wheel before. Spinning at regulated speeds, its centrifugal force substituted for the gravity that helped the heart pump the body's blood circulation to the feet. The group watched a version of the visualization helmet being fastened and adjusted over the astronauts on the wheel.

"This puts the astronauts in a world of their own," Marsha said. "We've already ordered the educational and entertainment software libraries for these units. The micro computer disks are easily stored, as well as updated and individually personalized as the crews are selected. These units are also equipped for TV satellite transmission from Earth and mission control."

The sea gull sailed by the window again. This time Bryan thought he saw something in its beak.

"Another plus for these pod units," Marsha said. "They have built-in exercise slots for arms and legs."

On the video the astronauts pushed the exercise bar pads up and down in their slots. The wheel spun around, slowly gaining speed as the astronauts went through their paces. After a few seconds at its top speed, the wheel slowed to a stop. The astronauts were unstrapped and they floated freer seemingly invigorated from their ride. Dianne smiled in a pumped-up pose for the camera.

"We edited out her throwing up," Ed chuckled and glanced at Dianne. Some smiled, others didn't. It wasn't funny.

"Just kidding," Ed added. "She did great."

The tape ran out and the screen went blue. Marsha set the VCR into rewind.

"Believing this unit to be successful," Marsha said. "we're already thinking of double-sided, eight pod wheels. And there have been suggestions for double pods for the couples who might be aboard the Station." The tape rewind stopped. "Anyone want to see portions of the tape again?" No one did. "Any questions?"

Radford stuffed his cigarette, put on his glasses and thumbed through his report, again. Miller flipped to the back of his and ran a quick check on the cost figures. Marsha ejected the tape and placed it on the blueprints.

"How long does the stabilization effect last once they're off the wheel?" Deerwood asked.

"About fifteen minutes." Dianne said.

"Not long," Radford said, and closed his report.

"Dianne was only on the wheel for a short time," Ed said. "Five minutes, at the most. That's about all we can get out of a dead fall. We really won't have any detailed results until it's tested on a flight where the astronauts can stay on as long as they need to. But so far the test figures look real good. Even for the short run, the muscle strength was up and that's good. And that's what we're really looking for here, isn't it?"

"Might be what you're looking for." Radford stated, staring at Ed. He didn't understand gays, didn't care for them. "What we're looking for here is a cure for weightlessness sickness. The curse of space flight." He sighed and glanced at the others, needlessly reminding them of their focus. "It has to be solved before we send anyone up to that Space Station. And if it's not, don't even think about the Mars trip. If this doesn't do it, all I can say, is, you'd better have a damm good backup plan.''

There was dead silence for a long, tense moment.

Finally, Marsha said, ''It'll work. I have all the faith in the world in this one.''

''I've never put much faith in contraptions,'' Radford said.

''We know what we want,'' Bryan said. ''Maybe, just maybe, we're not going at it the right way. I believe there's something out there we should be taking just a little bit more seriously.''

He had their full attention. What could possibly be more serious than weightlessness?

Well aware of Bryan's history of radical ideas, Radford dared to ask. ''What's that?''

''The aura,'' Bryan said, confidently.

They stared, puzzled.

Radford frowned. ''The what?''

''The aura,'' Bryan said, glancing around, judging their expressive need for clarification.

Bryan grabbed his briefcase, opened it and took out the video tape. ''I've put together something you need to see.'' He stepped quickly to the TV and shoved his tape into its VCR. Marsha frowned and glared at him as he took the remote. He pushed the play button and pictures of the silhouettes in the fog surrounded by the rainbow auras began to roll.

''We've all seen the auras around the astronauts in the test chamber,'' Bryan narrated. They had. It was a standard radiation test for the crews before and after each flight. ''Colorful, aren't they? Before. After. Before. After,'' he said, as the crew names rolled by. ''Not much radiation there, but we all know what that aura is.''

''It's body energy,'' Marsha huffed. ''What's your point?''

''Body energy's the point,'' Bryan said, as he strolled

behind their chairs. "In the before tests the energy aura is relatively small, in some cases, not extending more than five feet from the body. Now, in all the after flight tests the extension of the energy aura has increased, in most cases it has doubled in its size. And on all subsequent after flight tests of the veterans their aura is even larger and somewhat stronger. And the most intense auras recorded are those around the crews who have been the deepest in space . . . to the Moon."

They watched the tests flip by. Marsha closed her eyes as if she felt a headache coming on. She knew where he was going.

She'd heard him expound on his new thought theories which began to surface after his personal enlightenment from studying a set of books called, A *Course In Miracles.* He had tried to explain the theories to her, but they were so completely crosswise with her traditional Catholic heritage that she rejected them without a second thought. She cringed at the thought of him attempting to attack the technical minds of the Directors across the table.

"Not so much body energy but spiritual energy," Bryan continued. "It's what we're all born with. It's the energy that makes our muscles pump the heart and lungs, we live and breathe. Now," he pointed at the TV picture. "What makes this energy double its intensity in space? Where are the astronauts getting that boost of energy? Maybe a release? Maybe a recharge? Maybe both."

He had circled back to his briefcase, reached in, took a handful of folders and tossed them over the blueprints. He opened several on top and spread their contents. "These are charts on each astronaut on that tape, showing the correlation between their auras, expansion, the energy changes and growth of the astronauts' societal and attitudinal perceptions which, in turn, have affected their psyche and goal structures."

Marsha rose, leaning on the table, "What the hell are

you talking about?'' she snapped in a manner that relieved her of all responsibility for his actions. She didn't swear often, but when she did, it was at a screw up beyond her control.

Bryan leaned on the table, pointing the remote at the TV. "I'm talking about a force, a universal energy out there that's collectively connected to the spiritual energy in everyone of us. A powerful, universal energy force, an incredible intelligence that we might, could, somehow, use to stabilize our bodies in space.''

Marsha stood. "That's the most ridiculous thing I've ever heard. How do you come off proposing such a preposterous idea?''

"Easy.''

"Well,'' Marsha said. "Tell us. Just how do we use this aura, this universal energy, to stabilize weightlessness?''

He ran a hand through his hair. Oops. He had thought they would just accept the idea without a detailed explanation of its use. Now, how could he explain without revealing the alien technology they had in the shed. He was up against it now. He had to come up with something. While he thought he pressed the stop button at the TV, then the eject. "I don't know,'' he slowly confessed, as his tape popped out. "I hadn't worked that part out yet.''

"Just as I thought,'' Marsha snapped and took her seat. "All talk and no real substance. What does it matter? Just another one of your way-out ideas.''

"Wait a minute,'' Radford injected. "I want to hear some more of this.'' He frowned at Bryan. "Societal and attitudinal perceptions? What the hell is that?'' He shuffled and glanced at Bryan's graphs and pie charts.

"It's how we relate to the universe and each other,'' Bryan said. He wanted to say God versus ego, but he didn't want to offend anyone's religious conceptions of God. If he had to explain the differences he could talk all month and still they probably wouldn't understand. "Weightlessness and the close quarters over long periods of time have a direct affect on how we adjust to each other when we travel in space. It affects some astronauts more than it does others. And, we don't know why. We've already seen those differences the farther out we go. Astronauts not in equal balance with their body and spiritual energies will have trouble adjusting to a space environment. Those tests charts prove it.

"Space sickness is just a warning. I believe we should be designing a system that will support our needs in and beyond the biofield vectors."

"We're a long way from biofield vectors," Radford said.

"Maybe, maybe not." Bryan shrugged. "The aura's energy is our means to accessing other dimensions. It wouldn't hurt to start work on those systems now. They'll need refining as we go. And I believe the aura is telling us where we should start."

"And where's that?" Deerwood asked, his interest piqued.

Bryan said a silent prayer, *Holy Spirit, I need your help. I release this to your perfect outcome.*

"With onboard computers," Bryan said, confidently, suddenly gathering what he knew from the ship and funneling it toward a solution they could understand without raising suspicions. "We have computers, good computers, and they're getting better all the time. But they're a long way from being anywhere close to the greatest computer of all, the human brain and its spiritual energy. We know that a computer is no greater than its memory capacity and we know that there is no greater memory capacity right now than the brain. We know that when each of us is born we take on a spiritual energy from the universe that fuels our bodies. With this energy comes a spiritual intelligence that is programmed into the memory banks of our new minds. Sort of a universal DOS. We all have it, but most of us aren't using it because we don't know it's there. What we're seeing in the aura is its release, as it is re-energized by its original source.

"Now, think about what we could accomplish if we programmed our astronauts to use the onboard computers to reconnect their own spiritual energy into this universal intelligence."

Confused and dumbfounded, they stared at him. Clearly, his idea was going to need more explanation than he could possibly give them. He felt his mistake in even bringing it up. Their beliefs and reasoning weren't ready for such a drastic change.

"You mean, hook their brains to the computers?" Radford frowned.

Bryan shrugged. "Well, sort of. Hook their spiritual energy into the computers."

"Their spiritual energy into the computers?" Radford asked, incredulously. "How're we, you, gonna do that?"

"I don't know," Bryan said. "We'll have to work it out."

Radford looked at Marsha, who pinched her brow as if she had a larger headache. "Obviously, it's the first time you've heard about this," he said. "What do you have to say?"

Marsha was Bryan's superior strictly by seniority. Radford respected her experience, but she had just been upstaged by what he assumed was a reasonable cognizance, but far beyond his comprehension.

She opened her eyes and blinked at Radford. "He makes a vague supposition sound urgent. That bothers me more than a lot of pretty rainbows. Forget about it. For now, I believe the new Simulator will work just fine."

"I agree with Bryan," Ed said. "If it's out there then we should be using it to upgrade our systems. As it is, when it comes to putting bodies in space, we're still far behind.''

"Behind who?" Radford snapped.

"We know the aliens have been using that energy in their onboard systems for millions of years," Bryan said. And after he said it, he suddenly wished he hadn't.

A heavy silence fell over the room. Eyes popped and jaws fell. Bryan froze, as they stared at him. How could he? Aliens were never mentioned above a whisper at NASA. Maybe with friends behind closed doors, but never in an open meeting with a Program Director. It was against company rules. People had been fired on the spot for less.

Bryan saw his ally, Ed, recoil.

Radford's move. Avoiding the other's sheepish glances, his eyes dropped to the report under his arm. He studied its cover thoughtfully for a long moment before he glared up at Bryan.

"We know this?" he growled. "How do we know this?"

Bryan tossed the TV remote on the table in disgust. It slid toward Radford. "We've known this for a very, long time," he said.

"No. We don't know this," Radford snapped, cutting him short. "And never have. Is that clear?"

Suppressing further confrontation, Bryan and Radford stared across the table. The room was too quiet. No one moved. Half of them knew that Neil Armstrong had quit the program for not being allowed to talk about the aliens they'd seen on the Moon.

Radford finally broke it off and began rolling blueprints. "Ladies, gentlemen," he said. "I believe we can leave it at that. I believe we have a workable system in this new Simulator. So, let's get back to work."

DURING THE KOREAN WAR, Dean Radford easily reached the status of ace fighter pilot by deftly destroying the qualified number of enemy MIGS. He spent his final service years as an instructor at Desert Rock Top Gun. After resigning his commission, he managed and flew some for an air freight line before accepting a position at NASA through a recommendation by his old friend, Colonel Shorty Powers.

Lt. Colonel Radford's first encounter with an alien space craft, a UFO, as they were called since the summer of '47, was in April of '53 on a routine flight over the Kaesong Valley. It was not an exclusive sighting, his wing man, Colonel Calvin Fuller saw it too. They had heard rumors of such craft, but to actually see one, its shape, its speed, its maneuvers, put any doubts of their reality to rest. Recovering from their astonishment, they reported the disk craft to Command before attempting a chase that ended quickly when the craft just disappeared.

When they returned to base they were debriefed for days by the OSI and ONI Pacific Command. Questioned separately, their stories matched. In the end the ONI convinced them their best story would be that it never happened. And it was best for their military careers if the incident was never mentioned again. They were promoted and sent stateside, Radford to Top Gun, Fuller to the Pentagon.

While at Desert Rock, Radford had seen four or five UFOs over Nevada and New Mexico, but never reported or mentioned them to anyone. Checking in at NASA he signed form 146-E, as all NASA employees did, stating that he would never reveal, by oral or written statements, any unusual circumstances involving sightings or encounters with any strange or alien forces during official NASA space flights. The penalty assigned to breaking this agreement was a stiff ten thousand dollar fine and ten years in prison. Most thought the form was a joke, since they had no evidence that alien's existed. But having had prior experiences with these craft and the Guardians of the Secret, Radford knew they were deadly serious.

Bryan's incident aside, Radford thanked them for coming and a job well done, shook hands politely and with Miller, Deerwood and Farrell in tow, quickly marched from the shattered meeting.

Marsha fumed silently as her entourage gathered the extra report folders, blueprints and tapes from the table. Briefcase in hand, she stalked from the room leaving Bryan to struggle with the bulky roll of blueprints. Ed and Dianne lingered between, helping and muffling grins.

They caught up with Marsha at the elevator. With others aboard, not a word was exchanged on the way down, through the lobby and out the front doors. They had seen her silent treatments before and knew the storm clouds were gathering.

Marsha stopped in the sun at the top of the front steps. "Why, why, why?" she cried, to some imaginary audience. They pulled up short in the glare of solar spotlight and she turned on Bryan. Ed and Dianne sought a neutral position. "Why, in heavens name, would you embarrass us like that? Why didn't you tell me what you were going to do? Standing up there stuttering like that. It was dumb, dumb, dumb! So damn irrational! I've heard you say some ridiculous things before, but that takes the cake. I can't believe you could conceive of such a stupid notion. It has absolutely nothing to do with the Simulator."

"Oh, but it does." Bryan defended.

"On second thought, I believe you could," Marsha added. She bounded down the steps as they followed close behind.

"It has everything to do with what we're doing," Bryan said, catching up. "The stupid part is no one around here can see it. It's high time we all put our cards on the table. There are aliens out there and they're flying craft faster than the speed of light, and they're not having any problems with weightlessness."

"I hope to God Dean doesn't think I had one iota to do

with your accosting their intelligence.''

"But, Bryan's right, Marsha," Ed pointed out. "No matter what conditioning or survival support we come up with, there's just no way we can expect these bodies to live in space without some support from out there.''

"Dianne, surely you can see what I'm saying?" Marsha pleaded.

"Sorry, Marsha," Dianne shrugged. "I've been there and I know what space flight can do to a body. Muscle strength, bone structure. No amount of exercise, or fooling the mind, can prevent it. You're smart enough to see that. It's not Bryan's idea that you're upset about, Marsha, it's the alien thing, isn't it?"

"We can all get fired!" she cried to the heavens. "They can destroy us.''

Ed laughed. "It's incredible the way we have to treat this damn secret," he shrieked. "Marsha, we all know they're out there. For God's sake, we have tons of evidence. All the crews have seen them. Big deal. Tell her, Dianne.''

Dianne glanced to her right, then left. "They're there, okay? They don't do anything. They don't say anything. They just fly around watching us. Now you see 'em, now you don't. Spooky.''

"For Christ's sake, Marsha," Ed snapped. "Neil and Buzz took pictures of them on the moon. So, tell me, why won't NASA admit there are superior beings out there?''

"Because," Bryan said, balancing the blueprints. "Then they'd have to admit to everything else they've been covering up. And if they did that, the people of this country would have their butts. At least, I hope the blind will finally see.

"They've had alien technology for fifty years.''

"They, they, they!" Marsha yelped. "Who are they?''

"The secret government, MJ-12.''

"You've never proved that," Marsha snapped.

"Oh, I believe we can."

"We?" Marsha huffed. "We, meaning you, John Sherman and all those other weirdos in that, that club?"

"Can't say it, Marsha?" Ed smiled. "UFO Club. And searching for the truth doesn't make them weird."

Marsha shot Ed a look. "You coming out for them too, Ed?"

"Around here?" Ed scoffed. "Heavens no, dear. But you will allow me that one last closet, won't you, Marsha?"

They walked on in silence toward their building. Bryan and Dianne grinned at Ed's mocking Marsha's manner behind her back.

"Anyone for lunch?" Bryan asked.

Dianne and Ed declined.

IT WASN'T OFTEN that Bryan and Marsha had lunch together. At the most three or four times a month, and usually with three or four other people from the office, and mostly in the Center's cafeteria. It wasn't that they didn't get along, they did. It was just that they didn't have that much in common. Marsha's life outside the Center was quiet, peaceful and rather ordinary. To Bryan's, conservatively dull. Bryan was Chicken Little to her Henny Penny, trying his subtle best to alert her to the new extremities of life. Married thirty years to Andy, a bank vice-president, their two children were grown and gone, married other fine people and brought them three or four grandchildren. Bryan couldn't keep count, but their smiling pictures lined her office shelves. She stubbornly existed in an unexciting, unchangeable world of peaceable compliance, teeing the line, holding tightly to her rock in the stream of fearless, adventurous life.

They drove off campus to one of those fast food places out on El Camino Real. Half the patrons there wore security badges denoting the many companies supporting the space industry.

Marsha got a salad, Bryan a chicken sandwich. They sat at a corner table in the solarium room under the hanging plants.

"I know what you were trying to do," Marsha said. She put her napkin in her lap and dumped a half a packet of Equal in her tea. "It's from that course, isn't it?"

Bryan was surprised that she recognized his idea's basis.

"And you can talk till you're blue in the face," she added. "And you're never going to convince anyone that belief in any of that spiritual stuff is practical."

"Why?" Bryan said, cutting his sandwich in half. "Because you couldn't see it doesn't mean no one else can. It was worth a try. I don't regret doing it."

"And you don't regret your belief in that Course destroyed your marriage?" Marsha smirked. She dipped some salad in a cup of dressing.

"No, I don't," Bryan said. "The Course's truths are meant to help marriages, not destroy them. The problem was, it just wasn't Cheryl's time. She hadn't recognized her pain of hanging onto her fears. It was her decision not to return to love. And I forgive and support her decision. The Course's purpose is to help us see our separation from our true spiritual self to the belief in our illusioned ego. Simply, from love to fear. The Course is there to help us release our fears and get back to love. And I think those principles apply to what we're trying to do in space flight. And the aliens *are* involved."

Marsha grinned. "Really, Bryan. Get serious. I just hope Radford's not already signing your pink slip."

Bryan shrugged. "If they can kill a president, getting rid of me would be nothing."

Marsha had heard Bryan's theories of JFK's assassination; in an effort to prevent JFK's exposing their covert activities with the alien and drug deals, MJ-12 had contracted the NSA/CIA and the Mob to eliminate him. As with his theories about the aliens and the Course, she believed it too lacked facts. And to let that sleeping dog lie, she quietly picked at her salad.

"The difference between you and me, Marsha," Bryan said. "Is I don't fear them, you do. And that's exactly where they want you and all the rest of the people in this country. As long as you're caught up in your fears you can't see the truth of your reality. Until you realize how they've got you believing in your fears, you'll never regain your spiritual truths. MJ-12 traded our realities for alien technology. The aliens tricked them, and now we're all paying for their mistake with our pain in the separation from our spiritual reality."

"Why are you so complicated all the time?" Marsha asked. "Why do you insist on pushing your belief that our government is involved with these aliens, when you know there is no proof that any of it's true?"

"You mean, why don't I submit to their lies like the rest of the country?" Bryan said. "No, thanks. That's not me. I guess it's just my analytical personality. When I see something that's not what it seems to be, there's this little voice inside that says, Whoa, here! Something's not right. Listen up. Better take another look. This is not the truth. Why is the truth being hidden? Why is there a need to lie? Why the cover-up? Find the evidence, find the proof. And we've found plenty of proof."

"Then show me something. Some solid, tangible proof."

"Believe me, I could," Bryan said, thinking about the craft in the shed. "But the government has you and ninety percent of the people in this country in such a state of denial that you'd never believe it. I don't think you'd believe it even if I introduced you to one of the little aliens sitting behind a desk in the Pentagon. Or, if they'd let me, I could take you down to the Pentagon's basement, sixteen floors down, and show you an alien space ship. How'd it get there? The aliens put it there. Would you believe that? We have an eyewitness report.''

Bryan took a bite of sandwich and watched her nibble salad and a melba cracker. He wanted so badly to put her back in the car, drive her out to the shed and walk her through the alien space craft. "Look," he said. "They're not going to fire us. MJ-12 doesn't care what NASA does, how much money we spend. We're a diversion. The public watches us, not them. As long as we keep plodding along, wasting taxpayers' money, we're doing just fine. We're part of their cover-up. It's when someone stops pointing at our outdated technology here and starts pointing at the hi-tech alien craft being flown out of such places as Groom Lake and Lancaster that gets them upset.''

"MJ-12 this, MJ-12 that. Who are these people you're always blaming?'' Marsha frowned, waving her fork. "I've never heard of them. Where are they? Give me some names.''

"Oh, I could,'' he grinned. "But they'd deny it. You know some of them. They're some of the people you hob-nob with on those funding junkets to Washington. Most wear uniforms and hide behind friendly, devious little smiles, knowing they're the ones in control of everything, even our lives.''

"That's ridiculous!'' Marsha snapped. "Those are good, conscientious, intelligent, honest, hardworking people. They would never do any of those things.''

"Yeah, right. Wake up, Marsha,'' Bryan said. He wiped his hands on his napkin. "Tell you what, Marsha. Next time you're having a drink with your old friend Henry Kay, ask him to give you a tour of his Groom Lake facilities, or better yet, Montauk and the Brookhaven Labs, and see what he says.''

"I wouldn't think of it.'' she huffed.

"Of course you wouldn't,'' Bryan grinned. "Let me

go in your place next time and I'll ask him.''

"Henry's a close and dear friend. I wouldn't embarrass him with your ridiculous accusations.''

"Okay, fine," Bryan laughed. "Maybe he'll call you as a character witness at his hearing.''

"What hearing?''

"If Congress gets the guts, the Congressional one,'' Bryan said. "The one where MJ-12 has to fess up to everything after we blow their lying cover wide open.''

"After WE blow it wide open?'' Marsha laughed. "You mean, you and your weirdo friends? That's a laugh. How're you gonna do that? Where's the proof?''

Bryan grinned, slyly. "We have proof. All the proof we need. Believe me.''

"What?''

"The coup d'etat''.

"Don't give me that. Show me.''

"Sorry. You'll have to wait until we're ready.''

"Ha! When will that be?''

"Soon.''

Marsha took a final sip of her drink, tossed her napkin on the table and pushed her chair back. "I'll believe it when I see it,'' she huffed, grabbing her purse.

Bryan grinned, wiped his mouth and slid his folded napkin under his plate's edge. "Is that a promise, Marsha?'' he said, as he followed her out. "You'll finally believe something?''

AS AN INTERNATIONALLY known UFO investigator, John Sherman was one of three people Bryan knew who had actually gotten into Dreamland's S4 Section at the Groom Lake Test Site in central Nevada without being a member of MJ-12, and come out alive. Myra and Frank were the other two.

John's investigating began as a freshman at Cal Tech. He and his roommate, Allan Chin, started with a summer vacation side trips in New Mexico looking for clues to the "crashed weather balloon" of July '47. The government's stories didn't jibe. And they were right. What they found was the front end of the Greatest Coverup in the history of mankind. Thereafter, they began collecting every piece of information about UFO activity they could find. After graduation they continued, even though miles apart, John at McDonnel-Douglas in Huntsville, Alabama and Allan at Martin Denver. Their files bulged with reports and sightings from all over the world. Through their activity, they quickly became well known for their intense interest, and that notoriety put them high on the government's list of those being closely monitored.

John and Allan married women who were sympathetic to their cause and all four enjoyed their summer vacations digging for clues around reported crash sites. Unfortunately, that was during one of those summers, when John and Ellen were at NASA in Clear Lake and Allan and Su Lin with E G & G in Las Vegas, that they decided the '53 crash at Kingman, Arizona would be their next project.

Although it had been nearly ten years, they found people in Kingman who remembered the rumors and the place where the crash was supposed to have happened. They found the place in the mountains where the trees and brush had been cleaned away and never grew back. During their poking around they found an eyewitness, an old mountain man who had seen the whole thing, from the crash to the government cleanup. Hidden, he watched the whole thing; saw them take the space craft away in two pieces, covered on several trucks. And when the military left, he discovered two long, thin pieces of strange metal that they overlooked. The pieces, which resembled small I-beams, had some strange symbols imprinted on their sides, and proved to be indestructible. They eventually talked the old man out of one of his pieces and were on their way back down the mountain when, mysteriously, the brakes failed on Allen's car. They plunged over a steep curve and down a two hundred foot drop, smashing through boulders and trees. After spending a month in a Kingman hospital, John was the only one who came out alive. A mechanic at the garage, where what was left of Allan's car was taken, showed him unmistakable proof of brake line tampering. Local authorities pursued the case for a while before filing it for lack of evidence. John never found the little I beam with the strange markings, neither in the wreck, nor at the wreck site.

John met Myra when he was investigating a UFO incident that happened on a road outside Dayton, Texas, a small town north of Houston. One night shortly after Christmas, Betty Cash, Vicki Landrum and Vicki's grandson, Coby, were going home from a bingo parlor. Their trip was interrupted by a huge, diamond-shaped craft spewing flames and descending on the road in front of them. Getting out of their car for a closer look, they were consumed by the intense heat and later found to have been badly burned by radiation from the flames. Within minutes, they saw twenty-three black military helicopters arrive, surround the recovering craft and quickly escort it away. They followed behind the aerial phenomenon until the strange craft took off and disappeared.

A skeptical Myra covered the story for the *Houston Chronicle*. When she saw the victims's burns her interest shot from mildly professional to intensely personal. Doctors eventually diagnosed the burns as cancerous. The women hired a lawyer and sued the government — because of the helicopters' involvement — in federal court. The government denied knowledge of the strange craft, or the military helicopters. The ladies, lawyer asked John's help as an investigator to find some hard evidence of government involvement. John knew, from information he had gathered over the years, that MJ-12 had over a dozen flyable alien craft in their Dreamland S4 mountain hideaway

at Groom Lake. Taking advantage of Frank's Charter
Service, they flew to Vegas and after surviving days of
harrowing adventures in the mountains, broke into Groom
Lake's Dreamland S4 section and took pictures and videos
of the alien craft and alien beings before they were caught.
Their film and cameras were confiscated and their lives
spared by the S4 Commander, General Cal Fuller, who
decided, since most everyone would doubt their credibility
anyway, and the fact that their permanent elimination would
draw an unwanted investigation, Fuller set them free after
some debriefing and a stern warning to leave the issue of
the government's involvement with aliens alone, or the next
time MJ-12 wouldn't be so nice.

Dejected, the brave trio returned to Houston empty
handed. Confronted with a panel of government debunkers,
they didn't even attempt to tell their incredible story. The
ladies' case was thrown out of court for lack of evidence —
discounting the burns, of course, which were cancerous and
getting worse.

A nice thing did come of the event; three months after
the trial, Myra moved in with John.

An hour after lunch with Marsha, Bryan took the
elevator to the Engineering Department of the McDonnel-
Douglas building. He looked official with a roll of
blueprints under his arm. He went through the front doors
and marched past rows of honey-combed cubicles, each
with a large drafting table, drawing implements and a
draftsperson seemingly busy concentrating over complicated
plans. Serious people drawing tedious diagrams of wires
and connections, red, blue, green, yellow, black, all pieces
of the great puzzle that will eventually culminate in a
cooperative product sitting atop a pad at the Cape. Those
of this creative mass would be gathered around their TV

sets in a few days holding their breaths and hoping for the
sake of the astronauts they all got it right one more time.
He felt some of the passion and dedication that drove the
minds and bodies of those who could do such beehive
tasks. Yet, he had to wonder how John could hold his
composure while watching his fellow aerospace engineers
toil with these complications when, in fact, he was one of
the few people on Earth who knew it didn't take miles of
wires and tons of metal and fuel to fly in space.

Along one side of the open room was a row of private
and glassed offices. He hesitated at one, its door slightly
open and marked, John Sherman. He tapped lightly before
pushing through.

"Hi, John," he said. "How's it going?"

John looked up from some paper work. "Hi, Bryan."
He pushed strands of his silky blond hair back from his
forehead. "What's that?"

"Gravity Simulator," Bryan said, tossing the blueprints
on John's desk.

"How'd it go?" John asked. He started to remove the
rubber bands.

"Okay," Bryan shrugged. "Looks like a go. Radford
will send the orders through next week."

"Good," John said. "Then it can wait." He labeled
the rolled sheaf and dropped it into a sectioned ben holding
many others. "Glad you came by. I was gonna call." He
shoved his chair back. "Come on, I'll buy."

Very business like. But that's the way it went in their
offices. No getting around it, they had found the bugs. If
they removed them, they were replaced. Whoever it was
should know by now; John and Bryan talked only business
in their offices.

John punched two diet drinks from a vending machine

as they passed through the refreshment lounge. They popped the tops and stepped out onto a balcony overlooking Clear Lake streets, homes and shopping centers, all nestled in pillows of leafy green that stretched toward the Bay. They sipped and leaned on the railing.

"I hear you sounded off to Radford at the meeting this morning," John said to the landscape.

"Who?"

"Ed. I saw him and Dianne in the cafeteria."

"Damn. It'll be all over the Center."

"Your timing's really bad," John frowned. "They seemed to have given us some slack. But we don't need them watching us any closer. Not now."

"Sorry. I wasn't thinking," he sighed, regretfully. "I had this idea and, well, one thing led to another. And all of a sudden I was telling them how it all tied in with the way the aliens. Well, you know? I don't see how you can keep from sounding off once in a while."

"I know. It's frustrating," John sighed. "But, look, watch yourself, okay? We're too close to having our day."

His plan gone awry he felt bad for screwing up around John. They sipped cola.

"You coming out tonight?" John asked.

"Yeah, sure," Bryan said, puzzled at his asking. "What's up?"

"I want you to see something," John said. "I just picked up a new book on the latest crop circles. I think you'll find some of the new formations rather interesting." John smiled.

"Yeah?" Bryan returned John's smile. In their research of the Nefilim/Blonds John had discovered that the circles played an important role in the Blonds' ability to time travel. Throughout their history on Earth the Blonds had placed circles on Earth's energy grids. Stonehenges were the most famous of markings and were found positioned around the Earth at energy grid crossings. The circles proved to be the key portals for the Nefilim/Blonds time travel and when the crop circles began to appear around the world on the energy grids, the researchers had more proof that the Nefilim/Blonds were back.

"Such as?" Bryan added.

"It's not something to tell," John said, squinting into the bright sunlight. "It's something you have to see."

Bryan took the last swallows of his drink. "Okay," he said. "I'll see you there." He crushed his drink can and tossed it in a trash container as he started to leave.

"Something else," John said. Bryan stopped and waited. "I got a call from a gal in Galveston. Said she'd seen me on that talk show last month. She said she'd been abducted by some aliens a couple of years ago. She wanted to know if we'd be interested in hearing her story."

"Is it bothering her?" Bryan asked.

"She didn't say."

Bryan shrugged. "We have abduction stories out the gazunga. What's one more?"

"Well, this one's a little different." John smiled, slyly. "She said the aliens let her fly their ship."

A wide smile crept across Bryan's face and he scoffed, "You're kidding."

John slowly shook his head.

"Damn!" Bryan gushed. "We never had a pilot before. You think she's on the up and up, that maybe she really did?"

John shrugged. "Only one way to find out."

"When?"

"I told her maybe next week," John said. "After we

get the Shuttle back.''

Bryan leaned on the railing again and the two of them studied each other's thoughtful expressions.

"Quite a coincidence, wouldn't you say?'' Bryan puzzled. "I mean, with the way things are, our immediate need. You think they know? You think this could be, some sort of a setup?''

John looked down at his hands clasped around his drink can. "I thought about that. I don't know. Let's see.''

Chapter Four:
The Message

AFTER BRYAN LEFT John he spent what was left of his afternoon going over some astronaut applications in preparation for their upcoming personal interviews. By four o'clock news of a countdown hold at the Cape had swept through the Center causing those involved, Bryan and Marsha included, to consider possible alternate plans for the weekend. How long? No one knew just yet. It was rumored a booster fuel leak. They could be looking at least a week, maybe more. This was a heavy flight. A military spy satellite was involved and deployment would be blacked out. The flight's liftoff time was crucial to its success. Control's computers would be working overtime to reset. In the meantime, everyone involved was on standby.

It was almost five before Bryan left his office and headed for the parking lot. Remains of a sudden thundershower steamed over the lot's hot surface. A few wet cars still waited in their yellow striped pens; dry rectangles marked those departed. Bryan was thinking of calling Susan, maybe doing something on Saturday. He unlocked his car and swung the door open wide. A rush of hot air wafted around him. Suddenly, while he waited to ease into the car's warm interior, a dark shadow passed over him and a flapping near his head startled him. He ducked, throwing up a protective arm.

Caw! Caw! Caw! Caw! He was being attacked. He squinted into the setting sun and made out the shape of a sea gull. Something smacked his head. Bird crap? No. It bounced to the ground. A pebble. A damn sea gull was throwing rocks at him.

The sea gull circled, floating to a webbed-footed landing atop a low lighting post at the edge of the lot. Bryan saw the bird's whiteness sparkle in the clear light, quickly bringing to mind the sea gull he had seen that morning by the lake and again out the conference room windows. The bird ruffled its feathers, shook its tail and pranced a lively, webbed two-step.

Recovering from the sudden shock, Bryan found the incident amusing, if not puzzling. He glanced around; not a soul of an audience to share a reasoning explanation. The gull danced and bobbed its head. Cautiously, Bryan stooped and retrieved the pebble. On closer examination he saw what appeared to be a piece of broken sand dollar. Still puzzled, he studied the gull, then the piece of sand dollar. The bird bobbed, then tilted its head to watch Bryan with one eye. To the finder, a whole sand dollar meant good luck. A broken one, worthless. "This for me?" Bryan softly mouthed his words.

The gull bobbed his head, agreeing.

"Well, thanks." Bryan smiled. Meaningfully, he rubbed the fragment between his fingers, feeling it's rough groves. He nodded to the bird and then dropped the broken piece into his shirt pocket; for what reason, he didn't know. Maybe later.

The gull lifted up from its perch and flew south, over the lake. Bryan watched until it was just a dot in the sky.

BRYAN UNLOCKED THE DOOR into the shed's warehouse area and stepped through. The buzzer alarm stopped as he locked the door behind him. The others were there already, gathered around under the lights of a work table to one side of the ship's open ramped door. They looked up at the buzzer, waved and went back to their business while he slipped into his shiny heat suit.

Zipping his suit, he approached the table. He saw they were huddled over opened pages of some large picture books; one he assumed was the crop circle book John had mentioned. Frank, Boyd and Myra watched John sketch symbols from the books onto a pad of paper. Bryan leaned in next to Myra and Boyd, shoving aside a collection of used Styrofoam cups and fast food boxes.

"Bryan," John said, looking up from his sketch. "This is the book I was telling you about." John turned the crop circle book so Bryan could see its slick, full color reproductions.

Bryan studied the pictures; sharp, professional aerial perspectives of crop circles. He had seen many pictures of the now familiar formations since they began appearing in fields all around the world. First, there were just the simple circles, then smaller circles attached with lines, circles inside of circles, then outcroppings, straight lines, crosses and curved sections. As the formations progressed in time they got more complicated. But the pictures Bryan was looking at were the most complicated he had ever seen. He flipped several pages and saw more, each more intricate than the next.

John held up a couple of his sketches. "See anything that looks familiar?"

John had sketched several of the new formations' outcropping designs. Bryan studied them. His jaw dropped and he glanced at the ship.

John smiled. "That's right, the symbols on the panels."

"And look at this," Myra said, slipping another big coffee table book from beneath the crop circle book. It was a colorful photo collection of artifacts and museum pieces. Myra had the book open to some pictures of ancient decorative pottery and urns. She held the book for him to see and tapped her finger on several pieces in the photos. Bryan saw the words, 1st Millennia Babylonian and Sumerian in a bold heading under the picture.

"Same symbol," Myra said.

Bryan recognized the similarities. A tight smile crept across his face. When he looked up, they were grinning, proudly. "I'm not surprised," he said.

"Come on," John said, gathering up his book and sketches. "Let me show you in the ship."

Myra grabbed the museum book and they followed John up the ship's ramp. Each closed their suit a little tighter and pulled up their hoods. The geiger counter clicked at a fast and steady beat behind the big chair. John led them around the chair and placed his sketches and open crop circle book atop the console. Myra slid her open book next to John's. They gathered around and compared symbols, book to panel.

"This one's up there," John said, pointing at a section of a crop circle formation and a matching symbol on the panel. "This one's there," he flipped to marked pages. "This one and this one are over there, and this one's right down here." He pointed to the console.

"And the one on the pot," Myra said,, pointing from her book. "And a couple from the urn are on that side panel."

Bryan took the crop circle book and held it up next to the symbols, comparing and inspecting each at close range. He ran his gloved fingers across the panels, tiny engravings. No doubt about it, they were the same markings, the same language.

"This is a Nefilim ship," John said. "But, maybe not *just* a Nefilim ship. Look at where we found it. I checked my energy grid calculations from *The Earth Chronicles* and the Barrett's ranch is on a north/south grid. It's also between the 29th and 30th parallels, between two rivers —

the Colorado and the Brazos — and approximately thirty miles inland from the Gulf. What does that tell us? When the Nefilim first splashed down on Earth it was in the Persian Gulf. Their first colony was thirty miles inland in Shumer. Shumer is located between the 29th and 30th parallels and in the delta of two rivers — the Tigris and Euphrates. The Nefilim God, Enlil, first son of Anu, led that landing party." He glanced around the ship. "This could be the ship of a Nefilim God. Maybe Enlil's, maybe Enki's."

"Anu had a daughter, too," Myra said. "Ninhursag. It could be her ship."

"Come on," Boyd snorted. "How could they still be alive. We're talking over 500,000 years here!"

"Not impossible," John said. "They were recorded as still being around after the Flood, and that was less than 14,000 years ago. Their longevity genes are quite strong. Death is not an option. They could, and would, live forever."

"Okay," Bryan said. "Say it belongs to one of the Nefilim gods. What's He, or She, doing back here, and in Texas, and just where is He, or She?"

"Maybe not just Texas," John said. "These crop circles are all over the world. In the back of this book," he thumbed to the back pages where the more complicated formations were. "These researchers, investigators, are saying these crop circles are beginning to have messages. Those who can read this language are saying whoever is making these formations are beginning to complain about how humanity is destroying this planet.

"There's a story here about this group of investigators who came together one night in a field close to a recent formation. They began to meditate, telepathically sending a message, 'Talk to us. Please, talk to us.' After about an hour they gave up and started to leave. When they turned around they saw, in a field behind them, a new formation that wasn't there before. They had neither seen, or heard, anything. They took a look, but it wasn't until in the light of the next day that they could see what it was.'' John turned to the page and held the book so they could see the picture. ''The Mandelbrot.'' They were looking at a very intricate cross-patching weave in three circles of different sizes. The larger circle looked like a rounded heart shape with six smaller circles attached. ''In mathematics,'' John said. ''This is the universal symbol for *chaos*.''

''Chaos?'' Bryan puzzled. ''What're they saying?''

''They're saying, everything's all screwed up,'' Boyd said.

''Well, we can certainly vouch for that,'' Myra said.

''Could it be that's why they're back?'' Bryan asked, ''to straighten us out?''

''Like a judgment, maybe?'' Frank said.

''Could be.'' John mused.

The geiger counter clicked in the long silent moment. They glanced at each other and around the hallowed vehicle in which they stood. The ship glowed in response to their newly garnered respect, a new meaning. A reverent presence closed around them. John and Myra closed their books and, one by one, they slowly backed toward the door and out down the ramp. They stood staring back into the ship's open door.

''Having this ship,'' Myra said, ''needs some more thought.''

''Did you tell them about the abducted pilot?'' Bryan asked.

''Yes,'' John nodded.

''SINCE THE SHOT'S been delayed,'' John said to Bryan as they were taking off their heat suits. ''I thought I'd call that lady in Galveston, see if she could come by this weekend, maybe Sunday night. How does that sound? Think you can make it?''

Bryan thought about it as he ran a geiger counter over

his suit. There were clicks, but unsteady and way below the danger level. "Monday night would be better for me," he said.

"Okay. Monday. I'll let you know."

Once they knew the atomic fuel source in the craft was Element 115, and would be transmuted to Element 116 in the ship's reactors, wherever they were, and converted into anti-matter when the ship's engine was started, they had abandoned their first thinner heat resistant suits for the thicker models, much like those John had seen at Groom Lake.

When the Gray Zetas delivered the bartered ships to MJ-12 in '53 each ship contained a full load, two hundred and thirty two grams, to run each ship for many light years. But, with the next delivery of new ships ten years later, MJ-12 had talked the Gray Zetas into including five hundred pounds of the atomic fuel they harvested from some distant Nova. The excess fuel seemed sufficient for the ships MJ-12 had on hand, but, by the early seventies, when MJ-12 began to design and build their own ships, and in an effort to distance themselves from their dependence on the Gray Zetas' Nova source, MJ-12 decided to try producing Element 115 on Earth.

Their scientists knew they could not stabilize the weight of 115 within Earth's gravity levels without a SuperCollider. Funds from their drug operations and black budgets were not sufficient to cover the addition of a SuperCollider. A decision was made to fund the project through a Congressional budget under the guise of, 'searching for an energy that is the origin of the universe.' In other words; to find an access to the strong force.

Their plan worked perfectly; Congress bought it. So much so, they sold the idea to other countries, Japan, Germany and Russia, who contributed millions, borrowed through Congress for humanitarian purposes, and then donated back to the project.

A site was selected, Waxahachie, Texas, just south of

Dallas, farmers relocated, and digging the big hole began.

A year before the public decided knowing the origin of the universe wasn't worth twelve billion and Congress was forced to close their prized SuperCollider, John, Myra and Bryan paid a visit to the site off I-35W. Myra, with her credentials of doing a feature for *The Houston Chronicle*, got them a VIP tour. She took many pictures of the expensive two-hundred-fifty ton tunnel boring machine chewing away at its fifty-four mile track through rock and dirt. If everything had gone as planned, MJ-12 would have gotten their Element 115 atomic fuel and the public would have gotten the shaft. If, after its completion, anything had gone wrong, a hundred square miles of Dallas would have been dust. And a lethal radioactive cloud would have spread across the land killing every living thing in its path, a death that would have lasted for, at least, two hundred years. Just as it had after the first atomic war on the Sinai Peninsula in 2024 B.C. A fact they knew to be true; around the time after Sodom and Gomorrah. The Bible had the word, and NASA had space photo evidence of the radioactive gray ash still in the desert sand.

"You have big plans for the weekend?" Myra asked. She hung her suit in the storage closet.

"Don't know, yet," Bryan said.'

"Susan?" Myra grinned. "How are you two getting along?"

"Okay, I guess," Bryan shrugged. "We talked a lot. I mean, I talked a lot." He smiled and nodded. "She's a good listener."

"Well, give her credit for that," Myra said. "You'll have to admit you're quite a challenge."

Myra knew that to be true. John and Bryan were probably two of the most intelligent, focused, dedicated and driven men she had ever known. Their absolute honesty was overwhelming and disarming; their truth seeking, calculated and thorough. Until John, these kind of men existed only in her hopes and dreams.

Myra Bennett grew up on a ranch in West Texas. Her

daddy was a cattleman and she was a cowgirl. Her life was boots, jeans, horses, cowboys and pickups. In high school she raised a couple of blue ribbon steers for 4H and sold them at Livestock Shows. But the ranching life was not for her, she lived for reading, writing and her dreams. An English major at UT she studied and longed to be as good as her favorite writers; Twain, Hemingway and Steinbeck. But before she graduated and wrote the Great American novel, she married Tyler Buck, heir to a growing oil empire, and definitely her opposite. Her social life took a drastic change. She became a world traveler as Tyler learned his father's business. Europe, Asia, Middle East, Far East, Mexico and South America were stops along the way and filled pages in her journal. It wasn't until Central America that the truth of politics and the oil cartels exploded her bubble of truth. A local drug czar destroyed half a refinery because, Tyler told her later, they were trading too freely with a local General. That's when the Mob and CIA bodyguards entered her life. Tyler bought her a .45 and gave her shooting lessons, which came in handy during the next two years as an involuntary member of the company's running and gunning drug business. What an adventure. If she survived, it was going to make a great book.

As fate would have it, her father-in-law was elected Vice President of the United States. He put Tyler in charge of the Company with a desk job in Houston and a big home in River Oaks. Tyler still traveled, making deals and politics, and she was at home trying to write. Their time apart wasn't working, her heart wasn't in her writing and she was bored. She sold some picture features to the local papers and eventually took a position as a part-time writer at *The Houston Chronicle*. The marriage fell apart under the weight of Tyler's absence and his deeper involvement with the company's illegal activities. Their divorce was a quiet one. It had to be. She got a nice settlement, ten million; payment for her silence. The tell-all book was shelved, an ending she would live with. She slept with the .45 for a while, then she met John, and her truth crusade took on renewed dimensions.

John turned out to be the element that was missing from her life. Circumstances being as they were, if she hadn't met him first, Bryan would've been her next choice. She readily admitted to loving them both. It was Bryan's unfortunate destiny to knowingly outdistance two wives. Myra had empathized with him through the end of his last mistake: Cheryl.

"John was lucky," Bryan had bemoaned to Myra. "There aren't many intelligent, loving women out there. They're hard to find, and I've lost my patience to fix any of the others."

Sadly, Myra knew Bryan had reached his limit and had withdrawn from all flirtatious contacts. And she went along with his celibate declaration, for he had shared his knowing experience with her and John, and she understood, that is, until she met Susan. She had recognized in Susan that eager desire for some truthful answers she herself was experiencing at the time she met John. Myra hated to share Bryan, but she knew Bryan was what Susan was looking for, and, in turn, Bryan needed someone like Susan, who definitely had a need to know.

"So,," Myra said. "When are you going to see her again?"

"Don't know," Bryan shrugged. "Tomorrow, maybe."

Encouraged, Myra grinned. "That's a good sign."

Chapter Five:
The Tell

BY FOUR-THIRTY SATURDAY afternoon, Bryan and Susan were hitting balls on the tennis courts at the Bay Area Racket Club.

Susan cut a fine, athletic figure in her smart tennis outfit. Bryan soon realized Susan hadn't gotten her tan lounging around a pool. She was an above average tennis player, returning ground strokes and countering his deft strategy with her agile quickness. Both had good games, and just short of showiness, amiably accepted the other's challenges. They played a couple of sets and Bryan survived strictly on the strength of his serves.

Near spent, they toweled off while graciously complimenting each other. Bryan got drinks from the bar and they cooled down at a shaded outside table.

"How long have you been playing?" Bryan asked.

"Since high school." Susan smiled. "And you?"

"Oh, ten years, maybe," Bryan admitted, rattling the ice in his cup. "What about your ex-. He play, too?"

Susan nodded. "Not at first," she said. "He took it up for me. He got to be pretty good, but not as good as you."

Bryan grinned. "Thanks," he said. "It began just for the exercise. Then I figured, since I was out there, I might as well get serious. So, I pretty much taught myself and practiced on anyone who'd take the time. I like the challenge of knowing everything about something that interests me."

"So I've noticed," Susan smiled, slyly, and took a sip.

He grinned, and took a small swallow of his drink. "What does your ex- do?" he asked.

"Fred? He's a lawyer."

"Where'd you meet him?"

"At Southwestern," she said. Bryan knew the University to be in Lafayette. "He was from Crowley. When he graduated he went to South Texas Law and I transferred to UH. Somewhere in there we got married. Steve was born while I was getting my Masters. I had a younger brother who was killed in Viet Nam. My father was a rice farmer. He passed away several years ago. My mother still lives in Iota, and I visit her at least once a year. We don't get along. When Steve was about ten I caught Fred having an affair. We tried to put it back together, but never could. He married soon after we were divorced and they live on the other side of Houston. Happily, I presume. I've had no major illnesses and have no major debts. Not very exciting, but that's me in a nut shell. Might as well get all that out of the way right up front. How about you? Your ex- play tennis?"

Bryan chuckled at her sudden and simple directness. In a sense, that was what dating was all about. "Yes, she played" he began. "And like your ex-, just for me.

"I'm a middle son. My older sister and my parents are gone. My brother is a high school principal back home. I met my first wife when I came to Houston. We had three children who are all grown and on their own. I left my first wife for the second. She had three children. We were the Brady Bunch, three boys, three girls. We divorced shortly after I caught her in an affair. She married the guy. I have no major illnesses, nor any major debts. How's that?"

Susan grinned. "Fertile ground for questions, but I'll

leave it at that, for now. Any unresolved pains from your past?''

Bryan shrugged. ''No pain, no gain. You?''

Susan made a pair of scissors out of her fingers and pretended to cut imaginary strings above their heads. She waved her hands and blew as if shooing released balloons. ''There,'' she said. ''Say goodbye to your past. Anyway, we didn't even know those people.''

Bryan knew she was right. They watched imaginary balloons filled with their just declared past float away. ''There's another exercise where you write em all down and throw 'em in the fire.''

She looked at him and smiled. ''Something from one of the many recovery seminars I went through after Fred. Did you . . . '' she caught herself. ''. . . of course not, you're a psychiatrist. You know all that stuff. You're not supposed to screw up. Right?''

Bryan smiled and shrugged. ''Sometimes we do. When we take on a patient as a personal project.'' He finished his drink.

''You have anything planned for the evening?'' she asked.

''No, not really.''

''Good,'' she said. ''What say we go back to my place. We can take a dip in the pool, rustle up something to eat, and maybe go for a walk. I have a ton of questions.''

''Sounds good.''

BRYAN CARRIED A bathing suit in his tennis bag for just such occasions. They changed in Susan's townhouse and tossed their tennis clothes in the washer and grabbed some towels. At the pool they swam a few laps before sitting in the spa. They talked of books, movies and the latest news stories, and in general, were getting quite comfortable with their similar attitudes. It could have been from that pleasurable content of inner discovery, but Bryan felt a sensual decision that Susan looked even better in her bikini than she did in her tennis outfit. On the way back to her townhouse she pointed out the jogging track around the bayou and the complex's exercise room.

Susan showered and changed while Bryan's clothes dried. He browsed her space while he waited. Her decor was tastefully feminine, flowery and smelled of potpourri and spices. Her bookshelves were full of hardcover and paperback novels, self-help and the writing craft. Upstairs, there was a frilly master bedroom. An answering machine was on one nightstand, a copy of her first *Earth Chronicles* book on the other. He was flattered that she had sought out the books and was reading one. He wondered if she was doing it for him, or herself. He wanted to think it was a little of both. Across the hall was a guest bedroom and a workroom with a computer, printer and files. And there was a calico persian in a cushioned rocker who seemed to ignore him with a "just another guy" look. Susan had said her name was Missy. He offered a friendly pet, but she scooted from his touch.

While Bryan showered Susan grilled two chicken breasts and prepared a sauce. She set the table with boiled rice and steamed vegetables. When Bryan was ready she let him pull the cork from a bottle of chablis.

"Umm. This is very good," he said, taking a bite of the quick low fat, low cal meal.

"Thank you," she said, slicing a piece of chicken.

"You always eat this healthy?"

"Fish or fowl." she said. "Rice and veggies. We always had rice in our family. Should you expect less from a rice farmer's daughter?" She smiled. "But there was always red meat before. Fred was from a ranching family and a hunter. After he left I decided a change was in order. Healthy, or otherwise, I haven't eaten red meat since. I changed my diet, changed my lifestyle. It's turned out to be healthier. I feel better about myself. How about yourself? You cook?''

"If it's in a box with directions,'' he chuckled. "I eat a lot on the run . . . sandwiches: chicken, turkey, ham, once in a while. Bachelor stuff. But, like yourself, I've about eliminated red meat, too.''

"Hmmm,'' Susan grinned. "Something else we have in common. Will the list never stop?''

Bryan took his glass and offered a toast. "Well, let's hope not,'' he said. They happily clinked glasses, and sipped.

"It's funny,'' Susan said. "Us meeting like we did. Your spending all that time in my home town. What if we'd met way back then?''

"Wasn't suppose to be. We weren't ready.''

"Did you ever play on the old fire escape at the school?''

"You mean, the twisting tunnel?'' he grinned. He remembered the slick slide barrel-roll from the school's top floor to the ground. "Yeah. You?''

She laughed. "Every kid in Iota played on that thing. It was our theme park ride.''

They laughed, amazed at the coincidences, shaking their heads, then studied each other as they ate.

"Isn't it strange how people get together?'' Susan said. "Become friends, maybe fall in love, get married. And then, find out they're so different from what we thought they were. Believe me, I've looked for answers, and I can't seem to find any that work. Churches, philosophers, psychiatrists, psychologists; so many books, so many theories. You're one of these so-called experts and you've voiced some opinions about the human conditions. Why can't we get along with each other? What's wrong? Any theories?''

"The answer to that,'' Bryan said. "Can be just as easy, or just as hard as you want it to be.''

"Okay, what's the easy way?"

"First, we all need to discover who we really are, our real selves," Bryan said. "Our real origins, our real forefathers and our real Creator."

"You mean, what's in *The Chronicles*?" Susan said.

Bryan nodded. "I noticed you've read a hundred pages."

"They're pretty heavy. Not exactly a fast read."

"Have you read the Bible?"

"Uh huh. Tried to."

"Opinion?"

"It's a history book," she shrugged. "Transcribed from ancient allegorical metaphors."

Bryan grinned and shrugged. "But, can you imagine teaching and swearing by a history book that brushes aside about 400,000 years of our inheritance with just a mention in a few verses?"

"The Nefilim?"

"Their Hebrew name." Bryan said. "The giants who came down from Heaven to Earth. The Annunaki from Nebiru, which means 'The Crossing'. Marduk with a new name."

"I haven't gotten that far, yet," Susan said. "I'm still in the astronomy part where their planet, Nebiru, was caught up in that 3600 year orbit between Mars and Jupiter and around Sirius. One of Nebiru's moons has just knocked a big chunk out of Tiamat, Earth's original name, and spun it off to where Nebiru runs into it a couple of orbits later, and smashes it into the Asteroid Belt. Right?"

"That's pretty good," he smiled, pleasantly surprised she had committed so much to memory so quickly. A teacher's skill. "So, what do you think?"

Susan shrugged. "Possible. It could happen, I guess."

"The story gets better," Bryan said. "Remember the first part, where the Blonds were running from the Zetas, and they met again on this new planet, had another big war that knocked the new planet out of its solar orbit?''

Susan shrugged. ''That planet was Nebiru, right? And the Nefilim were the Blond giants? The Annunaki?''

''Right,'' Bryan said. ''Can you imagine these beings on that planet, sailing around the universe, whipping through our solar system for hundreds of thousands of years, before deciding to risk an expedition to this beautiful, watery, blue sphere?''

''I guess I can imagine that,'' she said. ''If they can hop to all those other planets, why not this one? They needed another place to hide.''

''Not originally.'' Bryan said. ''They were looking for gold. They had heard from one of their exiled leaders, who had been here that there was plenty of gold on this blue planet, Earth. So, they sent exploring parties who set up mining colonies in what was Persia, and later on, in Africa. They were mining gold and shipping it back to Nebiru in their space ships. They were scattering the gold in Nebiru's atmosphere to solve some sort of environmental problem, like keeping their planet's heat from dissipating on their long orbit between stars.

''Ever wonder how gold got to be such a valuable metal? That's how. It came with our inheritance. People digging it up and taking it to these ''Gods'' for favors.

''The mining operations is the part where man, Homo sapiens, came into the picture. But first, let me give you some names of the main Annunaki characters, The God Council. There was Anu and Antu; they were like the king and queen of Nebiru. And they had three children; two sons, Enki and Enlil, and a daughter, Ninhursag. Enki's wife was Ninki and Enlil's wife was Ninlil. And from them came the direct descendant grandchildren; Ishkur, Nannar and his wife, Ningal. And then the great-grand-children, Ishtar and Shamash. There were more, but those are the twelve who made up the God Council and made the rules.''

"How can you remember all those names?" Susan frowned. "That's amazing."

"Easy," Bryan shrugged and smiled, proudly. "When you know their places in our history, it's as easy as Washington, Lincoln and Roosevelt. These descendants of the Blonds from Nebiru turned up to be the Gods, with different names, in the mythology of all the civilizations on Earth. You'll see when you get into more of the books, but now, for the Creation of Homo sapiens you only need to remember the Father, Anu, the sons and daughter, Enki, Enlil, Ninhursag and Enki's wife, Ninki.

"Enki and Enlil led the first expeditions to Earth," Bryan said, as he refilled their glasses. They had finished eating and shoved their chairs back. "The brothers headed up an initial force of fifty Anunnaki — troops, so to speak, later to be known in history as God's helpers, angels. Some of the Elite Guard even wore uniforms that had wings on the back. As things got going on Earth, more Anunnaki came to set up more colonies and mine the gold.

"They mined a lot of gold in Persia/Mesopotamia, but they needed more. So, Enki took an expedition south where he found more gold in Africa. And it was there that the Anunnaki miners decided they were too good to be slaving away in the mines, and so, they mutinied.

"Well, now Enki didn't have any miners and Enlil decided to close down his operation. But Enki said no, that he had an idea where they might create their own mining slaves. As chief scientist and medical officer, Enki's plan was to use his labs for genetic manipulation and vitro fertilization. He took the egg of a female apewoman, Homo erectus, a Cro-Magnon, native of Africa, and fertilized it with the Nefilim sperm. It worked, then Ninki, Enki's wife, volunteered to have the fertilized egg implanted into her womb. And in a few months Adamus, the first hybrid Homo sapien Neanderthal was born.

"Then through some lab techniques, Enki manipulated

Adam's X and Y chromosomes in the bones of his DNA string and created a female hybrid, Eve. With the experiment proven, Enki and Ninki set up a production line of Anunnaki Birth Princesses, and began turning out a hybrid Homo sapiens slave mining force.''

Susan laughed. ''We all started out as slaves?''

Bryan smiled and nodded. ''Wild, isn't it? All humanity has a blond father and a black mother.''

''Is there more?''

''Oh, much more,'' Bryan said. ''We're only up to 300,000 B.C. But, of course, they didn't know it was B.C. at the time.''

''Well, let's put away these dishes,'' Susan said, as she stood and began cleaning the table. ''We can take the rest of this wine out on the patio.''

''THE GARDEN OF EDEN was one of Enki's projects,'' Bryan said, sipping his wine in the soft patio light. ''Basically, it was a genetics lab and botanical garden. The Nefilim were bringing animals and plants from Nebiru and propagating them with the Earth stock.''

''Where was the Garden of Eden?''

''Northeast of the Persian Gulf,'' Bryan said. ''About where Iraq is today. You have to realize it wasn't all sand in those times. It was a jungle then, a virtual paradise. The last of it was wiped out during the Flood and the atomic cloud from the war of 2024 B.C. in the Sinai.

''The Garden was Anu's pride and joy, and on one of His 'state' visits to Earth he toured the mines and saw how well the hybrids were working out and asked Enki to send a few to work in His Garden.

''Enki was proud to send Adams and Eves to work in his Father's Garden; at the time he had plenty. But shortly thereafter, the Birth Princesses on Enki's production line decided that they'd had enough, and they quit. Enki's plan was wombless.

"Well, this threw Enki's mine production into a slow down. He decided the only way he could replenish his slave force was to fix the hybrids so they could reproduce; the very thing Anu had forbid him to do. So, Enki headed for the Garden, and his labs. He was in luck, Anu was, 'out of town', back on Nebiru. So, Enki called in the Eves in the Garden and began working on their DNA-RNA genetic strings, manipulating them so they could produce a seed that would not reject the Adams's sperm. After a few trials and errors, he got a match. It worked. And from that day, Primitive Man and Woman, the Neanderthals, descendants of the Gods of Nebiru, a place to be known in biblical history as Heaven, began to procreate, and the evolution of mankind took a giant step into its dark destiny."

Bryan raised his glass in a salute and said, "How's that for a start?"

Being the student she was of religious Bible teachings, Susan asked, "Where's the snake come in?"

"Oh, yes," Bryan recalled. "I forgot to mention that Enki was known as the Serpent God. In all of the pictured text from that time Enki is shown as wearing robes with an emblem of a winged disk and double helix serpents. You know, like that symbol you see in doctors offices, on medical diplomas. Enki was the scientist, the medical engineer."

"He wore the caduceus on his robe?"

"Yes. I think that's its official name."

"What about the apple?" she asked.

Bryan shrugged. "Ovary. Seed."

Susan sipped her wine while she thought, then, "The tree of knowledge?"

"DNA strings," Bryan said. "The helix. The family tree. The Tree of Knowledge." He took a sip from his glass and sat up. "You see, that was it, the knowledge of the ego, the thing Anu didn't want man to have. Up to then, man was a slave. He was dependant upon the Gods for his thinking. Now man was separate. Man had an ego, he could do his own thinking and feel his own emotions. Man could create. Man was co-creator. Anu had warned Enki that man would not be able to adjust and handle the emotions that came with the knowledge of self. And when you look back and look around today, you have to realize, Anu was right.

"Can you see that?" Bryan said. "See what the Bible left out: the space ships, the space ports, the tenth planet? The Creation and its reasons?"

"Having studied the history of early man," Susan said. "The caveman, the Cro-Magnon, the Neanderthal, it's hard to imagine that kind of technology, atomic powered space ships, DNA genetic labs. Everything seemed so primitive."

"It happened," Bryan assured her. "The Annunaki were doing all that stuff eons before they brought it here."

"What about Cain and Able?" Susan asked. "Where'd their wives come from? And Seth's?"

"Well, if you know the real history," Bryan said. "You'd know that there were Anunnaki females all around outside the Garden. Integration. And there were also their cousins."

Susan smiled on realizing the truth in Bryan's answers. She took the last swallow of her wine, set the glass down and looked at him. "Let's go for a walk." She stood and stretched.

Bryan swallowed the last of his wine and followed her out the back gate.

"IF YOU READ the Bible with the knowing that these 'Gods' were flying space ships back and forth to their planet and all around the Earth," Bryan said, "you'll understand its history." He and Susan were walking down a lighted path by the bayou. His words had a background chorus of crickets and bullfrogs. She took his hand and held it for a ways. He felt some reassurance to go on.

"The Nefilim had space ports all over, on every continent, as they were at that time. Take the Giza pyramid and the Sphinx, for instance, they were built on Earth's energy grids to line up with Mount Ararat to mark their landing patterns for the space ports in the Sinai, Persia and Lebanon. All of these space ports were well guarded by the Anunnaki astronauts, whose special uniforms were marked by wings on their backs. Hence, when you hear stories of God's helper/messengers, angels with wings..."

"Anunnaki astronauts?"

"Right." Bryan said. "Take the story of Sodom and Gomorrah. When Marduk, Enki's son, and two Anunnaki astronauts, angels, showed up at Abraham's camp he knew immediately who they were. How? Because, besides their auras, the astronauts were wearing their winged uniforms. Marduk told Abraham His Father was appalled at the degradation within the cities and that He was going to destroy them. Abraham began bargaining for sparing of the cities if Marduk could find ten righteous souls within. The angels went to the cities and found only one righteous family, Lot's. But Lot didn't move fast enough, so the astronauts lifted his family and put them down outside the city. Airlifted them. They told Lot to take his family and flee, and don't look back. Marduk then leveled the city with atomic weapons. Lot's wife stopped and looked back. She was reduced to vapors by the heat from the aftershock. Now, doesn't the story make more sense when you know what was actually going on?"

"Yes, I suppose it does," Susan I said. "But it's hard to believe our Creators could be so heartless."

"Oh, but they could," Bryan said. "They were still ticked off at Enki for giving Homo sapiens an ego and separating them from their righteous law. Look at what was going on in those cities. It was proof positive of what Anu had told Enki would happen.

"Another prime example of Anu's frustration with humanity's fiasco was the Deluge,'' Bryan went on, entering matters that were dangerously deep. He felt he should be talking of other things, things women wanted to hear, but he also felt he needed to see her reactions to a reality check. ''The Nefilim Gods knew what was about to happen. On its next crossing through our solar system, Nebiru would pass so close to Earth that their gravity waves would collide. Our Sun's planets orbit counter-clockwise, Nebiru orbits clockwise. The crossing would be like an eighteen wheeler passing a car on a two lane highway. The buffeting on the car, or Earth, would create earthquakes and waters from the rains and subterranean caverns would cover the Earth. Anu was so disgusted with the decline of humanity that He made the Nefilim declare that they would not tell any human what was to happen; the scourge of mankind would be eliminated and the Nefilim could start again.

''Well, Enki had to agree with his father; mankind hadn't turned out the way he had planned. But there was one human Enki thought was more righteous than any, Noah. And Noah had taught a righteous family and stayed connected to God's spiritual law. So as not to break his pact with his Father, Enki got an indirect message to Noah; to build the Ark, gather the animals Enki had worked so hard to create in the Garden labs, and when Noah saw the light in the East, get on the boat. The Nefilim space port was east of Noah's Ark and the light was the Anunnaki taking off in their space ships, heading for the safety of Nebiru, Heaven.''

He paused, watching and waiting for her reactions. There was none, but she still seemed interested, so he went on.

''You've read the story in the Bible, about how angry Anu was when they came back after the waters receded and found Noah and his family had survived! He was going to kill them, but Enki fessed up and pleaded his case; that he had decided they would need righteous seeds, such as Noah and his family, to restart a better human species. And, of course, the animals. Eventually, Anu saw Enlil's point, His heart softened and humanity was given another chance.''

They reached the end of the lighted path and Susan led Bryan in a turn back to her home.

"So, that's some of it," Bryan shrugged, hoping he hadn't stretched his points. "The Bible's a good history book when you know how to fill in the mystery blanks."

"It's just hard to imagine space ships and atomic weapons here before the cavemen," Susan said.

"There's plenty of evidence," Bryan said. "In the ancient Assyrian, Sumerian and Babylonian texts. Even in the Bible, but you have to realize those scribes didn't have access to the space ports. It was Anu's law that no human would ever know the secrets of their space ships and their atomic power.

"There were plenty of stories around: Gilgamesh's search for immortality, and Enkidu, and how they looked for the space ports and a way in. They wanted to ride a space ship to Heaven and become immortal, as Elijah had done. They never got in.

"Take the Tower of Babel. What do you think all those people were doing?"

"Well," Susan said, cautiously. She knew what she'd read in the Bible, but now it sounded dumb. "They were building a Tower to Heaven?"

"A Tower to Heaven," Bryan repeated. "That sounds a little illogical, even for that time. What they were doing was building a space port, a launch pad, a gantry. Where they were going to get the space ships, heaven only knows. But when Anu saw what they had done, He had it destroyed.''

"And confused their speech," Susan added.

"And scattered their leaders across the lands. No communicating, no more planning." He was pleased that she readily saw the connection. "So, you see, there is plenty of evidence."

"But man did eventually get atomic power and fly in space."

"Yes," Bryan sighed, sadly, "but not from the Nefilim. They got both from the Gray Zetas, the Nefilim's arch enemy, after they broke into the hyperspace at Philadelphia Harbor in '43. Actually, the Zetas gave the secrets to both sides during WW II. It just happened the Allies figured it out before the Axis did. The Zetas loved doing that. They thrive off of our conflicts. Which brings us back to how I got started on this in the first place; why can't we get along with each other.

"It all started back at the Garden of Eden when Enki gave the hybrids an ego, an access to the knowledge of self, and the separation from God's spiritual knowing. The Annunaki Gods gave us the spiritual knowing of a universal God, their Father and Creator, and implanted it within mankind through birthing. This knowing is the very thing that the Zetas began to lose through cloning and are seeking to regain through us. It is our egos that gives them access to the knowing. Anu was aware of this, and why He was so angry with Enki for giving man an ego self. But, maybe through luck, Enki had created a block that would prevent the Zetas from interbreeding with us. But that's a whole other story, and I don't know if you're ready."

"No, wait," Susan said. "What is it? You can't bring me all this way and leave me wondering about that."

"The block's in our genetic chromosomes," Bryan said. "You see, in order to save their dying race the Zetas need to regain their spiritual powers and they can only do that by procreating through birthing. Spiritual energy can't be passed on through cloning. And since they can't find their Annunaki brothers, the next best thing is man. But Enki set up a block; the Zetas can't get a direct match into our DNA because of the chimpanzee link."

"You're kidding." Susan said. Bryan shook his head. "You're not kidding."

"Trying to integrate, all the Zetas got were mutants."

She seemed disturbed, "The Zetas tried to integrate with us?"

Bryan decided hearing about the Zetas' abductions, the implants, impregnations and space nurseries might be too much for her now. He sought an easy way to drop the subject. "I know it sounds a little scary, but there's not much we can do about this conflict between the Annunaki and the Zetas. We're pawns caught up in Earth's middle ground. Our only means of surviving is to recognize our problem: our egos. It's the way the Zetas get to us, through illusions, stirring up our emotions, our fears. They feed off our fears. Man has to recognize his ego illusions, settle our conflicts, inner and outer, get back into the knowing of spiritual self within and its connection to our Creator and the spiritual energy of the universe. Then we'll be okay."

They strolled the last few yards of the path holding hands and inner thoughts. Bryan wondered if maybe he had pressed for an understanding a little too fast. Susan led him to the patio gate and opened it. Entering the soft light from the house, they saw Missy sitting in the kitchen window washing her face.

"How about a cool bowl of ice cream?" Susan asked, opening the patio door.

"Yes, that would be nice," Bryan said.

"Chocolate marble, okay?" she asked at an open freezer.

"Yes, that's fine." Bryan leaned against the kitchen sink and watched her get the bowls and spoons. He held a hand out to pet Missy. She recoiled, laying her ears back, tensing for his touch. After a few soft strokes she blinked her eyes and eased her back up to meet his hand.

"I think she's finally decided she likes you," Susan

said, handing him his bowl of cream. She smiled. "I
noticed she went into her curiosity mode the minute she
saw you." Bryan followed her into the den. "She and Fred
tolerated each other," Susan added. "But they never really
got along."

"How old is she?" Bryan asked. He sat next to Susan
on the couch. Missy followed them into the den, hopping
onto the coffee table and staring at their bowls of cream.

"Uh, twelve years," Susan said. She picked up the
TV remote from an end table. "You wanna watch the
news?"

Bryan shrugged. The news came on and Susan punched
the volume down. They watched a few minutes while they
ate. The big stories were a drive-by shooting and a refinery
fire in Baytown. After a bit, Susan asked. "How, or why,
did you get into all these things we've been talking about:
space ships, aliens, and the Bible? Obviously, you've done
a lot of research."

"It came with my job," Bryan said. "To answer the
question you asked a while ago; why can't people get
along, what makes us do what we do to other people, even
people we profess to love. Look at what is going on." He
nodded at the TV. "Where does that come from? It comes
from our ego emotions, from our fears. Enki made sure of
that hundreds of thousands of years ago. He gave us
knowledge of illusioned fears. They came with our egos.
We had love, it came with our knowing of spiritual self at
birthing. That light of love energy from universal spirit
was passed on by our Creators. And it's still there, in
everyone of us. But, most of us don't realize it because
we've let our egos' illusions take control of our lives.
That's the cause of all the discord in today's world; egos
fighting egos. Fear against fear. Hate against hate. Greed
versus more greed. Where's love? What happened to
love? It's still there. We haven't lost love. We can't. But
our egos won't let us see love. If we did, our egos would

lose control. And egos don't like that. Egos don't like being put in their place.

"Anu warned Enki, a lower humanity wouldn't be able to handle the knowledge of an ego, and He was right. Take a look." Again, he motioned at the TV. "The effects of not knowing the cause. The Zetas love it."

Susan reached for the remote and clicked off the TV. She finished her ice cream and set her bowl on the coffee table. Missy was quick to check what was left, giving it a tongue test. Susan got up, went to the stereo and turned it on. Soft, easy listening music flowed from speakers at each end of the room. Bryan set his bowl on the coffee table and Missy sized up her next cleaning job. He leaned back on the couch in casual anticipation. Folding her leg beneath and between them, Susan eased onto the couch beside him. She braced an elbow on the back of the couch and leaned toward him.

"Would you say my problem is a big ego?" she smiled, her face close, eyes focused on his, her voice soft and sexy.

"A problem for all of us," Bryan said. "Size is relative."

"Relative?"

Bryan moved a little closer. "To whether or not you have it under control."

"Oh," she said. "And do I?"

Bryan shrugged. "That depends, on whether you've recognized the difference between your ego's emotional illusions and your love in spiritual reality."

"What's an emotional illusion?" She leaned closer, kissing him softly on his lips. He kissed her back.

"This," he whispered. "It's your illusions of a relationship versus mine. If neither has a reality base, we're headed for a disaster. If both are centered, with love in control, it can be a very strong and beautiful connection."

She snuggled close, their arms slipping around each other. "That sounds complicated," she said, before they kissed.

"It's a grounding for respect," Bryan whispered.

She kissed his cheek and nibbled his ear. "Are you going to sleep over, or not? We can talk about respect in the morning."

His hands were already probing her firm, curvaceous body bcneath her shirt. "If you think we can handle the pressure."

She took his hand and pulled him from the couch. "Let's find out," she said, and led him toward the stairs.

Chapter 6:
The Symbols

SUSAN AND BRYAN slept late. It was nearly eleven when, after another round of love making, Susan entered the shower. Afterwards, she went downstairs while Bryan showered. Before he finished she was back with two bowls of fresh fruit, toast, hot tea and the morning paper.

As always, the paper was full of stories of world turmoil; countries fighting each other, religions fighting each other, greed fighting greed, egos fighting egos, fear against fear.

Susan folded back her section after turning a page. "You suppose these people would quit fighting each other if they knew the difference between their ego and spirit?" she commented.

Bryan glanced at her. "I don't know," he said. "Maybe. It's a long stretch back to love for some people. There's so much in our societies that provokes our fears: religions, politics, education."

"Education!" she snapped. "How?" He'd hit close to home.

"Everywhere," he said. "Our education systems teach the fear of not knowing. We would get better results if our learning centers taught the love of knowing, the knowing of love. Everyone enters each life already knowing. We should encourage them to remember their knowing. Instead, we teach them illusioned ego fears. And what we get is their forgetting knowing love.''

She tossed her section and rolled toward him. ''I don't know,'' she grinned. ''I thought we did pretty good.'' Her hand slipped under the sheet and rubbed his chest.

Bryan dropped his section of paper. ''That depends,'' he said, putting an arm around her, ''on how many illusions our egos have created about what happened and what was said. And whether or not our love can put those illusions in their perspective place. That's the pressure of handling the ego.''

He pulled her close.

''It's a good beginning,'' Bryan whispered, responding to her touch.

IT WAS AFTER FOUR before Bryan came through the back door of his townhome. In his bedroom the message light was blinking on his answering machine. He pushed the replay button and began stripping out of his tennis outfit, shoes first.

''Bryan,'' the message started. ''John. This is Sunday noon. Where are you, buddy? We just got a fax of symbol translations from New York. They look great. We're on our way to check them out. Can't wait. Come out when you can. See ya. Beep. 12:20.''

He moved at a quicker, excited pace. His mind raced with the possibilities of discovery. He shaved and cleaned away any evidence of the past twenty four hours. He was dressed and back in his car in twenty minutes, heading for Alvin and the shed.

When Bryan came through the shed's door the others looked up at the sound of the buzzer. Frank and Boyd were beneath the ship and John waved him on from its doorway.

Quickly putting on his heat suit, Bryan noticed something different about the ship. It was brighter, more lights for some reason.

Bryan zipped his suit as he hurried toward the ship. He could now see that Frank and Boyd were probing in an open panel in the ship's underside. Frank was helping Boyd check several fax sheets of symbols against wires and blinking lights within the open section. Frank glanced at Bryan, smiled and gave him a gloved thumbs up. They had scored. Anxiously, Bryan turned and raced up the ramp and into the ship.

The geiger counter clicked faster than ever. Little lights, colorful and blinking, lit up the panels around the console in front of the chair. The panel lights reflecting in their heat suits, John and Myra's beaming anticipation welcomed him aboard. They, too, held fax sheets of symbols in their gloved hands.

"It's on!" Bryan gushed as he spun around, taking in the incredible display. "How'd you do it?"

John held up the sheets and pointed to a spot high on the edge of the console. "That little symbol right up there says ON." He moved around with Bryan and showed him the mark high above their heads. "It's way back behind there," John said. "I had to stand on Boyd's shoulders to reach it." He laughed.

"Why didn't we think of that," Myra grinned. "If you're seven to eight feet tall and you didn't want short humanoids starting your ships, it's logical you would design a switch out of our reach."

Bryan laughed. "The ON switch!"

"Isn't this incredible!" Myra beamed, gesturing at the pulsating display.

"Fantastic!" Bryan gleamed. "We're moving now. What else have you found?"

"Well," John said. "We've found some 'dangers, sensors, gravity amplifiers, and the reactors, but so far nothing that indicates a starter switch."

"Here, give me some of those and I'll help you look,"

Bryan said, reaching for the sheets. John and Myra divided their sheets with him. "Where've you checked already?"

"Pretty much all this side of the console," John said.

"What about the chair?" Bryan asked.

"No, not yet," Myra said, as she and John resumed their search of the console.

Bryan started with the front of the chair.

"See Susan this weekend?" Myra asked her fax sheets and the console.

"Huh?" Bryan said, knowing the question was meant for him. "Uh, yeah," he said, continuing to search the chair's back high and low.

"How'd it go?" Myra probed.

"Okay, I guess," Bryan shrugged at the bottom of the chair.

"Spent the night," Myra grinned over her shoulder. "It must have been better than okay."

"Yeah," Bryan admitted. "She's better than okay."

"Did you give her your test?" Myra asked.

"Test?" Bryan peered around the chair.

"Don't play dumb with me," Myra said. "I know you'll test any woman you're attracted to. Did she know the difference between her ego and spirit?" Behind her John kept searching the panels and listening.

Bryan stood and leaned on the chair. "Yeah, I think she does," he said. "At least, she didn't say I was nuts. But, like anyone's initial experience, it's going to take a lot more time to de-program her illusions and re-program her reality."

"Did you tell her about your out-of-body abduction?" Myra asked. Myra and John had heard Bryan tell of his experience several years ago, right after his divorce from Cheryl. How tall, blond beings abducted his spiritual self right out of his body and taken him on a reality check of his universal knowledge. His remembering of the *knowing*. An earth hour with these super beings was a lesson in pure truth. Bryan told Myra and John his return to his body had the same excruciating effects as being born again. And, as is true to the birthing process, his memory of what he knew to be true was dimmed. The past years since, he had gathered Earth proof of that truth, and in doing so, had recalled most all of the knowing.

"No, I didn't tell her." Bryan said. "I don't think she's ready for that bit just yet." He came around and slid into the chair and faced her. "I like her," he smiled. "I think she has the intelligence and desire to grasp the reality concept. But like everyone, she's searching for the perfect relationship without realizing that the perfection starts with her. And, as we know, that could be a long process."

Myra nodded. "That it is," she said, remembering the years of Bryan's help in finding their own truth.

"Took her forty years to build her illusions," Bryan said. "Could take half that to replace them with the truth."

"Then she's above average," Myra smiled.

Bryan shrugged. "She might even be a good candidate for the quick fix."

"Quick fix?" Myra frowned.

"I was thinking, on the way out here," Bryan mused. "What if we did it the way the astronauts do it."

"The way the astronauts do it?" Myra puzzled. "What are you talking about?"

"The aura. The rapture, Myra," Bryan said. He smiled, spreading his arms, gesturing to the ship. "Out there. Take her for a ride. Jolt her truth to life."

Incredulously, Myra stared at him. She turned to see John eyeing the both of them over his shoulder. Bryan stood and faced them.

"You hear what he's saying?" Myra asked John, then turned back to Bryan.

"Yes," John said. "I heard what he said."

"I don't know," Myra said. "I thought it was just going to be the five of us."

"It is," Bryan explained. "But we could take another, easy. It could be an experiment to see if it really works, you know? We've almost got this thing going."

"If works on Susan," Myra snapped, "then it's the rest of the world? Is that it, Bryan, you want to fix the whole damn world?"

Bryan grinned. "I hadn't thought about it, but, yes, that's a good idea."

"Sell tickets, why don't you?"

"Right!"

"John," Myra pleaded, turning to him.

John threw up his hands. "This is something we can discuss some other time," he said. "First thing we need to do right now is find that starter switch, and we won't do that unless you two get busy.

"What've you found on the chair?" John asked Bryan as he turned back to the console.

"Well," Bryan said, glancing at the chair's arms. "Looks like there's a danger and a *something* on each arm, but no 'Ons' and 'Offs'."

"A *something*," Myra muttered, returning to the console. "Don't you tell Susan about the ship until we say so."

"I won't." Bryan said. He leaned over the chair's arm and began searching its sides.

"How're you doing over there?" John asked Myra.

"Nothing yet," she said. "How about you?"

"No."

Bryan ran his gloved hand along the chair's sides searching for the slightest indentions. His fingers pressed into several grooved rows just beneath the chair's left arm and he leaned to get a better look. He thought he could see a small line of symbols above the indentions and he slid over the arm and dropped to the floor. When he held his fax papers up to the light to get a clear comparison he noticed a small panel on top of the chair's arm had flipped open.

Bryan stood and looked inside. "Hey! What's this?!"

John and Myra spun toward him. The three stood staring into the little open recess. Inside were two quarter-size buttons, one red, one white. Each had a lightning bolt engraved on top.

"How'd you do that?" Myra exclaimed.

"Well," Bryan recalled, repeating his motions. "I put my hand here and crawled over the arm. That's when I noticed it was open."

John inspected the spot where Bryan gripped the chair's left arm. "Must be a pressure point under there," he mused. Realizing the ship's design symmetry, John moved quickly to the chair's right arm and lined a grip of the arm with Bryan's spot and pressed heavily with his fingers. A twin panel on the right arm flipped open exposing a matching recess and two identical buttons.

"Bingo!" John yelped. "Looks like we're in business!"

They stared at the buttons on one arm, then the other. They were anxious, but cautious.

"What do the lighting bolts mean?" Myra asked.

All three flipped through their fax sheets. Finally, John stopped and held his papers, pointing to the lighting bolt symbols. The translation words beside them were, power and fire.

"Power and fire," John read.

"Power and fire," Bryan repeated, staring at the buttons.

"It could mean power to fire her up," John said.

"Yeah," Bryan mused. "And if you read them the other way, it's fire power."

They glanced at each other, pondering the possibilities.

"You mean, fire power as in guns?" Myra asked.

Bryan shrugged. "Guns? On this ship?" Bryan corrected. "Lasers, more than likely."

"Did the Annunaki write from left to right, or right to left?" Myra asked.

"I don't know," John snapped, frowning pondering their quandary. He ran his gloved fingers very gingerly over the buttons in the left arm. "Ignition. Guidance, right, left, up, down," he said.

"Only the person sitting in that chair knows for sure," Myra said.

As if seeking some decision, John turned and cautiously slid into the big chair. He rested his arms on the chair's arms to where his fingers could reach the buttons.

"What do you think?" Myra asked. "Do we dare?"

"Feels right," John said. "Maybe we should."

Myra glanced at them. "Wait! What about Frank and Boyd?"

John's fingers wiggled above the buttons. "They're okay," he said. "They're outside. They've got their suits on."

Myra recoiled. "Maybe we should wait outside, too."

"And, maybe, close the door." Bryan added.

"No," John snapped. "We're not going anywhere. We just want to start her up."

"Yeah," Bryan said. "We've come this far. Might as well."

"Okay," John said, his fingers steadying over the buttons. "Ready, or not, it's time to see what this baby has under her hood."

Myra and Bryan backed away and braced themselves against the console. "God be with us," Myra whispered. "Hope He's not mad at us for stealing His ship."

They held their breath, staring at John's fingers resting on both sets of buttons.

"The right side first," John said, as he pressed.

A soft whirring-whine-swoosh stirred under the chair and the lights dimmed ever so slightly. A blue flash popped outside and bounced through the door. John released the buttons as quickly as he had pushed them.

They heard a hissing and a crescendo of heavy clattering and clanking as metal crashed onto the concrete floor outside.

"Hey! What the hell!" Boyd yelled, as the commotion began to settle down. "Geezus! What're you doing in there!"

John leaped from the chair and scrambled through the open door behind Bryan and Myra. They saw an alarmed Frank and Boyd peering from around the backside of the ship. They cringed as another heavy metal pipe rattled to the floor in front of the ship. And as if a final note, a big rusty pipe with a sheered end rolled-out from under the trailer.

"We pushed some buttons," John admitted, as they carefully crept down the ramp.

"What buttons?" Boyd demanded. He and Frank joined them at the bottom of the ramp, all eyes searching the damage in front of the ship.

"Some we found in the chair's arms," John said.

The old drill pipe that they had stacked against the wall in front of the ship was scattered like pick-up sticks across the floor. They stepped carefully around and over the clutter. Gathering in front of the ship, they stared up at the wall. Above where the pipes had been were two round, smoking holes, each about six inches in diameter and about four feet apart, drilled all the way through the black-painted plywood and the rusted tin outer shell. From beyond, the starry sky twinkled back at them.

"Fire power, "Bryan commented.

"Yep," Myra agreed.

"Damn!" John snarled. "I thought we had it."

"Had what?" Boyd asked. He scrambled up onto the trailer to get a closer look at the holes.

"Ignition," John said. "But it was the lasers."

"Yeah, sure enough," Boyd said, as he examined some

"Yeah, sure enough," Boyd said, as he examined some little open areas that had opened on the front edge of the ship. "Right here. There's two more on the other side."

Frank climbed up beside him and both stood on their toes to peer out the holes.

"Wonder what their range is?" Boyd said. "Hope we didn't hit something down in Alvin."

"It's hard to say," Frank said, straining to see out the hole. "But it looks like we've got a little fire in one of the trees out there."

"Geez!" John sighed. The enormity of what they had done, could've done, or might've done, slowly began to settle over the three instigators. John, Myra and Bryan seemed frozen to the spot as they stared at the holes and then each other.

Frank and Boyd hopped down and started for the front door. "Better get it out before it catches." Frank said. "We sure don't want any fire departments out here."

"You guys see if you can find something to patch those," holes Boyd ordered, grabbing a fire extinguisher.

They didn't move until Frank and Boyd were out the door and the buzzer had stopped.

"I think we'd better be careful about pushing buttons," Bryan said.

"I'll buy that," Myra said.

They began to search for spare plywood.

Chapter Seven:
The Mission

IT WAS AFTER NINE when Bryan strolled into the reception room. Gail looked up from her first chore of the day, the crossword in the morning paper. "Hi."

"Morning," Bryan smiled.

"Oh, Bryan!" He stopped. "What's a five letter word, starting with C, ending in S, meaning confusion?"

Bryan thought about it. "Try *chaos*," he said, finally, a word still fresh on his mind. Coincidence?

"Yeah," Gail brightened. "That might work." She printed. "That's good."

"Anything else?" he asked before continuing to his office.

"Yes," Gail said to her puzzle. She looked up. "Steve Burris is waiting in your office."

"Steve Burris?" he repeated, glancing at his closed office door. "Isn't he supposed to be at the Cape?"

Gail shrugged. "He's in there." She nodded at his office. "Said he'd wait inside."

"Did he say what he wanted?"

She shook her head. "No."

His back to the door, Commander Steve Burris stood at the window staring somberly out into the bright morning. His arms were folded across his chest. He spun around as Bryan pushed through the office door. He forced a smile and dropped his arms. Bryan knew right off that here was a man who had plenty on his mind.

"Hey, Steve," Bryan grinned, mustering all of his cheerfulness. "Surprise. Thought you were holding at the Cape."

"I was," Steve shrugged, stepped away from the window and around Bryan's desk. When they shook hands, Bryan could feel Steve's suppression; something was not right. In the years he had known Steve, interviewing, testing and helping him adjust, they had become friends, not great buddies but good friends in a business sense, but Steve had never just dropped by.

"It's good to see you," Bryan said. " Looking fit as ever. So, what's up?"

NASA's official insignias and flight patches gave Steve's casual sonic-blue jumpsuit an informal aire, even though he was the pilot of the Shuttle sitting on a very busy launch pad down at the Cape. That, in itself, was enough for him to be a little up tight.

"Just a little emergency," Steve said.

"Yeah? Other than what they're holding for?" Bryan moved around his desk, but did not sit in his chair.

"My oldest boy got hurt in a Little League game."

Bryan grimaced. "Not bad, I hope. Well, uh," He shrugged. "Must be, or you wouldn't be here, eh?"

"No, no, he's okay," Steve assured him. "Just fractured a bone in his foot sliding into third base. It's in a cast. He'll be on crutches for a while. But he's tough, he'll be okay."

"Well, That's good." Bryan shifted, uncomfortably.

"The hold's gonna be longer than they expected. We got a break. They said we might as well wait it out here."

"Well, it's good to see you, man." Obviously Steve wasn't there to talk about his son's accident. They both shifted, nervously, from one foot to the other. "Can I get you a cup of coffee, or something?" Bryan added.

"Yes. Yes. That's fine," Steve muttered, thoughtfully. Bryan started for the door and the coffee hutch.

"Wait," Steve stopped him. "On second thought, why don't I buy you a cup?" He nodded at the window. "It's a nice day. Let's walk while we talk."

Yes, talk, that's what this is all about, Bryan thought. But of all his sessions with NASA's astronauts he had never done one outdoors, at least, not that he could remember. But, no one had ever asked for the informal privacy of a walk. "Yeah. Sure. Good idea," Bryan said, returning to his desk. "Should I take my pad? My recorder?"

"No," Steve demanded, then smiled. "That's why we're taking a walk. No notes, no recordings. Okay?"

Bryan shrugged, complying, and ushered Steve out the door.

Passing through the reception area, Bryan told Gail he would be back shortly. They stopped in a downstairs lounge area where Steve purchased two cups of coffee from a vending machine.

"You don't mind about this, do you?" Steve asked, as they doctored their coffee at a condiment table.

"No, not at all," Bryan assured him, hiding his puzzlement. "It's unusual, but I'm flexible."

Steve held the door as they went out. "Ever thought about the amount of information NASA has on all the personnel involved with the space program — on paper, on tape, on disks, videos?"

"It's a lot, I know," Bryan said, and tasted his coffee.

"Thanks to micro chips, they can store more stuff than they'll ever need." Stepping off the steps, Steve glanced side to side, as if searching for someone. Bryan noticed, and it just added to the strangeness of the event.

"That's true." Bryan agreed, and he too, glanced around. He didn't see anything out of the ordinary; some grounds people. "You know?" Steve mused, after a sip of coffee. "I'll bet there's enough tape on me, just me alone, to reach to the moon and back.''

"Yeah, you're probably right.   I've never thought about it,'' Bryan commented.   Maybe he's upset about invasion of privacy, Bryan thought.   He and Marsha alone had tons of info.   "Does that bother you?''

"Yes.   Yes,'' Steve said to a tree they were passing. "At times it does.''

Good! That's it, Bryan thought.   "Well, you never mentioned this before.''

"Well, it's beginning to,'' Steve said to the pebbled walkway.   He kicked at a small twig under foot.

Bryan shrugged, consoling.   "It comes with the territory, you know?   You can't complain.   You signed up. You weren't drafted.   You knew what you were getting into.''

"I thought I did,'' Steve mused, distantly.   He squinted in the bright light.   "But, maybe I didn't know about everything.''

Bryan frowned at him.   "What's that supposed to mean?''

"Do you have any idea what's going on around here?''

"Well,'' Bryan stalled, mentally listing all the things he knew and the trouble he'd be in if he were to say.   "I don't know,'' he added.   "What do you have in mind?''

"Take these secret missions for example.   Putting those spy satellites in orbit.''

Oh, so that's it, Bryan thought, not the tapes.   "You mean, like your flight?''

"Yes.   To be specific.''   Steve took a swallow of coffee.

Bryan wondered how specific Steve was going to be. It was against NASA policy to discuss the secret missions, and he didn't need more subversive trouble.   He suddenly felt uncomfortable with the direction their conversation was taking.   He made another quick survey of the area.   His coffee was making the warm day even warmer.   He wiped

at the perspiration that trickled down his face. He wished
he had gotten a cold drink.

"I have to tell you something you mustn't repeat to
anyone, understand?" Steve said in a side glance. "I know
you can do that, because that's what they pay you to do."

"What do you mean, have to tell *me?*"

"Because it's something that's bothering me," Steve
said. "That's your job, isn't it, to help us handle things
that are bothering us? Things that might keep us from doing
our job the way we're suppose to? Rationalize?"

"Well, yes, I suppose, if it's something I can help you
with." A calculating thought about Steve's situation, pilot
of this secret mission, crossed Bryan's mind. "It's not
something about this flight, is it? Something you're not
supposed to tell anyone, even me, is it?" He prayed it
wasn't.

"Yes, it's about the flight," Steve admitted. "And I
can tell you because I know you won't tell anyone else.
Right?"

"Well," Bryan stalled. "Are you sure you really have
to?"

"Yes," Steve snapped, tiring of Bryan's prevaricating.
"I can't tell Jan, and I can't carry this back to the Cape."

For several steps they studied each other. Can't tell his
wife, Bryan mused, seriously. "You're sure there's no
other way?"

"Sure," Steve nodded.

Bryan shrugged and nodded. "Okay, let's have it."

They threw their empty cups into a trash can. Steve,
then Bryan, glanced right and left. There was no one in
fifty yards.

"The spy satellite on this flight isn't just a spy satellite," Steve began in a low tone. "It doesn't have any
cameras, none of the usual stuff. It looks like the others all
right, but this one isn't."

"Wait, wait! Hold it!" Bryan said, waving his hands.

"Can you tell me what's bothering you without telling me any secret stuff?" He was high on NASA's radical list as it was, and after that meeting last week, they were probably watching him a little too much. And if Steve knows something really big, really bad about that satellite, something that would rip NASA, he probably hasn't been out of their sight since he found out. And he knows something bad. That's why he's been looking over his shoulder.

"I *have* to tell you the secret stuff," Steve said. *"That's* the trouble."

Bryan closed his eyes. Oh, Gezzus, he thought, I don't need the military any further up my butt. Not now, for sure, not now. But the damage is already done. They know Steve's talking to me, and no matter how much he tells me, they're going to know I know everything. He opened his eyes and nodded. "Okay, let's have it?"

"This satellite." Steve continued. "Where the cameras are supposed to be, well, there's two of the largest missiles I've ever seen. None of those little Nuke things. These babies are loaded. I'm talking hi-tech, super-neutron warheads."

"Geezus!" Bryan gasped. "Why me?"

"I need you to help me deal with putting those son-of-a-bitches up there," Steve hissed. "Spy satellites are one thing, but nuclear missiles, that's something else. I can't handle that. I couldn't live with myself. I had enough problems with what I did in Nam. You know, you helped me. Showing me how to forgive and forget. And the rapture — out there — you helped me with the changes. I just can't do this. No way."

Indeed, Bryan had helped Steve with understanding his attitudinal changes taking place within himself as Bryan had with all the astronauts who had sought his help. Steve had been, and was, an adapt student of the differences that took place within the body/mind/spirit when an astronaut is exposed to the timelessness of deep space. Steve had come

a long way in understanding the knowing of his spiritual
self and his earthly self ego.

"How'd you find out?" Bryan asked, his mind racing
for a solution that would benefit both of them.

"There were certain procedures that I would have to
implement before the satellite was deployed," Steve said.
"Two days before the intended launch, they took me
through the procedures. It was obvious, to me, these
procedures had nothing to do with the operating functions
of cameras. I've had experience in the arming of bombs
and missiles, and I knew what I was doing. They didn't
seem at all surprised that I would discover the fakes. I
believe they had chosen me specifically, to do just that and
to do this job. After I found the missiles, they acted as if
they were going to tell me all along. So they went ahead
and showed them to me. They made out like it was no big
deal and that I should be honored to be the one to carry out
this very important mission."

"Who told you?" Bryan asked.

"Two Air Force Generals. Defense Department. Joint
Chiefs, I believe. They wore NORAD shoulder patches."

"Names?"

"General Calvin Fuller," Steve said. "Four stars.
And a three star, Walter Rawlins."

"Hoo-boy," Bryan sighed.

"Sounds as if you know them."

Bryan massaged his forehead as if he felt a headache
coming on. And, he did. "I've heard of them," he said.
Not only had he heard of them, he knew them to be MJ-12.
Now, not only did he know that Steve's telling him about
the missiles would bring on more surveillance, but the
surveillance would be MJ-12.

Steve noticed Bryan's intense expression. "What've
you heard?" Steve asked. "From your reaction, I'd guess
these brass are more to worry about than the missiles. Just
how much power do they have?"

Bryan wiped the sweat from his face again. "You saw them," he said. "You heard them. They have all the power. General Cal Fuller is Above Top Secret Pentagon. That means, above the President, Congress, everyone. He's MJ-12 and he answers only to the Ruling Council."

Steve was shocked. "Ruling Council? How do you know this?"

Bryan took a deep breath and sighed. "It's a long story," he said. "And you probably wouldn't believe me if I told you."

"Try me."

"You thought understanding yourself in space was difficult," Bryan said, shrugging him off. "You saw the missiles?"

"Yes."

"Describe them." Bryan glanced around, hoping not to see any dark figures bearing down on them.

"Well," Steve began. "They were about six to eight feet across and maybe, twenty, twenty-five feet in length. They had the usual cone noses and fins. They were facing opposite directions and designed to detach from the satellite carrier once they were in space."

"Did they tell you why they were putting them out there?"

Steve shook his head. "No," he said. "They indicated all I needed to know was to get them out there, and arm them."

"That's a lot of responsibility without clarification."

"Tell me about it," Steve said. "In Nam I could go out, blast the jungles, shoot down a Mig, if we saw one, and never give it a second thought. A computer game, our job. We never saw the bodies. At least we could sleep nights. But this! This is something else. Can you imagine the destruction those things can do? Aren't we supposed to be cutting back on nuclear arms? Where'd those monsters come from? Who are they for?"

"Did you ask them?"

"I tried."

"What did they say?"

"A matter of national security."

"Their standard 'none of your business'." Bryan glanced around, again. "Where are you parked?"

Steve nodded toward a parking lot. "Over there." They reset their direction. "You seem to know these people," Steve said. "What do you know about them? What's going on? What would warrant their use of these monster missiles?"

Bryan shrugged. "Just a guess," Bryan said. "With General Fuller involved, several possible targets are already bouncing around in mind. A couple are too far out for anyone who doesn't know their history to believe. And I don't have time to bring you up to date. Not today, anyway. I only know of General Fuller through John Sherman. He had a run-in with Fuller at one of MJ-12's secret test sites, Groom Lake. You know Groom Lake?"

"Sure," Steve said. "Everybody knows Groom Lake. That's where all the super-tech stuff is developed. All our Star Wars technology comes from there. I've flown by there many times."

"And you can bet those missiles came from there."

"You think, maybe, they're meant for the Middle East?"

"Not necessarily," Bryan mused. "They could be for any place MJ-12 decides to stir up trouble. Or, wherever their trouble gets out of hand. It's part of their job; keeping world turmoil and the economy going."

"And slaughtering innocent people."

"That's life on planet Earth," Bryan said. "Hell, isn't it?"

They came to the parking lot and Steve stopped in front of his car. "You see the problem I'm having here?" he said. "So, how can I justify doing this?"

"Well, you were okay until you knew."

"Yes. But now I know," Steve said. "I can't pretend I don't know. I can't eat, can't sleep. I don't even know if I can pull it off once I get out there. Can you imagine the guilt? God! I don't see how they can stand it."

"It's easy," Bryan said. "They've been brainwashed. You know, you were there once, but you've escaped, and their mistake was not knowing that you had. However, at the moment, I can't rationalize your rejoining them in their madness."

"Taking another life, even one, is inconceivable," Steve growled. "I just can't do this. It's insane!"

"They're not going to let you walk away," Bryan pointed out, emphatically. "Listen to me. I know these people. You already know more than you'll ever need to. You screw up, and *they will kill you* and your family. And now they know that I know."

Steve frowned hard and glanced around. "How?" he gasped.

"There's a secretary in my office who works for them," Bryan said. "See that maintenance man over my shoulder, by the building?" Steve squinted into the distance. "That's not a transistor radio he's listening to, and there's a boom mike in that rake handle. He's CIA."

"My God!" Steve whispered. "Are you sure?"

"It's a burden of knowing."

"I'm sorry, Bryan, I didn't realize."

Bryan shrugged. "I know you didn't. It's okay. It's done."

Steve blinked and swallowed hard. He cleared his throat and whispered. "Is there anything we can do?"

"Well," Bryan smiled. "There's nowhere to run, if that's what you mean."

Steve forced a smile and took another look around. Bryan sighed. "Look. When are you due back at the Cape?"

"A week. Maybe less."

"I want to run this by someone."

"But, I..."

"Don't worry," Bryan assured him. "He's okay about this. If he can't help, no one can. But, listen, if I don't get back to you before you leave, just buckle up and do exactly what they've told you to do. They won't do anything unless you try to force their hand. Okay?"

Steve shook his head, incredulously. "I can't believe this."

Bryan shook his hand and patted his shoulder. "Welcome to the real world."

BY TWO-THIRTY that afternoon, with the Burris event resting unobtrusively in the back of his mind, Bryan quietly made his way down the short hallway toward Marsha's door. In his hand he had a craftily made gift; an office UFO, two paper plates paper clipped together with an inverted Styrofoam cup tooth picked to the assemblage's topside.

Marsha's door was slightly ajar and Bryan carefully eased it open, poking his head inside. Their offices looked basically the same; the basic books, the basic file cabinets, TV, stereo, and memorabilia. A typical government space, except Marsha's had floral patterned drapes, matching upholstered chairs and couch, and a color coordinated oriental rug that spread under and in front of her antique desk, behind which Marsha was busy studying paper work.

Bryan slipped his paper UFO through the partially opened door and wrist flipped it like a frisbee. The tiny paper ship sailed softly, spinning to a skipping landing across her desk and coming to a skidding stop against her coffee cup.

Marsha jumped, startled, and caught her cup, barely keeping it from spilling. She looked up, wide-eyed and aghast.

Bryan stood, smiling, in the open door. "Space visitor," he announced.

Marsha's flashing eyes jumped from her cup, the model, to him and back. "You're damn lucky you didn't spill my coffee all over these papers." She cautiously picked up the little model and examined its creative design.

"An invitation to an abductee's story," Bryan said. He strolled in without her invitation.

Unimpressed and a bit appalled, Marsha wrist flipped his model back to him. He caught it in his gut before he could step onto her fancy rug.

"Bryan, you're incorrigible," she sneered.

He fumbled with the toy. "Is that a no?"

"No!" she huffed. "Most definitely, a no!"

"My guest," he offered again. "Used my influence. They said you could sit in." They didn't, but she wasn't going anyway.

"I wouldn't dare be caught sneaking out of one of those cult meetings."

"Still angry about yesterday?"

"No." She leaned back and her high-backed leather chair creaked. "Why?"

"Just wondering." He glanced at the couch. She hadn't asked him to sit. "Heard anything from Radford?"

"Yes, as a matter of fact," she smiled, coyly. "He called. He apologized for the way he'd ended the meeting so abruptly. He complimented me again on our work."

"Anything else?"

She shrugged and leaned forward again. The chair creaked. "Yes," she said, twisting a pen in her fingers. "He wanted to know if there was really anything to that aura business. I told him I didn't think it held any real merit."

"And?"

"He said they decided to ignore your other remarks. And he suggested we get back to business as usual." She tapped a stack of folders in front of her. "He wants our evaluations on these applications by next Thursday."

Bryan smiled. Well, he thought, Radford hadn't heard about his latest caper, or if he had he wasn't going to mention it to Marsha.

"No problem," he grinned, confidently. He turned to leave, then another thought stopped him. "Eh," he said over his shoulder. "Would you go to the abductee interview if I promised you proof positive of the real thing?"

"Out!" she barked, flinging finger and arm at the door.

He grinned and nodded. "What if I told you I had a real alien space craft parked in my garage?"

"What if I told you I was going to have you committed? Out! Not another word."

Chapter Eight:
The Pilot

JOHN'S HOME WAS a total experience for any serious Ufologist. He had everything except the beings themselves. His former second floor game room and a bedroom overflowed with his filed reports and memorabilia collection from thirty years of investigating extraterrestrial visitations all over the world. In the midst, a computer, printer, copier, fax, TV and VCRs surrounded his desk at the top of the stairs. Hundreds of books, magazines, chronicles and recordings filled the shelves on every wall. Six legal sized file cabinets were filled with newspaper clippings and correspondence from fellow investigators on every continent. If there was an E.T. incident not in John's files it had not been heard or seen by man. Only two centers held more information on the subject; one was in the Pentagon's Defense Department, the other in MJ-12's S-4 division south of Groom Lake, Nevada.

Bryan loved visiting this Mecca of extraterrestrial lore and browsing its nooks and crannies. But tonight his presence held a different purpose, one that he'd experienced many times, but not with the fervent expectation as this abductee visit.

In the years Bryan had been a member of the Club, he'd been privileged to attend dozens of abduction interviews. John had helped write the UFO Field Investigators Manual and had the sessions of questions down to a science. Bryan knew this one wouldn't be conducted any differently. Few, if any, abductees had ever objected to having John record their experiences. Each was asked to start from the beginning and tell as much as they could remember. Once the pictures began forming in the subject's mind, John would probe for details that verified authenticity, such as a particular alien group; their appearance, their ship, method of communication, method of teleportation, duration, purpose — whether experiments were conducted or omnipotent knowledge was revealed — etc. Sometimes the victims, as they might be called, would bring photos of bruises, scratches, and burns they had received during their encounter. A few still had needle marks and skin scoops where the aliens had taken tissue samples. John would photograph these. Afterwards he created a file under the abductees code name that contained the interview tape, a transcription, photos and copies of photos. John's files were categorized as to species of aliens; Zeta Grays, Sirians, Orions, Nordic/Blonds, Pleiadians, Zeta Reticulian, Antarean, Arcturan. Repeat abductees, alien favorites, even had their own thick files covering many years of experiences, some dating back to their childhood.

"Once your vibrations are programmed into their computers," John had explained to these recalls, "they can lock onto you at any time, any place on Earth." John had many first and second kind reports of UFOs' blue beam sweeping an area for vibrations.

Most abductees insisted their sessions take place in their own space. John had no problem accommodating, since they felt comfortable and talked freely in those surroundings. Without asking, Karen Coe had suggested she come to John's place.

"Fuller *and* Rawlins?" John frowned as he gathered his recording equipment from a den cabinet.

"That's what he said," Bryan confirmed.

"Must be really something big going on to bring both

of them out of the mountain,'' John mused. He searched a drawer for blank tapes. ''And Burris came to you seeking help?''

''He seemed plenty shook,'' Bryan said.

John chuckled. ''Yeah. I would be, too,'' He said to a stack of tapes. ''Fuller has a way of scaring the hell out of you.''

Having never met General Fuller, Bryan had to take John's word for it, and Myra's.

''You can say that again,'' Myra called from the kitchen where she was putting together some refreshments. ''He sure did a number on us.''

''Burris brought you his problem, and now our problem,'' John said, selecting a couple of tapes. ''And, that *problem* is Fuller and MJ-12.''

''Yeah, I know,'' Bryan sighed. ''I saw them, already. With their boom mikes. They were all over the place.''

''They picked up on you?'' John asked. Myra leaned in the kitchen doorway listening.

Bryan nodded. ''I'm sure they did. But, they kept their distance.''

John glanced at a concerned Myra, then back to Bryan.

Bryan shrugged. ''Can they watch us anymore than they already are?''

''Damn right!'' John said. He tossed the unselected tapes back into the drawer and slammed it shut. ''MJ-12 can get real serious about their business. Especially, if we're in it.'' He took the tapes and recorder into his den and set them on the coffee table. He glanced at the front windows. ''They're probably sitting out front with their boom mikes right now.''

John went to an end table, picked up a pen and wrote on a small pad that was by the phone. Finished, he showed it to Bryan and Myra. *From now on any direct references to the ship will be written. We'll have to use the mall maze to lose their tail.* After they'd read it, he ripped the note into tiny pieces and dropped it into the disposal. "Maybe they'll ease up after that satellite's in orbit," he said, when the grinding stopped.

"Well," John said, as he came back into the den. "What did you tell Burris to do?"

Bryan shrugged. "I told him to do exactly what they told him to if he wanted to keep himself and his family alive. And, I told him I'd talk to you, and you'd come up with something."

"Oh, yeah, great," John snorted. "Talk about pressure. And just what do you think I, *we*, can do about it? NOTHING." He shouted for the benefit of any big ears listening.

Bryan grabbed the pad and wrote. *I had an idea. When we get the ship to flying, we could go shoot the missiles down.* He handed it to John.

"Ha!" John snorted, before showing it to Myra. Myra read it and he ripped it off and wrote. *We don't have it flying.*

Bryan read it, ripped it off and handed it to Myra. He then wrote, *we might after tonight.*

John read it, ripped it off, handed it to Myra and wrote, *Maybe. How would we know which satellite it was?*

Bryan read it, ripped it off and handed it to Myra and wrote, *We could tag it somehow.*

John read, ripped, handed it to Myra and wrote, *How?*

Bryan read, ripped, handed it to Myra and wrote, *I don't know. Think of something.*

John read, ripped, handed it to Myra and wrote, *I'm sure they're going to let us waltz over to the Cape and put a tag on their satellite.*

Bryan read, ripped, handed it to Myra and wrote, *We could get Burris to do it.*

John read, ripped, handed it to Myra and wrote, *Without them getting suspicious?*

"Think about it, okay?" Bryan said.

"Right. With everything else I have to think about," John said. He took the notes from Myra, tore them into tiny pieces and stuffed them down the disposal. He clicked it on and it ground slowly, laboring.

"You keep talking like this," Myra said. "And you're gonna clog up our disposal."

They smiled. It did sound ridiculous.

Bryan followed John back into the den. "You have any idea what they're for?" Bryan asked. He did a missile motion with his hand.

John shrugged as he sat on the couch. "Couple of guesses," he said, pulling the recorder to him. "They're probably Excaliburs."

Bryan waved his hand. When John looked at him, he was jerking a thumb toward the front windows.

"Oh, hell," John said. "They know we know about the Excalibur."

And indeed John did. The Excalibur missile was a black budget project at Groom Lake that his late friend, Allen Chin, had worked on before he was killed. Allen had told him it was designed to penetrate the Earth's crust up to three thousand feet. Its nuclear warheads could destroy the deepest enemy bunker, no matter what its material or construction.

"They probably don't know that we know," John said, going back to the recorder. "That their first test firing from land based rockets — Redstone, Atlas, Saturn — only penetrated about three hundred feet. So, my guess is that they've improved it, and they're going to try it from a much greater height." He ejected the cassette slot open. "How's that grab you?"

"Not so good." Bryan glanced at the front windows. "Who do they have in mind? Saddam Hussein?"

"They did everything else to him from those satellites," John said. "Why not this?" He put a one-hundred-twenty minute tape in the recorder and closed the slot.

"What's your other guess?"

"Okay. Try this one," John said, leaning back into the couch. "Remember that underground alien city that's supposed to be outside Dulce, New Mexico?"

"The Zeta's genetic labs?"

John nodded. "And remember several years ago, the rumor that MJ-12 had discovered that lab and had a big battle with the Zetas over their cloning and implanting way over the limits of their treaty, and a whole force of Black Beret got wiped out?" Bryan nodded. "Well, back then, Allen hinted that the Excalibur was to be used in the destruction of those labs."

"MJ-12 is Zeta controlled," Bryan said. "They wouldn't let that happen. Not to their own."

"Well," John shrugged. "I said it was just a guess. They've been known to slaughter their own. We know that's the way they destroyed all the life forces on the other planets unfortunate enough to be in their way."

Bryan sighed and looked at the front windows. "I hope if there is some intelligence listening out there, they're getting the message."

THREE MINUTES PAST the designated hour, Myra was relaxing on the den couch next to John. Bryan pushed a lounge chair into the circle around the coffee table.

All three glanced up at a car door slamming in the street followed by light footsteps up to and outside the front door.

The doorbell rang.

Bryan was the closest, so he opened the door, and was immediately stunned.

Karen Coe was beautiful. A gorgeous blue-eyed blond with a deep tan. She glowed in a white silk, spaghetti-strapped sundress that showed off every curve right down to her long legs and white sandals. She smiled, and her aura swept over his.

"Hi. Karen?" Bryan managed, with a smile.

"Yes, hi. John?"

"No. Bryan," he said, inviting her in and shaking hands. "Bryan Mayfield."

"Karen Coe."

Their eyes locked on and both held onto the moment. "Yes. Yes," he stammered. "Come in, come in." He held her hand as long as he could. It had been a while, but he knew how smitten felt. Silly and dumb, and he hoped she hadn't noticed. John came up behind Bryan and extended his hand.

"Hi, Karen. John Sherman."

They shook hands. "Hi, John. Hope I'm not late."

"No. Not at all. Have any trouble finding us?"

"No." She saw Myra beyond John.

"Come in," John said, ushering her into the living room.

Bryan followed, taking in a pleasingly perfect all around view. Damn! he thought, The aliens' taste in female abductees had greatly improved. His next thought; was she married? John hadn't said and he hadn't noticed to look for any rings. If she was, why was she here alone? Maybe she had one of those husbands who thought this kind of thing was dumb.

Myra welcomed her in. "Hi, Karen. Myra Bennett." They shook hands.

"Hi, Myra. Good to meet you."

"Come on in. Make yourself at home," Myra said, leading the way into the den.

Karen glanced around. "You have a very nice place."

"Thank you."

"I was just getting some refreshments together," Myra said. "Can I get you something? Diet drink? Iced tea? Lemonade? We don't have anything stronger than a Lite beer."

"Iced tea is fine," Karen smiled. "Herbal, if you have

it.''

"We do. Any flavor?'' Myra called, going into the kitchen.

"Whatever you're having's fine.''

John offered her the stuffed chair at the end of the coffee table in front of the recorder. "You can sit here if you like.'' She did, putting her shoulder bag on the floor beside her. Her mini dress rode up exposing more thigh. Bryan pulled the lounge chair closer before he sat.

"Well,'' John said, settling onto the couch. "We're glad you've decided to come and tell us your story. We're very interested in these kinds of experiences. Every one of them adds to the validity of the alien visitors. Have you had more than one?''

"No,'' she said. "Just this one, as far as I know.''

"Did you have any trauma with, or after, your abduction?'' Bryan asked. He had to keep reminding himself not to stare.

"Well, yes, and no,'' Karen said. She blinked her gorgeous blues at him, looked down and tugged at her skirt.

John reached for the recorder play button. "You mind the recorder?''

She shook her head. "No.''

"Good,'' John said. "Might as well get on with it then.'' He clicked the recorder on. "So, you're from West Beach,'' he began.

"Yes.''

"How long have you lived there?''

"Two years.''

"A native Texan?''

"Yes. Born in Houston. My parents still live in the same house, over on the West Side. Memorial area.''

"Uh huh,'' John mused. "What's your father do?''

"He's an executive with Exxon.''

"You married?'' Bryan asked. Out of the corner of his eye he caught a sly smile from Myra. Karen looked straight into his eyes and said quietly, "Widowed." They held the look a long moment. Myra noticed. Well, goodbye Susan, she thought.

"Sorry," Bryan frowned, looking sincerely sorry. Inside he fought off a delighted grin. Over Karen's shoulder he caught a glimpse of Myra's, "Awww, isn't that a shame," pantomime in the kitchen.

Myra entered with a tray of iced drinks. "Here you are," she said, passing them around. "It's not often we meet a native Texan anymore," she said, giving each a napkin and coaster. "I'm originally from West Texas myself, Midland. John's from Ohio and Bryan's from Louisiana." She took her drink and sat on the couch next to John.

"How long have you all been in this UFO club?" Karen asked.

"Five or six years, I guess," Myra said. "Ever since I met John. John's been in it forever. He started it. We're sort of a branch of the national club, MUFON. Bryan's been a member since, when?"

"Nine, ten years," Bryan shrugged.

"Then, you've seen UFOs?" Karen asked.

"We've seen our share, I guess," Myra said, thinking of the ship in the shed, as John and Bryan did, too. They were also conscious of those who might be listening outside. And if they were, they had already taken down Karen's license number, called it in and probably had her name and complete background. "Ever been on one?" she asked.

Myra took a quick glance at John and Bryan, like who's supposed to be asking the questions here. They'd had their suspicions about Karen from the start, showing up at this time, saying she had flown an alien craft. While preparing for the session they had set their rules about what information was to be voluntarily exchanged and what was not. This seemed like a loaded question. Back to Karen, she said, "No. We haven't. But we hear you have."

"Yes," Karen said. "About three years ago."

"Three years?" John said. "Why this long in wanting to talk about it? Did it bother you?"

"For a while," she said to her tea. "It took me over a year to realize what had happened, and another year of hypnosis to bring out all the details. I don't talk about it to just anyone. I'm sure you know how that is. I saw you on a local talk show about three months ago," she said to John, "talking about some of your cases, and I thought you might be interested in mine. It was rather unique."

"Yes, like any abduction, we're interested," John said. "Why don't you tell us, just start from the beginning."

She shifted in her chair, crossing her ankles and tugging the short hem toward her knees. She seemed conscious of the extra close inspection she was feeling from Bryan. Except for a few glances at John and Myra, he had barely taken his eyes off of her since he opened the front door.

"Well," Karen began. "It happened the summer my husband, Jim, and I decided on a camping trip to the Big Bend park."

"That's three years ago?" John injected.

"Yes. '92. We were living outside San Antonio at the time. I was teaching and he was doing oil exploration for the Gulf Oil Company. Chevron."

"What did you teach?" Myra asked.

"Painting and Art History at San Marcos," she said. Myra nodded, and she continued. "It was the third day out. July 10th, I'll never forget the date. We had our camper set up in Santa Elena Canyon, down where Terlingua Creek joins the Rio. It was real early in the morning, about two o'clock. Jim and I were asleep in our camper."

"What kind of camper?" John asked. Details again.

"It was one of those low-ride trailers that folds up and

out into a mobile tent.'' She fashioned the shape with her
hands. "The top's covered but the sides are netting.
That's why the ship's bright lights woke us up. Jim first.
He sat up and said something like, 'What time is it? It's
bright as day?' When I managed to get my eyes open, I
saw the clock. That's when we heard the sharp humming
sound. It kept getting louder as the light got brighter. We
could tell from the shadows that whatever it was, was
coming straight down out of the sky. Jim jumped up and
grabbed his rifle. 'Helicopter,' he said. 'Must be border
patrol looking for wetbacks.'

"Well, we were up, running around in the tent,
grabbing stuff to cover with. Jim got his pants on, and we
both got to the tent flap about the same time. We peeked
outside and it was bright as day, out to about so far, like
we were in a spotlight, and it was right above us. We
looked up, and were almost blinded by this one, huge light.
We squinted and shaded our eyes with our hands.'' She
animated with hands and body again. "We could see it
was no helicopter. 'Holy Jesus!' Jim said, 'what is that?'
There was this great ring of fiery orange almost right above
us. And roaring heat. Like looking into the exhaust of a
jet engine. It came down toward us, real slow, and we
could make out this huge craft. Big and round, maybe fifty
or sixty yards across, maybe three stories tall. There was
a dome on top with little lighted portholes around the sides.

"Damn!' Jim says. 'What is it?' I said. It was a space
ship. Just like those you see in the movies. Lit up like a
Christmas tree with these orange, green and white lights, all
around it, blinking on and off, spinning,''

"Your typical UFO,'' John said.

Karen nodded. "Sort of like the one in that movie,
Close Encounters, but it wasn't as elaborate, not as many
lights. This one was like a toy spinner top, you know, but
bigger, and it hummed just like one, too.''

"What happened next?'' John prodded, moving her

story along.

"Well, we just stood there looking at it. And it was sort of looking at us. Then all of a sudden this blue beam shot out and shined right on us. And boom! That was it. The next thing I remember, Jim was leaning over me, trying to wake me, and he was dripping wet. He said he woke up on the other side of the river. He had to swim back. He was really upset. I tried to move. I was sore all over, my arms, legs, back, neck, head. I felt as if I'd been drug up the mountain and back. Jim was in even worse shape. He helped me and we struggled outside and looked around. The sun was coming up. It was almost six o'clock. The only sign the UFO had been there was some cracked rocks and burned bushes. And there was a funny smell in the air, like battery acid. Burnt electricity. That's the only way I can explain it. We wandered around in a daze for a while, trying to put the lost hours together. We decided we weren't going to spend another hour there, so we packed up and left."

Karen took a long sip of her tea and glanced at them, waiting for their next question.

"You never left the camper?" Myra asked.

"No. I didn't think I had."

John asked, "What about being on the ship?"

"At the time, neither one of us could remember being on the ship," Karen said. "On the way home, we each recalled what had happened in the beginning and the end of the event, and tried to find some explanation for the missing time. Before we'd gotten back to the Park Headquarters, Jim broke out in a rash, and he got violently ill. He was delirious, and that's when he began saying we were on the ship with these, beings, aliens."

"Radiation poisoning," Bryan said. "That's what he had."

"That's what the doctors said, too," Karen said, sadly. "Strange thing was, we couldn't figure why he had it and

I didn't."

"You didn't?" Myra questioned.

"No."

"That is strange. You never did?"

"No. Not to this day."

"You tell the doctors about the UFO?" John asked.

"I told them we'd seen one."

"What'd they say to that?" Myra asked.

"They listened," she said. "They didn't say they believed us one way or the other. They were very skeptical. They asked, how close it was, and I told them, within twenty yards, I guess. They did what they could for Jim's burns. His hair was beginning to fall out in big clumps. The next day some government people came around. They flashed CIA badges. Jim was pretty much out of it by then, so I told them as much as I could remember about the incident. They did a video interview, took some pictures and a bunch of notes and left."

Myra glanced at John. "Sounds like the Cash/Landrum thing all over again." They remembered the radiation burns on Betty Cash and Vickie Landrum from the case where she met John.

"You mean those two ladies up north of here?" Karen said.

John nodded. "January '80. We investigated that case. They had the same sort of burns as you described."

"I saw the story of their experience on TV," she said. "On *Unsolved Mysteries,* or one of those kind of shows."

"They've done the story several times," John said.

"How're they doing? The ladies?" Karen inquired.

"Not too good. Betty Cash still has cancer."

"That's a shame," Karen said, sadly. "I guess Jim was luckier. The doctors made him comfortable as possible, under the circumstances, but a week after it happened, Jim was gone."

Karen hadn't meant for them to be so somber. "That's

life," she smiled, quickly, with her chin up. Bryan felt a little guilt for being happy before when she said she was a widow.

"Sorry," John said. Myra and Bryan nodded.

"What was the hospital?" Bryan asked.

"Brooks Army. That was after the local doctors."

"You never had a mark on you, anywhere?" John puzzled.

"Well, I did have a little redness on my face and arms," she said. "Maybe it was from looking up at the ship, maybe it was from the trip. I don't know." J o h n took a deep breath. "So, when did you remember you were on the space ship?"

She shifted and recrossed her legs. "Over the next year I kept having these strange dreams about these beings, and that experience, that time. Mixed up things. The dreams began to fit some of the things Jim had told me in his delirium. Us being on the ship, you know? Like being with them. For a while I thought my dreams were influenced by what Jim had told me! I did some paintings of the dreams and a feature writer from the San Antonio paper saw them in a gallery showing. He was interested and asked if he could do a story on me and my paintings. I said yes, and it was during the interview that he suggested I see a psychiatrist friend of his and have him use hypnosis to uncover my blocking of that experience."

"Did you?"

"Yes. It was strange," she said. "The session revealed I *was* on the alien ship, but my body *wasn't*. It was still back in the tent in Big Bend."

Her interviewers shot quick glances at each other. Out-of body abductions were not that common. There were basically two categories; physical and spiritual. Physical ones were the most traumatic. Conducted mostly by the Zeta Grays, these were rather painful experiments for extracting tissue, blood and semen samples. Spiritual contactee abductions, performed with or without the abductee's body, were peaceful and enlightening as they always involved some exchange of knowledge. These type of abductions could be done by any of the benevolent groups. Any investigator, knowing their history, knew that the Zeta Grays had little reason for teleporting just a soul.

Bryan sat up, leaned forward and asked, "You were out-of-your-body?"

Karen nodded. "You know? Spirit form, just energy mass."

"We know," Bryan said. "But Jim wasn't? That's strange."

"Doesn't sound like the Zetas," John mused.

"Why would they take one out, but not the other?" Bryan puzzled.

Karen shrugged. "I suppose they had their reasons. But that's why when they took us for a ride Jim's body got the full charge of radiation, while mine was still back at the camp."

"Did these beings have something on their ship to protect, or contain, your spiritual energy while you were on the ship?"

"Not really," Karen mused. "I guess, it sort of contained itself, within an image, sort of. Jim wouldn't have seen me if it hadn't. And he said he saw me onboard with the aliens. That's the way I remember the aliens were, the big ones, like me, but much taller. I could see their bodies, but I could also see their spiritual being, radiating, like a bright aura."

"Did you see any little aliens around?" John asked. "The ones about four feet tall, big head, big black eyes. You know the ones. You've probably seen pictures of them?"

"No. Just the tall ones. They were magnificent giants."

Giants! That's the word they wanted to hear. They

were getting somewhere now.

"Giants?" Bryan inquired.

"Yes," Karen smiled. "Blond. Sort of like super beings."

"Blond?" Bryan asked. "Shoulder length blond hair?"

"Yes."

"Angels?"

"Yes. I guess you could say they were angels," Karen mused.

They had a sort of glow, an iridescence, about them. And, I do remember, some of them seemed to have wings."

John, Myra and Bryan exchanged glances. That was what they wanted to hear. She was abducted by the Annunaki/Nefilim.

"And they took you for a ride?" John asked.

Karen nodded. "Flew all over the place; around stars, planets, galaxies. It was spectacular; fantastic!"

"It must have been," Myra smiled.

"And fast. Incredibly fast," Karen added.

"And they let you pilot their ship?"

She smiled. "Yes. It was great!"

"Do you remember how you did it?" John probed. "I mean, were there any controls? Buttons, switches, levers to push?"

Her head tilted back and her eyes searched the ceiling as if the answer might be seen there; "No," she said, slowly, as she looked back at John. "I don't recall handling any controls." She smiled. " There were controls, but I didn't have any hands, remember? It was like, well, they told me, think about what I wanted the ship to do and it did it. Right, left, fast, slow.

"It was strange. When I was in spirit, just spirit, I knew everything they knew. All knowledge. Everything about them, their ship, the universe, everything. I was one with them and everything they were. It was the most fantastic feeling I ever experienced, but back in my body, I didn't remember any of it."

John tried again. "If you weren't touching any physical guidance systems, there must have been something that connected your spiritual self to the ship?"

"Well," Karen said to the ceiling again. "I later remembered there was this place on the floor and one just like it in the ceiling right above," She looked at all three. "And when I was between them. It was as if I became the connecting link in the ship's power. I was one with the ship. I was its mind. I was its being. It went up, down, back, forward, spin around, fast, slow. It was easy. The aliens were pleased I took to that, actually recalling that *knowing,* so quickly."

"They were pleased?" Myra said.

She grinned. "That I was special. No fear. Not everyone can conquer that fear. Few people know we have that much power in spirit. What they showed me was a gift of life; the knowing that I was one with them and the universe."

The *circles!* On the ship's floor and ceiling! All three remembered seeing the circles; They hadn't thought much about them, except that maybe they opened to some compartments, or whatever, but they didn't open. Now, they knew. She was on a Nefilim ship, much like theirs, or she was sent with that specific information to get them to admit they had a ship.

Myra asked, "Were those places on the floor and ceiling, circles?"

"Yes. I believe they were round."

Myra qualified her question. "Others reported that, too."

Bryan reflected on Karen's description of the knowing. The way she described her out-of-body experience was exactly like his own. He began to understand what had almost knocked him over when he opened the front door.

It was her aura. Her spiritual power had been recharged, her aura expanded, and her's had touched his. He had experienced a little of the same with the astronauts, but nothing like what he had with hers. And, as close as they were at the moment, they were still caught up, plugged in. Incredible.

Finally, John asked. "This knowing, your spiritual power, is that the key to flying the ship?"

"Yes, of course," Karen grinned. "The *knowing* is the key to everything." She glanced at Bryan, and he had to wonder if she was as plugged in as he was?

"Obviously, you've recalled this *knowing* in recalling your experience," Bryan said. "Describe this *knowing*. How does it feel to know everything, all knowledge?"

She grinned. "You mean, describe knowing who we are? Knowing why we're here? Where we came from? Knowing the meaning of life? Knowing the pure energy of spiritual love? That would take a while. What're you doing for the next six hours?"

Bryan glanced at the clock and shrugged. It was 9:25. He was game. He settled back, leaning toward her.

She uncrossed her legs and sat up. "Myself," she said, reaching for her bag. "I can't spare that much time right now. I have some errands to run on my way home. You've heard my story, but if you're really that interested in the *knowing,* I had three more sessions with the psychiatrist, and I have tapes you can listen to at your convenience."

"YOU DON'T MIND making us copies?" Bryan asked Karen, as they walked to her car. After saying their thanks and goodbyes, John and Myra had closed the front door behind them. Myra had watched through the window until John pulled her away. Or maybe they were checking the street, as Bryan had done, looking for anyone sitting in a strange car, or van, trying to look as if they were from the neighborhood. Bryan didn't see anyone. They either hadn't been there, or they had left already.

"No," Karen said. "It's no problem."

Being that close, walking in her aura, Bryan felt the pure, intoxicating affects. She really had it. Everything. Looks, intelligence, the charisma of knowing. She was a perfect being, a perfect woman. She didn't need fixing, teaching. She knew the pure separation of her illusions and her reality. As a matter of fact, she could probably teach him a thing or two. He wondered if the reason she was still single is because, the same as himself, she couldn't find that spiritual match? He wondered what she felt about him? He pushed for a way to see her again.

"When can I pick up these tapes?" he asked.

"Well, I could have them ready by Thursday. Is that soon enough?"

He'd hoped for sooner. "Sure," he said, covering his disappointment. "I'll take off early." He walked her around her little white sports car.

"Good," she smiled and flashed those killer blue eyes. She had a great smile, perfect white teeth, and sensual lips. Oh, how he wanted to kiss her. Instead, he opened her car door. "Why don't you bring your family and we'll have dinner."

"There's no family," he smiled. "I'm divorced."

"Well then, we'll be looking for you late afternoon." She slipped into the bucket seat behind the wheel and he reluctantly closed the door.

"Late afternoon," he muttered. Her *we'll* had caught him right in the gut, right in his dream. All night, she hadn't mentioned anyone else, not even a pet. He thought about asking who *we* included, but decided not to damage his fantasy any further.

She started the engine. "Call me, and I'll give you directions. Bye."

"See you Thursday. Bye."

He watched her drive away.

As he went to his car, he waved bye to Myra's shadow in a front window.

Chapter Nine:
The General

DEEP IN THOUGHT, General Calvin Fuller paced the carpet in Dean Radford's office, stopping in front of the wide windows, his troubled eyes pondering the landscape without really seeing it. Under his bushy, gray mustache an unlit cigar rolled to one side of his mouth and clinched in his yellowing teeth. Dark, prescription glasses reflected what he wasn't really seeing. Thinning hair and a face weathered by experiences reflected in the four stars that sparkled on the epaulets of his Air Force dress blues. Campaign ribbons, so many half were hidden under his lapel, a Strategic Air Command and a lighting bolts NORAD patch added a shock of color to his formal military crispness.

Radford leaned back in his chair, lit a cigarette, his second of the day, and casually studied his old friend's demeanor. He blew a heavy puff of smoke over Fuller's dark blue military hat, with its Air Force metal and scrambled egg bill, that lay on a corner of his desk.

The General removed his cigar. Holding it behind his back in clasped hands. He flicked his corona, irritably.

"Burris sure disappointed me, Dean," Fuller said to the sky beyond the window. "First person he runs to is Mayfield. Burris has put us in a very precarious position."

"All the astronauts talk to Mayfield about their problems, Cal. It's Mayfield's job," Radford argued, drawing a drag on his cigarette and blowing smoke. "What's to worry?"

The General turned halfway and glared at Radford over his shoulder. His name stood out over his breast pocket; Calvin D. Fuller. "There wasn't supposed to be any problem," he growled. "I asked for your toughest, most trustworthy pilot for this mission, Dean. A gung-ho-All-American-Hero is what I wanted. Someone who puts our country's great ideals first. Someone who has almost as many kills as you and I put together. Not some conscious-ridden, bleeding heart, do-gooder."

"Burris was a perfect choice." Radford puffed.

Fuller ignored the remark, spun and strode slowly toward the desk, shoulders squared. "I wanted someone who could do this job without asking questions. You got anybody around here that can do that, Dean?" He dropped into one of the leather covered chairs in front of the desk. Clasped his hands, with cigar, in his lap and glared at Radford. A curl of smoke rose from Radford's cigarette.

Radford blinked and shrugged. "There was no better vet than Burris."

"Bullshit!" Fuller snapped. "Your choice was crap, Dean." He put his cigar in his mouth and rolled and chewed its end. He looked down his nose at Radford. "Against direct orders, he spills everything to Mayfield, and Mayfield runs and tells John Sherman." He removed the cigar and picked a tiny piece of tobacco from his tongue. "If it wouldn't draw an inquiry, I'd court-martial the son-of-a-bitch. As it is, we might have to eliminate all three of them. Sherman is long overdue. He's known too goddammed much for too long."

"Eliminate?" Radford swallowed. "That's pretty drastic, Cal. What the hell do you have on that satellite worth killing three people over?" He crushed his cigarette in an ashtray and reached for another. He needed it, what's the harm in three.

"Need to know, Dean," Fuller glared. "Need to know."

"You forget this is my show here, Cal?" Radford glared over lighting up again. "NASA's my baby. My butt's in the crack if something goes wrong out there. I want to know how big a crack."

Their thoughtful, smoke-screened stare-off weighed their many years of frequently interrupted friendship. It was evident neither knew all there was to know about each other. Finally, Fuller blinked. "There're a couple of missiles on that satellite."

"Missiles!" Radford snapped. "What kind of missiles?"

"Big ones."

"Who for?"

Fuller inhaled and sighed. "You've run out of a need to know, Dean."

"Don't give me that!" Radford huffed a stream of smoke. "I know what the hell you're doing out there in your big hole in the mountain. You come crawling out here, looking like a dried up ol' mole, threatening my people. I want to know what's going on. I want to know just how bad it's gotten that you have to up the ante on Pentagon stupidity."

Fuller dropped his head and rubbed his forehead between his fingers, pinching the pain of an aching head. After a long moment he straightened up, placed his wet, smelly cigar in the ashtray and looked Radford in the eyes. He sighed. "This place clean?"

Radford nodded. "Far as I know, it is."

Fuller allowed himself a tight, disbelieving smile.

Radford shrugged behind a curl of smoke.

"How long have we been friends, Dean? Flight school. The fifties. Korea. Damn, we were young and innocent, weren't we? Thought we knew everything. Crap, we didn't know shit, man.

"The day we saw that space ship over the Inchon valley was when our education started. We should've never backed down on what we saw. We should've stuck to our stories. Maybe things would've turned out different. Maybe they would have canned us both. We'd been better off owning a hardware store somewhere.

"There's a lot of weird stuff going on, Dean. More than you could ever imagine. Things that'd make your hair stand on end, your skin crawl, your heart stop and your stomach do flip-flops. Things that would scare hell out of everyone on this damn planet."

"We've seen the aliens, if that's what you mean," Radford said. "And their ships. We have pictures."

"Pictures!" Fuller scoffed. "You've never talked to 'em, Dean. Sat in one of their ships. Seen what the hell they can do. Had one of them turn your world upside down. They're so far ahead of us, it's incredible. Time travel, atomic power, laser weapons, computers, electronics, cloning, mind control, things we never even imagined fifty years ago. Scares me just to think about it."

Little aliens and the things they could do was nothing Radford could be afraid of. "Aliens are not my problem, Dean," he said, slowly and distinctly. "Remember? They don't exist. Now, what about those missiles?"

"I'm getting to it," Fuller said, his hands gesturing for a little patience and compassion. His eyes narrowed with his next question. "You remember reading about that Tunguska thing in Russia? That atomic blast in Siberia long time ago?"

Radford searched his memory. "Yeah. A little. 1908. Something like that, wasn't it?"

"June 30, 1908. Everyone thought it was a meteor, comet, or something. Nobody on Earth had an atomic bomb, missile or anything then. We didn't even know what atomic was back then. No one was around who could remember the atomic wars, way back — four, five thousand years ago. You know the ones — Sodom and Gomorrah, Jericho, the Sinai?'' Radford shrugged. ''Hell, Dean, NASA has space pictures of the ash still in the sand.''

Radford nodded. ''Uh huh. Seen 'em. So?''

''And you know that it wasn't until after Hiroshima, after we saw what kind of destruction the bomb could do, that they finally figured that thing in Tunguska was an atomic blast. That right? You reading me okay?''

''Yeah.'' Radford took a drag and blew smoke.

''And since no one here on Earth had an atomic bomb,'' Fuller went on, ''then it had to have come from somewhere else. Outer space. Extraterrestrial, right?''

Radford shrugged. ''So, some aliens took a shot at us. They didn't kill anyone.''

''That's my point,'' Fuller said. ''They could have. But, they zigged and zagged it, and blew up a bunch of trees. Then it must have been fired at us for some other reason, right?''

''I suppose,'' Radford shrugged. ''And what was that?''

''To adjust the Earth's orbit.''

''To *adjust* our orbit?'' Radford frowned, was this getting crazier, or what?. ''What for?''

''Well, we figured some of it,'' Fuller smiled. ''But then we got complete verification from another source.''

''Another source?''

''The aliens themselves, Dean.''

Radford's brows shot up, it's crazier, he thought. ''The aliens told you? Why?'' he asked, dutifully, taking another drag on his cigarette.

Fuller shifted in his chair and reached for his cigar. ''The blast shifted our axis wobble by three degrees and slowed our orbit so we wouldn't be in their planet's path.'' He gripped the butt with his lips and rolled it to one side.

''Which planet?''

''The tenth planet,'' Fuller snarled. ''You know about

the tenth planet, don't you?''

Radford blew smoke and shrugged. "I've heard rumors.''

"That big planet, Nebiru, that comes through here every thirty-six hundred years. You know the one.''

"You mean, it's really true?" Radford asked, incredulously. "There is a tenth planet?''

Fuller nodded. "Of course," he grunted. "These little aliens, the Zetas, plotted it out for us. It's dark, in the time portals, or something. But it's there, all right. And it's getting close, on another pass.''

"Why did they want to adjust our orbit?" Radford coughed as he dashed his cigarette in his ashtray.

"So they wouldn't run into us," Fuller said. "Like they almost did, way back, during the Flood. You know, you've heard about the Flood, haven't you?''

"Yeah, sure," Radford mused. "I suppose if the planet is really there, like you say, then I guess I can believe a close pass could cause the Flood.

"But, what does this tenth planet stuff have to do with your missiles?''

"Figure," Fuller said, waving a pointed finger. "What if these aliens need another adjustment, and take another shot at Russia? Who gets blamed this time? Us.''

"Your missiles are for the aliens?" Radford popped another cigarette in his mouth and lit it. A fourth wouldn't hurt at a time like this. He could back off again tomorrow.

"Either way, Dean," Fuller said. Up, down, in, out. Take your pick. Whatever comes first. We're ready.''

"Did you tell Burris that?''

"Hell, no. He doesn't have to know that to do his job. He just has to do it. Damn it, Dean, I don't have to justify it.''

"Maybe you should have told him." Radford blew smoke.

"And have him tell Mayfield and Sherman? Burris

knows too damn much as it is.''

Radford stared at him. "Cal, is there such a thing as knowing too much?''

"I see you don't realize what we're talking about here, Dean." Radford blew smoke. "What I see is our fearless leaders loading up to get us involved in a space war. And that scares me.''

Fuller reached for his hat and stood. "I'm glad you see it our way." He placed his hat at its correct angle on his head; its bill two fingers width above the eyebrow. "Come on, I'll buy lunch. I feel a need to talk about better times. The simple life, when we didn't know crap."

Taking a last drag on his cigarette, Radford shoved his chair back. He came around his desk, stubbing his butt in the ashtray and erupting into a coughing fit.

Fuller stopped and stared at Radford, concerned. "Hey, man, you okay?" he asked, after Radford recovered. Radford nodded, his face a choking red. " You better cut back," Fuller said. "You light those things and they'll kill you.''

Chapter Ten:
The Disks

BRYAN HAD TROUBLE getting to sleep the night he met Karen. Tossing and turning, thinking about what could be. He'd never had a woman that beautiful, that perfect, walk into his life out of the blue. He'd never even imagined there could be anyone like her anywhere on Earth. If this was what love at first sight felt like, then he had never felt it before. He'd long ago realized his reprogramming through his experience of knowing spiritual self, and now that programming had found a purpose. He agonized with his anxiety that perhaps this beautiful, super person had already connected with someone else now in her life. Luckily for her another super person, or, maybe a near-super person, as he had with Susan. There were many scenarios keeping his mind busy. But once he calmed his ego's building fearful illusions of loss, he relaxed and slept. Everything in truth was as it should be.

He awoke late after a weird dream of him having a vacation with his ex-wife, Cheryl, in a place they had never been before. It had completely faded before he finished shaving, and he spent breakfast and his drive to the Center comparing the women in his life to this new feeling aroused by Karen. Again, realizing they were just playful illusions, he put them in their egoical place.

In his office he spent a productive morning doing the work that they were paying him to do. John called by midmorning and set a luncheon meeting with him and Myra at the Yacht Club.

The three sat in the cool shade of an umbrella table on the Yacht Club veranda with their luncheon special, tuna salad.

"No question about it," Bryan said. "She's been there. You could feel her energy. Didn't you feel it? It filled the room the minute she came through the door."

Myra grinned. "I noticed she knocked you for a loop, if that's what you mean."

"But did you feel it?" Bryan said. "That fantastic energy?"

"Yes, I felt it," Myra admitted. "She's very beautiful."

Bryan turned to John. "You felt it too, didn't you?"

"Yes, I felt something," John said. "She's authentic."

"And her experience," Bryan went on. "It was just like what happened to me; the out-of-body, meeting those super beings, the angels, knowing the reality. We've both been through the same experience of knowing. The same as I taught you guys to realize your spiritual being. You both possess a sense of knowing, not as extreme as a pure separation, but, even at that, you should have felt a connection."

"All right, already," Myra said. "We all felt something. So when are you gonna see her again?"

Bryan sat back and finally faced her sly grin. "Thursday evening."

Myra winked at John. "I knew it."

"To get the tapes," Bryan added. "She's making copies."

"That's a convenient excuse," Myra said.

"When she drove off," Bryan said. "She said *we'll* see you Thursday."

"Oh," Myra said. "Well, with the connection you two made, I'll bet that's a done deal."

Bryan shrugged. "My bet is," he said. "That she

could stand between those two circles on the ship and start it.''

They both looked at John. ''Maybe so,'' John said. ''But with all this energy bouncing around between us, I say we should give it a try first ourselves. I called Frank and Boyd. The mall maze is on, starting tonight.''

BRYAN CROSSED THE Baybrook Mall's west lot, found Boyd's van in the A section, jumped in and slammed the door shut behind him.

''See anyone following you?'' John asked. He and Myra sat on a bench seat behind Boyd in his driver's seat. Boyd, sitting sideways, leaned against his door with his right arm over the back of his seat.

Bryan settled into one of the contour seats across from Myra and John, shaking his head as he said, ''Nope.''

''See Frank?'' Boyd asked. Frank was the only one still negotiating the escape maze, which began with parking in the Mall's southeast parking lot, walking through the length of the mall and exiting to the northwest parking lot and into the van.

''No.''

Boyd grinned. ''I hear the pilot was a looker,'' he said. Myra chuckled.

Bryan glanced at Myra and John. ''That's just the half of it,'' he said to Boyd. ''For sure she's flown a ship something like ours. She's met the Nefilim.'' He looked at Myra and John. ''Did you tell him?''

John nodded. ''Yes,'' he said. ''We told him about the energy and the circles and her description of the guidance system.''

''Guess that's why we couldn't get those plates open,'' Boyd said, and chuckled. ''They don't open.''

''You think she was setting us up?'' Boyd added.

Bryan shrugged. ''I don't.''

''With everything else that's going on,'' John said.

"We'll have to wait and see."

"You told him about the missiles?" Bryan asked.

"Yeah," Boyd sighed. "Ain't that a bunch of crap?"

The van's passenger door flew open and Frank jumped in, glancing around at the others. "What's a bunch of crap?" he asked.

BY THE TIME THEY reached the storage shed Frank had heard all about the missiles and Karen's story. Encouraged by the fact that they could now start the ship, and flying it was just a matter of doing it, they began tossing around ideas for marking the satellite for their shooting it down.

"How about a flag?" Frank suggested. "A big American flag. Patriotic. Memorial Day, and the Fourth's coming up. They'll love it. No one will suspect what it's really for. Burris could tag it on the satellite's tale."

"I like it," John said. "Let's give it some thought. Run it up the flagpole and see if it flies."

Their hopes soaring, they quickly slipped into their heat suits and hustled aboard the craft intent on applying Karen's experience on the secret of the circles.

John turned the ship's power on. The console and panels lit up and the geiger counter clicked faster. John, Frank and Boyd got down on their knees in front of the big chair and gave the twenty inch circles a close inspection. Bryan and Myra stood on the chair's arms and stretched to do the same for the disk in the ceiling. They ran their gloved hands over the smooth surfaces. Except for the slightest ring of an assembly line the circles appeared no different than their surrounding material.

"We've all stood on this thing a thousand times," Frank said."

"Yeah," Boyd said. "But we didn't have the juice on."

They rotated, swapping gloved circle inspections.

John slapped the ceiling disk. "Remember, they're tall," he said. "Maybe we have to be touching both at the same time."

"Give me your hand," Boyd said to John, as he stood on the floor disk. They held hands as John pressed against the ceiling circle. Nothing happened.

"Karen's only about five-eight," Myra said. "Unless spirit energy stretches, she couldn't have been touching both."

"They're not on," Bryan said. "Remember? She said they were glowing when she stepped between them."

"Yeah, that's right," John mused. "There must be a switch, button, lever, or something on the console that turns them on."

John and Frank hopped down from the chair and they gathered at the console.

"We've pulled and pushed everything," Bryan said.

"Maybe it's a combination of things," Boyd said.

"Okay," John said, taking a position at the console. "Let's start pulling and pushing."

They joined John in pushing switches and buttons in combinations with pulling levers. After each try they would look at the disks. Nothing.

"This reminds me of the transporter on *Star Trek*," Boyd said. "Remember how they'd stand on the circles and begin to dissolve?"

"Yes, it does," Myra said. "Wonder if whoever did that set design got it from an alien snip?"

"Wouldn't be hard to do," John said. "They've been around since before the beginning of time."

After about fifteen minutes of trying combinations they noticed the geiger counter clicks speed up.

"Ho! What've we got here?" John said.

They stared at the disks. They couldn't detect a glow.

"What were we doing?" Boyd asked.

"I was pulling these levers," Myra said.

"Okay," John said. "We've got the right set of buttons and switches and the right levers lined up. Which way were you pushing the levers?"

"Down," Myra said. She stepped back letting John take the levers in hand.

Everyone watched the disks as John slowly pulled the levers down. The geiger counter clicked steady. Both disks began to glow a brilliant white.

"All right!" Boyd shouted. "We got her!"

"Kick her over!" Frank beamed.

John pushed the levers to their limit. The geiger counter clicks blurred. The disks glowed a pure, bright white, but they didn't hear a starting hum from the ship's engine.

John backed off on the power levers. The geiger counter's clicks slowed and the disk's white faded to metal. They glanced at each other's puzzled and disappointed faces.

"I hate to say this," Bryan said. "But, I think the missing link, spark plug, so to speak, is spiritual energy. Someone with the pure knowing of their spiritual being has to be standing between those two disks.

"That's the key. That's why the Nefilim God could leave his ship parked anywhere he wanted. He, or she, knew that there was no human around who could start it. No one on Earth could bring up their pure spiritual, pure God energy, to start this ship."

"But, Karen did it," Myra said.

"She was out of her body, pure spiritual energy, remember?" Bryan pointed out.

"Well, you've been out of your body," Myra said. "You can do it."

"What? Get out of my body?" Bryan recoiled.

"Yes," Myra answered. "You've done it. Do it again."

"You kidding?" Bryan snorted. "I wish. No way. Not that I haven't tried. I've tried many times. But, I can't. I can't do it. Not like they did."

"You can bring your energy up to full intensity," Myra said. "I think I've seen you do that."

Bryan shrugged, then got her drift. "What?" he frowned at Myra. "You want me to stand between the disks, while you pull the levers? Is that it?"

She glanced around. "You're the only one here whose been through the same, 'pure separation', as Karen. Isn't that what you said?"

Bryan stared at her, then glances at the others. "Well, I.." He studied each circle, cautiously, while they waited. Was that pure radiation, he wondered, flowing between those circles? He could be fried. Turned to salt, or ashes, like Lot's wife.

"Can you project beyond your suit?" John asked.

Bryan tried to think, clearly, beyond fear. "I don't know."

"I know this is a lot to ask," John said, glancing at the others, verifying his right to speak for them, too. "But, are you up to giving it a try?"

Bryan looked at each helmeted face. He saw hope, but he didn't see their confidence in him that he needed. But they'd all come this far, doing their jobs, in this, together, to the end. There's no fear in dying, right?

Bryan shrugged and stepped toward the floor disk. "I'll nod when I'm ready," he cautioned. "And if I begin to feel the heat, I'm stepping out."

"That's all we can ask," John said. He reached the levers and stood ready.

Eyes closed, Bryan stood quietly on the floor disk, centering himself, going within, reaching for his spiritual reality, projecting. He brushed aside images of Betty Cash's burns. Once he settled his fears he had a grip on his pure love energy. His breathing was slow and steady. After ten minutes he felt he had his energy about as projected as he The disks glowed above and below and the geiger counter clicked steadily. They listened for the engine to hum. Down, down, down John pushed the levers. They watched for the slightest reaction from Bryan. The intense light reflected in their shiny suits. Bryan stood steady, his suit glowing. They held their breaths as John pushed the levers to their limits. Full ignition and the engine didn't kick on. John held the power surge as long as he felt it safe, then quickly backed off.

The disks ceased to glow, but Bryan hadn't moved. They watched him, still as a statue, for a long, tense moment. John and Myra rushed to him, saw his eyes were still closed, and shook him. His eyes popped open. They breathed a sigh of relief and helped him off the disk.

"You okay? How do you feel?" John probed.

"Okay, I guess," Bryan said, and smiled. "What happened?"

"Nothing," Myra said.

"Did you feel anything?" John asked. "Heat, or anything?"

"No," Bryan assured them. "Not a thing."

"Well, all we can say, is, thanks, Bryan, for putting yourself on the line like that," John said. "We're glad you're okay, and nothing drastic happened. I don't know what we would've done if it had, but she didn't kick over."

"Sorry," Bryan shrugged.

"It's okay, hon," Myra said. "You did your best. We're not about to ask you to do it without the suit."

John sighed, "So, now what?"

"Go for our next option," Bryan said. "Karen. Maybe she can get out of her body. Maybe her tapes . . ."

"Her tapes?" John puzzled.

"Maybe the answer to pure knowing is on her tapes," Bryan said. "Maybe the Nefilim told her how they did it. We get her tapes and learn how to do it."

"And, if we can't?" Myra asked.

Bryan shrugged. "Anyone have a better plan?"

They thought.

"Guess not," John said.

Chapter Eleven:
The Planets

AN OFFICIAL DARK blue Air Force sedan with a four-star plaque on its license plate rolled up 288 toward Rosharon. A sharp, 2nd Lieutenant aide drove. General Walt Rawlins scanned the landscape from the passenger's seat. On the back seat, Dean Radford and General Fuller rode in quiet thought. The plush, executive interior was pressurized with high level intrigue.

"It's only that we've been friends for so long, Dean, that I would even think about showing you this," Fuller said to the back of the Lieutenant's head. "This is above Top Secret. I'm risking national security just to give you some idea of what we've been forced to deal with. It's none of our doing, you understand. It's just the way things are."

Fuller turned to face Radford's stoic stare. He felt the wariness behind Radford's eyes. Radford blinked and turned away, wishing for a smoke. They rode on in silence.

The driver made a left off 288 onto FM 1462 just north of the Prison Farm. Farther on, they crossed Oyster Creek, then the Brazos River and took a right on FM 762. The narrow road wound through a thick brush forest. Suddenly, a white observatory dome appeared above the treetops. Radford recognized the area and the road as a back entrance into Brazos Bend State Park. The driver turned onto an unmarked road that dead ended at a guarded gate entrance to a secluded contemporary building. An armed guard stepped out of his booth, looked them over and waved them through. The driver pulled into a parking space by the front steps. He jumped out, ran around opening doors and saluting as the Generals exited.

Radford could barely see the one small building sign almost hidden in the lush landscaping: JPL-NASA. "JPL?" Radford said, behind the quick stepping Generals. "I didn't know we had a unit out here."

"There's no need for you to know," Fuller said to the front steps.

Radford felt ostracized. Resigned, he followed the generals up the steps to their reflections in the wall of black glass. Rawlins jerked a card from his coat pocket and shoved it into a slot in a small metal facing. A door-sized opening in the wall slid open and Rawlins, card popped back. He put it away as they filed through. The opening slid closed behind them.

"Trappings of the CIA," Radford muttered, as he fell into their march step down a long hallway, its blankness marred by five doors marked only with numbers and metal card slots on the wall opposite where the door handles should have been.

"This is one of three observatories," Fuller said. "Here, California, and Virginia. They're all tied into terminals at Los Alamos, Groom Lake and Lancaster."

Stopping at the 5 door, Rawlins did his card trick again. The door slid open and they stepped into a big room filled with computers, scopes, charts, space maps, recording machines and wall-sized video screens. Radford was amazed, he had no idea.

Three men in the maze of equipment looked up as they came in. One approached as they made their way around an aisle. Young and bearded, he wore thick, horn-rimmed glasses and a lab coat with a red-trimmed security badge clipped to the pocket. His stoical manner never changed as he shook hands with Fuller.

"Doc, how's it going?" Fuller greeted him.

"Quiet, as usual, General." Doc returned his greeting.

Fuller glanced at Rawlins. "You remember General Rawlins." The two men nodded as they shook hands. "Dean Radford, from NASA. Dr. Jack Harrington, Chief JPL Astronomer." Fuller said, as Radford and Harrington shook hands.

Radford noticed Harrington's badge picture looked much younger without his beard. Radford glanced around taking in the wall screens display.

"Dean's an old friend," Fuller said to Harrington. "Head man over at NASA's Shuttle Project."

"Yes, I've heard the name," Harrington said. Radford was looking past him at the mass of hi-tech equipment.

"Since we're using the Shuttle for the Lancer Project," Fuller said. "We thought we could give him an idea how big this thing is without getting him more involved than he needs to be."

Harrington's eyes darted between Fuller and Radford. His expression barely showed the hint of a smile as he made a quick judgment of Radford's IQ. "Fine, General. Where would you like to start?"

"Show him some charts," Fuller said, flipping a hand toward the room. "Give him a picture of what we're up against; you know, the planet."

Harrington led them past rows of computers. He stopped at a giant machine with blinking lights and a large keyboard. He set his fingers on the keys and softly clicked out a code. A wall-sized screen came alive with a 3D depiction of the solar system and makeup of the adjoining universe. The familiar nine planets, Mercury, Venus, Earth, Mars, Jupiter, Saturn, Uranus, Neptune and Pluto revolved in floating orbits around the Sun. Radford saw something different immediately. Another planet, ghostly, the size of Jupiter, with four moons larger than Earth's, was in a projected orbit between Mars and Jupiter that swung wide and deep out into space toward a distant galaxy.

"There she is," Fuller said. "Planet X."

"Know anything about Planet X; Mr. Radford?" Harrington asked, watching the solar system's screen projection.

"Not much," Radford said, studying the astronomical wonder. "Mostly all speculation, I fear."

Harrington looked at him and smiled. "Never read the *Earth Chronicles,* eh?" he asked. Radford shook his head. "You should. They're ancient records of our ancestors. That's Nebiru, their home planet, our tenth planet. Its ancient and original name was Marduk, Nebiru is Hebrew for 'the crossing'. As you can see, Nebiru's orbit around our Sun is between Mars and Jupiter. It's farthest point swings around through Sirius, approximately thirteen light years distant. It is a rogue planet/comet that was knocked out of its orbit around its Sirius sun by an atomic war that changed its gravity field approximately 2 million years ago. Its complete orbit is equal to 3600 of Earth's. Subsequently, it comes through here every 3600 of our years. It's mass is believed to be more than ten times that of Earth's. Nebiru is inclined at about thirty degrees to the ecliptic and has a semi-major axis of about 101 AU, or a full major axis of more than 200 AU. Our calculations indicate Nebiru spends part of its orbit above the ecliptic, in the northern skies, and most below it, in the southern skies. As a consequence, our search for the planet is focused in the southern skies at a distance about two-and-a-half times farther away than Neptune and Pluto are now."

"It's a dark planet," Fuller added. "Hard to track, because it spends most of its orbit in dark space away from any light of stars. But we had confirmation from those aliens at Groom Lake that it's out there. Now, here's their story. The aliens calculate that Nebiru's crossing orbit this time through will bring it closer to Earth than it did some 14,000 years ago when its close passing caused the earthquakes, rains and subterranean flooding of the Biblical Flood.''

"Maybe close enough for one of its moons to collide with us as it did over several million years ago,'' Harrington added.

"It's coming right at us,'' Rawlins sighed.

"We wanted you to see just how serious this is, Dean,'' Fuller said. ''The beings on that planet know it's serious too, or they wouldn't have fired that missile at Tunguska, hoping it might knock us out of their way.''

Harrington said, "Since we can't see it, plot its speed, we can't project its correct orbit to ours. We never heard from the probe we sent to plot it's position. It might be pushing a heavy gravity field, like a black hole.''

"Like I was telling you, Dean, if they take another shot at us, we're in big trouble. We could have ourselves an atomic war like no one has ever imagined.''

"And if it hits us?'' Radford asked.

Fuller shrugged. "It's all over, anyway you look at it.''

"That moon that hit us millions a years ago,'' Rawlins said. "Killed everything — the dinosaurs, everything.''

"Knocked a big piece out of us,'' Harrington added. "On a subsequent pass it shattered that chunk into the asteroid belt.''

"And if it misses?'' Radford asked.

Harrington glanced at the screen. "It won't miss by that much. The least we'll get is the earthquakes and floods.''

"Anyway you look at it,'' Radford sighed. "We lose.''

"Big guy versus little guy,'' Rawlins added.

"The missiles have to be out there,'' Fuller said. "If worse comes to worst, we might have to take out one of their moons.''

Radford sighed, deeply. He studied the orbital map. "How long do we have? What's Planet X's ETA?''

"Roughly, calculating from an approximate date of the last Flood, adding 3600 year orbits," Harrington mused. "January, 2013."

THE LIEUTENANT DROVE while the Generals and Radford rode mute all the way back down the winding road. Radford stared out his window. When they turned back onto 1426, he turned to Fuller. "There's no way around it, Cal," he said. "We have to tell the public the truth. Everyone. The whole world."

"Bullshit!" Fuller snorted. "We don't have to tell 'em crap. What do they know? They're all so goddammed stupid, I wouldn't save one of them. Who needs them?"

"Well, at least, give them a chance to prepare ... build a boat, a whole bunch of boats, or something."

"No boat this time, Dean. This time it's airlift. The way those so-called *gods* did it 14,600 years ago. You should have read the *Chronicles*. They weren't going to save any of the people then either. We're the gods this time, Dean. By 2010 we'll have our own fleet of space ships at Groom Lake, and we'll have the fuel from that SuperCollider. And we're out of here."

"We?" Radford frowned. "Who is this we? MJ-12?"

Fuller allowed Radford a sly smile. "There's more than twelve now, Dean," he said. "Eighteen. Sixteen besides us. We're the Power. The Olympians, Guardians of the Secret, whatever you want to call us. We make the rules. We say who lives, or dies."

"Without any guilt about spending their hard-earned tax dollars to save your butts?"

Fuller chuckled, and sneered. "Guilt? Spare me your condemnations, Dean. People are stupid. They give us the money to build the SuperCollider and we'd have enough 115 to save their stupid butts. But no, it's too much. So, let them die. They're garbage. Who needs them? Only the smart ones get to start over."

Radford huffed, "You mean, the insane ones."

"Your streak of righteousness will get your ticket punched, Dean," Fuller warned. "I'm sure we can find someone who'll be glad to take your seat."

"I can't believe this."

"Believe it," Fuller snapped. "The Space Station's part of the great escape plan."

Radford frowned, puzzled. "Since when?"

"Since certain Congressmen realized that it might be their only ticket out of here," Fuller said. "Think of them as keeping it on the budget for you, Dean. They're planning on being on the last Shuttle flights out of here. And I'm sure you'll want to be right there with em, saving your butt, too."

Radford thought about it. He sighed, swallowed hard. He wished Fuller would let him smoke in the car. He was frightened to face the inevitable truth and ashamed to admit, even to himself, that Fuller was right. When it came right down to it, he would save himself before anyone. "Damn it!" he groaned. "It's not right."

"What's right, Dean," Fuller said. "Is us getting those missiles out there, and keeping our secret. Trust me on that."

BY THE MIDDLE of the afternoon Bryan called Karen to get directions to her beach house. It was a call he had rehearsed for a day and a half. All the important things he planned to say and ask he felt different about when she was on the line and he didn't. She said the tape copies were ready and waiting. He said he would leave early and asked if there was anything he could bring? She said no, they had everything. And, again, to save his fantasy, he refused to inquire about *they*, this other.

Within twenty minutes after Karen's call, Bryan got a call from Susan. He hadn't talked to her since he last saw her on Sunday. She didn't ask why, so he didn't have to hide the fact his interest had drifted to another project. Susan asked if he would be busy that evening. He said he wouldn't, and she said that since school was out for the summer she had some free time and she had a project she wanted to talk to him about. She wouldn't say what, except that it was possible they could both do a lot of good for world consciousness, and make some money in the process. She invited him to dinner and told him to bring his walking shoes, they had a lot to talk about.

He had barely gotten off the phone when there was a light tap at his door. He looked up to see Marsha peeking through the slight opening and motioned her in.

"Glad to see you buckling down," she said, gesturing lo the open application folders he was evaluating.

"That's what they pay us for," he smiled. "I'm eliminating every applicant who doesn't profess to a belief in metaphysics, new thought, aliens and UFOs."

She looked shocked. "You're not?"

He grinned. "Just thought I'd get your reaction."

She rolled her eyes before she sat on the edge of a chair in front of his desk and clasped her hands in her lap. "Forget your funny stuff for a minute," she said. "I want to ask you something."

He closed the folder. "Yeah?" he piqued, and leaned back in his chair.

"I ran into Dean Radford over at Control yesterday," she began. "And in the ensuing conversation, he asked me if I knew what Steve Burris came to see you about on Monday. Needless to say, I was surprised. I said, no, I didn't even know that the Shuttle crew was back from the Cape, much less that Steve had been here."

"You should get out more, Marsha," he smiled.

"You never even mentioned it."

"No, I didn't," he shrugged. "It wasn't important." He tossed the folder on the finished stack and centered another in front of him, as if he were ready to resume working.

Not to be dismissed or belittled, she stood, flinging her arms. "It must have been something," she demanded, "or he wouldn't have made a special trip."

"It was personal," he calmly declared.

"Personal? What's personal? There isn't anything we don't share about everyone on those crews. Why should his problem be exclusive of me?"

A gamut of reasons ran through his mind. Picking the most ridiculous one, he said, seriously, "Burris said he thought the rest of the crew was gay and he wanted off the mission."

Marsha was shocked, temporarily. "He did not," she huffed.

Delighted with her reaction, he stifled laughing out loud. While she glared at him his mind went to work concocting another even more ridiculous. But his creative imagination had stalled for the moment, and knowing she probably wouldn't believe the truth, he quickly decided he'd give it a shot. He sighed, "It was about the spy satellite on this mission. Burris had some bad feelings about it."

She frowned. "Well, that's understandable. But why should this one be any different than the others?"

"Several hours before they were to board the Shuttle, two MJ-12 Generals took him into the bay where the satellite was ready to go. They opened the camera casings and showed him what was inside. No cameras, just two giant neutron missiles with mega ton warheads. They didn't tell him exactly what, or who, the missiles were meant for, but he figured they were going to shoot them at someone, or someplace, or they wouldn't be there. He was shook up. His conscience was tearing him apart. He came to see me. He wanted me to help him deal with it."

Marsha gasped, slack-jawed and wide-eyed.

He sensed she was truly shocked. Stunned, even, he thought, as well as she should be. Even in his twisted attempt at humor, he enjoyed her expression, the way her jaw dropped. Then he felt the guilt of cheating Steve of the pleasure of any public revulsion. "That's it," Bryan shrugged, nonchalantly. "That's all it was." He opened the next folder.

"You mean to tell me," she gasped. "That our government is putting atomic weapons in space?"

He nodded. "Star Wars. SDI. MJ-12. The secret government."

"What for? We're not at war with anyone. Are we?"

"We could be, at any moment, Marsha," he said. Her innocent gullibility fueled his imagination. "Our valiant leaders want to be ready. On line. These aliens they've been dealing with are getting ideas of taking over this planet."

Her eyes narrowed, suddenly focused, and realized his humor in the undertow of his constant taunting. A smile crept across her face. "Oh, you . . ." She couldn't bring herself to call him an appropriate nasty name, even if she knew one. She shook her head. "You're not going to pull me into that. No, sir. You and your secret government and their so called, 'alien friends.' No, no. Not me." She leaned over his desk. "Now tell me what was really bothering him."

He leaned back and shrugged. "You got me," he grinned. "It was just something about one of his boys having some problems adjusting to not being able to play Little League ball. You know, baseball, father/son stuff. You wouldn't understand."

She pulled back, seeming somewhat satisfied she had found a true reason somewhere in his dichotomy. "Why didn't you tell me that in the first place," she said, flinging her arms, again. "Instead of all that other crap?"

He held his smile, still delighted with his opportunity to pull her chain. "Well," he said, "in the first place, Marsha, I was curious how Radford knew Steve was here. Since you're in the same office and you didn't know, how did he know? And another thing. Why didn't you ask him why he wanted to know? He's never been interested in these kind of things before."

"Hmmmm," Marsha pondered, tapping fingernails on the edge of his desk. "Good question. Do you know why?"

He leaned close and whispered. "Like ninety percent of the people in this country, Marsha, you wouldn't believe me even if I could tell you."

Chapter Twelve:
The Deal

"HI. DINNER'S ALMOST ready," Susan said, letting Bryan in through her front door. "Come on, you can help me. Glad to see you remembered your walking shoes." She was laid back casual in shorts and T-shirt and barefooted. He followed her through the den admiring the supple strength in her graceful body, one that fit his programming so neatly. Even in his enjoying the vision he had to constantly remind himself not to get caught up in the physical entrapment. For a slight diversion, he gave a passing stroke to Missy sitting on the coffee table. She rose to his touch, wanting more, friends now.

In the kitchen, after he washed his hands, she gave him a salad in progress to finish, while she returned to steaming the vegetables and rice. The main dish was to be broiled flounder in her special lemon sauce.

After exchanges of, how've you been and how'd your day go, were out of the way, Bryan asked, "So, what's this project you wanted to talk about?"

"Well," Susan began. "I've been doing a lot of thinking and reading since our talks. And I must say, you're the most interesting person that I've met in a long time."

Bryan smiled, self-consciously. "Thank you."

"No, really," she said. "You've helped turn things around for me. I got most of the books and have even finished some of them. And after listening to you, it's all beginning to make a lot of sense. I'm seeing this picture of reality. I'm beginning to look at my work and the kids in a different light, and seeing the testing processes we've been going through here at the end of the year, and I'm beginning to realize the truth in what you were saying about how the system teaches fear of not knowing. I find myself looking at the kids, and the teachers, and thinking about what you said about everyone already knowing everything. That everyone comes into life already knowing and it's society and our education systems that keeps them from realizing they already know, and how we should just help them to remember, and how they fit into life, and who they really are."

Bryan grinned, delighted with his impact, and sliced some tomatoes onto their salad plates.

"I see the kids who're the toughest to teach, Susan" went on. "And I realize their background, their parents and how they were never taught their knowing, either. And I see now how the parents passed their not knowing on to their kids. And I look back at my own parents and see now how they didn't know either. And I remember how they passed their not knowing on to me. Even the religious mysteries, but I realize they weren't to blame, because they were passing on what their parents taught them, and, I have to admit, there is something that has to be said for parental respect, to some extent.

"I see kids going astray, disillusioned with the system, with their lives, and I have to wonder, if these kids could've been led in the right direction, if they had only known the truth about themselves and everyone, that we all have this inherent knowledge of the gods and the universe right inside of us, that their lives would be so much better? We don't have to go looking for it, we already have it. And as a teacher, all I have to do is help them remember their reality."

Bryan nodded "That's right." He smiled, somewhat

self-satisfied and washed his hands. "As teachers who know, that's all any of us can do." He took the salads to the table. "The rest is up to the individuals."

"That's it," Susan said to pouring the vegetables into a serving dish. "Here's the deal. I want us to write a book."

"A book?" Bryan huffed. "There're books out there already. What good would another one do?"

"I know," she said, handing him the vegetables. "But they're books about this, and books about that. But there're not any books about everything. You know, about all the things you were telling me. About the history of how we got in this mess and what we have to do to get out."

You mean, the whole story?"

"Yes, the whole story. From the beginning to now."

"The Blonds, the Zetas, our creation, the conspiracies, the government, religions? Everything in one book?"

"Yes," Susan said to spooning the rice from a steaming pot. "The whole story. Why do we have to go to this book, and that book? Why not put it all in one book?"

"That'd be a big book. You're talking covering millions of years."

"No, no, listen." She placed the rice dish on the table. "We'd condense, simplify, make it fun to read, get them interested enough to know the truth that they'd go for the details in the other books."

"One problem," Bryan said. "The government won't let you do it."

"Why? How do you know they won't?" She pulled the bubbling flounder from the oven and neatly served each piece onto dinner plates.

"Myra's already tried." Bryan pulled out his chair at the table and sat. "The government owns everything, especially the media. That's the way their debunkers keep the public in denial. Myra can't even get any of what we know into her own paper. What truths they can't get around not reporting, they have to put the emphasis on the witnesses' credibilities. It's the law. If the truth were known, there'd be a national revolution. The Blonds and Zetas would be going at it again on this planet. And the winner, if there were one, gets what's left.''

Susan set the plates of fish on their place mats and sat. "Well, I say we write the book," she said. "We can worry about getting it published later."

"Who's gonna write it?" Bryan inquired, unfolding a napkin.

"We will. Collaborate. Me and you."

"You're the writer." He pointed out.

"Well, yes, I guess," she said. "But we'll do it together, and we'll use your name. You're the doctor, and your name would have much more clout than mine."

"Clout?" he laughed. "And I know who'll be delivering it: MJ-12. We'll use both names, die together, or we use a pen name."

"Okay, a pen name." She handed him the bowl of vegetables. Bryan began to doubt the fruition of this book since her suggestion that they write it together. Especially, when one of them was not a writer. He fought suspicions that her imagined collaboration was simply an attempt to keep their relationship ongoing, good, or bad. If their relationship didn't work out, neither would the book.

He spooned vegetables onto his plate. "Why don't you just write a story about your life down on the farm, or your divorce, or something romantics would do?"

"What good would that do?" she said. "I want to write this book."

"Then why don't you write it?"

"Because you're the one who knows everything. I need you to make it right."

He thought about Karen, and her possible other, and his fantasizing of something that might never be. "Okay," he agreed. "When do we start?"

"How about tonight?"

"WHEN WE KNOW the true history of our inheritance," Bryan said, as they walked in the twilight along the bayou trail. Susan held a small cassette recorder about chest high between them. "We can see that our problems stem from our not understanding the differences between our ego illusions and our spiritual realities."

"And this ego is what Enki gave the hybrid Homo sapiens in the Garden of Eden?" Susan asked.

"The Adam and Eve hybrids already had somewhat of a small ego," Bryan said. "They had gender, so they must have had individuality. Enki gave them the knowledge in procreation, which separated them from, and made them, and us, independent of their creator. Enki gave his hybrids an identity, so to speak, a personality, a persona."

"Big or small, good or bad, but an ego," Susan said. "Okay, so now, how do we explain an ego in simple terms?"

"Easy," Bryan said before he thought about it. "Everybody's born with an ego and a spiritual self. Standard equipment, they come with the body. Body, mind, soul. When the fetus is in its mother's womb, its growth energy is provided by its mother's energy. At birth, its appointed spiritual energy takes over as the baby's power source, bringing with it a slight remembrance of its past lives' egos. The new infant's brain comes with, an ego blank-tape, which is already programming its new identity: its immediate realities, being; its environment, hospital, doctors, nurses, its parents and siblings, survival and, of course, its name.

"The infant's spiritual mind, soul energy, also takes up residency alongside the ego forming in the new brain. And, although eventually overwhelmed and dominated by illusions of the new ego's programming and virtually forgotten, the spiritual mind always retains its connection to its reality in universal knowledge. Spiritual self knows it is a powerful fragment of the Universal God force, while the new ego programs its reality in societal and environmental fears and illusions, ego; the creation of man, spirit; the creation of the Universal God."

"Explain illusions," Susan said. "I'm still having trouble with that. I find it hard to grasp the idea that my concepts of parents and childhood programming weren't real,"

"As physical substance they are; or were," Bryan said. "But to our egos, they exist in the same programmed illusions that were passed on to you. As an example: parental responsibility doesn't include ownership, such as, my this, my that. We take on the responsibilities, but we don't own anything. Each of us experiences life for two reasons; to seek knowledge and to know love. One is the function of our ego and the other is the soul purpose of spiritual self.

"Whatever society you chose to be born into, your ego will take on the illusions of that society, whether it be in Africa, France, Mexico, America, or wherever, your ego is programmed to accept, get along, exist. But your spiritual energy/reality remains the same from lifetime to lifetime.

"Your parents responsibilities were to help you remember your true spiritual self. Instead, by not knowing themselves as such, they repeated the mistakes of their own parents by programming you with half-truths, those of their own society's ego illusions; fears, hates, greed, prejudices, you name it."

"Religion?"

"Right. Greatest sin of all," Bryan said. "Denying their own, and others', historical reality."

"Most religions believe Jesus was a super spiritual being, the Son of God," Susan said. "Did he have an ego?"

"Yes, he did," Bryan said. "Evidenced by his tirade with the money changers in !he temple. But it wasn't so large that he couldn't put it in its place. All bodies have an ego. And since Jesus was born of a body, he had an ego programmed by his parents society. But *knowing* that his spiritual being was a gift from his Father gave him his powers."

"Now, here's a good one," Susan smiled, holding the recorder closer. "Explain the immaculate conception, Jesus as the Son of God and his role as Savior?"

"Knowing our history, that one's easy to see," Bryan said. "Anu as God, Enki, or Enlil, as Lords, one of the three, impregnated Mary, probably Enki, through artificial insemination. We know that he was into that, so it's quite possible that's the way it happened. The angel messenger who came to her, setting the meeting, was one of the Elite Anunnaki Guard.

"Being in an earthly body, Jesus's ego programming covered his spiritual inheritance. Just like it does us. And, although he did have flashes of some remembrance that he had knowledge of a better life, Jesus led a fairly ordinary life up to the age of thirty. Then there was his forty days and nights wandering in the desert fighting the temptation of the Devil. Now, who is this Devil? His ego. Here again history; you know that the Gods were whipping around the skies in their space ships. Wouldn't it seem logical in their plan for them to watch over Jesus, their spiritual investment in humanity? I say yes, and I believe that there was no *wandering*. It was an abduction. I believe Jesus was a product of Enki, the old master planner himself. Trying to atone for his mistake in the Garden, Enki created Jesus with his knowledge of pure spiritual self to teach his message of love to a lost humanity. Enki waited thirty years. His plan had signs of faltering; Jesus's ego was blocking his truth, like our egos mask ours. Jesus wasn't remembering his purpose. So, Enki abducted Jesus's spiritual self, out of his body, separate from his ego, and showed him his reality; a pure, true Son of God. Then Enki put Jesus's spiritual self back it his body and sent him to spread that message, 'that, whosoever believeth in me shall have everlasting life.' In other words, 'believe me, that you are all the children of God, love one another, and have a good life.' And all of those who did believe were saved from a wasted life. So, Jesus would have to be considered a Savior and Wayshower.''

"But Enki's plan didn't work," Susan said. "Jesus ended up getting himself crucified."

"True," Bryan said. "No one got the meaning of his message. Even his parables didn't work. No one could understand spirit and egos, gods flying around in space ships; a lot like today, they didn't understand they had the power and could do their own miracles. They only understood that Jesus had the power, he was the Miracle Worker, their Savior. They believed that only Jesus had the power to destroy the evil political and religious forces of that time. The people didn't understand that they too had the power to do it themselves. The evil forces knew that they could stop the Miracle Worker by eliminating him, and they did, with the conviction of the masses' not knowing. Enki had to sit back and watch his experiment fail, and listen to his Father saying: I told you so.

"Those same evil forces are in control today. And too, they know they will lose their control, if ever the people get the message that each of us must realize oui spiritual knowledge."

"Just knowing the difference between our illusions and our reality is all there is to it?"

"That's it," Bryan grinned. "Simple. Ego there, spirit here. This is that, that is this. Mind and spirit coexisting in one body. Mind connected to Earth, spirit connected to a universal God power. Sort it out, put it to use, and take control of our lives."

"You know," Susan said, after thinking about it. They made a turn back toward home. "The more I listen to you, the more I'm feeling that you know more than what's in those books. This knowledge had to come from somewhere else."

Bryan shrugged and grinned at his feet. An owl hooted in a tree in the bayou. "Would you believe me if I told you I got a verification of my spiritual truth through an out-of-body abduction/meeting with the blonds themselves? The quickest fix of all."

She didn't say anything for at least ten yards. In the dim path lights and spots of moonlight filtering through the trees he watched her studying his serious expression. "Yes, I might," she nodded. "Tell me about it."

Chapter Thirteen:
The Other

AS BRYAN EXPECTED, the southbound lanes of the I-45 freeway toward the island city and the Gulf coast bedroom communities were already heavy with the leading edge of rush hour traffic from the sprawling business complexes around Houston.

He reminisced, telling Susan about his experiences and the effects they had on his life; before and after. She had goaded him on long after she ran out of tapes. He could still see her look of amazement, and maybe a little bit of awe, and then the indecision of whether to believe him or not. That's what threw him off and he declined another offer to spend the night, saying he had an early morning meeting. As to her question of when they would get together again, he told her his free time would be uncertain the next few days with the launch nearing a ready, but that he would get back to her, and her book project, as soon as he could.

Atop the causeway bridge he squinted into the glistening reflection of a low sun on a rippling chop on the dark back bay waters. The quivering finger of light followed him all the way to the island.

As desirable as Susan was, he had to admit his illusions of Karen had tarnished his attraction to the near flawless coupling and left him with an early morning quandary as to what he might have to do should he and Karen hit it off. That is, if Karen was free and clear in the relationship department. And if not, how he should handle the progressing situation with Susan. Perhaps a solution was premature, as he didn't have a problem, yet. Last month there were no choices, now there were two. Well, maybe two.

On the median beyond the bridge the tall, multi-colored rows of oleanders were in full glorious May bloom; reds, whites and pinks. He turned off on the 61st Street island crossing toward the seawall and West Beach.

Joggers, bicyclists and skaters streamed in and around the strolling tourists on the wide walkways of Seawall Boulevard. The Gulf waters rolled in behind a four foot surf, seeming fairly calm and green beyond the fishing piers; a fisherman's delight, which made parking spaces a premium for several blocks either side of the piers' entrances.

Near the end of the seawall, the traffic slowed around a gray-bearded man feeding a flock of sea gulls from several large loaves of bread.

Traffic was lighter out the West Beach Road that divided the piered houses, beach and Gulf from the ranch pastures. Down the road early arrivals for the holiday weekend were already firing up barbecue pits at the beach camping parks.

Bryan had never noticed the beach road markers in all the years he had driven out West Beach. They had never been important before. Today he was counting each one after Eight Mile Road looking for Sixteen. On the wide beach beyond the boondocks just past Jamaica Beach he caught a glimpse of a volleyball game next to a couple of catamarans with bright, colorful sails.

Bryan turned toward the beach and a cluster of contemporary beach houses at Sixteen Mile Road. He did a right on the first road as the directions said and counted for the fifth house with two tall palms by the drive. Every house on the street had two palms, obviously, a builder's perk. All were guywired to the property and a few were dead brown, bone-rattling in the wind.

He recognized Karen's white sports car in a parking space between a row of heavy piers beneath a weathered gray two story. A woodcarved sign swinging on rusted hooks above the stairs to an entrance below the house read, ''Coe's Cove.'' His car's tires crunched onto the shell drive and stopped.

He stepped out into a steady Gulf breeze. Palm fronds above him fluttered and slapped. A leafy ground cover with tiny yellow flowers was quilted to the sand around the house. An empty space with worn ruts and oil spots beside Karen's car lent him dread of his worst illusioned scenario. He braced himself to face the facts, and the stiff wind.

Following a path to steps at the side of the house, he stepped up onto a footbridge that led over the boondocks and to steps and a deck around the front of the house.

On the deck, a three-by-four-foot stretched canvas bolted to a heavy, mobil easel rattled sideways into the wind next to a castered taboret and a scattering of deck chairs. He hopped up the stairs onto the deck for a closer inspection. Smells of drying paint and sea salt swirled around her painting in progress; a bright, colorful seascape. She was good and he smiled his approval.

Cupping his hands to his reflection in the house's front wall of windows, he peered in. No one. When he stepped back he saw Karen in the reflection, waving from the beach end of the footbridge.

He strode quickly, but confidently, toward the beach. Karen was a bodily vision to behold. A pair of cutoffs showed off her long, muscular, tanned legs. She had rolled the sleeves of her open shirt to her elbows and tied its tail tightly under her ample cleavage. Her blond tresses whipped around her face over a patterned headband as she propped an arm on the stair railing. His home-from-the-office attire was indeed a contrast, but no matter, he was in love.

"Hi," she grinned. "You found us."

Up close he saw paint smears on her shirt and cutoffs.

He returned her grin. "Hi. Yes," he said, wetting his lips.

"No problem." There was that *us* thing, again. He hoped she meant the house. He glanced at it. "Great place."

"Thanks. It's Jim's parents. They're letting me use it."

He noticed her legs were wet to mid calf and a powdering of drying sand covered the sides of her bare feet and red toenails.

"They live here?" he hoped.

"No. In Conroe."

"Oh." He nodded toward the deck. "That your painting?"

"Yes." She pushed her hair back. "That's my living. I show in a gallery down on the Strand and one in Houston."

"A painter, eh?"

"Art degree from UT, remember? Art teacher." She stepped onto the beach and backed away.

He nodded. "Yeah, that's right." He searched new avenues for conversation. "You teaching now?" He followed her onto the beach with an eye for her hip-swinging stride.

She shook her head. "No." She spun around. "This is my get-away-from-it time," she said. "Want to go for a walk?"

"Sure."

"Take your shoes off and roll your pants," she said. "I like to wade."

She waited as he sat on the steps doing as she suggested, left his shoes on the steps and hurried after her.

The wet sand was cool. She splashed the surf ahead of him. The foam washed around their feet.

"It's cold," she laughed. "Doesn't it feel great?"

"Yes, it does." He felt the chill up his legs. "You swim out here?"

"Some." She stopped to dig a shell with her toe. "Mostly on my float. And I surf when it's up. You come to the beach much?"

"Not as much as I used to." Family pictures flashed through his mind. "When the kids were smaller," he muttered. "With the family when I was married."

"What happened?"

"Divorce."

"And what keeps you from the beach now?" she asked, the surf sucking sand around their feet.

Bryan shrugged. "Sailing, I guess," he said. "John and Myra have a boat. Forty-two foot sloop. We sail out of Watergate. Fish sometimes, and race once in a while. You sail?"

"Yes," she smiled, glancing at him and squinting away from the low sun. "I love it."

"Maybe you'd like to go with us next time?"

She shaded her eyes and studied him for a moment. "Okay," she said. "I'd like that. John and Myra seem very nice."

He saw a big conch shell half buried in the sand. She watched him pick it up, a half of a once beautiful shell. He tossed it into the surf.

A MILE DOWN the beach they turned and headed back. Smells of barbecuing mixed with the breeze. Karen clutched a handful of pretty shells. They had found only one small colorful conch in good condition.

"Look at all the nice pinks and browns," she pointed out, while he admired it. "And the way it spirals. This is a beauty."

"You collect many shells?"

"Only the best. And sand dollars when I can find

them.''

"Living on the beach, you must have a big collection."

"Hundreds, thousands," she laughed. He liked her laugh. "To find any at all you have to get out early, before the souvenir shops run the beach on their motor scooters."

"You sell them?"

"I draw and paint them," she said. "They're good subjects. Some I glue right on the canvas and paint around them. They're vessels of life, our beginnings, washing up on shore and life crawling out." She washed a big shell in the surf and examined its colors and unique shape. "Makes one wonder where they came from."

He saw her shiver. "Cold?" he asked. The sun was halfway into a string of low, distant clouds.

"Just for a moment." She rubbed her upper arms.

Then he felt a sudden chill, too, on his arms and legs.

Karen hugged herself and rolled down her sleeves. Bryan rubbed at a rash of goose bumps on his arms. She untied her shirt and began buttoning it. They moved away from the surf. So quickly the warmth of the day had blown away.

Suddenly, as they neared her boondock bridge, Karen perked and grinned at her house. He looked. A man standing at the front railing of her deck waved. Karen waved back.

"David's back," she beamed. "Come on, I want you to meet him."

She led him in a slow jog to the stairs and up. He grabbed his shoes and followed, in no hurry to meet David, a man she would run to, or maybe she was just trying to get warm.

At the stairs to the deck Bryan saw a tan and green van with tall side windows parked under the house next to Karen's white sports car. Not what he wanted to see.

"Get everything?" she asked David, as they came up the stairs and onto the deck.

"Everything you asked for," David smiled and they kissed as if he had just gotten home from the office. Except he wore an open flowered shirt, cutoffs and sandals, as if he lived on the beach. David was tall, over six feet, like Bryan. He was heavily tanned, or dark skinned, with dark, bushy hair, matted with gray.

She turned to a disheartened Bryan, masking his disappointment with a forced smile. "Bryan, this is David. David, Bryan."

They shook hands. "Bryan Mayfield, David." David seemed much older than Karen, Bryan detected some telling wrinkles. He also felt a definite, but fleeting, warmth in David's touch.

"David Rodriguez, Bryan." He grinned perfectly white teeth.

Rodriguez. Latino. Mex, maybe, Bryan thought, that accounts for the dark skin. He didn't seem Karen's type.

"The NASA UFO man," David said, a mischievous twinkle in his dark eyes. "Karen's told me about you. Come. Sit." He swept an arm toward the chairs. "We'll talk."

"David's my friend I met in San Antonio a couple of years after the incident," Karen said, pulling a chair into the last of the sun's warm light. "He was the one who recommended the psychiatrist and the hypnosis."

"And look what it's led to," David said, selecting a chair.

"Karen tells me you're a psychiatrist, too, Bryan."

"Yes." He positioned a chair and sat.

"Fascinating!" David beamed. "You do hypnosis too?"

"No. Nothing like that. I work mostly with the astronauts. Testing, qualifying, attitude adjustments, things like that."

"David's a writer," Karen said, proudly. "He was with the San Antonio paper when we met." She grabbed her taboret and rolled it aside. "He did a feature story on my paintings."

Bryan jumped up to help her. "A newspaper writer?" he said. "Maybe you know my friend, Myra Bennett? She's a feature writer with *The Houston Cronicle.*"

Bryan positioned the taboret while Karen rolled the easel around next to it.

"No, don't think I do," David said.

"What!" Karen shrieked. "What is this!" She gaped at her painting, then glared at a slyly smiling David. "My painting! What did you do?" Her eyes darted across her painting and she began hugging and rubbing her arms. Watching her, Bryan suddenly felt a chill again himself.

"What's wrong?" David said, feigning surprise.

Bryan rubbed at a new set of goose bumps as he moved around the taboret.

"This!" she demanded and pulled the easel around for them to see.

Karen and Bryan stared at the painting. It was no longer a beautiful seascape. Its sand had turned to snow, the boondocks were now mountains and the sea grass was snow capped pines. Two nude figures, a man and woman, strolled hand in hand by an icy lake.

David chuckled, innocently. "What's wrong?"

Bryan didn't know why, but he felt colder. He was standing in a sliver of sunlight, but his temperature had taken an even deeper nose dive.

"Where's my seascape?" Karen demanded of David, her teeth chattering.

David shrugged. "It's there."

"Oh no, no, no, it isn't," she shivered. "That's snow and, and that's Bryan and me." She pointed a shaky finger at the nude figures. "Naked? Where's my beach? The sun?"

"That's us?" Bryan quivered.

Karen tensed her shaking. "Don't you fee-e . . . f-eel

it?''

Bryan couldn't believe what he was seeing, and feeling. She was right. The tiny figures were a very good likeness of the two of them. At least, he certainly recognized himself. And as hard as he tried, he couldn't quite focus on Karen's portrayal. They were freezing, while standing in the heat of a warm sun and Gulf breeze. For some unexplainable reason they had taken on the cold of their images in the winter painting. How could that be? Karen and Bryan stared at each other, shaking, and tried desperately to stop, but couldn't.

David rocked back in his chair, grinning from ear to ear. Definitely delighted in whatever was going on. Sweat beads glistened on his forehead while they shivered.

Bryan observed, David's sweating, and we're freezing.

"Damn it, David!" Karen snapped. She dropped into a chair and hugged her long, bare legs up to her chest. She watched Bryan shiver, his hands shoved deep in his pockets, and glared at David over her knees. "Do something! This is no way to treat our guest.''

Bryan jogged slowly in place, slapping at his body to ward off the icy grip. He blew a frosty breath and tucked his hands in his armpits.

David chuckled devilishly and shrugged, perhaps his game had run its course. He lifted slowly from his chair and sauntered to the taboret. Selecting a brush and inspecting its cleanliness, he dipped its tip into a glob of red-orange paint on her palette. He held the long, thin brush so both could see its swipe of hot hue. Facing the painting, at arm and brush length, he slowly and meticulously drew a glowing red-orange line around their small naked images.

He tossed the brush on the taboret, stepped back and wiped his hands together. Arms spread, smiling broadly, he presented them his finished masterpiece.

Magically, their cold vanished and they felt warm again.

"Thanks," Karen said. She unfolded her legs and relaxed as the warmth rushed over her. She stretched.

Bryan steadied and sighed. He felt relieved and somewhat comfortable again, but still mystified.

"Well?" Karen frowned.

David strode slowly behind her chair, grabbed its arms as he leaned over her. "Sorry," he said, and kissed her.

Karen mellowed and kissed him back. "What about Bryan?"

David stood, looked at Bryan and shrugged. "Sorry about that, Bryan," he smiled, dryly. He stepped around the chair and extended his hand.

Cautiously, Bryan took his hand and David gripped it hard, barely shook it, pulled closer and patted him on his back. "No hard feelings, Bryan," he said. "It was all an illusion," He laughed. "Just a little demonstration of some of the things I've learned from listening to Karen's tapes."

"It's not just *listening*, Bryan," Karen injected. "It's more like *studying*."

David glanced at her. She gave him a short smile.

"It's practice, practice, practice," David said. "Until you get the hang of it. That's what it's all about, isn't it, Bryan? Practicing the knowing? Getting it right?"

Bryan was confused. What was going on? He didn't know what to say. Karen seemed innocent and almost as bewildered and upset as he. "Yes," he smiled, nodding tolerantly. "That's what it's all about, illusions and reality."

"And that's what you're here for, the tapes? Right?"

Bryan didn't know how to take that. If David could do what he had just done, he could have just as easily read Bryan's thoughts about Karen. "Right," Bryan said. "The tapes."

David studied Bryan a long moment before he said, "Bryan, you have a deep, intricate and knowing spiritual mind. Much like Karen's. It's in your aura, just like hers. That's interesting. Both very strong, clear, accepting.

Otherwise, none of what you just felt could have happened. You're going to need a very open mind for her tapes.'' David looked at Karen. ''That right, hon?''

He reads auras, Bryan thought, then he knows.

Karen squinted into the sun behind David. ''This your test?''

David shrugged.

Karen draped an arm around the back of her chair and looked up at Bryan. ''When I told David I agreed to give you copies of my tapes,'' she said. ''He thought we should test you, see if you were ready. One has to be in their right mindset to receive the knowing. I told him I thought you and your friends were. It was just a feeling I had. He said he'd see. I had no idea what he had in mind, or that whatever included me.''

They both looked at David. He raised a brow. ''Passed.''

Karen stood and stretched. ''Enough of this. What say we throw together some dinner.''

BRYAN WAS GLAD to hear Karen verify her feeling something in their fast meeting. But David's energy was different, his was overwhelming. David's energy was probably greater than his and Karen's together. He couldn't figure David. Anyone who could control spiritual energy the way David had just demonstrated needed to be watched very closely.

They followed Karen from the deck through a sliding glass door. The interior of the big, open room was divided into three sections; a kitchen/dining, a den/sitting and painting studio, all facing high windows to the deck and Gulf. A utility, bath and storage flanked a stairwell leading below and up to bedrooms and an upper deck. Karen's paintings, drawings and constructions were everywhere. Several large canvasses, some still in progress, were stacked against her studio's back wall.

David followed Karen into the kitchen, leaving Bryan in

the center of the big room, gazing at the talent, amazed at the strong display of creative spirit.

Bryan wandered toward the walls for a closer, individual inspection while David helped Karen gather items to prepare.

"You an artist, too, David?" Bryan asked a painting in the dining area.

David looked up from emptying a grocery bag. "What? Me?" he questioned and shook his head. "No."

"But, but, what about that out there?" Bryan nodded toward the deck.

"That?" David shrugged and glanced at the canvas on the deck. "I told you. That was an illusion, Bryan. It wasn't real. I never painted anything." He stepped around the breakfast bar and faced Bryan's confused expression. David nodded at the deck. "Take a look," he said.

An eye on David, Bryan strolled to the window and looked hard at the painting rocking in the breeze on the deck. David was right. Karen's seascape, the one he had seen in the beginning, looked back at him. No snow, no mountains, no frozen lake, and no nude images with a red-orange outline. Incredible!

Now he was really confused. Blankly, studying the painting, his mind fumbled for an answer. How could this be? The seascape was the painting's reality all along? Who was this David and how could he do that? No man could have that much power over ego minds. It was a trick. That's what it was, a magical trick.

"No magic," David said from the kitchen.

Bryan spun around, alarmed that David could read his mind.

David took lettuce and tomatoes from a bag. "If I'd been wearing boots and a cowboy hat," David said to a cutting board he took from a cabinet, "would you have thought I was a cowboy, or a kicker? A hard hat, a construction worker?"

"Well, I don't know," he mumbled, wondering where David was leading him now.

"Everything's perception, Bryan. You know that." He washed the lettuce and tomatoes in the sink. "Society is an illusion. It isn't real. We made the rules. And being that we created it, we can change it any time we choose. What if, suddenly everyone in the world were to realize that there was about to be a great catastrophe, like the end of the world as we know it?" He took a big knife from a drawer and chopped the head of lettuce in half. "Say, something like the Great Flood, and everyone who was bad and mean was going to die. And the only way any of them could save themselves was to change their ways, change their attitudes toward humanity and life. Know each other as brothers. Return to the love of spirit and start living the Ten Commandments."

Karen, suddenly aware of his tone, looked up from her tuna mixing and saw him angrily butchering the lettuce. Bryan quietly slid onto a stool at the breakfast bar and observed David's fury.

"Be kind and love thy neighbor," David railed. "Can you imagine what this world could be?" He grabbed a tomato and began viscously slicing it. Bryan noticed Karen's concern. "No one would lie and cheat ever again. No one would steal or kill. No more wars. Everyone would reject anger and fear. Remember they were love and be good, gentle, forthright and honest. Most of all, *honest.*"

Karen put a hand atop his and stopped the knife. "Did you go to Charlie's again?"

He looked at her, realized, calmed and shrugged. She let go the knife and he slowly sliced the tomato. He drew a deep sigh, "Charlie Bolivar is a tiny-brained, conniving, little cheat, who delights in persecuting his fellow man. He will have his day of judgment. Believe me."

"Be that as it may," Karen said, going back to her task.

"But I told you to go into the SuperMarket."

David waved the big knife, cutting air, "I refuse to let a little weasel like Charlie Bolivar make *me* drive halfway to Galveston."

"Then you should have stopped last night, like I told you."

Grabbing a cucumber, David attacked it with the knife. "The little prick is a blight on humanity."

Karen saw Bryan fidget uneasily. "Sorry, Bryan," she said. "You'll have to excuse him again. Charlie's Pak 'n Sak prices are the highest on West Beach. There's not another store for miles." She glanced at David. "He's spent months trying to alter Charlie's attitude, bombarding him with spiritual love."

Bryan smiled, passively, thinking, this Charlie must be a super negative.

"How can he exist?" David growled. "His concept of goodness is blackened by a terrible fear of lack. If I thought it would do him any good, I'd tie him up and make him listen to the tapes twenty-four hours a day."

Annoyed with his manner, Karen turned on him. "So," she sighed. "Was that it? You failed with Charlie again, and you came back here looking to prove yourself on us?"

"Well," David admitted and shrugged, regretfully. He raked his cuttings into the bowl. "I was close, oh, so close," he said, measuring the closeness between his fingers, then grinned. "It's taking time to find Charlie's level, but I'll get him. One of these days, I'll get him." He grinned, slyly.

FROM THE UPPER room's sitting area they could see miles up and down the narrow beach; Galveston's city lights to the east, a brilliant orange, pink and violet sunset to the west. A string of pearls sparkled in between; porch lights, flashlights, street lights, bonfires, headlights. An evening dressed in glitter.

Over the course of their light dinner they swapped tales of their past. Due to the strangeness of their first encounter, Bryan was more than curious about David's background, and even more interested in his involvement with Karen's. David was even polite enough to inquire into Bryan's. It was a face-off that Karen found intriguing.

David's life was fairly average for someone from south San Antonio. Finished high school there before joining the Navy in the early fifties. A tour as a Merchant Marine took him to the Pacific and the Korean War. Afterwards, he spent his GI Bill on journalism at San Marcos, then twenty years as a reporter for the *Austin Statesman*. Married once, no children. His wife died ten years ago in an auto accident. Three years ago he moved to the *San Antonio Express News*, met Karen and they moved to West Beach.

"Saw my first UFO in the Pacific," David said. He pushed his plate away and leaned back into the couch. "Summer of '54. We were somewhere east of Korea in the Sea of Japan. I was doing nightwatch, early morning shift, when it happened. I saw these lights in the water, under water. Yeah, under water, can you believe it? And they came up real fast, broke the surface and, there it was, a huge disk, big as a city block, with lights all over it. Scared the hell out of me. It sort of hung over the water a second or two, wobbled a couple times, then took off, straight up, out of sight." He slapped his flat palms together and speared his right an arms length above his head. "A red blur.

"Well," he glanced wide-eyed side to side. "I looked around to see if anyone else had seen it. No one. I called the watch officer. He was on the opposite side of the ship, and he comes over. I showed him where the thing came out of the water and where it went and he looks at me like I'm crazy, or drunk. But while he's standing there wondering what to do with me, the damn thing came back. He and I both saw it go right back into the ocean, and sink out of sight. We stood there looking it each other. We couldn't believe what we'd just seen. No way. It was incredible. I'd heard stories about pilots seeing them in the air, but I never expected to see one in the ocean."

"At least you had a witness," Bryan said. "Did you report the sighting?"

David laughed. "You kidding? Report what? There're space aliens living under the Sea of Japan? They'd throw us in the brig for being drunk on watch. You tell anyone the first time you saw one?"

Bryan smiled and shook his head.

"Why not? Where was it?"

"In the Army, late fifties. I was finishing basic at Fort Bliss, El Paso. This sound familiar? I was walking guard duty at this gunnery range in the early morning hours, about 2:30. It was almost overhead. I got a good look at it. Sleek, shiny disk with lights. Didn't make a sound. It banked to its right and I saw a fiery, orange ring underneath, up inside. It was heading north, real fast, toward White Sands.

"There were six other guys walking guard duty that night. Far as I know I was the only one who saw it. And, no, I didn't report it. Those were the days of atomic bombs, space shots. I didn't know what was going on then. Today, I do."

David smiled. "When did you find out?"

"After I came to NASA. I saw the pictures, talked to the astronauts and met John Sherman. When did you?"

"I guess I came in the back door," David said and glanced at Karen. She lounged on the L-couch, the other side of him, a foot and leg tucked under her. A screen save pattern flicked on a computer behind her. Printer and copier sat next to it. Boxes of used pencils and pastels were open on an end table. A large drawing pad leaned against the couch's arm completing, what was obvious to Bryan, a cozy hideaway duo working space. Things creative that they had in common were adding up.

"It was the Kennedy assassination," David went on. "I was there, traveling with the Texas press corp. I witnessed a lot of things that didn't add up. And then the Warren Commission's coverup, that really got me going. I found some people who would talk, most of it deathbed confessions. A picture began to fall together. The CIA, FBI and the Mob were heavily involved, and a U.S. drug cartel. Everything pointed to some high level group of people in the government putting out a contract on Kennedy."

"MJ-12," Bryan said.

David smiled. "You know the group."

Bryan nodded. "They had to kill him so they could keep the war going to protect their heroin supply and General Khun Sa."

"You know that story, too," David grinned. Bryan nodded. "Well, the more I investigated the government's involvement in drug activity, the more I found out just how big it really was."

"The biggest," Bryan nodded.

"Double-digit billions a year. Millions, right here in Texas. I couldn't believe the people who were involved in the government's cartel. Seemingly honest, respected, public people. I reported, wrote plenty of scandal stories. I was threatened. By my own paper, yet. The cartel said they would kill me if I didn't cool it. I left Austin, got the day job in San Antonio, and kept out of their way. But the question remained. Why? And what were they doing with all that money."

"Funding black budgets," Bryan injected.

"Yes," David smiled and nodded. "And I found that the biggest slice of those budgets was going to places like, Groom Lake, Los Alamos, Brookhaven National Labs."

"Lancaster and Montauk," Bryan added.

David studied him. "Right," he said and grinned. "You seem to know as much about this as I do."

"Most of the money was going to fund government in-

volvement with alien technology,'' Bryan sad. ''It's been
going on since the mid forties, since the Philadelphia
Experiment, since their treaty with the Gray Zetas in '52.''
''Did you know they were doing cloning at Los Alamos
and mind control implants at Brookhaven?''
''And time travel at Montauk?''
Karen watched the facts flying back and forth like base
line strokes in a tennis match.
''That they accidentally created HIV and the AIDS virus
at Brookhaven while screwing around with implanting alien
mind control links into human DNA?'' David said.
''And the implanting destroyed our immune systems,''
Bryan added. ''And that they were looking for a plan to
reduce the world population from eight to two billion by
the year 2000, so they started by introducing the AIDS
virus into the Belgian Congo through free polio serum?''
Both realized each had run the gamut of their test and
both knew who they were and what the they were doing.
They stared at each other. Finally, Bryan said, ''Welcome
to the club.'' David laughed.
''You're all right, Bryan,'' he said. ''Smart fellow.''
''Thanks,'' Bryan said.
''When I went to San Antonio, and met Karen,'' David
said, ''I realized she might've actually met these beings I'd
heard about, and maybe she had some information, 'from
their side of the cover-up,' that could fill in some of my
blank spaces.''
Glancing at Karen, they both saw she was looking at
something out the window, beyond the deck, in the sky.
She rose slowly. ''He's late,'' she said, and began gathering
scraps of bread onto her napkin.
Bryan and David watched her and then the sea gull
floating concentric circles over the upper deck. Karen
scooped up her wayfarer's handout and headed for the deck
as the bird fluttered to a perfect landing atop a railing post.
Something about the way the bird did that reminded Bryan

of another incident.

"Hey, guy! You're really late today," Karen said, stepping onto the deck and into the sunset's golden light. She slid the glass door closed behind her. on seeing the bread, the bird pranced and bobbed its head. Again, another familiar movement to Bryan, but didn't all sea gulls do that?

The bird lifted up above Karen, keeling steadily in the brisk Gulf breeze, waiting patiently for her to toss the first piece. One after another, the bird caught each morsel and quickly gulped it down. It was an excellent catcher.

"Did she tell you she was impregnated by the aliens?" David said to the scene on the deck.

Bryan glanced at him. "What?" he gasped.

David looked at him. "She didn't tell you she had an alien baby?"

Bryan glanced back at Karen. Her fantastic body suddenly took on another illusion; pregnant with an alien baby. "No. She didn't," he said around his shock. He turned back to David, but found he couldn't look at him, not wanting to reveal the effect his bit of news had had.

"I suppose she still can't talk about it," David said, as seriously as he could, and watching Bryan. "They impregnated her after they brought her back that night. She carried the fetus three months and the aliens came back and took it. Somewhere out there she has an alien son."

"I've heard stories of those kinds of abductions," Bryan said, watching Karen feeding the bird on the deck. "But, Karen?" The mother of an alien being? He wondered how David felt about that? He wanted to ask, since David was so close to her. David's answer might help to clear up his sudden disheartening concern. But Bryan decided he'd keep as many of those little secrets to himself.

"A mutant, probably," David said. "You know the aliens have trouble matching into our DNA?"

"Yes," Bryan mused. "So I've heard."

The two studied each other for a long moment, both aware that their confrontation had suddenly taken a curious turn.

Karen tossed the bird her last piece of bread. It gulped it down and she waved the empty napkin. All gone.

"Look," David said. "I guess she's still a little sensitive about the baby thing. So, don't say anything about it. Okay? Just forget I even mentioned it."

Bryan nodded, but there was no way he could forget his new image of Karen. From then on every time he would look at her he would think about her alien baby. She was no longer pure, so to speak. She was defiled. She was a mother to a child somewhere out there, with the aliens, flying a space ship.

David secretly enjoyed Bryan's sudden change of interest.

Karen stepped inside the door and they watched the bird fly away. "That's Stanley," she said to the winged speck against the darkening sky.

"Stanley?" Bryan puzzled.

She closed the door. "He's our vagabond spirit."

"Stanley?" Bryan questioned, again. "Why Stanley?"

She began stacking their plates. "Because someone already named one Livingston."

Karen folded back onto the couch, in the same spot, sitting on the same foot.

"And then you met Karen." Bryan said to David, prodding him on.

"Oh. Yes," David said. He shifted, recrossing his legs. "It was at one of her gallery exhibits in San Antonio. Her paintings seemed to give off this glow of energy, this, this inspiration of spiritual creations. I knew I had to talk with this beautiful person. So, I set up an interview, and as we were talking, she began to tell me how she received her inspirations through a spiritual muse. And that this opening, connection, seemed to have happened several months after her abduction experience with these aliens. Well, with what I already knew about the aliens, without ever having met one, and here was someone who had. I just had to know, if in fact, these aliens were dealing with the government. Heal it from the other side, as it were, since the government was so secretive about its side of the story.

"As we talked it was obvious that Karen could only recall bits and pieces of what these aliens had told her. There was a block somewhere, so that was when I suggested she see a hypnotist. And that's when the whole story came out. Everything that she'd experienced. Their history, our history, everything. All about their brothers, the Gray Zetas, the wars, their coming to Earth and creating us, the Gray Zetas tricking our government so they could destroy us and get to the others. It's just incredible."

"The Annunaki," Bryan said. David looked surprised. "The Blonds, Nordics, the Nefilim. Karen was abducted by the Nefilim."

"Yes," David puzzled. "You know them, too?"

"Yes," Bryan nodded, feeling a surge of one-up-manship. He glanced at Karen. She didn't seem to be all that impressed. He could have said he too had met the Nefilim the same way Karen had, but he decided to hold that ace, just for her. "There are books, *The Earth Chronicles,* ever heard of them? And the Bible. The Nefilim history is all through them. they're the Annunaki, our *gods* from Nebiru, their planet that comes through here every 3600 years?"

David nodded, still amazed. "Yes," he said. "It's all on Karen's tapes."

"Sounds as if you already know what's on the tapes," Karen said.

"Maybe, maybe not," Bryan smiled, locking onto her probing, killer blue eyes.

"Just what is it you're searching for?" Karen asked.

Bryan glanced from Karen to David, David to Karen. Both had him pinned with steady inquiring minds. God, what energy, he thought, the two of them together. How much could a person take?

"The knowing," he said.

"The knowing?" Karen said.

"Yes," Bryan nodded. "You said that when you were with the Nefilim, you experienced the knowing, out-of-your body, in pure spiritual being. That's what I want to know."

"How to get out of your body?" Karen grinned.

Bryan shrugged. "If that's on the tapes, yes."

Karen thought about it. "I suppose you could say that the tapes are an instructional manual to remembering our spiritual power," she mused. "But getting that energy out of your body, I don't know."

"Once you know your spiritual power," David said. "It's just a matter of practice to realizing its potential."

"That what you did?" Bryan asked him.

David shrugged. "After you know, practice the principles, that's the key." He smiled and winked.

"Then that's what I want, the *key,*" Bryan said. He studied both for any response to their subtle references to the *key.*

Karen slowly rose, unfolding again, from her nest on the couch. "I'll get the tapes," she smiled.

They watched her go around the coffee table and into the master bedroom. Bryan tried not to think of what probably went on in there, what he *knew* went on in there. Then he remembered that David could read his thoughts. He fumbled, nervously, with a broken sand dollar on the end table next to him and tried to think of something else.

"You know," Bryan said to David while tapping the piece of sand dollar on the table. "If it hadn't been for the religious and government conspiracies to hide the truth, just think where we would be today."

Bryan saw some tiny pieces fall out of the sand dollar. He carefully picked up the fragile fragments and tried to put them back into one sand dollar's hollow center.

"Yes," David said, watching Bryan worry with the sand dollar pieces. "It's a pity that some beings need to steal the powers of their brothers to make themselves whole."

"You didn't break it," Karen said. She was standing by the table with the tapes. "Stanley dropped that sand dollar on the deck one morning last week. It broke in two. He took the missing piece and flew off with it. Strange. I don't know why, but I kept that piece. Broken dollars aren't worth anything. One of the doves is even missing."

"Doves?"

"Dove bones," she said. "Those little bones you're trying to put back inside. They're called doves."

Bryan examined them closer. True, they did resemble little white birds in flight.

"Don't you know the legend of the sand dollar?"

He shrugged. "No. Guess not."

Karen set the tapes down and took the broken sand dollar and its dove bones in her hand. She sat down beside him, close, touching and leaned toward him. Her smell was pure, clean and delicate, salt of the sea, unencumbered by artificial perfumes. He felt a surge of sensual pleasure. He wished David would make himself vanish.

"In a way, it's sort of spiritual," Karen said, holding the dollar face up. "See the flower?" she pointed. "The petals? Five of them. Some say it's an Easter Lily. Some say it's the Christ. See the head, arms, legs? Like on the cross. The three holes at the edge? Those are the holes the nails made in his hands and feet. The hole in the middle? That's the one the Roman's spear made in His side."

She spread the dove bones in her hand. "There're five doves inside every sand dollar. Legend says, that when the sand dollar is broken open, the doves fly out, carrying the Christ message across the land." She grinned. "Neat, huh?"

"Hmmm," Bryan nodded. "I thought Stanley looked familiar. He brought me the missing piece, at NASA, last week."

"Yeah?" Karen said, raising her brow. "Interesting." She reached the tapes and handed them to him. "I guess these must be for you."

Chapter Fourteen:
The Plan

BRYAN LISTENED TO Karen's tapes on his car's tape deck all the way home. With his concentration so intense and Karen's hypnotic tone it was a wonder his automatic pilot got him home safely. He finished the last tape early the next morning barely staying awake to the end. He was exhausted and disappointed; nothing he hadn't read in *The Earth Chronicles* and *The Course in Miracles*, or heard from the beings themselves. Karen had gotten the same lesson. The tapes hadn't revealed any instructions on exactly how to apply the principles to get out of the body. He sighed a couple of times, hoping that maybe the secret was hidden in something he'd missed, or wasn't aware of. He would have to try again. His head hit the pillow and he was out, his mind racing away to dreamland.

The next morning in his office, Bryan took a cup of coffee and closed his door. He slipped some blank tapes in his recorder and began copying from Karen's first tape. He stretched out on his couch, relaxed and tried to concentrate on every word.

It was all there: the Nefilim history from their Lyran home planet, the wars, the Vegans, the Rigelians, the Zeta Reticiuli, the Sirians, Procyon, Nebiru, coming to Earth, the creation of Homo sapiens, the Garden, the Deluge, all of it just as it was in the *Earth Chronicles*. There was the knowledge of humanity's separation from spiritual self with the creation of the ego, all things that Bryan had experienced himself through his own incident. Could it be he already knew all there was to know and it was as David said, *the knowing's* power came through a concentrated practice; controlling ego illusions? He felt some jealousy that David could accomplish that so easily and more so that he used it to be in that presence with Karen. But he also had to admire David for just being able to do it. And it said something for a man, a perfect man, who could understand and accept his girlfriend having an alien baby. An unconditional love. The tapes, he had to concentrate on her tapes.

Over Karen's voice he heard a tapping on his door and Marsha was standing in its opening before he could come upright. She listened to the tape as Bryan got to his feet.

"What're you listening to?" Marsha inquired.

"Oh," Bryan said, casually, strolling to his stereo's power controls. "Just some abductee's hypnosis session. The one you turned down."

"Wasting your time, again."

He held his fingers on the off buttons. "You want to hear? She actually flew their craft."

"Heavens, no," Marsha huffed. "It's just a lot of silly nonsense, Bryan. There are no craft to fly. Get real."

Bryan shrugged and clicked off the tapes. He glanced at her as he went to his desk. "You'd be surprised just how much you could learn from one of those sessions."

"I doubt it."

"Yes," he sighed. "You're right. You won't report me, will you?" He forced a smile.

"I've got more important things to do."

"Such as?"

"While you were out of it," she said, "they put the shot back on. The next window's Monday morning."

"Memorial Day?"

"What's a holiday with a Shuttle ready to go?" she said. "I expected as much from you, so I've already arranged for myself and Ed to take the first shift.''

His phone rang.

"They're shooting for a 5:45 liftoff."

The phone rang, again. He moved around his desk, picked it up and held his hand over the receiver. He looked at her.

"You and Dianne have the second shift," she said, moving toward the door. "Be there by ten. Any questions, see me later." She closed the door behind her. He answered his phone.

"Hello?"

It was John. "You get the tapes?" he asked.

"Yes."

"Well? Have you listened to them, yet?"

"Twice. Not much there we don't already know. I'm making you copies. I'll bring them over this evening."

"Fine," John said. "Bring them to the boat. We'll be over at the marina after five."

"Okay."

"See ya there. Bye."

JOHN AND MYRA'S forty-two foot sloop, *Star Mist,* rocked in its slip at the far end of Watergate Marina's pier nine. Bryan sat in one side of the cockpit sipping a soft drink, the tape copies by his side. Myra squinted at him from the rear of the cockpit. The setting sun was just above his head.

"So, she has a boyfriend," Myra said. She took a sip from her drink and glanced back at John, halfway down in the engine hole, tinkering with the boat's diesel. A heavy duty battery charger sat by the hole at the end of a thick red cord that ran to a plug on the pier.

Bryan nodded. "Yeah. They're living together."

Myra grinned. "You're not gonna let that stop you?"

"You don't know this guy. Or, maybe you do. Says he was an investigative reporter with the Austin and San

Antonio papers.''

"What's his name?"

"David Rodriguez."

"David Rodriguez" Myra said. "Yeah, I've heard of him. Long ago. He dug up a lot of graft on some big political names. Drug, mob connection, money laundering stuff. Last I remember hearing, somebody tried to kill him, shot at him, ran him off the road, something like that. I think he got their message; quit, sort of, dropped out of sight.''

"To hear him tell it," Bryan said, "they almost did kill him. It was MJ-12 he was bugging. Followed the laundry right to their black budget funding: Groom Lake, Los Alamos, Brookhaven, Montauk, everything. He discovered the whole history of the Zeta connections, and when he met Karen, heard she'd met some aliens, he got her to do the hypnosis, thinking she'd tell him the alien's side, only it wasn't the Zeta's lies, it was the Nefilim's truth. So, now he has all the alien history, Nefilim and Zetas, and the knowing. It's all on those tapes."

Some clanking and grunting came from the engine hole and John stood up wiping his hands on a grease spotted rag.

"It's all the things we already know," Bryan added. "All the knowing of spiritual self that I've already told you from my experience. Nothing new. No secret method."

John hopped up from the hole and sat beside Myra at the end of the cockpit. He wiped his hands on a clean towel and asked, "You didn't find *anything* new? Nothing that would help you get out of your body?"

Bryan shook his head. "Nope."

"Not one tiny little thing?" Myra frowned.

Bryan shrugged. "Well, maybe one thing," he said. "David."

"David?" John puzzled.

"Yeah," Bryan sighed and glanced down the pier. "Whoever he was before he met Karen and heard her tapes, he isn't now.''

"What do you mean, isn't now?'' Myra asked.

"I don't know,'' Bryan mused. "From the minute I met him, things began to happen. Strange things. He can change things.''

"Like what?''

"Reality. Illusions,'' Bryan said. "He really gave my ego a shot. Showed me just how vulnerable it still was. Karen, too.'' Remembering the painting incident; Bryan shook his head, incredulously.

"What did he do?'' Myra questioned.

"Don't know exactly,'' Bryan said, reflectively. "Best way I've been able to figure, he projected an illusion, got us caught up in our imaging, and pushed it with the power of our combined energies until it became our reality.'' He shrugged at their blank, but confused, expressions. "The non-locality thing. That's the only way I can explain it. He's developed this, this, incredibly powerful energy. He, and Karen, said he got it from studying and practicing the principles of the knowing on her tapes.''

"Non-locality?'' Myra mused.

"You know, dimensions, consciousness, mind merging with matter,'' Bryan said. "I've explained it to you, remember? The holographic imaging thing; the mind storing information in a holographic, or non-local situation. Dimensionality.''

"Oh, yeah,'' Myra said, but not real sure.

"It's like the aliens' propulsion systems. We know that they travel in other dimensions — the strong force, gravity that's not abundant here. They access their gravity waves with their gravity amplifiers. The energy that drives those amplifiers come from the reactors fueled by element 115, also something we don't have here. It works the same way with the spiritual power of mind. Once we get pure access, it's possible to push mind power out of the locality of three dimensions into higher dimensions: fourth, fifth, sixth, and higher. It's what the astronauts get into outside Earth dimensions, automatic release. That's just about the best way I can explain it."

Myra and John turned and stared at each other, questioning whether either one understood what Bryan had just said. They didn't. They looked at him and blinked.

"Guess you would've had to have been there," Bryan said.

"That's the power, the knowing, that will start the ship?" Myra asked.

"That's it, spiritual power at it's highest decimal."

"Think we, any of us, could get the same results just by studying and practicing from her tapes?" John asked.

"Suppose it could be done," Bryan said. "Depending on the focus and intensity; but it still takes time. I've been at it for more than two years and I'm no where near doing what David did."

"Hmmm," John mused. "This David sounds like someone we'd like to meet." He looked at Myra, she was already way ahead of him.

"Why don't we invite them on the boat with us," Myra said, her mind running through possible plans.

"Yes, good idea," John added. "We're taking the *Mist* out for a shakedown Sunday. Let's invite them along."

Just the plan Myra had in mind. "Make it a day," she said. "A picnic. Drop anchor on the other side of the bay."

"It's a holiday weekend," Bryan reminded. "They could have plans, you know."

"No harm in asking," John said. "Where's the phone?" He glanced, searching around.

"I left it down in the cabin," Myra said.

Bryan got to his feet and headed down the stairs. "What time?"

"Eight," John said, as he went back to the engine.

A boat motored up the channel and Myra exchanged waves with their crew. Its wake rocked the *Star Mist* and the halyard clanked against the mast.

Bryan was grinning when he hopped back up the stairs. He had a happy report. "They'll be here."

"Good," John grinned around the engine cover. "That'll give us some time to study those tapes. We'll be ready for your mysterious Mr. David."

Bryan leaned down and looked into the engine housing. "You need any help finishing up?"

"No. Thanks. We've just about got her."

Bryan sat back down. "Look," he said. "Is it okay if I ask someone else to come along?"

Myra grinned and exchanged a quick glance with John. "Susan?" she asked.

Bryan nodded and returned her grin.

"She ready for this? You know, David?"

"I think so," Bryan said. "I've told her enough that she's writing a book, *we're* writing a book."

"Oh? And she already understands everything?"

"Not everything," Bryan said. "But she's getting there. I'm going to let her listen to the tapes. They're better than my repeating everything. And David, well, that's another chapter."

"Sure, bring her along." John smiled. He started to go back to the engine, then a thought stopped him. He squinted up at Bryan. "I'm sure you've heard the launch is on for Monday?"

Bryan nodded. "Already have my shift."

"I talked to Burris today," John said. "I told him we came up with something that would save him some worry. We're meeting with him tomorrow morning."

JOHN PULLED HIS car into the parking lot of the building that housed the astronauts' physical fitness area. There was a small scattering of cars close to the entrance.

He saw Bryan's and parked in the empty space beside it. The two glanced at each other and got out together searching the area. A van with a trailer of lawn maintenance equipment was parked at one side of the lot. Two men behind mowers trimmed the lawn between the lot and the building. John and Bryan disguised a less than passing interest in the van and men as they met between their cars.

"Did you bring it?" Bryan asked on seeing John's hands were empty. He spoke away from the van and just audible enough to be heard over the mower's engines.

John nodded. "In the car. I'm keeping it out of sight as long as possible."

They walked together, saying nothing until they were inside the front entrance of the building.

"They haven't left him out of their sight since they told him," John said, commenting on the scene behind them. "Have you caught any watching you?"

"No," Bryan said. They were going through doors and walking down hallways. "But I know they're there."

"Yeah. And I get a real strong feeling that Fuller is somewhere in the area. He's going to want to watch the deployment, I'm sure, and the only place he can do that is right here in ficker three."

"You mean, I'm finally gonna get to see the infamous General Fuller?"

John grinned. "Things as they are, you might even get to meet him."

"I'll forego that pleasure, thank you."

They stopped in front of the exercise room windows and searched through the maze of equipment. Steve straddled a press bench, his muscles straining under a heavy load of iron. They went in and stood where he would see them when he finished.

"You think they've got some guys in here?" Bryan asked, as they surveyed the scattered activity in the room.

"I wouldn't bet against it."

"That's a lot of man hours."

"Two outside, no telling how many in the van," John counted. "Maybe two in here. Never take Fuller lightly."

"You think these people know why they're watching Steve?"

"No way."

After a bit. "Did you listen to the tapes?" Bryan asked.

"Uh huh."

"What do ya think?"

"Like you suspected;" John said. "You both met the same beings. Nothing we hadn't already heard. Certainly no instant key to starting the ship, not without a lot of practice time. We thought about what you said about the dimensions and we think it makes a lot of sense. But we don't have years to practice. Myra says we should start thinking about bringing Karen and David in as a last resort. That is, if he's as good as you say he is at cutting down learning time."

"Maybe you'll get a chance to see how good for yourselves."

Steve set the weights in their bar rests and sat up on the bench. He saw them waiting and John gestured that they would meet him in the lounge.

They were casually making selections in front of a vending machine when Steve came in toweling his upper body.

"Hi," Steve panted, as they shook hands. "How's it going?"

"You're looking pretty good out there," Bryan said. "What're you pressing? One-fifty? Two?"

Steve shrugged, modestly. "Something like that."

"What'll you have?" John asked Steve. He and Bryan had made their selections.

"Anything diet. Thanks."

There was nothing but diet in the machine. John

dropped in the coins, a drink popped out and Steve took it. They made their way to a table on the far side by a wall window overlooking a lush courtyard.

"When're you leaving?" John asked.

"First thing in the morning," Steve sighed, after his first sip.

"So," John said. "Is everyone up to speed on our problem?"

"I think you guys are more so than I am," Steve said.

"What is it you need to know?"

"What, or who, are those missiles for? You said they were Excaliburs. I've never heard of Excaliburs."

"Of course, you haven't. They're above top secret because of where they're developed and by whom. Their purpose was to penetrate the Earth's surface up to three thousand feet. Tests so far have been way short of that. We figure MJ-12 believes a shot from space will improve the Excalibur's performance capabilities."

"A shot? At who?"

"There're several possibilities," John said. "All of which may be wrong. The problem is that they're going to be out there. MJ-12 is going to make sure of that, and there's nothing we can do about it."

Steve shook his head, incredulously, "I still can't believe there's a group like MJ-12 running this country and the aliens. This is all just too much."

"We get into making you a believer, Steve," John said. "And you'll miss your flight. Bryan and I have come up with a plan. We can't tell you all of it right now."

John stopped as he saw the two men he and Bryan had seen exercising at the far end of the weight room come into the lounge. They toweled off as they selected drinks from the vending machine. Steve and Bryan glanced at the men as they made their way to a table within hearing distance.

"You know those guys?" John asked, his face turned away.

"No," Steve said, toweling his face.

"All we're asking you to do, John continued in a softer tone, "is your part. We'll do the rest."

Apprehensive, Steve glanced at their hopeful faces.

"It's important," Bryan assured him . "It's our only out."

Steve sighed and nodded. "Okay. What do I have to do?"

John shot a quick glance at the two men. They seemed innocent enough, but . . . "Why don't you shower and change," John whispered. "And meet us in the parking lot?"

Steve got their drift. They faked a big laugh about something they'd said and pushed their chairs back. "That's great! I love it," Steve laughed, looking at his watch. "I've gotta get going." They stood and shook hands. "It's great seeing you guys. We'll do some handball when I get back."

They walked out together. Steve headed for the locker room.

"Good luck," John called. "And the crew. Have a good flight. We'll be watching."

"THOSE THE TAPES?" Susan asked, seeing the cassettes in Bryan's hand when she let him in her front door. He had called saying he had some tapes that would help them in writing their book.

"Yes." He handed them to her. She had her hair pulled up and pinned. Shorts, T-shirt and silver sandals.

She took the tapes, bundled with a rubber band, and gave them a passing exam. "What did you say they were?"

He followed her into the den. "They're a hypnosis session of one of our abductees."

"I just made some lemonade," Susan said. She placed the tapes on the breakfast bar as she went into the kitchen. Her sandals slapped on the tile. "You want a glass? We can sit out on the patio. It's so nice out there this time of day."

"Sure," Bryan said. He glanced at the patio. It was nice and shady. She kept it swept and washed. Clean and neat around blooming flowers.

Susan put ice cubes in two glasses and poured lemonade from a pitcher.

"How's the book coming?" he asked.

"Slow."

"Have you started?"

She handed him his glass. "Sort of," she said, and led him out onto the patio. They sat in sling lounge chairs, their legs touching beneath a wicker end table. "Did you bring your suit?" Bryan nodded. "Good. We can take a dip later."

She took a sip of her drink, set it on the glass top table and stretched. "Ooooh, this feels great," she groaned. "I love this time of the day, don't you?"

"Uh huh. The golden hours."

"What I need is a form," she said to the evening sky.

"What?"

"A form. We've got plenty of content. What we need is the right form. Whether it's gonna be fiction or non-fiction. How can we present all that information, hundreds of thousands of years of history, and have the reader enjoy reading it. That's the key. What do people enjoy reading, fiction, a good story. But all the facts are true. Non-fiction might not interest the right people. Look at the *Earth Chronicles,* seven non-fiction volumes that few people have the courage to tackle. And you've already said there's no need to do more of that.

"I can't start until I have a form."

"You're the writer."

"Yeah, I know. At least, I think I am," she sighed. "So, what's on the tapes? Maybe something that'll help?"

"It's the experiences of a gal from Galveston," Bryan said. "Name's Karen Coe. She and her husband were abducted about three years ago from a camping site in the Big Bend Park. She was taken out of her body, he wasn't. He died about two weeks later from the radiation his body got on their trip.''

Without the slightest doubt of its truth, Susan frowned. ''Oh, that must have been awful.''

Bryan shrugged. ''Happens. We've seen a lot of burns, and cancers. Not too many die that soon. He got a heavy dose.

''The tapes are of all the knowledge she experienced from being out of her body and from being with the beings themselves.

''Pretty much like my experience,'' Bryan added. ''Listening to them, I would have to say, we were picked up by the same beings: the Nefilim. The knowledge, the history is the same.''

''The same?''

Bryan nodded. ''Might not be anything new, but I thought you'd like to hear them. Helps to hear it over and over, till you get it right. And practice it, so I've learned.''

''Is she pretty?''

Bryan weighed her question and his answer. ''Yes, she is. Why?''

''From what I've gathered listening to you talk about being out of the body, getting the knowledge and knowing the spiritual self makes one a beautiful person.'' She raised a brow. ''The perfect man, the perfect woman. Isn't that what you're all looking for?''

''We get perfect so we know perfect when it comes along,'' Bryan said. He took the last sip of his lemonade and set the glass down. ''She's living with a man who's taken perfect to its ultimate power.''

''The *ultimate* power of perfect?'' Susan said, incredulously. ''Now, that's someone I really want to meet.''

''Well, you can,'' Bryan smiled. ''His name is David, and he and Karen will be sailing on John and Myra's boat tomorrow, and you're invited. Wanna come?''

''You bet. What'll we bring?''

''Picnic stuff. Swim suit. And an open mind.''

Chapter Fifteen:
The Game

IN THE TWILIGHT on the other side of the county the lights at the Little League ballpark flooded on. Top of the third. The Indians, in red shirts and caps trimmed in black, were in the field. A skinny kid whose uniform hung like it was still on the hanger was on the mound slinging a baseball that appeared half as large as his head toward a stocky teammate squatting behind a mass of catcher's padding and a seat cushion sized mitt. A smaller kid, hiding in a black shirt with a yellow Pirate picture and lettering, short sleeves that fell past his tiny elbows, a bat two thirds his height and weight, peered from under a massive black helmet that protected everything including his seeing the ballgame, and got a glimpse of the ball falling in the dirt behind home plate and rolling to the backstop. A giant of an umpire with a small black air mattress protecting his beer gut yelled, "BALL," and dodged the little mass of catching geer scrambling after the elusive white missile. The stands behind the opposing dugouts along each baseline erupted in applause and a chorus of encouragement: "Way to go, Buddy!; Goodbye Eddie, goodbye."

Fathers watched the game, mothers gossiped with an eye for their little ones playing spontaneous games in the dirt behind the fences and under the stands. Teenagers hung out around the concession stand and flirted in the parking lot. A couple of toddlers had made fast friends chasing night beetles at the base of a light pole.

Mark Burris, his ankle in a light cast, sat at the end of the Pirates' bench swinging his crutch in the air when they did good and banging it on the ground when they did bad. He had dug himself a fine furrow.

Steve and Jan Burris were backing the Pirates half way up the third base stands. Most all on their side knew him as an astronaut, but at the games he was just Mark's dad. They had not expected to see Steve at the past three games, and then Mark broke an ankle. The Shuttle went on hold and there he was. Some had good naturedly kidded him about causing the problem so he could come to the game. If they only knew. His whole purpose in coming to the game was to try and think about something else besides what the flight was all about. He felt himself wondering what all of them would do if they actually knew the truth. What would they think of him if he were to march up to the scorer's booth, grab the PA system's mike and begin broadcasting the whole story. They'd think he had flipped. "Excuse me, ladies and gentlemen. I'm sorry to have to interrupt your ballgame, but this is Commander Steve Burris, and I have a very important announcement about some missiles on this Shuttle, and some incredible revelations about our secret government." What would they do? Probably put up a howl about him interrupting their ballgame. So, why bother? Let them be happy in their ignorance.

A veteran Pirate got a hit, Pirate fans got their chance to stand and cheer. The hitter slid into second following an Indian error. There was still hope. Bottom of the fifth, one on and two out.

In the excitement no one noticed the dark blue Air Force staff car creep around the far end of the parking lot down the left field line. Its headlights blinked off and its driver, a Sergeant Major, hopped out and opened its back doors. Generals Fuller and Rawlings, in civilian clothes, slid out and casually strolled to the outfield fence. Fuller, chewing on his cigar, leaned on the fence as they surveyed the field, then the stands. Finally, spotting what he wanted, Fuller beckoned the Sergeant Major and nodded toward the Pirate's stands. The noncom searched the stands as Fuller stated his orders.

The Sergeant Major marched up the fence line and around a group of Little Leaguers gathering for the following game. All the Pirate boosters at that end of the stands were surprised to see a uniform looking for a path through them. Steve was shocked to see the Sergeant. His heart leaped into his throat as he saw the Sergeant's look target him while winding his way up the rows through the scattering of spectators. The Sergeant leaned down when he reached Steve and whispered in his ear. Steve looked around the uniform and saw the civies-clad Generals leaning on the outfield fence.

Everyone in the Pirate's bleachers were now aware of the event and the game had suddenly lost their attention. An Air Force Sergeant Major doesn't search out an astronaut at a Little League game unless it's an emergency, especially if that astronaut happens to be the pilot of a Shuttle waiting to be launched in the next couple of days. Jan strained to hear what was being whispered, but couldn't. Steve looked her in the eye and patted her leg, assuredly. "It's okay, hon. I'll be right back." He stood and followed the Sergeant back down his path.

Deeply puzzled, she watched her husband and the Sergeant hop from the bleachers and march along the fence toward two men she did not recognize. If they'd had on uniforms she might have felt easier about the interruption. Those close by whispered questions to which she could only shrug. The mysterious incident rivaled the ballgame for their attention.

Steve's mind shuffled reasons for the generals being there. He was sure they knew that he had disobeyed orders and talked about the missiles. Bryan and John had made an issue of pointing out their agents. He summoned and practiced possible excuses he might need as alibis.

Fuller rested his elbows atop the four-foot fence, chewed his cigar and sought interest in the play afield. Beyond him Rawlins leaned on the fence with one hand and watched Steve approach. The Sergeant, mission accomplished, backed off and took a position by their car. Shadows, civies and time added mystery to this punitive meeting.

Fuller removed his cigar. "Your team winning, Commander?" he asked before looking at Steve.

"Not at the moment, sir," Steve said, puzzled at Fuller's interest. The missiles were the only business they had. Why not get to the point? Maybe that was the point, he thought, winning and losing.

"I never had much time to watch my boys play ball," Fuller said. He looked back at the game. "Always too busy, always on the go, always had a fire to put out. You know how that is, don't ya, Commander? The responsibilities?"

Steve nodded. "Yes, sir." He weighed the analogy to their purpose.

"Whenever I see something like this," Fuller said with a quick glance at Steve, "it makes me feel sad, real sad. All the family things I've missed in life, trying to make it safe for the people of this great country."

Steve felt the red, white and blue and apple pie speech was incongruous and a waste. He watched the game with Fuller and waited patiently for him to get to the point. The Pirates were in the field again, yelling encouragement to their pitcher.

"You get a chance to come back home, see a game,"

Fuller said to the field. "And the first thing you do is go straight to Mayfield and Sherman."

Steve feigned shocked innocence. "Sir?"

"You told them about the missiles, didn't you?"

"Well, I . . . I," he stammered.

"We know you did, Commander."

"Knowing about the missiles was a little heavy for me to handle, sir. I couldn't sleep nights. I had to talk to someone. I thought Mayfield would be the fight one to help me cope."

"You didn't indicate they bothered you at the time," Fuller said. "You should have said so. Not violated our trust."

"I . . ."

"Mayfield and Sherman aren't on our team, Commander," Fuller said. He flicked his cigar in clasped hands. "They don't know the problems we have out there in the real world. How much did you tell them?"

"Not much, sir," Steve said, as he thought over his situation. "They knew more than I did. They knew the missiles were Excaliburs."

"The Excaliburs, eh?" Fuller nodded and glanced at Rawlins. "What else do they know?"

"That they were designed for underground bunkers," Steve said. "And that they had been ineffective fired from land-based rockets and that you will be looking for better results when the missiles are fired from a greater distance."

In front of them the Pirate left fielder settled under a high fly ball.

"Hmmm," Fuller moaned and glanced at Rawlins. He coughed and spit a flake of tobacco. "What else?" He asked, turning back and glaring at Steve.

Steve shrugged. "That's about it."

"And you're okay with that?"

"Yes, sir." Steve relaxed.

"In that case," Fuller grunted, stepping back from the

fence, "I guess we can feel assured that there are no further problems, Commander?"

"Not that I know of, sir," Steve said, then smiled for the first time, "Except, maybe, in getting it off the pad."

"Good," Fuller nodded. "That's what I wanted to hear." He flicked his cigar. "You know, Commander, you could have come to us with your problems. We thought we gave you enough information to do your job. We figured you were the type who would be proud to carry out this mission for your country and the peace of the world. Mayfield and Sherman? Sometimes they don't see eye to eye with us, and what little information they've been able to get through their little covert activities, they don't know what's going on, and their imaginations work overtime, you know? Knowing who our enemies are. Most of the time they don't have the straight poop. You understand what I'm saying?"

Steve forced a grin, "Yes, sir." All he wanted to do was get away from the two generals, back to the safety of people who didn't know.

"Good, Commander," Fuller smiled, confidently. "We knew you'd understand." He nodded his cigar at the field. "Sorry about the intrusion. Didn't mean to cause a scene. we just wanted to make sure we're still on the same page."

Fuller stuck his cigar in his grin and extended his hand. "Have a good flight, Commander," he said and they shook hands.

Fuller and Rawlins turned and headed for their car. After a few steps, they stopped. "Oh, and Commander," Fuller said over his shoulder. "If anything goes wrong, and we're confident that it won't, you won't have to worry about your family. We'll make sure they're well taken care of. Just thought you'd like to know. Good luck." He threw an informal salute and Steve returned it.

Watching them get into their car and drive away, Steve

did an instant replay of what was said. He thought he had satisfied their inquisition, so what did Fuller mean by, "taking care of his family?" He wondered if they knew about what Bryan and John had asked him to do? If so, should he proceed as planned? Was the risk greater than the safety of his family? Heading back up the fence line he thought of the implications. Did they know, or didn't they? Was this Fuller's way of covering all the bases? There wasn't time to check with Bryan and John. Should he go ahead, take the risk? Appointed heros carried heavy heads.

The game was between innings. He felt everyone watching him wind his way up the bleachers and settle beside Jan. She felt his diluting a stressful situation with a forced smile.

She took his hind and frowned. "What was that all about?"

"Nothing," he shrugged, pressing against her shoulder and squeezing her hand. "Just some flight changes they needed to tell me before I got away in the morning. Secret stuff. Nothing for you to worry about."

Chapter Sixteen:
The Sail

"HEY, OUT THERE!" a radio disc jockey bellowed. "Can you believe this day? Not a cloud in the sky. Beautiful. And hot. Ninety tops, weatherman says. But, listen up, we're gonna be COOL! YEAH. ALL DAY! Right here at KGAL 93.6. Going to the beach? Take us with you. But, HEY! Don't all of you rush down here at once, you'll tip us over. OKAY! ALL RIGHT!" A shattering of fender guitars, booming bass and blaring drums stomped on the tail of the DJ's "BOBBA LOBBA LU." The early morning vibrations came from stereo speakers in the cabin of a big boat Susan and Bryan passed as they came down pier nine carrying their picnic contributions and outing gear. Bryan spotted a couple of teenagers passed out on cushion pads in the forward cabin of the rocking yawl.

"Any of yours?" Bryan asked after they had gotten past the noise.

Susan shuttered a "No" beneath her pink and orange windbreaker. A wide-brimmed cap was pulled down over her pony-tailed hair and dark glasses. She wore a loosely-buttoned shirt and shorts over a two-piece swim suit. Bryan looked seaworthy in his pullover and thigh-length shorts. They shuffled along the weather-warped pier in their running shoes toward the *Star Mist's* slip.

Myra was watching for them and waved from the bow as Susan and Bryan saw her.

"Hey! You made it!" Myra greeted. She ushered them down to the open life line.

"Hi," Susan grinned. She was impressed with the size of the boat and its sleek colors.

Myra offered a helping hand onto the deck. "Hi, Susan. It's good to see you?"

They hugged. "It's good to see you, too. Hi, John. How've you all been?"

"Fine. Just fine," John grinned. "We're glad you could come."

John stepped in to help Bryan with their gear.

"Thank you," Susan said. "I'm so happy you asked me. I've just been so busy with the end of school. It's nice to have a chance to get away."

"Have you sailed much?" Myra asked.

"Not a lot, but I'm ready to get with it again."

"Did you see Karen and David?" John asked Bryan.

"No. Maybe I'd better go back to the lot and show them the way." He jumped back to the pier.

"Let's get this gear below," John said, taking their drink cooler and picnic boxes.

"You brought your swim suit?" Myra asked.

"Yes. Wearing it."

"Where we're going's not always a great place to swim," John said. "But you never know."

"Here they come." Bryan said as he reached the bow pier.

The little group stopped and watched Karen and David coming toward them. The mysterious David drew their focus. At that distance he didn't seem all that spiritually powerful. Bryan waved and Karen waved back. Their pure white tops and shorts glistened in the bright morning sun.

"Hi," Bryan grinned. They shook hands beyond the bow. "Glad you could make it. Hi, David."

"Us, too," Karen grinned.

"Hi, Bryan. Good to see you again." David shifted a

cooler to his left hand before shaking Bryan's.

Bryan ushered them toward the life line opening. "Come on. Meet everyone."

"Hi," Karen said, taking Myra's hand as she stepped on deck.

"Glad you could make it," Myra said.

"So nice of you to invite us." Karen glanced at Susan. Karen, this is Susan Sullivan," Myra said. Karen smiled and extended her hand.

"Karen Coe. Hi, Susan," Karen said, as they shook hands.

Karen turned, taking David's arm. "David," she said. "This is Myra, Susan, and Joan. This is my friend, David." Graciously they shook hands. "Ah! The mysterious David Bryan has told us so much about you," Myra said."

"All good, I hope, David smiled and glanced at Bryan. Bryan shrugged.

"I'm with the *Houston Chronicle,*" Myra added.

"Ah. yes," David said. "You're the writer. That's right, yes."

"Can I help you with those?" John asked, reaching for their Playmate and small duffle.

"Thank you," David said. "I'll do it, if you'll just show me where to stow them."

"Sure. Just bring em below."

John led the way into the cockpit.

"Here," Myra said, following behind David. "Let me help with those."

"She's a great looking boat, John," David said, standing in the companionway looking into the cabin. "Isn't she, honey?"

"She's beautiful, hon," Karen gushed. She strolled toward the bow, grasping shrouds and looking up the mast.

Bryan and Susan watched and exchanged looks.

"We ready to get underway?" Bryan asked John.

"She's ready," John said, from the back of the cockpit.

"All I need to do is crank her up and someone to cast off those lines." He reached for the starter switch.

"Grab the bow line, Bryan," David said, jumping onto the deck. "I'll get this side."

The engine kicked over, belching a puff of smoke.

Myra popped up the companionway stairs with her camera and shot pictures of all their crew's activity forward.

Bryan and David cast the lines, gave the boat a shove and jumped aboard. Slowly, the *Star Mist* drifted backwards into the channel. When she cleared the slip John spun her wheel and shifted her engine. She jolted forward and chugged along through the marina channels. John piloted with the help of the others atop the cabin housing. They motored by the lake and into the channel under the tall 146 bridge and by the Kemah restaurants' row and the markets. Susan glanced at Bryan as they passed Fishbone's, remembering their first date and seeing the restaurant from another side.

"This is gonna be a great day!" Myra said. "Feel that wind!" She tucked her whipping hair back under her cap.

"Oh, yes!" Karen said. They were looking at a medium chop on the bay and holding onto the mast and leaning against the boom and mainsail.

"Bryan says you two are writing a book," Myra said to Susan.

"Trying to," Susan said. "But it's awfully tough."

"You're a writer, too?" David asked Susan.

"Sometimes," Susan said. "I'm a high school English teacher on vacation."

"Half the crew are writers," David grinned. "What's your book about?"

"It's about alien history, our creation, heritage and our government's involvement since WW II," Susan said. "The *Earth Chronicles* and the knowing that Bryan and Karen experienced during their out-of-body incidents with the Nefilim.''

"Bryan's had an out-of-body experience with the Nefilim?'' David frowned, glancing at Bryan, out of earshot, sitting on the front end of the cabin housing.

"He didn't tell you?'' Susan said. She hoped she hadn't said something out of turn.

David shook his head and winked. "Nope, didn't mention it.''

Myra grabbed for the bundled jib. "Let's have a hand here!'' she yelled above the stiff breeze.

David and Bryan helped her set the jib lines and the headsail popped full. The *Mist* lurched forward picking up speed, cutting the chop and throwing a spray. They passed the 3 buoy and the 10 mph signs, or was that knots?

John cut back on the engine. Myra led the others untying the mainsail. The 4 buoy drifted by.

"5 buoy!'' Bryan yelled and grinned at Susan. "She goes up.''

He patted the mainsail and took a position by the halyard winch with David. Myra went aft and took the mainsheet and got ready for the close reach in the southeasterly.

The bow was barely to the 5 buoy when Myra yelled, "UP!''

Bryan cranked the halyard winch, David set the mast links, Karen and Susan fed the sail and the mainsail billowed. The boom swung leeward, running the traveler and the boat heeled. Myra caught the mainsheet and tied it off just as the lead halyard link reached the top.

John cut the engine and set the boat back on course. The *Mist* leaped into the chop. The spray was strong and stinging cold. The mast rigger crew quickly retreated to the shelter of the cockpit.

"Wanna try the spinnaker?'' Myra shouted to John.

John shook his head. "On the way back. In the tail wind.''

"YAHOO!" Bryan yelled, wiping spray from his face and hair. "Is there anything better than this?"

They leaned back in the cockpit on the topside of the heel and rode into the wind.

SUSAN WAS TAKING her turn at the wheel, learning the art of tacking, when David came down the stairs into the cabin. Myra was there popping the top on a canned drink. Her wet hair below her cap was stuck to the side of her face. She pushed it back.

"She rides real nice," David said. He opened the ice chest and hunted for a drink.

"When're you gonna take your turn?" Myra asked.

"In a bit. I'll wait."

"You sail a lot over there in the hill country?"

David laughed. "Not a lot."

"Why not?"

"Guess I'm just a land lubber at heart." He popped the top on his drink can. "Not enough time." He smiled and sipped without taking his eyes from hers. "It's quite a drive to the Gulf."

"Bryan says you really got into MJ-12's business."

He nodded. "Drugs, black budget funding, alien technology, implanting — the head of the monster's MJ-12. But you all know that."

"Why'd you stop?"

"You should know," he grinned. "If we can't get them to admit what they did, whose gonna believe us? Besides, they tried to kill me."

"I heard," Myra nodded. "But now you have the proof in Karen's tapes."

David chuckled. "The Nefilim? A hypnotic regression from an out-of-body knowing with these superbeings? Come on, get real. First, we have to get around their propaganda denial that there are such beings from another star system."

'Yeah, we know,'' Myra sighed. ''Got any solutions, outside of having the aliens capture Carl Sagan and Phil Klass?'' David laughed. ''Maybe. You?''

''We're working on something. All we need is one key element.''

''What's that?''

Myra shrugged. ''Don't know yet,'' she said. ''We'll let you know when we figure it out.''

HALFWAY ACROSS THE bay the *Mist* crossed the Houston Shipping Channel. The water's color suddenly turned to the muddy side of green. The boat sliced through a wide path of thin, spectrum-reflecting oil slicks snaking over the waves. A dotted line of freighters, about two miles apart, lay at anchor, waiting their turn to head on up to La Porte, Morgan Point, or Baytown to unload their cargo and load another.

David had stepped in to take his turn behind the wheel. He proved to be an adept pilot, although, he said, inexperienced. Around the cockpit, they all watched, tentatively, reticently aware, forewarned, that at any moment, with David in charge, reality could suddenly slip a dimension gear.

All was smooth sailing for almost a mile and their close attention relaxed, wandered to other boats, a bird, the sky, the spray, and that's when it happened. David spun the wheel in a sharp leeway tack. The boat heeled, the boom slid toward the water pitching the starboard cockpit high. Everyone grabbed for a life line, anything. Water sprayed over the leeward side, drenching John, Susan And Bryan. Susan and Myra screamed. And just as quickly as David had spun the wheel to port, he spun it starboard. The boom kicked across, the mainsail logging its wind and the starboard side dipped, drenching Myra and Susan clinging to that side of the cockpit.

Then another sharp tack, and back, another tack, and

back, tossing them back and forth, holding on for their lives. The force was the only thing that kept John from reaching the wheel. At one point John thought he felt the boat leave the water when it leaped a wave and its own wake.

As suddenly as David had jerked the boat, he brought it back on course, sailing as smooth as ever. Water washing around his feet, he laughed and yelped like a mad pirate.

They picked themselves up and clambered back onto the seat cushions. An urge to kill seething inside, they glared up at David. He was calmly holding the wheel and studying the compass as if nothing had happened. They looked at each other, puzzled. They were wet, but they had been before. There was no standing water in the cockpit as there should have been. John looked back at their wake. It was as straight as it should be. John was amazed. He stepped in front of the wheel, looked at the compass then stared at David.

"How'd you do that?" John demanded.

"Do what?" David asked, innocently.

"That tack without flipping her over?"

David shrugged. "Tack?" he frowned. "What's a tack? I held her on course just as you said."

John glanced around at the others, all barely recovering. Bryan was shaking his head, incredulously. He smiled, slyly. *Okay, he got us. That's one for David.* When he looked at the two, John turned to him with a curious, puzzled look. Bryan managed a shrug and a knowing nod.

"Ok. You did fine," John said, taking the wheel. "I'll take her. We're coming up on the island and I know where the channels are. Thanks."

David eased back and slid onto a place beside Karen. Her eyes narrowed as he grinned at her. "Great boat," he said.

SMITH ISLAND WAS a scrubby little sandbar island about twenty miles across Galveston Bay halfway between Smith Point and the Bolivar Peninsula in East Bay just north of Hanna Reef. It wasn't a picturesque place, uninhabitable, not something to write home about or plan a vacation around, much less a picnic. Any vegetation was brought there by the winds and birds. The effect was something like raw nature with a tangled burr cut. Boaters used it as a reference point and fishermen used it as a sometimes favorite fishing spot. Shielded from the shipping channel by the reef, its waters were fairly clean and fishable; redfish, trout, crabs and catfish; no sharks to speak of, so if you fell out of your boat, or just took a mind to jump in, it was safe to swim there, as long as you didn't swallow anything.

While his crew pulled in the jib and lowered the main sail, John started the engine and circled the island to the southeast where the sandbar ran long and shallow. With Myra and Bryan eyeball sounding in the forward pulpit and the others standing atop the cabin housing, John slowly motored the *Mist* around the sandbar and toward the island.

"Not much of a place, is it?" Susan said to David as they surveyed the cove and approaching island.

"Imagine what it used to be before man discovered oil down here," David said.

"That'd be a real stretch."

David laughed. "Nothing is, if you really wanna do it."

"Yeah?"

David nodded. "Take your book, for instance," he said. "You couldn't do it unless you really wanted to do it."

"I really do. I believe the message is really important and we could make a lot of money. People are ready for this."

"Is it the message, or the money?"

"If it was the money, I'd do a children's book, or a good mystery."

"There's a lot of 'who done it' mystery in this story."

"True," Susan nodded. "There're plenty of clues, too. And the resolution will take a great deal of brevity."

"Left, left," Myra yelled and waved to John. "Port, port!"

"I hear you didn't have any trouble *getting it* from Karen's tapes," Susan said to David.

David shrugged. "I found it rather easy."

"I listened to the tapes last night and I'm still having trouble separating illusion from reality."

David grinned. "Takes patience, discipline," he said. "This is illusion, that's reality. Ego, spirit. Easy. You'll feel a sudden exhilaration, a high, when your power comes free. A beautiful rush. That's when you know. It's a dimensional thing."

Susan couldn't imagine, but nodded behind a smile.

Fifty yards to the island, the keel barely drug bottom.

Bryan and Myra felt the jolt. "That's it!" Myra shouted.

John reversed the engine and shut it down as Bryan tossed the anchor. He and Myra watched it hit the water and sink, not into olive green muck, but crystal clear blue water. Astounded, they followed the chain and anchor all the way to the bottom where the prongs kicked up a cloud of white sand.

From bow to stern and all the way to the island they saw the waters were now as pure and bright as a Caribbean bay.

Myra and Bryan looked at each other. They blinked. The water was still ice blue. Incredible! They walked slowly aft, watching the water as they went.

"Hey! Get a load of this!" Bryan shouted to the water.

"You see the water?" Myra said to David, Susan and Karen as she passed them. They were staring down from the life line.

"What happened?" Susan puzzled. She and Karen looked to David.

David grinned at Susan. "You must have wished awfully hard."

"But I . . . I didn't . . . " Susan stammered.

Excited, Myra jumped into the cockpit where John had just finished locking the wheel. "Did you see the water?" she gasped.

John saw her astonished manner and joined her in gaping down and around at the sudden miracle of the waters. Ice clear and inviting, they saw the boat's shadow rippling on the bottom sand.

"Did we just sail into the Bahamas, or what?" Myra said.

"Ever see the bay anything like this?" Bryan shouted. "All around the boat, all the way to the island, clear as glass!"

John shook his head. "Impossible! Not in these waters."

"It was yucky bay water a minute ago," Myra said, gawking at the schools of fish, flitting here and there, more surprised and delighted than anyone.

"We tossed the anchor," Bryan said. "It hit the water, and, boom, just like that it turned as crystal clear as the club pool."

Myra and John turned on David, and Karen. David didn't seem as astonished as he should have been. "You did this," Myra said. "Didn't you? Bryan told us about things changing when you're around. This is an illusion, isn't it?"

David shrugged and glanced at the bay. "Looks like beautiful clear water to me," he said, and grinned, mischievously.

"You both did it," John said, including Karen with a nod.

"Who? Karen?" David glanced at Karen. She didn't know what to say. "No," David said, and turned to Susan. "It was Susan who made the wish for a better place."

"Me?" Susan gasped. "Well, I did think something like that."

David grinned at her. "Looks great! Accept it. Thanks."

Susan was startled, aghast.

"Well, argue about who did it if you will," Bryan said, unbuttoning his shirt. "But I'm going to take advantage of our good luck before it goes away. And take it from me, it can."

THOSE WHO HADN'T worn their suits donned them and were on deck ready to dive in. All five looked to David to be first, as if the water might not be there, clean and clear, as it seemed, if he wasn't. David felt their suspicions and to prove its reality, stepped to the open life line, gripped the toe rail, and dove, arching as far as he could, knifing the water with a perfect ten, cutting a curving, bubbling trail deep down through the icy blue and kicked far from the boat. Karen hit the water right behind him and followed his underwater trail. David broke the surface about thirty yards out shaking the water from his, dark, glistening hair.

"YE-E-E-0-0-W-E-E!" he yelped. "Fantastic!"

Karen popped up in front of him, shaking her hair and wiping it back from her face.

"Come on!" Karen shouted. "It's beautiful!" David splashed a handful of water at her. She splashed back.

John hung the boarding ladder over the side and Myra threw in a couple of floats she and Bryan had pumped. She grabbed her camera and shot pictures of the others diving, or jumping, in. She took a few more shots of them in the water, wondering as she did, if an illusion would show up on film. Stowing her camera, she dove in, too.

Bryan swam over and steadied a float as Karen climbed aboard. She straddled it as she lay face down on its pillowed end.

"Thanks," she smiled.

"My pleasure," he smiled. "Tell me, honestly," he added. "Do you believe David did the water?"

She squinted at him. "Honestly, I don't know," she said. "But I know he wouldn't be in it the way it was."

He was struck by her plain beauty; no makeup and a mop of wet hair. He glanced at David, with Susan by the other float. A shadow whipped across them. Together, he and Karen looked up, shading their eyes. A lone sea gull floating thermals, circled the boat and settled on a spreader bar at the mast's top.

"Stanley?" Bryan said.

"Uh huh," she said.

"What more are we to expect today?"

"I haven't the slightest."

Chapter Seventeen:
The Island

THE SWIMMERS DIDN'T HAVE long to wait. John was the first to see the lush, green tropical isle. His brow pinched in, squinting, as he shaded his eyes. Blinking a couple of times, he threw water on his face and blinked again. The phenomenon was still there, right where the former scrubby little Smith Island had been. Incredible!

"Would you look at that?" John said to the island and to the closest, Bryan.

"What?" Bryan said, treading water just above the bottom sand.

"Tell me you see a tropical island where Smith used to be."

Bryan swam up to him. "Yeah. I think I do" he said. He rubbed his eyes and looked again. "Now what? First the water, now this." He saw David talking to Susan while holding onto her float. "Maybe it's an extension of the water miracle."

"Come on," John said and began swimming toward the island. "I have to see if this is real."

"Hey, look!" Bryan shouted to the others and pointed to the island. As one, they looked at him and beyond, John swimming for the island. He waited for their surprised expressions, verifying that he and John were not alone in what they were seeing. Bryan turned and slowly paddled after John. One by one the others followed, kicking and pushing the floats.

An amazed John waded onto the island's glistening white, sandy beach. Bryan was close behind and just as bewildered. They stood dripping water, squinting across the sand at the green thicket wall of jungle paradise.

Myra and David helped Susan and Karen drag the floats over the blue surf and drop them on the beach. They split suspicious looks between the island and David. He seemed as befuddled as they. He had, sort of, blamed the water on Susan's wish, but an island's transformation was way out of her range.

John kicked the dry sand and it sprayed up in front of them. "It's real!" he said, making a point of looking directly at David. "Can you believe this?"

David, hands on hips, was surveying the wonder as a modern Columbus in swim suit.

"Hell, if we could believe the water," Bryan said, picking up a double handful of sand, "we can believe this." He let the fine powder sift through his fingers. It blew in the wind.

Sand sticking to their wet feet, Susan and Myra plodded up beside them and helped stare.

"What is going on?" Myra huffed.

Where there was once sea grass and scrub bushes now stood tall swaying coconut and date palms, avocados and mangos, pomegranates and papayas, breadfruits and banyans, mangroves and shiffaleros. And an abundance of flowers; those they could see from the beach were orchids, hibiscus and passion flowers.

The four turned on David and Karen. Stories Bryan had told of being around them were gaining in evident validity.

"We've been out here a few times before," John said to David. "Nothing like what's going on has ever happened to us. And you're the only new ones on this trip."

David shrugged. "I'm as dumbfounded as you. Honest."

Karen glanced at David. "I don't know," she said. "I've never seen anything like this."

John turned and led them across the beach toward the lush jungle. As they trudged through the deep sand they didn't seem to notice, or feel, that at each step, changes were taking place. First, their swim suits disappeared, and their nakedness began to be covered by a fine, thick body hair, and their bodies began to take on the posture of the ape man, Homo erectus Neanderthal hybrid. Except David, who took on the appearance of a giant blond wearing gold snake armlets and a white, gold-trimmed robe sporting a golden snake entwined winged-cross caduceus.

Into the jungle they wandered and wondered.

Susan asked, "What be this beautiful place?"

"Tis the wonderful Garden," Bryan said.

"Tis Eden," David said. "Our Garden of Creation."

"None such as we are allowed here," Myra cowered.

David laughed. "Be not afraid," he assured them. "Our Father hast chosen ye to tend his famous Garden."

"Why us?" John asked. "What have we done to receive such an honor, as to see such a magnificent place?"

"Cheap help," David shrugged. "Father wants to get the most from My creations. I agreed, tis a good deal. Adams and Eves. Besides, I have use of thou in My own needs, my dear Eves."

They pushed on into the Garden's thick growth, astounded by the magnificent beauty of plants, fruit and flowers never before seen. Above, brightly colored birds darted through the trees, calling and singing. Wild animals of all descriptions, large and small, watched and roamed at close proximity. Two by two. "Tis much better than working the mines," Bryan said.

"Oooh." Karen cooed. "See the flowers. I've never seen such beautiful colors." She caressed them to her face. "Oooo, what heavenly smells."

"Those were brought here from our home: Heaven,"

David said. "Actually, our planet, but we won't get into that. We mated them with many found wild here. Tis a most glorious result, eh?"

David picked a flower and stuck it in Karen's hair, which was just about anywhere, but he chose above her ear. He smiled. She felt happy inside and copied his smile. "Ye are a beautiful creation," he said. "I must remember to offer my congratulations to the Birth Princesses, *former* Birth Princesses, I should say, for their added perfection."

John picked a huge pink flower, an orchid, and placed it in Myra's hair. They felt a happiness and copied a smile. Amorous desires were contagious. Bryan snapped off a big red flower and stuck it in Susan's hair. They too felt a joy inside and smiled.

It was fun. John picked another flower and placed it in Bryan's hair. They smiled and grinned.

"Well now, I don't know," David laughed. "Maybe that's not exactly how it should be." He scratched his chin. "But, perhaps, that can be fixed."

Karen picked a flower and placed it in Myra's hair, and Susan put a flower in Karen's hair, and Myra put one in John's, Susan stuck one in Bryan's, Karen put one in David's hair, and they were picking flowers from all over and putting them in each other's hair. They laughed and giggled with the strange feelings of newly discovered love. They got so carried away they even felt like hugging each other, and they did. And they felt good. A feeling they had not known before.

They pushed on into the garden picking flowers as they went, putting them in their hair and stringing them together around their necks. They put flowers in David's hair and he gave flowers to Karen, Myra and Susan, but he would not give flowers to John or Bryan. They puzzled over why he did not feel joy in knowing happiness with John and Bryan.

"Tis not natural," David said.

"Why?" Karen said. "What be this feeling?"

David thought about it. "Tis love," he finally admitted. "Tis the spirit of your creation."

"Tis not natural?" John said.

"No. Well, sometimes," David said.

"It feels happy," Karen said. "Why is it not natural?"

"Because it isn't," David said. He led them on into an orchard where all the trees were heavy with their fruit. "We know better than thee. Thou are different. Pure. Thou knowest love, but thou hath no knowing of self."

"Knowing?" Myra puzzled. "What be this knowing" David picked an apple and rubbed a shine on it against his robe. "Thou were created as servants, workers," he said. "The perfect worker. Thou will not be burdened, distracted with any pleasures or pain of sexual desire's." He took a big, juicy bite from the apple.

"Sexual desires?" Karen said. "What be that? Tell us."

"No. Tis forbidden by My Father. Thou are not programmed for handling emotions."

"Why?" Karen said. "What be these forbidden emotions?"

He offered her a bite of his apple. She took it and bit into it as he had. She chewed and its juices wet her lips. "Tell us," she smiled, slyly.

"Thou art a temptress," David smiled close to her lips. In his eyes even a Neanderthal hybrid seemed desirable for his purpose. They could be taught to shave. "Tis against the law."

The other four, eager to participate, began picking fruit from the trees around them and ate as David and Karen had done.

"Law?" Karen continued. "God's law?"

"To thee, yes," David said. "Father, to me."

"Thou art God's son, art thee not?" Karen cajoled.

David shrugged. "That I am. And thou My children."

She grinned, a devilish glint in her eyes. "So. He will

not punish thee if thou tellest us.''

"I am far from his favorite.'' David said. "He awaits any chances for specifying faults.''

"He be not here. We are alone,'' Karen pointed out. "He will never knowest.''

"Oh, but He shall,'' David said. "Trust me.''

"How will he knowest?'' Susan puzzled.

"The seed of knowing arouses desires thou cannot control,'' David said. "Desires thou cannot hide. Thou will know ecstasy and pain as thou hast never imagined.''

"These desires,'' Karen mused. "Be they as we felt with the giving of the flowers, the hugging?''

"Even greater,'' David smiled. The sun glinted off his snake armlets.

"Greater?'' Karen beamed. "How can that be? Oh, we must know these desires. Tellest us, showest us!''

A chorus of, "Yes, tellest us,'' gushed at him from the others.

"Tellest us, now,'' Karen pleaded. "Or, we shall tell God thou brokest His law and He will punish thee anyway.'' Certainly not the first time he'd been blackmailed, but this time was the sweetest.

David weighed the issue as he studied their eager faces. His Birth Princesses had mutinied; the only way he had of continuing a production of his hybrid worker force was to correct Eve's slight deficiency by introducing her to the seed and have them procreate on their own. The needed process he had in mind was going to be easier than he had planned; His Father was "off the planet" and His subjects were ready and primed. But His Father's warning still rang in his ears; "Give them the knowing of creation and thou separate them from their knowing of spirit. Thou will give them the fear of separateness, a forgetfulness of knowing. Thou will give them an ego with emotions they will never be able to handle. Thou shall destroy their perfect way.''

But, as the scientist who had created them, He knew

there was no other way. Even their creation had been a risk, and now this; the greatest risk of all. Any punishment that might be dealt from His Father was worth the pleasures of unleashing the sexual fires in this most lovely, flower bedecked, creature with the doeful, begging eyes.

"So be it," David, reluctantly, relented. "Come, my pure ones," he beckoned, moving through them and strolling into the orchard. Gleefully, they followed. "Thou secret seed be within the tree of life."

David pushed on, deep into the orchard, finally stopping before a great, fruit-ladened tree. He selected a fat, reddened sample, gripped it forcefully with both hands, twisted and split it in two. He handed one-half to Karen, the other to Susan. "Thou fruit of passion," he grinned, gallantly. "Eat and drink heartily. It's juices be sweet and sour, and will drive thee crazy with desire."

David broke open another plump selection and handed a half to Myra. John reached for the other half. "No," David snapped, and tossed it away. "Thou hast always had thy half."

"Oooo, this is wonderful," Karen cooed around the juices and seeds dripping from her lips. "I've never tasted anything so delicious. What is it?"

David smiled, confidently. "Pomegranate," he said.

"Pom-e-gran-ate?" Karen frowned, tasting its sharp sourness.

"Yes," David nodded. "A Garden-spliced concoction of love's bittersweet seeds. It will mend thy genes and link thy blood strings."

The passion fruit was so stimulating the Eves needed no further explanation. After only two pieces, the forbidden fruit had reached its desired affect. David was delighted. The seeds' hosts began to feel desires they had never experienced before. They felt the rapture. They turned on the Adams, dancing and grinding to a seductive rhythm. David joined in, encouraging Bryan and John to submit to their own ravenous stirrings.

David was elated. He grabbed Karen, holding her, dancing, rubbing body to body, heating uncontrollable desires, hugging, kissing and fondling. Susan and Myra, following Karen's lead, enticed Bryan and John to fan their fires. They saw David was well-versed and they copied his moves. David kissed Karen passionately on her open mouth, and all over. Bryan and John tried the same on Susan and Myra, and it was good and it drove them wild. As was David, they were excited, their blood ran hot and heady, and their manhood became hard and stiff. They lost control of their senses. They saw David atop Karen, thrusting his hard member between her legs. They had a great desire to do the same with Myra and Susan, and they did, and it was good. And they had thoughts they seldom knew. Their desires flowed from them. David called it copulation and fornication and it was good. They loved this, this, copulation. They loved it so much that they began to experience its varieties with each other. They were swimming in ecstasy. They were having an orgy.

So engrossed in their new freedom of expression, they didn't notice a darkening in the sky, or the wind rustling the tall trees. Suddenly, the moment felt cool to their hot, sticky bodies, their hair matted slick all over. Dark clouds rumbled and rolled above them. Lightning struck the ground, thunder clapped and it began to rain, blowing hard and cold, squelching their sexual fires. Sand and tree branches whipped around them. Leaves and fruit flew in the wind and slammed hard against them.

"Hell beset thee!" David yelled, as he rolled off Susan, dragging his member in the sand. "He wasn't supposed to be back until next week!"

His great space ship hovered above them, and His great voice roared and rushed on the wind, "GET YE THE HELL FROM MY GARDEN!" And He meant it. He wasn't taking any excuses.

Terrified, they scurried this way and that, falling over each other in their confused directions. The blowing sand stung their skin, now without the thin ape-like hair, and for the first time they recognized their nakedness. Running before the Great Wind, the Wrath of God, they grabbed at leaves and vines to cover their shame.

Among the stampede of fear-stricken birds and animals, they ran from the Garden, stumbling, falling, and crawling, lightning bolts crashing Paradise all around them. Onto the beach they ran not daring to look back.

The Great Wind forced them into the water where high, heavy waves washed them under and they groped for each other, and for anything that could float — the floats.

They swam and swam hard and fast, faster than they had ever swam in their lives. Gasping, they gulped and spit water.

Soon they were exhausted and the waters calmed around them. Clinging to their floats they hung limp in the water. Coughing and sputtering they slowly collected themselves. Each bewildered glance got another one in return. They felt a shame and dared not look back at the island.

"Tell me it's not there," John coughed and spit.

Bryan sneaked a peek. "It's gone," he sighed, relieved.

Bewildered yet, each slowly turned and helped Bryan stare in wonderment at the lowly, scrubby Smith Island in all of its' barren plainness.

John sought out David among the bobbing heads and panting bodies. "What the hell was that all about?" he gasped.

Without taking his eyes from the island, David muttered, "It was about . . . what it was about."

A shocked and confused Susan stared wide-eyed at Bryan. What their eyes said couldn't be put in words.

Chapter Eighteen:
The Light

BACK ON THE BOAT, they sprawled, exhausted, on the deck and in the cockpit. Some collected their thoughts with eyes closed. Others stared at the scrubby little island through narrowed eyes. All, in their own way, slowly recovered from some strange unimaginable ordeal. They just couldn't figure what. Hazy flashes of Paradise, sex and terror filtered through each's memories. Who would dare say what they had done, what it all meant? And at the bottom of it all were their suspicions of David's involvement. He was stretched out in the back of the cockpit with his feet propped on the engine housing, seemingly in a state of nonassumption. Karen was huddled in a corner of the cockpit resting her chin atop hugging her knees.

For a while, the guilt of what each could recall doing made it difficult to look at each other. Somehow, they felt glad to be back in their bathing suits.

John sat up, looked around and found Myra staring at him. Together, they glanced at the little sandbar of an island.

"Did we . . . ?" John stammered.

Slowly, Myra nodded. "Yeah," she sighed. "I think we did."

John frowned. "This is crazy."

"I should've never gotten involved with this," Susan said, ruefully. She was staring blankly at the cockpit deck.

Bryan sat atop the cabin, his legs dangling above her. He massaged his forehead. "I shouldn't be here," Susan added. "But, I am, and I just can't remember why I thought I could handle this." She wished she was back on the rice farm starting over.

Bryan felt the guilt of setting them up when he knew all along that something like this could happen. But this was too much. The Garden of Eden was more than he had bargained for. He looked up, right into David's slit-eyed stare. David fashioned a crooked little smile.

Nodding at the island, Bryan asked David, "Can you explain that?"

David shrugged. "Maybe."

The others tuned in.

"How? Why?" Bryan asked. "Logically."

"The tapes," David said. "We've all heard the tapes. Some of us have even studied, practiced them. Some of us even know more than what's on the tapes. But we all know our history. And we all know of our true power. The Garden of Eden is embedded in our history, in our true spirit, in our knowing. It's our beginning, our origin, our ultimate, authentic experience we all share. We carry it with us always, and pass it on from lifetime to lifetime. it would be logical that we could all recall the same experience at the same time. A daydream, a wish, our knowing energies connected, and our combined power created a mighty strong thought, so powerful that it became its own reality, creating a conscious dimension."

"We were screwing," Myra frowned. "We were having an orgy. Was that our daydream, our wish? Is that what we were all thinking? All wanting?"

David chuckled and shrugged. "That's what the Garden of Eden was all about," he said. "Our need to experience copulation, and creation."

"I distinctly remember the Garden as Enki's big screw-up," Bryan said. "It was where Enki went against His

Father's order and gave us separation through our knowledge of ego. And I faintly recall Enki being in our, our
created dimension, or was it just one of us wearing Enki's
robe.''

"Yes," Myra beamed. "I recall that, too." And with
the dawning of another thought, she got up and went down
the cabin stairs.

"Anyone else remember that?" Bryan asked.

"I do," John said.

"Me, too," Karen said.

"Susan?"

"I don't know," Susan said. "I'm still trying to sort
it out. But I do recall someone in a robe with a golden
caduceus.''

"And golden snake armlets," Karen added, eyeing
David.

Myra came back with her camera and began to shoot
candid shots. She sat down by John.

"That was Enki," Bryan said. "Anu's son, scientist,
doctor, genealogist, Creator, serpent in the Garden. The
winged disk, serpent-entwined cross, the Great Doctor
himself: Enki, the Son of God." Bryan stared at David.
"Was it my imagination, or an illusion, that you were
wearing Enki's robe?''

Myra's camera clicked.

David grinned. "My illusion," he said. "Ever since
I've heard the truth, I've imagined myself with the power
of an Enki. What a goal ... the Son of God. After all,
we're their offspring, their children. It's not inconceivable
that we also have their powers, their spirit, and we do. I
think we will all agree that we just had an experience of
that power of unity. The power of truth.''

"That was truth?" Susan snapped. "Running naked
for my life in someone else's day dream?''

"I wished I'd had my camera," Myra said. "I'd loved
to have had a picture of all that.''

"Us rolling around in the sand?" Susan shook her head and covered her eyes.

"Can you imagine what a story that'd be?" Myra snapped a group shot. "The truth about the Garden of Eden. With pictures."

"Enki's big screw-up," Bryan added.

David grinned. "Perhaps, perhaps not," he said. "Enki had a lot of faith in his creations. Maybe more than man had in himself. But that can be corrected. When we realize the mistake wasn't His, but ours, then that's when we can correct it."

"That's true," Bryan said. "But do we need a lesson that debilitating?"

David laughed. "It was rather severe, wasn't it."

Myra ran off a couple more pictures. "Anyone hungry?" she asked, putting her camera down. "We brought a real nice lunch."

Susan made a sour face. "Maybe something to get rid of this bittersweet taste. Yuk."

BACK TO THEIR ROLES, the guys strung up a yellow plastic canopy over the boom and cockpit while the gals went below and broke out the food and drinks. Each, in his own way, was gradually making an inner peace with the trauma of their collective experience. It was beginning to fade like a bad dream in the bright light of present day. A tought lesson not of their doing.

They streamed up and down the cabinway, playful and bantering now, bringing their selections up to eat in the mellow shade of the cockpit and deck. The boat rocked and reflected slivers of rippling aqua sunlight snaked across them as they settled beneath the canopy. The halyard clanked against the mast to the rhythm of the easy listening music from the stereo below.

Myra set a tray of fruit on the engine housing and sat back with her camera.

Susan giggled at her sandwich, then glanced at David. "I can't believe we did what we did. Really."

David smiled. "I'm glad to see you can laugh about it now," he said, grinned and winked. "It was great, wasn't it?"

"Yeah," she giggled. She glanced at Bryan. He was grinning and he winked. They looked at the others. Everyone was looking at each other and laughing, unabashedly.

Susan added, coyly. "I was hoping I would remember a lot more about my first orgy, except that our Father came home early and caught us."

They laughed. The incident's seriousness was fading along with their guilt of the original sin's separation. The fact that each was comfortable with their own sexuality made acceptance of the truth much easier.

"I don't know about the rest of you," Susan said. "But I still can't understand how all of us could make it happen."

"It happened in the collective power of our spiritual minds, in the combined energy of our thoughts David said. "It was as real as any thought we can create."

"In our minds? It didn't really happen?" Susan pondered.

David set his plate down. "A thought is the most powerful energy that we can project," he said. "Its full power comes from spiritual being. The knowing of our spiritual energy unlocks our full power of spiritual being. We had six spiritual minds on, or near, full power. We all projected on the same thought, and the energy created acted like a hologram, creating the reality."

"That was more than holography," John said, after reflecting on Bryan's explanation of the mind's power to create strong holographic dimensions. "That was more like a time warp."

"Virtual reality," Bryan injected.

David nodded. "True," he said. "Same principle, but

a time warp would have affected everything within the time portal. This was just a projection of a thought."

Susan looked confused. Myra took her picture. Susan raised her brow and looked wide-eyed into the lens. "Do you understand any of this?" she asked Myra. "Tell me I'm not the only dense one here."

Myra lowered her camera and smiled. "You're not," she said.

"And you will realize how simple it is, eventually. But I have many reasons to believe that there is much more going on in our universe than we can comprehend immediately. Reality is not what it appears to be. We live in a three dimensional world, but there are many dimensions we can access with the right power source."

"Oh," Susan mused, not clearly understanding.

"Man's realizations come from the knowing," Karen said.

"And I have to get out of my body to realize the knowing?" Susan asked.

David spotted a light bulb stuck behind the wheel housing. "Not necessarily," he said. He leaned down, picked up the bulb rubbed it between his hands and taking the metal end in his fingers, showed it around like a magician about to perform. "You understand how light bulbs work, don't you?" David asked Susan, holding the bulb between them. "You put a little energy right in here." He pointed out the bulb's conductor. "It goes through the stem, heats up the filament and emits a glowing evidence of its presence."

Susan shrugged. That was simple science.

Taking the bulb's glass end with his other hand, he touched the conductor end to his index finger. He set a focused stare on the bulb's filament as he concentrated on his inner energies.

"What we're going to do here," David said, slowly, as not to break his concentration. "Is for all of us to project our energy into the lighting of this bulb's filament. Believe it.''

Susan glanced at the others. They were mesmerized, staring at the bulb. She returned to the bulb and David's eyes beyond. She concentrated, projecting her belief in her power, her energy into the bulb. She gave it all she had.

"The light company," David slowly said to the bulb, "gets its power from the universe, same place we got ours.''

At first it was just the slightest glow, then brighter and brighter until the filament burn was equal to about twenty-five watts. They were amazed and elated at their success, but held to their intense concentration. Myra was so busy concentrating she couldn't think to take a picture.

The halyard clanked against the mast.

"There's your proof," David grinned. He lifted the bulb from his finger and its filament stopped glowing.

Susan smiled, slyly. "A trick bulb. I've seen them in novelty shops.'' She could say that after the island bit?

David arched a brow. Shoving the business end of the bulb toward her, he demanded, "Show me.''

Her bluff called, she froze. Maybe it wasn't a trick bulb. After all, she wasn't so sure about everything else that had been happening. And David did seem to be the root force.

"Come on," he grinned, confidently. "It won't bite you.''

Ever so slightly, Susan shook her head. "Maybe I was wrong.''

"You were, but that doesn't matter," he said. "Hold out your finger. You want something for your book?''

Glancing at the others, Karen hoped one of them would step in and rescue her. Do one did. They watched and waited.

"Any finger will do," David said.

Slowly, she extended her hand and an index finger. A

nice long finger, strong from hours at the keyboard. David carefully placed the bulb's conductor to its tip. No one moved.

"Now," he said. "Once again, we're all going to believe and project our spiritual energies into Susan and the light."

The halyard clanked in the silence of their concentration.

After a few seconds the filament began to glow, not as bright as on David's finger, but glowing as it was. Susan's eyes got wide as saucers and she jerked her finger away, killing the glow.

"Can't deny it," David grinned. "That's the power of your knowing. It's in everyone of us." He sat up. "All of you touch the one closest to either side. Make a circle."

Karen led the way by taking David's hand and Myra's. All around the cockpit they took the hand of the one next to them. To complete the circle Bryan placed his hand on David's shoulder since he was holding the bulb at arms length in front and toward the center of their circle.

Every eye was focused on the tiny filament. "Let's think about pushing our energies into this little light," David said.

Before his words were out the tiny filament begin to glow. Brighter and brighter, they couldn't take their eyes from its brilliance. The more they wanted it to happen the stronger it glowed.

Suddenly a blue arc leaped from the bulb. Susan screamed. It shot through David, sparked around the circle of heads and back through David into the bulb, exploding its thin glass dome. Susan screamed. Snapping and crackling, the static arc leaped from the bare stem to each head. Susan screamed, again.

Sparks jumped from each head and fizzled around them.

They fell back, breaking the circle and reducing the arc

and the stem to a sparkler in David's hands. Their Memorial Day fireworks finally spewed to a puff of smoke. David tossed the spent stem onto the deck where he had found it.

Cowering on the cockpit's seats, they stared at each other through the clearing smoke. Unscathed, David glanced around as each slowly began to recovered. "How about that?" he gleamed. "Powerful! Pure, collective energy! Proof positive we are greater than we have ever believed."

They eased to sitting positions, rubbing the numbing and tingling in their limbs. Susan clung tightly to Bryan's waist, her face pressed against his chest. Through total amazement, they stared at David. Again, they searched for some reality in what they had just done. Was it he, or was it all of them?

"Damn!" John gasped. "I'm glad there was no water standing on the deck."

"You can say that again," Bryan added, checking to see if Susan was all right.

Susan rubbed her arms and hugged herself. Then felt the top of her head for any singed hair. "No one will ever believe this," she said.

THE CANOPY CAME DOWN, the anchor came up and the *Star Mist* motored out of the shallows. Beyond the reef her sails billowed quickly with a stiff southeast wind and Smith Island with all its strange happenings drifted far behind in the fork of their spreading and fading wake.

With the wind at her back the *Star Mist* heeled to the starboard running high and fast. Her crew had performed admirably. Into the bay they broke out the spinnaker and it filled quickly. The *Mist* jumped, *took the bone* and plowed a smooth, shallow furor. The crew whooped! Blaring strands of *Rocky's* conquering theme roared from the stereo below. The whooshing of winds in her sails, the sloshing swish of a rushing wake and the slap of spray over her topsides set the tempo of her racing mode. She flew across the waters. John and Myra beamed with pride, she was beautiful, she was the most powerful of all boats. It was a great and beautiful time. They soared on their incredible high of full, free energy.

Before the five buoy they had to pull down the spinnaker. At the five buoy they pulled down the main sail and they motored toward the channel. The crew rode her proudly by the restaurants and open markets, waving triumphantly. They chugged up the channel and across the lake toward a setting sun. Bryan, Susan and Karen helped Myra with the buttoning down chores, sacking the spinnaker and lashing the mainsail to the boom.

Karen caught Susan stealing glances at her, again, as if she were holding something she wanted to say. The next time she did it, Karen was there first and held her eyes. They smiled.

"I think I need to apologize for David," Karen said.

"What for?" Susan said. "We were forewarned. We were all to blame for anything that happened. No apologies necessary."

"Thank you," Karen smiled. "I think it's very courageous of you to try and put some simple meaning to all this. I mean, you're writing a book."

Myra overheard the conversation and moved closer.

"I've seen so many books with just pieces and parts of the puzzle," Susan said, tying another sail strap around the boom. "But, I don't know, when I think I've got it, there always seems to be something else. I suppose it's so much easier to discover the knowing the way you and Bryan did. Pure, no hang-ups. He said the aliens even let you fly their ship. What was that like?"

Tying a sash, Karen shrugged. "It seemed to come natural."

Susan chuckled. "Words couldn't describe it?"

"Sorry. I don't know any that do."

Susan tied the last strap and glanced at David, sitting behind the wheel with John. "David certainly seems to have gotten the full message of your tapes. What's it like being with someone that's, that's, so together...has all the answers?"

"He does seem to," Karen grinned. "It can be fantastic when the connection is mutual in every aspect. When you match up on the same level of knowing, the experience is very gratifying, very loving."

"Yes. I can see that," Susan said. "That's why Bryan's been so patient with me, bringing me along, wanting me to reach that level. Knowing that that's the only level where relationships really work. And I'm really trying, not for him so much as for myself. But, it's really tough, I don't know if I'll ever reach that level."

"Sure you can," Karen smiled. "Anyone can. Just don't listen to your ego saying you can't. But don't use David as your goal, even I can't reach that. Don't know anyone who could."

"EVER READ THE *Earth Chronicles?*" John asked David, as he guided the *Star Mist* up the marina channel.

"I hadn't before I met Bryan," David said. "He mentioned them. Said they were about our ancient history with the Nefilim, same as on Karen's tapes. I found some copies and read them. And those other books he mentioned, *A Course in Miracles.* Great books. And you know what? They're right on."

"You read all those books since you met Bryan?"

David shrugged. "Sure."

John was amazed. "Two days? And you understand them?"

"Well, guess I had a head start," David grinned.

"When you already know, they're just a refresher course."

John nodded. "You're quite remarkable," he grinned. "Bryan said you got mixed up with MJ-12 back a couple of years ago."

"Yeah," David sighed to piers of moored boats.

"Ever get into any of their secret bases?"

"Are you kidding? But, most of my information came from people who had been there, seen it all. And that information was basically verified by the Nefilim."

"You mean, about the Zetas owning MJ-12?"

David nodded.

"Your opinion," John asked. "What do you believe the Zetas are up to? Taking over, or destroying us?"

"Both," David said. "The Zetas' taking over will destroy us. That's when they'll regain their lost brotherhood from the Nefilim."

"You think that's why the Nefilim are back, to prevent that from happening?"

David shrugged. "I don't think the Nefilim are looking for a fight, but it's possible," he grinned. "If I see any eight foot blond giants around, I'll ask them."

"How'd you know they were eight feet tall?" John mused. "Karen didn't mention that on her tapes."

David grinned. "It's in the books, remember?"

JOHN SWUNG THE *STAR Mist* into her berth and threw her engine into reverse. She drifted toward the bumpers while the crew scurried onto the pier to fend off and tie down her lines. Spent and sunburned as they were, all stayed to help wash her down and close her up. By sundown they were hauling their gear back up the pier as the marina lights came on.

In the parking lot they hugged, shook hands and said how much they enjoyed the day and how they should do it again soon. "We'll call you," John said to David and Karen, as they went their way. "There's lots more we have to talk about.''

"Anytime," David called. "We'll be there."

Scattered trunk slamming, car doors closing, motors revving, headlights popping on and the crunching of shell preceded their departure. There were a few parting waves as they jockeyed for the marina's exit road and gate. At the highway they turned in different directions, their tail lights fading toward home.

"Well, that was interesting," John said to Myra, as they sped down the highway toward League City. "Any opinions on David?"

"My opinion of David?" she repeated, as she searched for the right words. A writer's ploy, she used often. "Handsome and charming. Sly as the proverbial old gray fox," she said. "Highly intelligent, extremely enlightened and very into himself. Whatever, or whoever, he was before, he's much more than he appears to be now, or says he is. A big mystery. Can't say I really bought his explanation of what happened out there. Although, it did somewhat match Bryan's."

John nodded. "Yeah, my thoughts exactly."

He turned north at the Highway 3 light. "What d'ya think about showing Karen and David the ship?"

"You mean, we see if their knowing is the right key?" she said. "Like those little plastic prize keys we get in the mail, 'If your key starts the car, you win it?''

He grinned at her simile. "I have this nagging feeling, they could already be winners," he said. "But I'm going to ask Bryan to give them one more test."

Myra arched a brow. "What we saw wasn't enough?"

John glanced at the road. "Tell you something even better," he said, patting her leg. She took his hand in hers and waited. "That bulb he used? I took it out of the pier light the other night because it was burned out."

SUSAN BURST THROUGH THE back door of

her townhouse and dumped an armload of towels, sunglasses, lotions and her wind breaker on the floor. Her face, arms and legs were showing a little reddening around her shirt and shorts. "Whew! It feels great to get some AC again," she sighed. She kicked off her shoes while unpinning her hair. It fell down in strands that showed the dry torture of sun and wind.

Bryan came through the door carrying a half empty cooler. He stepped around her and set it on the kitchen table.

"God, I feel cruddy," she groaned. She reached beneath her shirt and unsnapped her bikini top as she padded to the utility room. "I don't know about you," she said. "But I think I still have some of that sand in my nooks and crannies from that little imagined escapade." She slipped her top from beneath her shirt and dropped it in the washer.

"You shouldn't," he said, "if it wasn't real." He was enjoying her strip tease. Her oversized cambric shirt fell to mid thigh and clung diaphanously to all the right places.

She unzipped her shorts and they fell to the floor. She wiggled out of her bikini bottom, stepped out, toe-hooked her shorts with a leg kick and tossed them in the washer.

She slinked toward him rubbing her private places beneath her shirt. "Yep, sand," she said.

"Not salt?"

"No. Sand." She showed him the white grit on her hands, then slipped them around his waist and snuggled up close. "Imaginary sand. Wanna take a shower?" she cooed, batted her eyes and kissed his chest through his open shirt.

"Uh huh. I could go for that."

"I've got some lotion we can rub on our burn."

"Okay," he sighed. "Does it get any better than that?"

"Maybe," she smiled. "We can fix something to eat

afterwards.''

They kissed. She backed away and headed for the stairs. "Take your things off in the utility room," she said. "Don't want sand all over the house."

By the time Bryan got upstairs Susan was already in the shower. He was standing naked in the bedroom. "Come on in," she called from the bathroom. He tried not to get too excited an he saw her sensuous image through the fluted glass. He snapped open the shower door and carefully slipped in. She had the water at the right temp and the soap soft and bubbly.

"YOU KNOW," SUSAN SAID to the open fridge. "I think I need to talk to David some more before I start the book." She spoke over the washer's rumble from the utility room. Bryan chopped veggies at the counter, gathering them into a skillet to stir fry.

"Why?"

"Well, there's a lot more to know," she said. "And I want to know just how he accessed his power so easily." She took out a package of chicken.

"He told you. Practice."

"Practice?" she said. "Practice what?" She got out a cutting board and opened the package.

"Practice knowing the difference," he offered.

"Well, you and Karen know the difference between your ego and your reality," she said, getting a knife and spreading the chicken. "And I'm sure the both of you practice what you preach. So, why can't you do what he did today?"

"I don't know," he mused. "But, don't think I haven't wondered about that. Did he really do it?"

"You know what I've been thinking?" She sliced chicken.

"What?"

"I was talking to her when we were coming in this

evening, and I was asking her how it was, you know, living with someone who could use his power like that, and she told me, with a great big grin, that it was fantastic.''

"So. I can believe that,'' although he tried not to, "two people into their knowing would have a fantastic relationship.''

"No, no, no,'' she said, slicing away. "You're not getting my drift. It's sleeping with her. He got access to his power, the knowing, from sleeping with her.''

He looked at her and chuckled. "It's not like a disease.''

"I know that,'' she said. "But look, he didn't have it before he met her. He listens to her tapes, makes love with her and he's got it. He got his power charged from her.''

Bryan thought about Karen having an alien baby. If she had sex with the aliens, she could have passed it on.

"You and I have made love,'' Bryan pointed out. "Did you get anything from me?''

"What, two or three times,'' she figured and pushed the chicken slices aside. "We're talking about two years, maybe. It could happen.''

She went to the pantry for a box of rice.

"You're saying,'' he said. "If given two years of practice, you'd get it?''

"It's a thought.''

"I was married ten years, four of which were after the out-of-body, and Cheryl never got it. It just doesn't work like that. It's timing. Cosmic zero timing. When it's your time, you'll get it. That's what happened to Karen, then David. It was their time.''

Susan was uncharacteristically quiet, a silence he had, in their short time, grown to recognize as thought provoking. When he looked at her, she was standing in the open pantry door, holding a box of rice and a paper-sleeved light bulb, plainly marked GE soft light. His eyes locked onto hers and her daring thought.

She put the rice down and pulled the bulb from its protective sleeve. Holding it by its metal end, at arms length between them, she smiled around it, "Game?"

He slowly shook his head, incredulously.

She arched a brow and teased. "Afraid it won't work? And then what?"

"We've done that."

"Fear's what blocks it, didn't I hear someone say?" She gripped the bulb's glass dome and shoved the metal end toward him. "Come on, gimme your finger."

He relented, extended his index finger and touched the lead conductor point.

"Concentrate," Susan said, her voice a deep imitation of David's. "Think. Bring forth your spiritual energy, push it to lighting the filament, the light. Let our light shine."

They stared at the bulb's dormant filament for a long, tense and hopeful minute.

"Are you concentrating?" Susan whispered.

"Yes. Are you?"

"Uh huh."

Another minute. Nothing.

"Harder," she gritted and strained. "Push harder! Push!"

Bryan grinned at the sexual connotation in her desire.

"You're not pushing," she said, seeing his grin. Then his thought hit her when she realized what she had said, and they both laughed.

"Come on. You've gotta be serious. I know we can do this." She wet the bulb's conductor end on her tongue, held it to him and he touched his finger to it again. "Okay, be serious," she said. "Concentrate your energy."

And they did. At times with their eyes closed and with not a word being said for two, three tense, serious minutes. But the light wouldn't burn.

Finally, Bryan lowered his finger. Susan shook the bulb next to her ear. "Not the bulb," she said.

Undaunted, Susan smiled at him and shrugged. "Guess we need more practice."

"Or David's something more than we expect."

Chapter Nineteen:
The Satellite

BRYAN AWOKE A LITTLE after eight in his own bed. He rolled out and turned on his TV. The morning news program was standing by to cutaway when the Shuttle's lift-off reached the final countdown. Its time was scheduled for 8:26 CST and so far the count was going smoothly. He remembered earlier times when the news shows covered the launches for weeks, then days and now just ten minutes of the lift-off.

He watched and listened as he dressed on auto. Pictures of the Flight Control Room activities, Marsha and Ed on the medical row checking off the mission book and watching the numbers and the big screen, blanked his mirrored shaving image. He had done it so many times he knew exactly where they were. He could even smell the excitement in the room.

The TV anchorman announced the cutaway. He stopped and watched. A long shot of the Cape, gantry and shuttle. Zoom in, switch to close up. Steaming clouds of smoke boiled around the pad. Great picture, it was a beautiful day. *Twelve, eleven, ten* . . . He saw the digital numbers flipping in an insert. He imagined he could see Steve at the Shuttle's controls and the satellite in the bay area. A voice over, *six, five, four, three* . . . a closeup of the engine cones as they belched fire, *we have ignition, one* . . . the Shuttle shuddered and rose, *we have lift off.*

The Shuttle and boosters roared upward. A long shot,

the gantry's umbilical fell away. The Shuttle bird sprung
from its nest of rolling smoke. Hawking, roaring, she
streamed into the clear blue morning sky. *We have a go
for down range.* A shot up her tail pipes, a roll, *power up,*
higher and higher into the deep blue the billowing rope of
smoke tapered, almost out of camera range, *we have
booster release.* Her smoke trail faded and the picture
switched back to the news anchors.

Bryan saw a replay in the mirror as he finished dressing. His schedule for the next few days was set.

THE SHUTTLE HAD ALREADY drawn two
complete wavy orbit lines on the Mission Control wall-size
Sony tracking screen when Bryan strolled into the second
floor FCR. Marsha and Ed looked weary as they methodi-
cally watched check lists and monitors at their console on
the Flight Surgeons' row. They had been there since before
the astronaut crew had boarded the Shuttle.

Bryan stood behind them watching the blinking orbital
light on the third orbit and listened to control's communications. The TV pictures were of an open Shuttle bay.
Astronauts in backpack extravehicular suits, trailing tether
cords, worked around the satellites. The harsh sun light
flashed into a camera before they could switch to another.
They were just minutes away from blackout and deployment.

"How're they doing?" Bryan asked Marsha.

She looked up from a readout tape. "Hi," she sighed.
"The usual."

"Rookies had some irregulars," Ed said. "We had
them do a turn on The Box. They're okay now."

"Good," Bryan smiled.

"You timed it just right," Marsha said. She pushed
her chair back and rubbed her eyes. "Fickers' already up."

Bryan glanced at the door. "Yeah?" He grabbed his
Flight Book and flipped through pages. "Where are we?"

"Page 230c."

Bryan found the page and checked it against Marsha's book.

Ed yawned as Dianne came up behind his chair. "Hi, how ya doing?" she asked, and began massaging Ed's shoulders. "Oooo, better." Ed sighed and relaxed.

Bryan closed his book over his finger and started for the door. "This won't take long," he said to Dianne. "See ya when your picture comes back."

THE THIRD FLOOR FCR was exactly like the second floor FCR. It was used only for deployment black-outs and was restricted to NASA Flight Control and Military personnel. The communications to the Shuttle was switched to restricted channels.

When Bryan was cleared through the door he searched the room for the General. He didn't see him right off and settled into his place at the Flight Surgeons' consoles. He checked his monitors and readouts with his Flight book. Everything was in sync for a pass over. The big screen picture was of the bay area and the satellite and two astronauts working under the crane arm. Directly in line with the screen, and down, he saw John look back from his console in the Electrical and Environmental Control Systems section. John gave him a slightly detectable nod toward the Flight Director's consoles. Bryan stood and peered over the rows of computers. Two Air Force Generals and Dean Radford were just visible behind the FD's station. Bryan assumed the four stars was Fuller. As usual, they were trying to be as inconspicuous as possible, but everyone in the room knew they all were there whether seen or not. When Bryan sat down he couldn't see them at all.

Bryan checked his monitor and book and watched the screen. The Astronauts were adjusting the bay crane on the satellite. When the crane lifted the satellite from the bay, it was the first good look all but the Generals had of it. Bryan tried figuring where they could hide two missiles the size he had imagined. A central cylinder with a large cover panel seemed obvious to him as he remembered Steve's description.

There was some concern at his station over the increased heart rate of one of the payload specialists. They took a few minutes to get him back to normal which slowed the deployment. When Bryan looked up again, he suddenly found himself eye to eye with General Fuller leaning on the top of the computers behind the FD. For a short moment they stared at each other. Fuller's glare sent a message: If it were up to me, you wouldn't be here. Message delivered, both went back to the big screen TV.

All eyes in the FCR were on the TV picture as the bay crane lifted the satellite to launch position. The short, clicking communications back and forth between the Payload Officer and the Payload Specialists were the only sounds that scratched the room's tension. Bryan barely heard a beeping signal coming from one of his consoles. He checked. It wasn't an alarm and slowly faded away.

The crane swung the satellite out of the bay and the TV screens went dark. Ten minutes later their reception was back. The satellite floated away from the crane. That's when everyone in the room saw it. A good-sized American flag, probably ten by fifteen feet, was tied to the satellite and trailing close behind. Their sudden surprise was washed away with a wave of patriotic realization and the room erupted into applause and a small standing ovation.

Bryan applauded and grinned from ear to ear, seemingly as happily surprised as everyone except John, who also applauded just as vigorously. A sudden patriotic chill made goose bumps on his arms and the hair on the back of his neck stand up. Radford and the Generals were the last to stand and their applauding had a certain consenting propensity that was recognized by its lack of sincerity by only two other people in the room. The Generals and Radford turned to their right and left accepting congratulations and, obvious to Bryan and John, to purposely avoid any eye contact with either of them. As the commotion died down, Bryan and John exchanged grins, a sly wink and a secluded thumbs up.

Fuller whispered something into the Flight Directors ear and the FD switched off the blackout communications link. "Who do we credit the flag?" the FD said into the open mike.

"It was Scotty," the reply came back.

"Thanks. Looks good from down here," the FD said.

Radford, Fuller and Rawlins grabbed their briefcases and made their way out through the rows of consoles. Along the way they shook hands giving congratulations to those within reach."

They were out the door as half of those in the FCR were packing to return to the second floor FCR.

John was waiting for Bryan when he came out the door. John joined him in the scattered flow down the stairs.

"Well," Bryan sighed. "It's out there."

"Did you see how big that thing looked?"

"Yeah. Certainly doesn't justify cameras, would you say?"

"Hardly," John laughed. "Wonder how Scotty got the honor?"

"Steve must have asked him."

At the bottom of the stairs they saw the Generals and Radford conversing at the exit door. All three exchanged glances with John and Bryan before they went into the second floor FCR.

"Well, did you and Myra believe David?" Bryan asked. They'd stopped in back of the FCR computer rows. The picture was back on the big screen. The flagged satellite was not in view.

"We haven't reached any conclusions, yet," John said. "We tried to light a light bulb with our fingers. Concentrated with all our might. Never did."

Bryan grinned. "Yeah, Susan and I did, too. Same results."

"We did it once, why can't we do it again?"

"You'd think."

"Wonder how he got the power to do that?"

Bryan shrugged. "Same as the island, I guess. Practice."

"Yeah, sure," John nodded.

"If he was taller, I'd say we'd found our missing Nefilim."

"Are you going to ask them? You know, what we were talking about?"

"I'll give 'em a call after I check the schedule."

"PATRIOTIC, SMATRIOTIC," Fuller snorted. He led Radford and Rawlins through Radford's office door. "Nobody's gonna see the damn thing, way the hell out there in space." He took a cigar from his jacket's inner pocket and removed the wrapping. "No. I don't think so," he pondered. "You gotta get up pretty early in the morning to fool me. It's for something else."

"It's like a tag," Rawlins added. He set his briefcase on Radford's desk.

"Yeah, that's it." Fuller cigar pointed Rawlins. "A tag."

"A tag?" Radford puzzled. He tossed his briefcase on the credenza behind his desk. "For what?" He dropped into his chair. Rawlins took a seat. Fuller paced. Radford popped a cigarette from his pack, pulled it out with his lips and flicked his Bic.

"Yes, a tag," Fuller mused, tossing the wrapping in a waste basket. "I don't know why just yet, but it's something. I'll figure it out, you can bet on it." He bit off an end of his cigar. "Show him those pictures, Walt." He gestured with his cigar. "The flag's a clue. Your boys have something up their sleeves, Dean. Don't know what yet, but it's something."

Rawlins opened his briefcase and took out a folder which contained a handful of 8 x 10 photos. He spread them across Radford's desk. Radford randomly selected a handful for closer inspection. They were telephoto shots of Bryan and John on John's boat with Myra, Susan, Karen and David, and some shots of Bryan and John with Steve Burris in the exercise room lounge and the parking lot giving Steve a package.

"There are your boys, Dean," Fuller said, rolling the cigar across his lips. He pulled up a chair, sat and crossed his legs.

"All over the place, busy, doing something, ever since Burris told them about that satellite." Radford studied each picture and dropped them back on the pile under a puff of smoke.

"See those shots of them and Burris in the parking lot?" Fuller pointed out. Radford hunted, found them and fanned away the haze. "They're giving him a package. Burris carried that package with him to the Cape when he went back for the flight. Without Burris knowing it, we had our boys take a look at it. Guess what it was?"

Radford shrugged. "The flag?" he guessed, and puffed.

Fuller nodded. "Just an ordinary American flag," Fuller said. "We couldn't figure. No harm in that, so we let it go. And now, it turns up tagged to the back of our satellite. Why!"

Radford shrugged. "Why don't you go ask Mayfield and Sherman, or Burris, when he gets back?"

"We could." Fuller said. "Show 'em the evidence. But they wouldn't tell us the truth. We know that. The flag's just a tag, and we figure it's for something else.

"There's more. See those other shots of them on the boat?" Radford found a few and studied them. They were telephoto shots of the group boarding the *Star Mist,* motoring out the channels and coming back in. "See the Chicano? Name's David Rodriguez. He used to be an investigative reporter with the Austin paper. I say, *used* to be, because he's supposed to be dead."

"Dead?" Radford responded by blowing a stream of smoke and took another look at David's picture.

"That's right," Fuller assured him. "Several years ago he publicly revealed some alleged covert activities and subsequent involvement of a couple of our funding organizations. Got'em closed down for awhile. But he didn't stop there. He started putting a bunch of loose ends together, and began blowing smoke up our ass. Well, you know how I hate smoke, so we put out a contract on his butt and had him eliminated."

Radford coughed and crushed his cigarette in his ashtray.

"Now, a year or so later," Fuller went on, "he shows up here, with Mayfield and Sherman. Alive. How the hell did he do that? Is that some sort of miracle, or what?

"See the blond chick in the picture?" Fuller asked. Radford looked. "There are two."

"The one in the white outfit."

"Yeah."

"He's been living with her down on Galveston Beach." Radford waited. From the way Fuller had said it, he knew there was more about the blond chick.

"Her name's Karen Coe," Fuller went on. "Several years ago, she shows up at Brooks Army with a husband dying of a severe case of radiation burns. Her story: while on a camping trip, they were abducted by these aliens. We have her case on file. Her husband died. A couple of years later, a dead Rodriguez is living with her. He's dead because he knew too much about our involvement with the funding and the aliens. Maybe the same aliens who picked her up. See the connection there?''

Radford thought he did, but he wasn't going to say. Everything seemed to be getting way over his head and he wanted another cigarette real bad.

''Now, the blond and Rodriguez show up palling around with Mayfield, Sherman and his girlfriend; all of them knowing way too much about our operation.'' Fuller flicked his unlit cigar. ''See what I'm saying? Now they put a tag on our satellite. What do you make of that?''

Radford leaned back in his chair, swivelled, studying first Fuller, then Rawlins. ''Aliens, missiles, Tenth Planet, killing people.'' He sighed. ''Hell, Cal, you people are way down range. Out of my league. I have no idea. What?''

''Well, just the same, Dean,'' Fuller said, rolling his cigar between thumb and forefinger. ''We thought we'd give you a shot at it.''

Radford shuffled the photos into a stack, shoved them back into the folder and handed them to Rawlins. ''On second thought, Cal,'' he said. ''I don't want to know. What I do know, is that Mayfield and Sherman, and probably the others, are good people. Somewhere back there, you were too. I'm sorry you've all gotten yourselves involved with this whole sordid mess. Only thing I can say is, go round up all of your suspects and ask them what's going on. Maybe you could swap some secrets. The less I know, the better I'm going to sleep nights.''

Temporarily stunned by Radford's perverse attitude, Fuller shook his head. ''That's not the way it works, Dean. We can't jerk people around until they become a real threat. Otherwise, we find ourselves involved in a Congressional Investigation. And that's not good for anyone. Too much at stake to make a rash move. We bring in some more people, tighten the screws. Something's up, and that flag's part of it. We figure it out and get there before it happens.

Save ourselves a lot of trouble.''

Fuller stuck his cigar into his inside pocket, grabbed his hat and stood to leave. Rawlins snapped the picture folder back into his briefcase.

"Sleep tight, Dean," Fuller said, wheeled and followed Rawlins toward the door.

"Okay, Cal," Radford said, stopping them. Fuller glanced over his shoulder. "Just for curosity's sake, why do you think they tagged your satellite?"

Fuller faced him. "Well, Dean," Fuller smiled. He took a step back toward Radford's desk. "I thought you'd never ask. You see, when I tag something it's for identification purposes. So I know what it is and where it is. I figure Sherman and Mayfield think the same way. Right now I can't figure a *why,* but I'm sure they know. Tagging it tells me that. Pick 'em up, try and force it out of them? No. We act dumb. We let them think they're getting away with it. They get careless. We listen to their every word, watch their every move, we get the *why.*

"I should be on my way back to Nevada," he said, turning halfway toward the door. "But, now, I've gotta take some time to see a man about a ghost. See ya next time around."

DURING HIS FIRST BREAK, Bryan hurried to his office, closed the door, rounded his desk and dropped into his chair. Grabbing his phone, he punched in the numbers as he remembered them. He leaned back, swirled around and gazed out his window. He watched several sailboats glide across the lake and counted the rings click off.

What could she be doing? He had pictures; painting, sunning on the deck, running on the beach, four rings, maybe in bed with David.

Fifth ring. "Hello."

"Karen? Bryan."

"Hi." She stood in front of a large painting in progress. She balanced the phone in one hand, wet brushes between fingers of her other.

He pictured her in a tail-tied work shirt and shorts. And he was right. "How're you doing?"

"Fine. And you?"

"Okay. You busy?"

"No. What's up?" She cradled the receiver between shoulder and chin and began to swish each brush in a can of cleaner.

"I'd like to ask a favor of you and David."

"Sure. Ask."

"I'd like to have you and David go through our radiation chamber test."

She chuckled. "What's a radiation chamber test?" She wiped a brush on a paint rag and placed it in a holder.

"It's a test we put our astronauts through," he said. "We use it before and after space flights. It gives us a reading on the amount of radiation they pick up on each flight."

"You want to check us for radiation?" She wiped her hands with the paint rag and tossed it on her taboret.

"No. Not radiation, exactly," he said. "What I'm really interested in is your auras."

"Our auras?"

"Your energy auras," he said. "This test not only shows radiation levels, it also shows the strength of the body's energy. Its aura."

"What for?" She took the phone and flopped down on her couch. "Why do you want to check our body energy?"

"Well," he began, fashioning some reasoning to cover the real one. "Ever since we've been using this test I've noticed changes in the astronauts' auras. The deeper they go into space, they access stronger dimensions and the larger their auras are when they return. For some reason their energy has been expanded. And so, I figured since you've been deeper in space than any of them, I just wanted to get a comparison."

"David's never been in space," she pointed out.

Bryan sat up, whirled around and leaned on his desk.

"I know, but after last weekend there shouldn't be any question why I want to test him. Your tapes seemed to have released an awful lot of his energies. I've listened to your tapes and I want to check my aura against his. You know? Is it the tapes, or what?" Did any of that make sense?

"Well," she said, "David's not here right now, but I suppose it will be all right. I'll ask him later to be sure. What do we have to do?"

"Real simple. All you have to do is put on a jumpsuit and stand in the middle of this little room full of a special chemical fog while I take a picture of your aura."

"That's it?"

"That's it."

"Okay. When?"

"How about tomorrow evening?"

"Uh, what time?"

"Say, six?"

"Six?" Karen thought. "That might work out. David has a meeting in Houston tomorrow night, and he's taking my car. We can come in together, but you'll have to give me a lift back."

He grinned. "Sure, I'll be glad to. Least I can do." What a stroke of luck. No accident, it was supposed to be.

"Good. Where should we meet you?"

"Visitor's Center's fine," he said. "I'll be looking for you. Thanks. See you then. Bye."

"Bye."

Bryan hurried back to the FCR entertaining many amorous illusions of being alone with Karen, driving her back to Galveston. He thought a lot about what he would say, what he wanted to say.

He found John in the back of the room. The glassed gallery behind them was half filled with visitors and media personnel. John felt Bryan's smile before he patted him on his shoulder.

"We have a go for tomorrow night," Bryan said.

Chapter Twenty:
The Aura

THE CURSOR BLINKED INCESSANTLY at the beginning of a new paragraph while David gazed out the window. He had a commanding view of the beach from the third floor study. Something about two men fishing the surf had held his attention for some time. A curiosity nagged at him; they were fishing, but they weren't really fishing.

He went downstairs, strolled past Karen, who was so busy she didn't notice him go out the door and all the way to the end of the deck. He leaned on the railing and casually watched.

After a few minutes, it was obvious; the two men had all the right gear, but were no fishermen. They seemed to be somewhat interested in his watching them. Or, them watching him.

David left the deck, wandered down the boondocks bridge and sat on the steps at the beach. Around their antics of fishing, the two men sneaked a few glances at him. He recognized their shiny new equipment as some of the expensive stuff he had seen at Bolivar's. Charlie should have given them some instructions on how to use it. Their attempts at casting were laughable, and they didn't seem to be enjoying it all that much. Real amateurs.

If it wasn't their casting, it was the waders. Charlie had finally found someone to soak with the waders. No experienced surf fisherman would be caught dead in them, and that's what you would be. A wave would wash over their top, fill with water and a tow would take you down.

Then David saw the clincher, atop their expensive tackle box, a pair of fancy, government issue binoculars and a camera with a zoom lens. Agents! CIA! NSA! They had that look about them. Not top guys, rookies. How? How'd they find him? Charlie must have told them where he lived. But how'd they figure West Beach, or Galveston? Where'd he screw up?

One of the men fouled his reel, and they were trying to untangle it. They could have at least sent a couple of guys who knew what they were doing.

David left the steps and ambled across the beach toward them. They were aware of his approach and got even busier trying to untangle the line, like they knew what they were doing.

"Morning," David said. He stopped along side of them and watched their frustration. "Having any luck?"

"Morning," the closest one said with a weak smile. "No. Not yet. Just started." He picked at the wad of line on his reel.

"First time surf fishing?" David glanced at the camera and binoculars.

"Well, sort of. We'd been wanting to try it."

"Charlie didn't give you guys any instructions on how to use those things?" David frowned at their efforts to untangle their twelve-pound line. Twelve pound's a bitch. Most beginners would have given up by now, cut it out and started all over.

"Charlie?" the other questioned.

"The guy at the convenience store, where you got your gear. I've seen it there, many times. Love to have it. Cost too much." He stifled a grin.

"Oh, yeah, the old guy. Charlie. No, he didn't have to. We've fished before."

Not surf fishing you haven't, David thought.   "Well

then," David said. "You should know when casting sinkers that heavy to keep your thumb on the reel and stop it when your bait hits the water. You'll avoid a backlash like that." David moved around to the other agent. "Here, let me show you."

David reached for the agent's rod and he cautiously gave it up. David reeled in his bait and sinker to the end of the rod. The agents watched as he gave the rod a few whips to get its feel. He unlocked the reel and placed his thumb on the line spool. "See, you put your thumb right there, hold it tight while you pull the rod behind ya." David held the rod behind him, ready to cast. "And when you cast, you let the line go at the top of your arc." David did it as he said it. The reel whined. "And when the bait hits the water, you clamp down on the line with your thumb." The bait hit and David stopped the reel. "There. Just like that. Easy." David set the reel's gear and reeled the bait in.

"You think you've got the hang of it?" David asked. The sinker and bait came almost to the tip of the rod.

"Yes. Yes, I think we've got it," one agent said. "Thank you. That's very kind of you."

"Well, here," David said. "Let me try one more, and I'll let you have it." He whipped the rod a couple of times and let the line out about three feet. "You boys stand back there a little bit. I'll show you how to cast as far as you can. In case there might be a school running beyond the breakers."

The two agents stepped back. David took a few practice swings, and undetected by the agents, aligned the bait and hooks with the camera's strap behind him. "Now," David said. "This one's going way out there." He spread his stance, muscled up and let fly. The rod swished forward. Their camera clanked over their fancy bait box before it flew over their heads with the baited hook. Their camera sailed twenty yards into the Gulf surf.

"Oh, my God!" David shouted. "Your camera! Damn!

I just casted your camera! I'm sorry. Damm, man, I'm
sorry about that."

The agents were in shock.

"Son of a bitch! I'm sorry," David huffed. He reeled
in as fast as he could. "I think it's still on there. Yeah, I
feel it. It's coming. Yeah. We're lucky, it's still hooked."

The rod drooped under the camera's weight. David
lifted it, dripping sand and seaweed. He swung it in and an
agent caught it, and jerked the rod from David's hands.

"You jerk!" one agent snapped. "Gimme that!"

"I'm sorry, really, I am," David apologized. "It was
an accident. I'll gladly replace any damage."

"No. No," the agent growled. "Just get away.
Leave us alone."

"Maybe all it needs is drying out, and it'll be good as
new."

The agents were busy inspecting their ruined camera as
David backed away and made a hasty retreat for the bridge.

BRYAN LEFT KAREN AND DAVID'S names at
the main gate house. The guards would only be curious
about anyone coming into the center after hours during a
Shuttle Flight. Not that they would be up to no good, but
that they might be lost. It wasn't unusual to find tourists
wandering around the area during a mission. They figured
since they had just driven a thousand miles or so the family
should be able to come in and see how their tax dollars
were being spent. A majority of them didn't have the
slightest idea what they were looking at anyway, so the
security was there simply to keep them from getting lost, or
hurt.

Bryan glanced at his watch again and leaned on his car.
He watched what little activity there was around the TV
trailers. He remembered, again, the days when all the big
networks were doing a twenty-four hour watch during a
flight. They grabbed anyone who looked as if they knew

anything whatsoever about what was going on. Wear a
badge and they would interview you. He was asked a lot
of questions on the mental attitude of the astronauts on the
troubled Apollo 13 flight. About all he remembered saying
was that they were cold, but holding their own, doing fine
and would be all right. And they were. What happened
was supposed to.

A few minutes after six Karen's little sports car rolled
into the parking lot with David behind the wheel. Bryan
told them to follow him and he led them to a restricted
parking area at a back door to Building 9A.

Karen was radiant as ever, in white shorts, T-shirt and
sandals. She greeted him with a hug. David wore all dark
navy blue, not his usual matching white, open collar shirt,
slacks and a light-weight sports coat, as if he were going to
a party, or a meeting with someone he didn't want to
upstage. Subdued, dark, like the mystery he was.

Bryan unlocked the door and Karen and David
followed him into an enormous hanger expanse where the
crews practiced in the Shuttle mock-up. Doors slammed
and their footsteps echoed around the massive equipment.
Karen and David were impressed with what they could see
in the few lights Bryan needed to light their way. In
hushed tones, Bryan asked it they had ever taken the tour
of the mock-ups? They said they hadn't. Bryan said if they
had time afterwards, and wanted to, they could take a look
inside the Shuttle, sit at the controls. A side perk for being
his subjects of the day.

Bryan led them around the Shuttle, down a short
hallway and into a small room lined with computers and
high-tech equipment. In the center of the room was another
room, the Chamber. It had cinder block walls to four feet
and framed glass to its flat roof. There were doors at
opposite sides of the Chamber and a bank of spot lights on
its ceiling beams.

David and Karen wandered in, carefully stepping around

the support cables and pipes on the floor between the Chamber and the operating equipment. Bryan made his way around the outer room clicking switches and turning dials. Some computer panel lights came on and there were some hissing and humming sounds.

"So, this is it," David said. He nodded, looking around and smiled, seemingly impressed.

"This is it," Bryan echoed.

"How's it work?" David asked.

"Well," Bryan said to turning some valves at the Chamber's wall. "We fog the chamber with some gases, you stand inside, we bring the lights down and take your picture with the cameras at that end." He gestured at the video equipment at one end of the Chamber. "Who wants to be first?" he asked, anxious for the discovery.

"Ladies first," David said.

"Okay, Karen," Bryan said, motioning for her. "If you'll come over here we'll get you suited up."

She followed, David tagging along. Bryan opened a storage cabinet and rummaged through light colored jumpsuits on hangers, looking at marked sizes. He selected one and held it up to her. "Medium-large, off the rack." Bryan said. "Might be a little baggy, but it'll do."

It was lightweight and zipped down the front. She noticed the attached boots were oversized too. "Keep my sandals on?"

"Sure," Bryan said, rummaging for gloves and a helmet.

"This isn't dangerous, or anything?" Karen asked, zipping up in the suit. She had noticed the sharp lab smells.

"No," Bryan said, checking her fit. "The suit's to keep the dyes in the gases from getting on you, or in you."

He helped her on with the helmet and handed her the gloves. "Ready for the moon," David grinned. He tugged at the loose rear folds of the suit. Behind him the Chamber had almost filled with foggy gases.

"Just wait," Karen grinned. "You'll get your turn."

Bryan eased the helmet down over her head and set it into a collar ring.

"How's it feel?" Bryan asked.

"Okay, I guess," she said, her voice muffled in the helmet. "It could get hot."

"You won't be in it long," he said. "Now, let's get you inside."

Bryan took her hand, led her to the door and opened it. David watched as he strolled to the computer end of the Chamber. Some gases rolled out around Bryan and Karen. "There's a spot on a floor turntable in the center of the Chamber," he shouted. "It glows, so you can't miss it. Just stand on top of it."

She carefully stepped in and Bryan closed the door behind her. He made his way over the floor clutter around the Chamber to the computers and video equipment. He sat on a stool next to David and began to push buttons and click switches. Monitors and panel lights lit up as did the ready lights on the videocams. "Find the spot?" Bryan said into a mike.

"Yes," Karen's voice came back on a speaker. "I'm standing on it, I think." They saw her checking her feet.

"Good," Bryan said. "Don't move."

Bryan clicked more switches and brilliant lights on a light bar came on. He pressed another button and the light bar slowly swung down behind her. The light bar stopped at a vertical lock two feet behind her and her figure was sharply silhouetted in the fused light. A resonant rainbow aura glowed around Karen's silhouette on the video monitors. Bryan clicked a switch and the turntable began a slow revolution.

"Hmmmm," David grinned. He glanced from Karen's figure in the Chamber to her glowing image on the monitors. "How does it do that?"

"The light bounces off her body, through the gases and her energy vibrations activate the special dyes in the gases. The cameras' polarized lenses pick up the colors and the computers translate the patterns. What you see is her energy aura. As I suspected, she has a very strong, pure spiritual aura. Stronger than I've ever seen."

"Even yours?"

Bryan shot him a look. "Even mine."

"That's good?" David said to the monitor.

"It proves without a doubt she's experienced a complete realization of the knowing," Bryan said.

"You doubted it?"

"No," Bryan said. "This test is for intensity." He leaned into the mike. "Karen, I want you to bring up your energy. Think of love, all the love in the universe."

"Love?" Karen's voice asked on the speakers.

"All the love, all the knowledge, all the energy of your spiritual energy," Bryan said into the mike. "Concentrate."

For a long silent moment, Karen slowly revolved within the lighted gases. Bryan and David watched the monitors. Then, as asked, on cue, Karen's aura began to grow and glow brighter and brighter until it covered the screen in its pure white light.

Bryan and David grinned into the video monitors, glow, and then at each other.

"That it?" David asked.

"That's it," Bryan said, very pleased.

"How's that?" Karen said through the speakers.

"Fantastic!" Bryan said into the mike. "That's good. You can bring it down now. Thanks."

Karen's brilliant aura dimmed on the monitors.

"When the light bar gets all the way up, Karen," Bryan said into the mike, "just turn around and come out the door." He held the button down as the light bar retracted. Turning to David, he smiled. "She holds the record now. Want to see if you can beat it?"

"Me?" David shrugged. "I doubt it." He slid off his stool and followed Bryan around the chamber.

"Yes, you," Bryan said. "I'm betting you won't let me down."

Bryan helped Karen from the Chamber. "Pick out a suit," he said to David.

"How'd I do?" Karen asked, after her helmet came off.

"Better than I expected," Bryan said. "I'll run it back for you while David gets set,"

She dropped the gloves and unzipped the suit. David found a sizeable suit and sat on a bench to put his feet in.

"You'll have to take off those dark clothes," Bryan said.

"I will? Why?"

"Clothes restrict male energy," Bryan said. "Especially dark colors. I don't know why exactly. They just do. A little something we discovered after we signed female astronauts."

David began unbuttoning his shirt. He looked annoyed. Karen was out of her suit and Bryan put it, the helmet and gloves back on a hanger in the cabinet. "Come on," he said to her. "I'll show you your tape."

David was down to his pants. "When you get suited," Bryan said. "Go into the Chamber and stand on the spot like Karen did. And let me know when you're ready."

David had a sullen look Bryan rather enjoyed. *Don't like being ordered around, eh?* Bryan thought, *or maybe you don't like the attention I'm giving Karen? Well, at least, he's wearing white underwear.*

Bryan and Karen sat on the stools behind the monitors He ran the tape back and they watched her test. She was amazed at the technology and grinned excitedly. Her colorful aura almost filled the screen, then its brilliance spread. "Wow!" she gasped. "Is that love?"

Bryan nodded. "Yep. Pure love. Beautiful, isn't it?"

"Incredible!" she beamed. "I never knew you could see love."

"Feeling love is almost the same as seeing it," Bryan said. "I've never seen anyone knowing love that strong before."

"I'm on the spot," David's voice said through the speakers.

"Okay, don't move," Bryan said. He pushed the button that lowered the lights, checked the tape and switched the cameras on. When the light bar stopped behind David, his silhouette on the monitors stood in the center of an aura already as colorful and as bright as Karen's on full love. Intrigued, Bryan pouted a lip and arched a brow.

"How's that?" David said over the speaker.

"What are you thinking about?" Bryan asked into the mike. He had a fleeting thought it might be jealousy. His second thought was about what David could do to the Chamber, not to mention the equipment, if he turned it up full force. He set the turntable to revolving.

"Nothing really," David answered. "Should I be?"

Bryan studied the monitors. "Nothing?"

"Does that machine show what I'm thinking?"

"No," Bryan said. "Just emotions."

"Well," David said. "I'm thinking about being here and wondering what you're seeing. Is something wrong?"

"No," Bryan said. "I thought I was picking up some anger."

"What if I hold out my arms?" David asked, and did.

His silhouette's arms went straight out on the monitor and his aura went wild. Colors exploded in every direction.

"You ready for me to think about universal love?" David chuckled.

Bryan couldn't say. The monitors were going crazy.

"Here goes," David said. "I love you, Karen. I love you, Bryan. I love the whole world. I love the whole universe." His voice boomed over the speakers, and then he laughed, heartily.

The monitors went pure white. No silhouette, no colors, just intense, pure, brilliant, blinding white light glared from the monitors. Bryan and Karen squinted into the blinding glare. Their short hairs stood up and they had to turn away.

A computer hummed funny and spit a stream of sparks and smoke. Another's panel went crazy before its cables popped out of their sockets. Smoke bellowed from the generators and then from the monitors. Bryan fumbled for the control switches and quickly shut the system down. In the haze, everything hummed to a stop. Some final sparking sputtered from the computers. Bryan and Karen gathered themselves and sat up. David's silhouette in the Chamber was playfully waving its arms and gleefully jumping up and down.

"That enough love?" David boomed over the speakers.

Bryan leaned into the mike. "Yes. Enough, David," he said. "Thank you." He glanced at Karen's shocked look. "You may resume normal thoughts, and exit the Chamber. Thank you."

Chapter Twenty-One:
The Test

BRYAN STARTED UP THE equipment while David slipped out of the suit and dressed. There would have been hell to pay if he had destroyed the Chamber with an unauthorized test.

"Didn't break anything, did I?" David asked as he buckled up his pants.

"No. I don't think so," Bryan said. He checked for smoke and sparks. "Everything looks okay." He shut down the system and cleared the Chamber. The haze had almost settled.

David had his clothes back on and climbed onto a stool by the monitors wanting to see his tape. Bryan was reluctant at first, thinking what it might do to the equipment again, but with David calmly sitting beside Karen, he figured it might be all right.

They watched replays of both Karen's and David's aura test. David didn't seem to be surprised at all that his was as great as it was. Bryan thought David showed a little disappointment it wasn't greater. David gave Karen a kiss, more like an apology, for outshining her.

"How do you account for such an outpouring of energy?" Bryan asked David. "With no out-of-body and just a studying of Karen's tapes, how do you explain reaching those dimensions?"

"I don't," David smiled and shrugged. "It's your test. You figure it out." And that was that.

Outside, dusk had turned to night. Bryan thanked them again for coming. David said his good nights, kissed Karen goodbye, slipped behind the wheel of her car and drove off toward his meeting in Houston. Two blocks from his turn toward the guarded exit, a dark car pulled in behind him. Karen and Bryan didn't notice, but David did. He had seen the rookies follow them from the beach and now, without Karen, he was going to see just how good they were at holding a tail at high speeds.

"Any reason you have to go straight home?" Bryan asked Karen as they turned west out of the Center onto NASA Road 1.

"No, not really," she said. "Why?"

"I, we have something we want to show you."

"We? Show me?"

"John, Myra, myself and a couple of other Club members," he said. "You don't mind the little side trip, do you? Just the other side of Alvin."

"Depends," she shrugged. "What is it?"

Bryan smiled. "I'll let it be a surprise," he winked. "I think you'll find it interesting."

She grinned. "I like surprises." They stopped at the light at Highway 3. "The other side of Alvin?" she mused. "I can't begin to imagine." She was picturing open fields and farms.

Bryan drove under the freeway and west on 528.

"I noticed you were as surprised as I was at David's aura." Bryan said.

She nodded and chuckled. "I was surprised you got it without burning your tape. I hope he didn't do any damage."

"I don't think he did. Everything seemed okay." He sneaked another glance at her, reassuring his perceptions that she was indeed very beautiful in any light, even street lights. "Is he as big a mystery to you as he is to us?"

"He's getting to be."

"He wasn't like this when you met?"

She shook her head. "No."

"You're sure it was just your tapes?"

She shrugged. "So he says."

"He ever tell you anymore about himself than he's told us?"

"We met in San Antonio like I told you. We got to be good friends, and we've been together ever since."

"I mean, what about his background. Where's he from? His family? Ever meet them?"

"He's from Brownsville, I think," Karen said. "He doesn't talk much about his past. His wife died in a car accident. They had no children, and I think he mentioned his parents are gone, and he hasn't any brothers or sisters."

"So, it's just him?"

"Far as I know."

"It doesn't bother you he can do what he does?"

She shrugged. "Some of it does," she said. "Does it you?"

"Of course it does. All of us. John, Myra, Susan, we can't believe anyone can muster that much power just by practicing the knowing from your tapes. It's not normal."

Karen looked at him and grinned. "But, and you'd be the first to agree, the knowing is normal."

He had to agree. He watched the road and thought of another way to ask. "When's the first time you remember anything unusual happening when he was around, and you knew it was him doing it?"

She thought about it. "First time? Hmmm. Probably about six months ago. After we moved to West Beach. Just a little thing."

"A little thing?" He glanced at her. "What's a little thing?"

She studied him, weighing her opinion of a little thing. Finally, "He levitated the dining table and chairs," she said.

"He levitated the table and chairs! Just like that? Out of the blue?"

"Yes."

"And that's a little thing? How?"

"Well," she gestured. "He was just sitting there staring at them and they rose up in the air."

"How far?" Bryan asked. "How long did he hold them?"

"About two feet, I guess," she said. "And, maybe five minutes. He said he learned it from the tapes."

"You made the tapes. Can you do it?"

"I don't know. I never studied them like he does."

Bryan grinned at a surfacing thought. "You know?" he said. "Susan has an interesting theory how he got his unusual powers. In addition to your tapes."

She was curious. "How?"

"From sleeping with you."

She laughed. "Really?" she said. "I've never thought of it that way. Maybe. Ha! I'll have to ask him. Was it Susan, or was it what you think?" she added.

"It was Susan."

They were silent for about a half a mile.

"What's he doing tonight?" Bryan asked.

"Research. A follow-up interview for a story he started a couple of years ago."

"What's that?"

"Something to do with the government cover-up." She glanced at the landscape. "An AIDS researcher. A guy whose found one of the scientists who was at the Brookhaven Labs when the virus was accidentally created. He doesn't tell me too much. One way to keep me alive, he says."

After a silent space, she asked, "All your questions. Are you suspicious of his powers for any reason? Jealously, maybe?"

"Yes, and yes," Bryan grinned. "But you'll understand my reasons after you see our surprise.''

He turned off 1462 onto the old oil field road.

The road got rough all of a sudden and they bumped along kicking up dust around old oil pumps and by fenced pasture land. Searching the darkness beyond the weaving headlights, she felt some apprehension about their destination.

"Where is this we're going?" she asked.

"It's not much farther," he assured her.

"You're sure? I don't see anything out here."

"That's the reason it's out here."

Around a curve, across a gully bridge, up a hill and Bryan turned into tho rut road that led to the shed. The light above the front door barely lit Boyd's van, parked at the side of the building out of sight. He pulled in beside it. "Here we are," he said, and clicked off the lights. They got out.

"Keep out. Restricted Area. Radiation?" she read the signs as they approached the door. "Atomic Energy Commission? What is this? Are we authorized personnel?"

"Sure," Bryan said opening the door. The buzzers went off.

"Those signs are to keep away nosy people."

"Really? It would make me more curious."

"Curiosity killed the cat. Remember?"

He clicked on the light and she hesitated before carefully stepping into the dirty little front room. She waited as he unlocked the warehouse door. Another buzzer when it opened. She saw the light beyond and cautiously followed him through.

First sight of the ship shocked her. He watched her react, and wondered what she had expected. She froze, aghast, staring at the space craft, shining in the lights. The door closed and the alarm stopped. She glanced at the figures in silver suits coming toward her. Through her shock, she recognized John and Myra. Remembering the signs outside, she took a step backwards.

"Welcome to Alienland," John grinned. He took her hand and shook it, but she hardly realized it. She couldn't take her eyes off the ship. "Only have one ride," he said. "But it's a doozy."

She glanced back at Bryan, who was getting two silver suits from a storage closet. Another suit for this weird night! "See anything you recognize?" Myra asked her.

"Where'd you get it?" Karen gasped. "You build it?"

"Nope," John said, proudly. "It's the real McCoy. We found it."

"Found it? Where?" She started slowly toward the ship.

"Here," Bryan said. "You'll have to put on one of these." He held a silver suit for her. The others waited while he helped her put it on.

"Last October we found it on a ranch not too far from here," John said. "We've been trying to fly it ever since."

Bryan helped her zip up her suit. He handed her gloves and a helmet.

"This is Frank and Boyd," John said. "Karen."

They shook hands. "Nice to meet you," Frank said. "We've heard a lot about you."

"Yes, we have," Boyd said. "Sure hope you can help."

"Help? What do you mean? What can I do?" she said, wandering cautiously toward the ship and its open door. "This is really incredible. You *found* an alien space ship?"

"You told us the aliens let you fly their ship," John said, as they followed along with her, like proud car dealers showing off their new model. "We've tried just about everything we can think of. We opened the door and got the lights on, and a few other things, but so far we can't get the engine to kick over. Then you came along with your story about being a pilot, and the key. And, well, under the circumstances, you can't blame us for being a little suspicious at first. And then David. Well, he was something else. But we had one last test, and if you and David passed that, then it was agreed that you should be given a shot at starting the ship. You don't know how happy we were to see you. We hoped for David too, but that wasn't to be, so for now, we'll take what we can get.''

Karen was still awestruck. As John explained, she gave the ship a thorough, wide-eyed inspection. If it had had tires she probably would have kicked them. Gazing up at the ship she said, ''The ship Jim and I saw was much bigger. Maybe ten times as big.''

''Probably so,'' John said. ''More than likely it was a mother ship. This is a shuttle craft. It could have had a crew of one, or as many as four. We don't think more than four, because the owners are pretty good size. Seven to eight feet tall.''

''Seven to eight feet?'' she said. ''How can you tell?''

''By what's inside,'' John said. ''Come on, we'll show you.''

She followed him up the ramp with the others close behind in single file.

''What we need you to do is inside anyway,'' John said.

Inside, Karen continued her awestruck inspection. John checked the reading on the clicking Geiger counter behind the huge pilot's chair.

''What's that?'' Karen asked;

''A Geiger counter,'' John said. ''I don't have to tell you, the ship is loaded with radiation. The count's low enough right now that you won't need your protective gear, but keep it on in case we get ignition.''

''Ignition?'' Karen puzzled. ''You mean, you're gonna start it up?''

John got a foot boost from Boyd and reached high up behind the corner of the control console and switched the ship's power on. "Not quite," John said. Panel lights blinked on as did the floor and ceiling circles. With the colorful reflections vibrating on their suits and walls it was like a carnival midway at night. All they needed was the calliope music. "This is as far as we've gotten," John said, as he stepped down. "It seems as though whoever flew this ship here, might have the only ignition key. We know this is a Nefilim ship, the blond giants from the Tenth Planet. And from what you told us, we know that you were abducted by the Nefilim. You said that when you were flying their craft you were standing on a floor circle, and the ships energy flowed through you to the circle, up there." John pointed out the two circles and Karen seemed to have some recognition. "We tried standing between the circles, and nothing happened. None of us seemed to have the right vibrations, energy, or whatever the key is. You referred to that right energy as the knowing. Well, we listened to your tapes, hoping we could boost our knowing, and we tried it again and nothing. The Nefilim who left this ship on the ranch didn't have any fear of it being flown by an earthling without a pure and powerful knowing of spiritual energy. An extremely righteous entity.

"The Chamber test was to see if you could take your spiritual energy to a level that might start this ship. If you could, Bryan was to bring you here."

Karen glanced at Bryan. He smiled and nodded.

"I'm the key, is that it?" she asked, suspiciously.

"Possibly," Bryan said. "You, or David."

"Why are you so set on flying this ship?" Karen asked.

"A couple of reasons," John said. "One, to expose MJ-12's denial that there are aliens visitors and that they are covertly involved with them to destroy humanity. The second reason has an immediate urgency, which we'll reveal, if you are the key."

John offered her the circle on the floor. "We respect

your right to say no. And in turn, you must respect our right for secrecy.''

Karen studied them and the circles while she mulled their proposition. She tried imagining what might happen, and what might not. ''You're serious, aren't you?'' she said, glancing around at each expecting face.

''Yes. Very serious,'' John said.

''Do you know what you're doing?'' she asked. ''Have you any idea the technology you fooling with here? Atomic energy like you've never imagined. Radiation none of us would strive. I've seen it and it's not a pretty sight.''

''We're aware of the danger,'' John said. ''We're prepared and we're committed to seeing this project through to our goal, no matter the risks. It's something we have to do. We weighed the prospects of asking you and David very carefully. We would never have asked if we hadn't believed beyond a shadow of doubt that you could do this, that both of you were as dedicated as we in bringing the truth to the world.''

''What's the second reason?'' Karen asked.

''After you start the ship,'' John said.

''The first one's not good enough to risk it,'' Karen said.

John took a quick glance at the others. Tacitly, they said it was his decision.

''We've discovered a military plot to deploy atomic missiles in outer space,'' John said. ''There were a couple of their best on a satellite deployed on this last Shuttle mission.''

Karen stared at them. ''And you have to fly this craft to . . . '' she prodded.

''To take them out,'' John said.

''That's wild!'' she grinned, shaking her head. ''Like some heroes in a science fiction movie.'' She laughed.

''You're standing here,'' John exploded, gesturing at the ship, ''in an alien ship, talking about science fiction?''

Karen took another look, regaining her perspective. She knew the ship was alien, and real. She had met the Nefilim, and she knew the government was involved in a cover-up. These people staring at her, waiting, were serious. They knew what she had done. They had tried it and failed. They were desperate. She and David were their last hope. Perhaps they were asking more than she could give. She felt very small. She hadn't prepared for such a decision. The aliens never gave her a choice. They just took her, as if they had the right. Turned her life around. Maybe it was for this. Maybe it was for David. There are no accidents. What would David do?

"Yes, or no?" John asked.

Karen studied the disks, floor and ceiling. "You realize I was out of my body when I did this with them."

"We know," John said. "Can you do that?"

Karen shook her head. She stepped toward the floor disk. There were sighs of relief as hope bloomed.

"We'll take what we can get," John said. "We'll give you all the protection we can." He moved to the ignition controls on the console. "We'll shut it down the minute anything goes wrong." The others moving away, back with John, made her leery.

"Anything goes wrong?" she said. "Thanks, that's a relief."

Karen centered herself on the floor disk and glanced up at the ceiling disk. "How will you know when something's wrong?"

John and the others put on their protective gloves and helmets. "Now that's encouraging," Karen said. "Do I get to put on mine?"

"Can you project your energy through the suit?" John asked.

"I don't know. Remember? I've never done this before."

"Your energy will be the linking spark," John said,

hand on the switches. "Once she kicks on, we figure she'll revert to her own systems." John studied the situation, then shrugged. "Better put on the gloves and helmet, just in case we're wrong."

Bryan helped her. "Has anyone heard from the warden?" she joked as he adjusted the helmet. If anyone grinned it didn't show through their helmets. Bryan stepped back and she dropped her hands to her side.

"Now, Karen," Bryan said. "Bring your spiritual energy to its highest level. Just like you did in the Chamber tonight. Think of love. Project its power. When you believe it's at lull intensity, wiggle a finger or something. Okay?"

Karen nodded and resumed her quite meditation. John clicked on the switches and placed his hands on the right levers.

They waited, all eyes on Karen's suit and her gloved finger. One minute . . . two . . . three . . . A finger wiggled.

Slowly, John pulled the levers. The circles glowed and the ship hummed, brighter and higher, as the levers moved.

The levers went all the way. The ship revved at full power. Nothing happened. She wouldn't start.

"Did you do it, yet?" Karen shouted above the hum.

"Yes," John shouted. Disappointed, frustrated, he pulled the levers back and the ship settled down to square one.

Bryan stepped forward and helped Karen with her helmet. "It didn't work." he said. "Did you feel anything?"

"No. Should I try it without the suit?" Karen asked.

John sighed. "We can't ask you to do that."

She took off the gloves, tossed them aside and unzipped the suit.

Bryan said, "you realize your body could receive the same lethal charge as your husband's?"

"Yes, I know," Karen sighed. "Life's a risk." She stepped out of the suit and shoved it off the disk. "If I get my energy aura up to full power, it will protect my body." Centering herself she confidently looked at John. "I made that up," she said. "Okay, let's try it again," as calm as if she were jump-starting her little car.

"If you feel uncomfortable," John reassured her, "anything at all, step away."

Karen nodded, closed her eyes, took several, deep relaxing breaths and went into her centering meditation. Everyone in the room, first Bryan, then Myra, took off their helmets, gloves and unzipped their suits. They closed their eyes and consciously began to project their own spiritual energy into Karen's. If she could do it for them, they could do it for her.

John reached back and found the levers. He counted off the minutes and slowly pulled the levers. The ship glowed and hummed as it did before. John felt the levers hit bottom, full power. Nothing happened. Again, the ship wouldn't start.

John pulled the levers back and the humming died down. They opened their eyes. Karen saw they had taken off their suits and she smiled, stepping off the circle.

"Sorry," Karen shrugged, and rubbed at her body.

"How do you feel?" John asked. "You okay?"

"Fine, I guess," she said. "I'll let you know tomorrow."

"You did your best," Bryan said. "For all of us, thanks."

"There's still hope," Karen, said. "There's still David."

Chapter Twenty-Two:
The Sparks

"YOU GUYS REALLY SURPRISE me," Karen chuckled, pouring two glasses of wine at her kitchen bar. She stood in the light of her open refrigerator. Bryan wandered into her studio; admiring a painting in progress on her easel. "I would have never guessed, a Nefilim shuttle craft! I'm still in awe."

"It's been tough playing it cool this long," Bryan said to the painting. "We expected to be flying it by now."

"I think it's just too wild," she said, stuffing the cork back in the bottle. "You guys flying it to a football game? That's incredible!"

"The Super Bowl half-time," Bryan grinned. "Biggest TV audience in the world."

She placed the bottle in the fridge. "Did you guys ever give any thought to what would happen after that?" She came around the bar with the glasses.

"No, I don't guess we did."

"I mean, people see space ships all the time and never think anything about it. To a large majority they've become just another fact of life." She handed him his glass.

"Thank you. We figured everything would just take care of itself after the secret was out. MJ-12 would admit all their mistakes, religions would teach the truth, people would get their lives back, and everyone would have a happy, joyous, pain-free life. If it was supposed to happen, it would."

Karen held up her glass and Bryan tapped it with his. "Here's to knowing the truth," he said. She smiled and nodded.

After they sipped, she asked, "The painting: what do you think?"

"Huh? Oh." He took another look. "Very nice," he nodded. "What is it?"

"Life," she said. "Love. Whatever. Just a thought. It's supposed to make people think. Does anything come to mind?"

"Ummmm. I guess."

"What?"

He shrugged. "Like you said, love. You."

"Nothing deeper?"

"I don't know," he mused. "What's deeper than that?"

"You think anyone would get it who didn't already know?"

"Perhaps," he said. "But, I have to admit, your paintings don't play to simple illusions."

She grinned. "Come on," she beckoned, heading for the deck. "It's a beautiful night. Let's not waste it in here."

Bryan was delighted with her suggestion. Discussing her paintings was not what he'd had in mind. A romantic stroll on the beach was more like it, but he would settle for the deck. The cool Gulf breeze was rather mild and two foot waves calmly lapped the beach. A three-quarter moon and Venus looked as if they were somewhere over the Pacific.

"A night made for romance," Karen sighed, leading him to the far railing. Faint wisps of her perfume blended with the salty air.

They leaned on the railing, inches apart, aura's entwined. The steady wind whipped around them. Lights on the offshore rigs were pinpricks on the Gulf's dark horizon. A couple of shrimp boats passed each other a mile beyond the surf. Two lanterns on the beach shown light on the backs of several night fishermen. "I'm sorry I wasn't a match for your ship," Karen said to the Gulf waters.

"It's okay." He thought about giving her a kiss for effort.

"I don't know. Maybe I was afraid of it at first. The ship brought back so much of how awesome that whole thing really was. How powerful it was, how absolutely powerful the Nefilim are. They truly are gods. Reality can really turn your life around."

"I know." He wanted to kiss her for his reality.

"I've tried expressing that intense love in my paintings," Karen said. "But the medium is so limiting, so restricted, so earthly." She took a sip of wine and set her glass on the deck. "I think Susan has the right idea, a book would be better."

"Maybe. She's having a tough time getting started. You know, getting everything straight. I know it must have been as tough for you as it was for me, coming back into the body, all of that knowing is just too much to retain."

"Yes, it was," she said into the wind.

He nodded after a swallow of wine, his eyes absorbing her every sensual curve, thinking only of how beautiful she was and how so evenly they had been programmed, and that he'd rather be kissing her and making love to her right there on the deck. He wondered, having never been with a woman of his equal spiritual energy level, if their auras were plugged into their desires. He didn't seem to be picking up anything — but David in a jealous rage. And neither one wanted to see that. He took a final sip of his wine and set the glass beyond them on the deck.

He leaned on the railing, almost touching her. "It must have been pretty tough on you." he said. "The rape and all."

"The rape! What rape?"

She was shocked and confused. He backed off, groping for a way out of his faux pas. David had warned him, she didn't want to remember. "Well, the one that they, uh," he stammered. "I'm sorry. I forgot. David warned me you didn't like to remember having their baby."

"Having whose baby?"

"The aliens."

"David told you I had an alien baby?"

"Well, uh, yeah. He said you told him they raped you, you got pregnant and three months later they came back and took the baby."

She laughed at the absurdity. "Why would he tell you that?" She glanced at the house, but the culprit wasn't there. "It never happened. I never told David any such thing."

He felt some relief in that. "I don't know," he said. "But that's what he told me, that day, when you were on the deck feeding Stanley."

They stared at each other, pondering David's reasoning. She grinned and chuckled to herself. "That rat," she said. "He's up to something. It's one of his little tricks. You can bet on it. David was playing with your mind, Bryan."

Bryan tried to figure. Why?

"How'd you feel about me having an alien baby?"

"I don't know," he shrugged. "I didn't like it. I felt sorry they'd used you like that. I've heard stories of them having sex with abductees, and how traumatic it can be, during and after."

"Well, I can put your mind at ease," she said. "It never happened. Not that I know of. And if it did I certainly don't remember it — and I think I would have with the hypnosis. Don't you?"

"There are cases where patients have completely blocked out devastating events in their lives."

"They didn't even take my body on the ship," she pointed out. "How could they rape me without a body?"

"I don't know," he said. "Maybe they did it after they put you back in."

"Well, I would've known if I was carrying a baby, wouldn't I? That's pretty hard to hide, you know."

Bryan felt sorry that he had brought up the subject. He couldn't tell if she was upset at him for thinking she'd had an alien baby, or at David for tricking him, again. He hated David for getting in his way again, but he can't say he wasn't warned. "Forget it. Just forget I ever mentioned it."

"He has some explaining to do when he gets back," Karen said. She reached her glass and took a final swallow.

"Just when do you think that'll be?" Bryan asked. They

had been looking for David to return at anytime. They were waiting to tell him about the Nefilim ship and asking if he would be willing to volunteer helping start it.

"I don't know," Karen sighed. "Sometimes when he goes to one of these kinds of meetings he's gone all night."

"Really?" Bryan said, masking his inner joy. "Well, I don't suppose I can wait all night." He glanced at his watch. "It's late and it's a long drive back."

"Yes, it is," Karen said. She took his arm and patted his hand. "Thanks for the exciting evening, and bringing me home. It was a real adventure I won't soon forget." She laughed.

"It was my pleasure." Then he thought, maybe that was the wrong thing to say. He put his arms around her. "How are you feeling?"

"Okay. I'm okay. No fever, no rash."

"Yes, you do feel great," Bryan grinned. "I enjoyed being with you."

Her arms slipped around him. "Thank you," she whispered. When they looked into each other's eyes it just seemed natural that they kiss. Not a long kiss, just a friendly, feeling kiss, one that barely stirred the emotions. When they pulled back he thought he saw some sparks fall behind her. Maybe, static electricity.

"Could I ask you something?" she asked, looking into his eyes while they still held each other's arms.

"Sure."

"You said you would tell me why it was that you all were suspicious of David and the power he has, after you showed me the ship," Karen said. "Why?"

"It should be obvious," Bryan said.

"What?" she puzzled.

"The ship," he said. She didn't get it. "Well, here it is, we found this ship, and it has an earth-proof security system, and we know it's a Nefilim ship, probably belongs to a Nefilim God. And since we didn't find a body, it's logical for us to assume that he, or she, is out there walking around somewhere."

"David?" she gasped.

"David shows up in your life around a year before we

find the ship, and you say you don't know that much about him, and you'll have to admit, he's demonstrated some pretty powerful energy. And we don't believe he got it from studying your tapes. We believe he got it from somewhere else. And we believe that somewhere else has something to do with the ship and the missing god. Now that you've seen the ship, you know what we suspect."

Karen thought about it. "David?" she mused. "No. It's not possible."

"You're living together," Bryan said. "You've made love. What's he like? I mean, anything like on the immortal level?"

She grinned, reflectively. "Well, he's pretty good, better than what I was accustomed to, but," she chuckled, "I haven't known any immortals, that I know of."

"Nothing special? No special — magic?"

"Well, I guess you could say," she grinned at the thought, "but it could be me, or both. I don't know. David says it's me. From my trip."

"What?"

"Well," she chuckled. "There's these sparks . . ."

"Sparks?"

"Yeah. Like from Christmas sparklers, you know?" She put her arms around him and they embraced. "Here, let me show you. Keep you eyes open and watch around me."

They kissed, long and passionately. When she finally pulled back he saw a shower of blue and gold sparks fall from her. More than he had seen before.

"There," she said, breathlessly. "See them?"

"I don't know. Maybe we'd better give it another try."

He pulled her to him, and for the longest time, neither seemed to want to let go.

"There," she whispered, finally. "See them?"

"Yeah, I think so." The sparks were everywhere. But he was thinking about going for a Fourth of July display.

"David says it's an overcharge from being on their ship out-of-body. It happens whenever I get sensually over-excited."

"Yeah?" he quizzed. "That's cool. Let's see it again."

They laughed. And, both eagerly, for the fun in it, kissed long and hard in a shower of fireworks.

KAREN AWOKE EARLY THE next morning; her body alarm set at six no matter the hour of retirement. She ran her hand between the cool sheets in David's empty place and wondered what had kept him. She wasn't worried. Wasn't the first time. He always showed up later with some curious tale of government intrigue. She was aware he made enemies in his career and had assured her many times there was nothing to worry about. He could take care of himself. Knowing him as she did, worry was a waste of time.

She played with thoughts of Bryan before she rolled out of bed and slipped into a T-shirt and shorts. She gave her hair some quick strokes and gathered it under a headband. In the early morning light, she skipped down the stairs, grabbed a handful of grapes from the kitchen and burst onto the deck in the cool dawn breeze. She strolled across the boondock bridge eating grapes and contemplating the day's probable activities. A shell hunter on a motor scooter putted slowly up the beach past a lone fisherman casting into the surf. She padded onto the beach squishing wet sand with her toes. First the cold surf stung her feet, then out of its reach, she walked, then jogged and then ran. Great for getting thoughts straight.

Two miles later she walked back into a sunrise already scorching the horizon haze. Hopping up the boondock bridge steps she saw David sitting on the deck, his head barely visible above the top railing.

She hurried across the bridge and greeted him with a smile as she came up the deck stairs. He was still dressed in his navy blue from the night before.

"Well, good morning," she panted.

"Morning," he smiled and saluted her with his tall glass of orange juice.

She took it from him, dropped into a chair opposite him and took a long sip. Licking her lips, she handed it back to him.

"You were out late," she grinned, "or in early."

David shrugged. "When we got into it, things went on and on. He had a lot of evidence; photos, documents, names, places, orders, reports, videos. You name it. He has his butt covered."

"Hmmm." she nodded. "It took all night?"

He smiled at her inquisition. "I was back by midnight," he said to the Gulf. "Bryan's car was still here. I didn't see any lights — so. There was something I needed to check on over in Brazoria County. It just took longer than I thought. Sorry." He grinned, and to change the subject, "How'd it go with you?"

"We talked, watched stars out here," she said. "Waiting for you."

"Waiting for me?"

"Bryan had something he wanted to ask you."

"What?"

"After you left," she said. "He took me to see a space ship they have in an old storage building way out in the woods."

"A space ship?"

"You don't seem surprised."

"It doesn't surprise me they could build a space ship."

"It doesn't?"

He shook his head. "No."

"Why?"

She brushed sand from her bare feet, sank down in her chair and stretched her feet into a chair next to him. He touched her softly and ran his hand up her leg to her knee.

"They work at NASA," David said. "They have a UFO Club. They have access to a lot of information about space craft. They wouldn't have any trouble building one."

"Well, they didn't," she said. "They found it. On a ranch, somewhere out around West Columbia. It's a Nefilim ship. They figure some Nefilim God left it there." She noticed his interest didn't jump as much as she had expected. "This doesn't surprise you?"

"Yes. Sort of," he shrugged.

"They've had it since last October. They've been

trying to fly it. Thing is, they can't get it started.''

"Can't get it started? Why?" He took a sip of juice.

"Well, you see, it takes a special energy," she said. "Something as powerful as the knowing, pure spiritual energy. And since they knew I'd flown a Nefilim ship, and I passed Bryan's test last night, they figured I had enough power. But, I didn't." Again, she noticed his calm, mild interest. Here she was telling him about the biggest event that could happen in their lives and he was taking it like it was no big deal. Where was the amazement, the excitement? He should have been jumping out of his chair. All he was doing was staring at her with that far away, that deep thought look she knew too well. What was he thinking? She recalled Bryan's suspicions.

"How is it they figure this special energy can start this ship?" he asked.

"The ship is much like the one I flew," she said. "Same system, only smaller. The ignition key is missing. The key is a very powerful spiritual energy. Someone with this special energy stands on a circle in front of this big chair and their energy links to a power flow from a circle in the ceiling. I stood on the circle, they turned it on and nothing happened."

"Nothing?" he said and took a sip of juice. Beyond her and the boondocks, he saw the rookie fishermen strolling up the beach with their rods, but minus the waders.

"Nothing," she repeated, studying his reactions. "I didn't project the special spiritual power to make the link." Odd, she thought, he seems to be ignoring the fact that he would be their next choice. As if he hadn't heard what she had said.

"What?" he asked, feeling her intense scrutiny.

Her eyes narrowed. "Nothing," she said and shrugged. "They want you to try."

"Me?"

"Remember? You scored higher on Bryan's test than I did," she reminded. "And your showing off you're their next obvious choice. Not afraid you might be the one, are you?"

"No. I doubt I would be," he grinned. "But, I'd love

to see their ship.''

"Admission price is, they try your energy.''

"Oh. Well, in that case, let's see if I fit the lock.''

She nodded and grinned, took his glass of juice and almost finished it off in one swallow and handed it back to him. "Come on,'' she said, taking his hand. "Let's take a shower.''

BRYAN LEANED OVER THE phone at an empty desk in the FCR. "How're you feeling?'' he asked softly into the receiver.

"Fine,'' Karen answered on the other end. She sprawled on her downstairs couch in a tank top and cutoffs. "No rash, headaches, or anything. So, I guess I'll be okay.''

"I was worried,'' Bryan sighed. "That was a big chance you took for us. We can't say how thankful we are and that there were no disastrous affects. When did David get in?''

"Not until this morning.''

"This morning?'' Bryan uttered. "Did he say where he was?''

"He said after the meeting he had to check on something in another county.''

"Check on what?''

"He didn't say, and I didn't ask,'' she said. "He came by around midnight, saw your car.''

"Came by and didn't come in because he saw my car?'' he asked, twisting the phone cord.

"Uh huh.''

"That's strange, not coming in, don't you think?''

"No.''

"Like he was giving us the space.''

"Well, it is my house.''

Bryan thought of the times since, that he had checked to see if he had gained any special powers, such as trying to levitate a chair, or just a pencil, something. "Well, I'm glad he didn't come in,'' he said. "Aren't you?''

"Uh huh. It was . . . special.''

He'd never heard anyone refer to it as special. But it

was special. That had a softer ring than test, or favor.
"You think he knew what was going on?"

"Probably," Karen said. "I don't know. You know
David; there's not much I can hide from him, even if I was
trying. And I wasn't. I would've told him if he'd asked."

"But he didn't?"

"No. Of course not. I love him, and he loves me."

"Did you tell him about the craft?"

"Yes."

"What did he say? Was he surprised?"

"Well, I don't know," she said. "Maybe a little."

"A little? Not excited that we have the solid
evidence?"

"No. He seemed to take it as something he had
expected."

"Strange. You tell him what we need him to do?"

"Uh huh," she answered. "He said he would."

"He did? Just like that? Without giving it a second
thought?"

"He had some doubts about his power being stronger
than mine," Karen said, "even knowing the results of your
tests. But he did seem excited about getting to see the
ship."

"Hmm. Well, uh, okay. When?"

"Whenever you say."

"Well, I'm going to be pretty busy until the Shuttle
gets back," he mused. "How about Friday night?"

"Okay. Sounds fine. I'll tell him."

"Do you remember how to get out there?"

"No. It was dark. You'll have to take us."

"Yeah. Okay," he said. "No problem." He glanced
up at the orbit board as the Shuttle was coming around.
"Look, I've gotta go. I'll have to call you back, give you
time and place. Okay?"

"Okay. Bye."

"Bye."

THE NEXT DAY THE Shuttle returned, making
a smooth, three-point, parachute-braking landing at Patrick

AFB. Again, it was so routine the major networks didn't bother with news breaks to show it live. Only CNN took the direct feed and held it all the way through the happy, waving astronauts' disembarking, hugging and kissing their families and the short congratulatory speeches behind mikes on the bunting-draped platform. The public had seen the event dozens of times. Only the astronauts' names changed, which few casual viewers could even remember an hour later.

Bryan caught glimpses of the ceremony at the Flight Control Room as he and Marsha cleared their console desks. He walked out with John. They decided it would be better if Bryan met Karen and David in the Mall lot and brought them out in his car. Even though they hadn't detected anyone following them lately, the others would go out in Boyd's van as usual after doing the maze.

Bryan said, "Have you thought about what we'll do if David's not the key?"

John ran a hand through his hair. "No," he said. "Have you?"

"Put it on display and hope they'll believe us."

"We should live so long."

THE TV PICTURE WAS of a NASA news conference; a blue skirted table in front of a drape with a silk-screened NASA logo. Space Center Director, Donald Strake and Dean Radford flanked Steve Burris behind the table and tight cluster of mikes. All wore coats, ties and serious faces. The news camera zoomed in on Steve as he was saying . . .

" . . . my resignation of service to the space program in this capacity. However, I feel that I have reached a time in my life where I should think of moving on to less demanding endeavors." Steve seemed a little choked up and glanced down at his prepared statement on the table beneath his hands.

Bryan sat on Susan's couch watching her den TV. Susan came from the kitchen with two full wine glasses. They were about to celebrate her finishing the first chapter of the book, a printout of which Bryan had in his hand.

". . . spend more time with my family . . ." Steve went on.

Susan read the concerned look on Bryan's face. "Was he a friend of yours?" she asked handing him his glass.

"They're all friends of mine," Bryan said to the TV. "Thanks," as he took the glass.

"I mean, closer than the others?" She sat on the couch's arm and watched the picture of Steve.

Bryan shrugged. "Yes, he is."

". . . and as yet I have no immediate plans for the future," Steve said. "I have several offers to consider, all from space related companies."

"Did you have any idea that he was going to resign?" Susan asked. "You don't seem surprised more, concerned."

"I'm not surprised," Bryan said. He raised his glass to hers. "Here's to a great beginning." They smiled, glasses clinked, they sipped and he went back to her manuscript. On the TV a reporter was asking a question.

"Why?" she asked. "Why're you not surprised? Does it have something to do with the flight? Or, should I ask?"

The picture switched back to the news anchor. "Commander Steve Burris, pilot of the Shuttle Atlantis, returning today, and resigning from the Space Program this afternoon. In other news . . ."

"Yes, it had something to do with the flight," Bryan said to her pages. "And you shouldn't ask." He flipped the first page, reached for the remote and clicked off the TV. "This reads pretty good," he said, going back to her manuscript.

Susan stood and went back to the kitchen, saying, "I don't like to watch someone read my writing."

"Why? Writer's psychosis? Exposing your soul?"

"Something like that. I feel my presence taints any form of sincere attribution."

"DID YOU KNOW THAT women buy more books than men?" Susan said. She held Bryan's hand as they walked along the bayou trail. The sun had set and the June night was cooling very nicely. Heavy fragrances of gardenias and cut grass drifted on the humid air. From the bayou, a bull frog choral sang for rain. "Mostly they buy fiction and love stories. Men buy adventure and technical things. It's a fact. That's how I decided on my form. Marketing. There are plenty of non-fiction books sitting on the shelves that have all the details. You've already pointed that out, and we have most of them. What we want to do is give both sexes what they want and throw in enough of the truth to get them to thinking, and then maybe they'll go for the other books. I mean, why do we need to tell it all over again, when it's already there?"

"Yes, good thinking. Why re-invent the wheel?" Bryan mused, then laughed. "Marketing? Where'd you get that? I had you pegged as the romantic. Romantics aren't that commercially practical."

"I teach it to my kids all the time," she grinned. "No use writing something you can't sell. Get your feelings out there. Give the people what they want, better yet, give them what they need. And they certainly need this story. They'll buy a good storyteller any day."

"You think Karen will mind us using her abduction?" she added. "I'm not using her name, or anything, but I'm sure she'll recognize it."

"No, I don't think so. She told me she was all for your book."

"Our book," she reminded. "She told me, too. That's why I used it. Couldn't think of another angle for a love story."

"Love story?"

"Yes. She gets abducted by the Nefilim, see, and it's Enki. His planet, the tenth planet, Nebiru, is back. It's coming up on the next 3600 years. I figured it up, roughly. If you take the Flood somewhere around 13,000 B.C. and keep adding consecutive orbits, it comes out to where it's close to another crossing. So that's why I figured it was Enki who picked her up. And he likes her and tells her his whole history, and ours. She remembers all the details on her tapes. Enki figures he's in love with her and comes back to help her save all her people from the disaster of the next Flood, Armageddon, or whatever."

Bryan was astounded. Not only had she surprised him with how quickly she grasped the meaning of the knowing, now he couldn't believe how close she had come to thinking what he had been thinking ever since he had met David. Had she become so perceptive that she was now picking up on his thoughts? He had to fight the urge to break his promise and tell her about the ship. It would add so much to the reality of her story.

"That's a little rough," Susan said. "But that's basically the way I see the book right now. What do you think?"

"Are you gonna use the rest of us, John, Myra, me, you?"

"I don't know, yet. If it works out. Think I should?"

"You could use John for the technical things."

"Yes. That's good."

"What're you gonna do about David?"

"I don't know. He's sort of in the way, isn't he?" she mused. "Maybe, I could make it a triangle. That would add a lot of conflict. That's always good. How 'bout he's a Zeta clone, and that's where he got all his powers? He's working for the government, and that's where we get in all the government's cover up stuff, MJ-12, and all. And we kill him off in the end. How's that?"

Bryan grinned. "I like it," he said, "but how're you gonna explain a seven or eight foot blond giant walking around on Earth?"

She let go of his hand, shrugged and said, "I don't know, yet. I'll figure it out when it comes to me."

"When it comes to you?"

She laughed. "Honey, you'll just have to understand how writers work," she said, taking his hand again. "Sometimes we just have to wait until things come to us. It will. You'll see."

"You don't want to get too far out, your readers will think that it's all fiction." Again, he wanted to tell her all about the ship. "Worse, yet, science fiction."

"They might, for a while," she said, "but with a few more earthquakes and floods like we're having, they'll figure it out, too. If I can, they can. Nebriu's coming around again. That's a given."

Chapter Twenty-Three:
The Factor

LEAVING WEST BEACH, DAVID was aware of the tail car's headlights pulling in behind them two hundred yards back. He kept an eye on the rookies through Galveston and all the way up the freeway to Clear Lake. They hung in, close, not about to be shaken again. They learned fast, maybe from an ass-chewing. With Karen in the car, school was out this time. No need to worry her and have to concoct another explanation. David cooled it, but continued thoughts of how he could keep from leading them to the ship and not raise the other's suspicions that they were there.

It was after sundown when they pulled into the Mall parking lot with the tail car jockeying close. David tried circling the lot several times before stopping in a space on the east side as Bryan had told them to. Exiting their car and heading into the Mall, David glanced at the tail car, easing along behind. Not to be fooled by an innocent shopping trip, the tail car stopped in a red zone and the passenger agent hopped out and followed them into the Mall with a two-way radio.

They met Bryan under the clock in the Mall's concession area. After a short greeting, Bryan led them quickly through the shoppers in the arcade and toward an exit to the west parking lot. Weaving through the maze of benches, trees and potted plants, the rookie agent followed and when he realized what was up he radioed his partner to get to the west side of the Mall, fast.

David glanced back to see the rookie agent, with the

radio at his face, making his way through the rows of cars, Karen and David piled into Bryan's car and he headed out of the parking lot. They drove right past the panicked rookie. The last David saw of him, he was running as fast as he could, trying to keep them in sight and looking for his partner.

"KAREN SAID YOU FOUND this space ship on a ranch," David said to Bryan, as he leaned on the back of the front seats. "How'd you do that? What were you doing on the ranch?"

"The rancher found it," Bryan said to David's image in his rear view mirror. "We'd been down there investigating some of his mutilated cattle. He had a hard time believing who'd done it, but even more shocked that the government was allowing it. John left his card. When he found the craft, he matched it up with the picture on John's card and called us. We trucked it back up here, and have been working on it ever since."

"Since when?" David asked.

"Last October."

David sat back. "And Karen gave you the key to start it." He glanced out the back window. He was relieved, the rookies were no where in sight. "You guys were lucky."

Bryan smiled at Karen. "Yes. We were," he said. She smiled. She looked great in the same white silk outfit she wore the first time he had seen her. He wondered if David knew what had gone on between them? He had to remind himself not to think about it, David was too good at reading energies. Maybe he already knew. "But our luck might be running out," Bryan added.

"You mean, if I'm not the one?" David said.

Bryan looked at him in the rear view mirror. David sat in the middle with his arms spread across the top of the back seat, grinning, leading Bryan to wonder, what did he mean by that?

"That's about the size of it," Bryan said.

"Maybe it's not a Nefilim ship," David grinned. "What makes you think it is?"

"The panel markings, and the big pilot's seat," Bryan

said. "They were giants, you know."

"There are a lot of giants out there," David said, as he leaned forward again. "Maybe this isn't the way you start it."

"It's just like the one I was on." Karen said. "Only smaller." She wondered why he was still questioning the event.

Bryan turned off onto the oil field road and rumbled up the old shell road. The grasses alongside were getting thick again.

David searched the dark outside. "Where is this place we're going?"

"Middle of nowhere," Karen said. "They really have it well hidden."

BRYAN PARKED BY BOYD'S van out of the building's front light. David commented on the signs, same as Karen had. They stepped through the front doors. Buzzers sounded opening and closing the doors and they stood looking at the craft and the others, waiting around the work tables in their heat suits.

Same as Karen, David was awestruck when he saw the space craft. Bryan and Karen paid particular attention to his reactions. Was it an act? Neither detected any pretense. For a long moment he just stood slack-jawed and stared at the shiny ship before looking at Karen, then Bryan.

"That's incredible!" David gasped. "Absolutely incredible! It's real. You really do have a space craft."

"You didn't think we did?" Bryan laughed, judging David's surprise as a bit overdone. Had he doubted Karen and him? Where had he thought he was being taken, for a joke?

As with Karen, John, Myra, Frank and Boyd rustled over in their silver suits to greet them halfway. To David, they were a strange sight; in their outfits and coming from the open ship, they just added to the dramatic, other worldliness of the scene. John and Myra also tried to read David's reactions even though he had barely taken his eyes from the ship.

"Welcome aboard," John said, extending his hand.

Even in shaking John's hand David still looked around
him at the ship. He did smile at Myra while greeting her
and held eye contact for a moment with Frank and Boyd
when they were introduced.

"Glad you could come," Boyd said.

"After I heard, nothing could have kept me away,"
David said, slowly pushing past them to get a closer look
at the ship.

Bryan led Karen to the lockers for their suits and
David's.

"They say you're our last hope," Boyd added,
following along, watching David, trying to find some sign
of the wizard he was reported to be.

David shrugged. "That's a lot of pressure," he said.
He stared into the ship's open door as he reached the ramp.
"I don't know what it is you're expecting of me."

Boyd glanced around at the others. "To be the power
key to starting her. Didn't they tell you?"

"Yes. Yes, of course," David said. He stepped onto
the ramp. "Karen told me that she'd tried, but I still don't
understand why I should be any better."

He seemed anxious to get inside. John caught his arm
before he took another step. "Wait," he said. "Let's get
you into a suit. It'll be a lot safer if you start her, when
you start her."

David stopped. When he turned around he saw a suited
Karen and Bryan coming with an extra suit and helmet.

"This baby'll put out a dose of radiation when she
kicks on," Boyd said. "That's element 115 in there."

"It'll get intense," Frank added

"Yes. Yes, of course," David said. "I was so
excited, I forgot." Bryan and Karen helped him hold the
suit as he slipped his feet in.

"But, if you think you can stand it without the suit,"
Bryan said, exchanging a smile with Karen. "Then that'll
be all right too."

David shook his head. "No. No," he said. "I'll take
all the precautions I can get."

John helped Bryan pull the suit up over David's arms
and shoulders. He zipped it up, pulled on the gloves and

took the helmet. He took a look around at their anxious faces and led them up the ramp, hesitating briefly at the door, checking inside before stepping in.

The line of silver suits followed him into the ship and circled the pilot's chair. The geiger counter counted rapidly by their feet.

"It's bigger inside than it looks from outside," David said. He wandered around, glove inspecting the chair and control console. John and Bryan wanted to believe he was checking everything to see if it was still there and not broken.

"Yes, it does seem that way," John said. "It's probably a different dimension. The three dimensional outside is different than the time/space dimension in here. The ship creates its own electromagnetic field. It's basically a time machine. Its zero time reference to the cosmology of the universe is locked onto Nebiru's, its home planet. It was probably flown here through a time portal. What you feel is a residue of ET dimensionality. That's about the only way we can explain the distortion."

"With your knowledge of electromagnetic fields and time distortions," Bryan said, "you shouldn't have any problem with that."

A deadening silence engulfed the group as David stared at Bryan. Myra and John exchanged glances and shifted uneasily.

David nodded. "Yes, I see your point," he said and smiled that knowing smile all but Boyd and Frank had seen just before something happened out of their reality. He watched his gloved hand slide innocently across a panel. "A marvel of advanced technology," he said of the ship. "Don't you find it frustrating that the Nefilim never felt secure enough in our emotional stability to pass this knowledge on to us? Why? Why is that! Did you ever stop and think that there might be a logical reason. That if we had this power, what would we do with it? Are we prepared to take the responsibility for our decisions, our actions? What if you were to start this ship? Then what? What's the purpose? Outside of your going for a joy ride and probably getting yourself killed, what good would come of it?''

They glanced at each other and then realized that no one had told David their immediate reason.

"MJ-12 used this past Shuttle to deploy a satellite that is carrying two missiles with mega nuclear warheads," John said. "Their reasons for doing so are not certain, but we were going to fly the ship to destroy that satellite."

"Destroy! Destroy!" David snapped. "Is it any wonder the Nefilim never gave man the secrets of atomic power?" He studied them. "And just how were you going to destroy these missiles?"

"Lasers," Bryan said. "There're firing buttons in the arms of the chair."

David looked at the chair and ran his gloved hand across its arm, thinking. If he opens those panels, Bryan thought, we'll know, for sure. Only someone who knows the workings of this ship would know how to do that.

Suddenly, David looked up at the ceiling circle and then down at the floor circle. "These the circles?" he asked.

They glanced at each other, again, this time with somewhat relieved smiles he hadn't opened the panels.

"Yes," Karen sighed.

David stepped onto the floor circle. "I stand right here?" he asked. He checked his positioning with the ceiling circle. "That's it," John said, moving to the console and the levers. Frank gave Boyd a foot boost and he reached high behind the console panels and turned on the ship's power. The panels blinked on, the ship hummed and the circles began to glow.

Apprehensively, David watched them move to the console with John and don their helmets.

"Should I put on my helmet?" David asked.

"If you feel more comfortable with that," John said, as he adjusted his own. "Karen did it without her suit."

David looked at Karen. "I projected my energy," she said. "Its aura was enough to protect me from the surge, but not enough to start the ship."

David tossed his helmet. He unzipped his suit and shrugged it off his shoulders. It crumpled around his feet.

He stepped out, shoved it aside with his feet and recentered himself on the floor circle. "Okay," he said, hands at his side, head back and eyes closed. "Let's get on with it."

John clicked on the switches and gripped the levers. "Give us a signal when you're ready," he said.

"I'm ready now," David said to the ceiling circle, its glow stark white on his face.

John started the gradual descent of the levers. The circles glowed brighter and the ship's hum reached for a higher pitch. They watched in amazement and actually saw David's aura extend around his body and mingle with the shaft of light that flowed between the circles. John pushed the levers to their limit. They were nearly blinded by the intense light that swirled around David's body. Arcs jumped from the shaft to the ship's walls. The ship screamed and shook, but it wouldn't kick on. John held the levers at full power until the circles began to smoke. Fearing for David's safety, he pulled back to half power and the ship settled. Then figuring a sudden jolt might kick her on, like kick-starting a cold engine, he slammed the levers to full power. Again, the shaft of light suddenly glowed and swirled around David at a furious spin. Arcs jumped, the ship screamed and shook, but no connecting kick. She wasn't going to do it. John held the levers down until they saw David begin to fold within the vapor cocoon of light.

"Stop it! Stop it!" Karen yelled.

John slammed the levers to off. The light sizzled into a haze between the circles and the ship settled again. David sank to his knees, limp. They rushed to his aid. Karen and Bryan lifted him and sat him into the chair. His head hung, chin on his chest, and his eyes were still closed. Karen raised his head and checked for breathing.

"Oh, my God!" she gasped. "You've killed him!" She slapped David's face and lifted his eyelids. "His eyes are rolled back!"

"Oh, Geezus! What'll we do?" Myra moaned.

"Let's get him outside!" John shouted. "Quick! Grab his arms!"

John lifted David's legs, pulling him from the chair, with Boyd and Bryan at an arm and shoulder. They shuffled

under his weight around the chair, out the door and down
the ramp.

Karen and Myra rushed ahead of them. Myra tossed
her helmet and began clearing a place on the less cluttered
work bench. "Here!" Myra shouted. "Put him up here!"
"No. No!" Karen screamed. "On the floor! Quick!
Lay him down here! Hurry! Oh, God, hurry!"

Everyone was thinking, Call 911. But there was no way
they could. This was going to be a group effort.

John, Bryan and Boyd lowered David's body and his
weight spread on the floor. Karen tossed her helmet,
kneeled and bent over David's head. She lifted his chin,
opened his mouth and pinched his nose. "Someone pump
his chest!" she ordered before she cupped her mouth over
David's and began her CPR breathing.

Myra straddled David's hips and began aiding Karen in
her efforts. In, out, in, out.

The guys removed their helmets and stood helplessly
watching the gals breathing and pumping over David.
Everyone prayed.

In, out, in, out. They were sweating. In, out,
pounding, in, out. Finally, a response. David wheezed, a
little breath.

They sat up. David coughed, gasped and took several
deep breaths. He wet his lips and his eyes flickered open.
He was going to be all right. Well, at least, he was alive.

David rubbed his face, blinked at them staring down at
him and slowly lifted his upper body to his elbows. "What
happened?" he asked, dazed, looking around.

They smiled, relieved he seemed okay. "You passed
out," Karen said. "We thought you were a goner."

"How do you feel?" Myra asked.

"Okay, I guess," David said, rubbing his head. They
helped him to a sitting position. "How'd I get out here?"

"We carried you," John said. "You collapsed. I'm
sorry, it was just too much." He shrugged.

David looked at the ship. "Did it work? Did she
start?"

All of them shook their heads. "No," John said.

David tried to get to his feet and they helped him. "Damm," he sighed. "Why not? I gave her my best shot." They helped him to the work bench, still a little woozy, he sat. Myra found a clean cloth rag and took it to the restroom to wet it.

"Yeah, we know," John said. "It was a good shot. Couldn't have been better. But, she wouldn't kick over."

"What're you gonna do now?" David asked.

"I don't know," John said. "We wouldn't put either one of you through that again."

"No way," Bryan said. "You were our last hope."

Myra returned with the wet cloth. Karen took it and began to wipe David's face and neck. She checked for burns.

"We can't fly her, she's useless," Boyd said.

"Maybe not," Frank said. "We could call the media. Have 'em come out. Put her on display. Tell all about her."

David laughed. They felt good that he could. "MJ-12 owns the media," he said. "They'd be here first. Cart her away. Us, too. No one would ever be the wiser."

Frank nodded and sighed, "So any suggestions?"

"Well, I might have one," David said. "Might be your only one."

John and Bryan shrugged. "Yeah?" John said. "At the moment, we're open for anything."

"Take her back to the ranch," David said.

"Take her back?!" John snorted. Their prize? Give her up, just like that? Defeated? Who's he kidding?

David shrugged. "You can't fly her. She's useless to you," he reminded. "You've figured a Nefilim flew her here. A god, maybe. You've figured He, or She, probably parked it on the ranch and is somewhere, still in the area. Wouldn't you figure that if He, or She, parked it, He, or She, would come back for it, sometime?"

They mulled the thought as if it had never occurred to them and looked to their leader. John shrugged.

"Take it back to the ranch," David continued. "Put her back right where you found her, and wait for this god to show up. Maybe he'll give you the ride you're trying for.''

They thought about it. It would be tough to give her up.

"What else have you got to do?'' David added. "Maybe you'd get to talk to this Nefilim God. Maybe he'd tell you why he's here, what he's been doing.'' David grinned. "Not many living people have had an audience with a god. I know I'd like to talk to him. Interview Him. I've got some big questions.''

They thought about it. Finally, John sighed and said, "Yeah, I guess you're right. It's the only answer.''

"And MJ-12 wins,'' Bryan said.

"Maybe not,'' David said. "Maybe you win.''

"Will you and Karen go with us?'' John asked.

"If I'm able, I wouldn't miss it for the world,'' David grinned. "But, better do it soon.''

"Yeah, I guess,'' John said. "How about tomorrow?''

David glanced at Karen and they both nodded.

John looked longingly at the ship and sighed. He pulled his gloves back on. "Well, let's button her up.''

Chapter Twenty-Four:
The Call

TAKING THE SHIP BACK to the ranch had never been one of their options. From the day they found her the thought of not succeeding never entered their minds. They hadn't had time for a negative thought. Every failure turned into a success. One after another, as if being led through her mysteries by their faith, they never had a doubt that some day they would fly her.

For over an hour they moved sadly through the painful chore of closing the ship down, letting go of their dream. John and Boyd shut off her power, removed the geiger counter and closed the door ever so carefully as not to slam it shut. There was the possibility they would want to get back inside. They all helped with replacing the hay bales and fake sidings of plywood. Next came the tarp and the ropes lashing her to the trailer.

"Throw the suits on there," John said, as they stood checking for what else they should do. "You never know. We might need them, in case we get that ride."

Those who had taken off their suits, did, and one by one they tossed them under the tarp.

"Fire extinguishes, too," Bryan called.

"Anything else?" Boyd asked, going to the lockers.

They looked around. "No," John said. "Guess that's it. She's ready to go. Boyd, you and Frank go by the rental place in the morning, first thing, pick up the cab. Bryan and I will meet you out here and help you hook up the trailer and see you on your way. I'll make arrangements for an escort to meet you down at the highway." He glanced around at their sad faces. "Guess that's about it."

"Better call the Barretts," Myra said.

"I will," John said. "In the morning."

"I'd like to ask Susan to go with us," Bryan said. "She's writing the book and this would really help her. She knows about everything but the ship."

"Who's Susan?" Boyd asked.

"A friend of ours, and Bryan's," Myra said. "They've been dating. She's met Karen and David."

"Oh," Boyd said. "What kinda book is she writing?"

"About the knowing," Bryan said. He glanced around at them. There were no objections.

John shrugged. "Okay, you gonna tell her?"

Bryan nodded. "But I might need some help. I don't know if she'll believe me, you know, springing this on her after all this time. It'll be quite a shock. I'd like for you and Myra to come along, help me out."

"You mean, take some of the blame?" Myra said. "I know I'd be pretty pissed if you'd been hiding this from me all this time."

Bryan came back with, "We might have to explain to her why we didn't trust her enough to include her in our promise."

Myra smiled as she shook her head.

"Okay," John said, and they moved toward the door. "We'll meet you back at the Mall and follow you over to her place."

John opened the door and the buzzer went off. Karen, David, then the others filed through.

"How're you feeling?" John asked David.

"I'm okay," he said. "A little dizzy, but I'll be okay. I'm sorry I couldn't help you guys start her. But that's the way it goes sometimes, life on Planet Earth."

"That's okay," John said. "You really scared the hell

out of us. We couldn't ask for more than you gave.''

He closed the door and the buzzer stopped.

In the parking lot David offered his van for the trip out to the ranch.

"Frank and Boyd will be driving the truck." David pointed out. "Why don't the rest of us go in my van. It's plenty roomy. We can meet down at the beach, throw our camping gear in back and save taking two, three cars. I even have a lean-to tarp and poles that fits over the open side door.''

It was agreed. No telling how long they might have to wait. Their sudden plans were falling into place as they should.

The ride back to the Mall was somber, to say the least. David tried to make light of the incident. "I think it's great that you guys even had a chance at flying her," he said. "Not many people have even seen one, much less, been in one and try to start her up. That's fantastic! I love it!'' He yelped and slapped the back of the seat. He seemed to be recovering nicely from his ordeal. Back to his old feisty self.

"Yeah, flying her would've been great," Bryan sighed. "But exposing MJ-12 would've been greater.''

"True," David said. "I know what you mean. Maybe it's best it happened this way. You could've gotten everyone killed.''

In the Mall's near-empty parking lot, Bryan let Karen and David out at Karen's car. Agreeing to meet around ten or eleven the next morning, he drove on to the other side of the lot.

Going around to the driver's side, David spotted the rookie agents' car in a dark, secluded corner of the lot. He got in, started the car, wheeled it around so as his head-lights swept across them as they ducked. They pulled in close behind, determined not to lose him in the light traffic. Their car lights didn't come on until they hit the street.

Smart move, David thought, smiling at his rear view mirror. No need to attract attention in an empty lot.

John and Myra waited in their car while Bryan found a phone and called Susan. She was still up. Bryan made it short as he could. "John, Myra and I need to come by and tell you something," he said. "It won't take long."

"Well, what is it?" she wondered, picturing all kinds of crazy things.

"It's too long a story to tell you over the phone," he said. "We'll tell you when we get there. All I can say is it has something to do with the book. We'll be there in about twenty minutes."

Susan put on her tea pot and wondered, *the book?*

DAVID HAD THE LITTLE sports car up to seventy-five down the freeway. He glanced in the rear view mirror every time he upped it another five. The rookies were keeping pace. At that hour of night there would be state troopers every five miles on both sides of I-45. Many of them lived in the area and they liked pulling late duty close to home. Racing on their turf got their temper up, their adrenalin flowing. David knew they had a way; first unit would catch the one in back, second unit got the one in front. David wondered how the rookies would explain their caper.

Karen glanced around at the freeway lights whipping by and leaned toward the speedometer. "What's your hurry?" she asked.

David smiled. "Nothing," he shrugged. "I was all set for a space ride, tonight. Weren't you?"

She just looked at him.

"Thought, maybe, I'd make up for it."

The speedometer needle was pushing ninety. Karen had a fleeting thought that he intended on making her little car fly, levitate. She wondered if he could do that. She hoped not. But asking him not to only made him try harder.

It was the challenge of the thing. She watched him carefully before she said, "You know, Bryan and John have this . . . suspicion, you were, or are somehow connected to, the Nefilim god who owns that ship."

He let off on the accelerator and grinned at the freeway ahead. "Yeah?" he said, and looked at her, still grinning. No big news. "I guess we put that notion to rest, eh?"

"We?"

"They tried you, too. Remember?"

"But I never gave them any reason to suspect me."

"You didn't?" David laughed. "You flew with the Nefilim. You had all the knowledge, the powers of your knowing. You would've been my first choice if I had a ship without a pilot."

She shot him a glance. "I *know* I'm not an alien."

He grinned. "Neither am I. Even if I have to die to prove it." He looked at her. "Hon, if our forefathers came from another planet, to some degree, I'd say we're all aliens."

Karen sighed and looked into the night. "You really think there's a Nefilim god out there somewhere?"

He shrugged at the road, the lights from the rear view mirror across his face. "It's nice to think there is."

"They were so disappointed," she said. "If there's a god out there, I hope he shows up."

"Yeah, that'd be something." He reached over and took her hand. "You know Bryan's in love with you."

She looked at him, the lights of the rookie's car strong on the side of her face, dash lights soft on the other. "Does it show?"

"Uh huh."

"It's his fascination with a perfect relationship."

"Do you love him?"

"I'd like to help him, but I don't know how."

"You didn't answer the question."

"I thought I did."

"Then, do you love me?"

She searched her feelings. "Yes," she said, squeezing his hand. "I never felt it more than when I thought I had lost you tonight."

She leaned on the shift console and they kissed, softly, with strong feelings. The car's tires rat-a-tat-tated on the lane reflectors. She hugged him as he swerved back. He glanced at the rookies in his rear view mirror. He wondered how they liked their night so far.

They drove on into the night.

SUSAN POURED HOT WATER over tea bags in four cups. "I can't imagine what it is you wanna tell me. Must be important though."

"It is," Bryan said.

"Well, tell me," she said, bringing two cups to the table. "I can't wait." She set the cups in front of Myra and John.

"It's about a, about a trip," Bryan said. "A trip we're going on tomorrow, and we wanted to know if you would like to go."

"A trip?" Susan said, going back for two more cups. "What kind of trip? On the boat?" She had thoughts of visiting ancient places again.

"No, not the boat," Bryan said. "This is a special trip. That's why we thought it would take all three of us to explain."

"Oh, my goodness," Susan said. She set a cup in front of Bryan and one at her place.

"But before we get to the trip," Bryan said. "There's something else we need to tell you that will explain the whole thing. Sort of, you know, bring you up to speed."

Bryan started from the beginning, with John and Myra jumping in as the story unfolded. They told how they found the space craft last October, hid it away in the old storage building and had been trying to fly it ever since;

how they discovered it was a Nefilim ship and that they suspected the Nefilim, maybe one of the gods, was somewhere in the area. And the part about Karen's experience and how they had hoped she could help them start the ship, and then David's try that very night, only hours ago.

Susan didn't say a word through the whole story. Stunned, she tried assimilating the plots and characters the best she could. She nodded here and there and said, "Uh huh," and gasped "Oh, no!" a few times to let them know she was getting the picture. Knowing the *Earth Chronicles*, Karen and David and MJ-12 as she did, made the reality of the ship more believable than if she didn't. Whenever one of them paused to sip tea, so did Susan. And then another would take up the story.

"So, tonight," Bryan said, after his last swallow, "after David's try, we decided the only thing left for us to do was take the ship back to the ranch, where we found it, and wait, in the hopes that the Nefilim god will return and take his ship, and that we could talk to him, and maybe he would give us a ride, a trip, so to speak."

End of story. Susan stared at them. Bryan smiled. "We're taking the ship back in the morning," he said. "And we want you to come along."

"You're serious?" Susan said. "You have a Nefilim ship?"

They nodded. "Yes," Bryan shrugged. "That's what we said."

"And a Nefilim god is out there, waiting for its return?"

"Yes, so we think."

"You don't have to go if you don't want to," Myra said.

Susan studied them, and then her cup, as she turned it in her hands. What an incredible story, she thought, almost the same scenario as she had devised for the book. She looked at Bryan. "That was almost the exact plots I told you the other night," she said. "Why didn't you tell me about the ship then?"

Bryan shrugged. "I wanted to, but I couldn't," he said. "Not without the others' permission. We all had promised."

"The fewer who knew, the better," John said.

"It's not something you go around telling just anybody," Myra said. "We had to see how you would take everything, the knowing. Not everyone can, you know."

Susan nodded and shrugged. "True."

"But you were fast. Faster than anyone I've ever known," Bryan said. "Faster than John and Myra even."

"Could I see the ship, now?" Susan asked.

Bryan glanced at John and Myra. "You could, I guess," he said. "But it's covered, on the truck, wrapped and ready to go."

"You can see it tomorrow," Myra said. "Plenty of time."

"Are Karen and David going?"

"Yes," Bryan said. "We're going in David's van. We're to meet them at the beach tomorrow morning, after the truck and ship are on their way."

All the time she had been asking questions she had been weighing the odds. "You know," she said. "This is scary. Real scary. If what you say is true, you have a Nefilim ship, and there's a Nefilim god walking around out there looking for it, and that it's true these gods were our Creators, then what we're talking about here is, we're going to meet — God. Right? We're bringing His ship back, and He's going to be so happy to get it back that He's going to give us a joy ride?"

"Something like that, yes."

"And what if He doesn't?" Susan asked. "What if He kicks our butts for running off with His ship in the first place? You stole His ship!"

"Well," Bryan muttered. "We, uh . . ."

"Never thought about that, did you?" Susan said.

"We'll just tell Him it was a mistake," Myra said.

"As if stealing wasn't one of this God's commandments."

Myra added, "We'll say we didn't know it was His until we opened it up."

"He could just zap us," Susan said. "Take His ship and get the hell out of Dodge. What are we to this God? Nothing. It says in the books, we're nothing. Diluted beings."

John shrugged. "What can we say? Life's a risk."

"Think what you'll be missing if you don't go," Myra said.

"It'll mean everything to your, our, book if we get His story first hand," Bryan said.

"Let's say this god does take us for a ride." Susan mused. "Will he take us out of our bodies, like they did Karen?"

"We don't know," Bryan said. "We're taking heat suits for everyone, just in case he doesn't."

"Heat suits?"

"Those aluminum fire suits."

"Ummm," Susan mused. "You've thought of everything, haven't you?"

"We hope so."

Susan thought about it as she studied their faces. "Okay," she said, finally, sighing deeply. "Sounds crazy, but I wanna go. How could I not? Think of the paper I could write on what I did on my summer vacation. But, you have to promise me one thing."

Bryan grinned. "What's that?"

"That you'll make it perfectly clear to this god that I had nothing to do with stealing his ship. I'm just along for the ride."

Chapter Twenty-Five:
The Return

BEFORE MYRA AND JOHN LEFT, plans for the weekend camp out had been made. Everyone would take a change of clothes. There were facilities at the ranch house; it wasn't as if they would be isolated, they would be only an hour's drive from home. They could pick up food, drinks and ice on the way out. Two ice chests, two card tables and folding patio chairs finished out their to-do lists.

By the time they were leaving Susan's, satisfied they had thought of every conceivable detail and their plan was now moving along, another meeting atop a Galveston high-rise hotel began to gather slowly emerging details for a counter plan.

General Fuller strode from his fancy penthouse suite into the adjoining informal conference room. He wore Air Force blue slacks and a short-sleeve open-collar shirt. Four embroidered gold stars lined each collar. He carried a stack of eight-by-ten's and his unlit cigar between his fingers. A stern Gayland Harwell, Texas' senior Senator, in an expensive custom pinstripe suit, stood at the table. Around Harwell, General Rawling, as casually attired as Fuller, lounged in a side chair. Three Delta Force officers in dark black uniforms were at their scattered posts and the Master Sergeant mixed drinks at the bar.

"Sorry to take you away from your fancy dinner, Senator," Fuller growled, as he approached the table. "But, I think I have something here you're gonna find real interesting." He tossed the telephotos of David on the table and the stack slid to a stop in front of Harwell. The old Senator looked put out, the indignity of being ordered by the General to report to his quarters was more than his ego could handle. But MJ-12 ruled and when MJ-12 said jump, you jumped, or else you'd never have the chance to jump again. Reluctantly, he picked up the photos and began shuffling through them, stopping and studying each one. "See anyone you recognize there, Senator?" Fuller gloated. He stuck his cigar in his mouth, clasped his hands behind his back and waited, smugly rolling and chewing his cigar.

Harwell looked at every picture and dropped them back on the table. He looked at Fuller and shrugged, unimpressed. "Rodriguez," he stated.

Fuller removed his cigar, smiled and said, "I thought you would."

"So?"

"We took those pictures last week."

Harwell glanced down at the pictures again, then back at Fuller. The General wasn't smiling. "Impossible!" Harwell gasped. The thought of incompetence being piled onto his contempt for the General and MJ-12 was more than he could take. When would the deceit ever stop? How could he ever get out? Please let it be soon, he prayed, God help us. "How? Where?"

"He's very much alive, Senator."

A cellular phone rang and Rawlins answered it.

"I saw him dead, I saw pictures," Harwell said, covering his disgust for the ordered deed. "They tossed his body down an old well, somewhere."

"Your boys put one over on you, Senator. He's living with his girlfriend out there on West Beach. And he's hooked up with some people who're pissing in our pond."

"I don't see how he could still be alive. Uh, uh, I don't understand. We haven't heard anything out of him since that night."

"Well, we have now, Senator, and I don't like being made a fool of," Fuller growled. Rawlins approached with the cellular, motioning that there was a serious message on the line. Fuller picked up the stack of photos and shoved them at Harwell. "I don't want to hear any excuses about how you screwed up, Senator. Take those photos to your boys and see if they can do the job right this time. Have a good evening."

Fuller took the phone as Harwell gathered the photos and was escorted to the door by one of the Delta Force officers. "And, Senator," Fuller called, stopping Harwell at the door, "if Rodriguez did, in fact, return from the dead, I would appreciate your letting me know how he did it. That little trick might come in handy someday." Fuller laughed.

Harwell glared at him, turned and was let out the door.

The General turned his attention to the phone. "Yeah," he said, and listened. In a minute his brow pinched into a frown. "Jesus Christ!" he growled. "Yes, it's important! How long were they gone?" He listened, his eyes angry and pensive. "Stay there and don't let him out of your sight again. I'm sending a relief." Fuller slammed the phone down and glared at a waiting Rawlins. "Rodriguez and his girlfriend shook 'em at the Mall after meeting up with Mayfield. They were gone somewhere for three fuggin' hours before Mayfield brought 'em back. Something's going on." He nodded at two of the Delta Force officers. "Get out there and relieve those two. And I want you to report in every time he makes a move." The officers turned on their heels and were out the door. Fuller looked at Rawlins. "When they get back here, I want them on Sherman and Mayfield, round the clock. Something's coming down. You can bet on it."

SUSAN KEPT BRYAN UP for hours talking about the ship. She wanted to know how it felt to be inside, touching and handling something from another planet, from another civilization so far away. She wanted to know what sort of things they could ask the Nefilim god, in case he did showed up. Tops on Bryan's list was, why he was here and where had he been? A feeling Bryan couldn't share with her was his overwhelming disappointment in not being able to fly the ship and then having to let it go. Deep inside he was hoping the Nefilim wouldn't show up and that they could keep the ship and keep trying. He had to deal with the thought that they might not ever get another chance such as this.

"Now that I know about the ship," Susan said, adjusting her tape recorder between the fresh cups of tea on the breakfast table. "I want to know everything about it. As much as you, John, and Myra know."

"Such as?" Bryan said, squeezing his tea bag dry.

"Everything. What makes it go? How does it travel so fast? The working parts. You must know that? What made you all believe Karen and David could start it and you couldn't?" She test sipped her tea. "You know, things like that."

Bryan cautiously sipped his tea while he studied her and thought about what, how much, to tell her. He nodded. "Okay. How much do you know about physics?" He hoped she'd say not much at all and that would be the end of it.

She shrugged. "Not the greatest."

"It could get complicated."

She nodded at the recorder. "Simplify it for our book, okay? Pretend I just graduated from grammar school."

"Okay," he mused, arranging his thoughts. "Let's start with dimensions and gravity. Here on Earth we live in three dimensions. But Einstein discovered that the universe is made up of other dimensions, a fourth and a fifth, and other gravity forces. It was his unified fields theory. And once scientist got through that they discovered that there might be even more dimensions, if you believe in the String

Theory, there might be as many as ten, or more."

"What's the String Theory?"

"That's the Theory of Everything," he shrugged. "It's what is believed to be the knowing of energy forces that make up mass, and then matter. If you think the atom is small, think about what makes up an atom, and then what's inside them."

"Explain. Simply."

She watched him study the tea in his cup, then, "First you have mass, then you have matter. Mass is the infinitesimal particles that make up an atom; protons, electrons, neutrons. And then these atoms are what makes matter. The small gravity force that holds mass together is called subatomic, or the strong forces. To simplify, we'll call this force gravity A. The gravity force that holds matter, atoms, together is the big gravity wave that holds planets, stars, and galaxies together. It's not as strong as A. We can break this force with rocket thrust, or jumping up and down, so we'll call this force gravity B, or the weak force. Now, the String Theory takes in all those gravity dimensions that hold protons, electrons and neutrons together. But we won't get into that since we don't know that much about them. The problem we have is that we haven't even been able to access gravity A, yet. The aliens have. They have the power source to do that, we don't.

"And that's the difference between the aliens and us; their ability to access gravity A, and maybe the other smaller ones. It's easy for them since they live in star systems and galaxies where those dimensions are an everyday thing, like three dimensions are to us. Everything beyond three dimensions is a mystery to us. And this's why it's hard for us to understand time travel within the gravity wave, which is basically gravity A. The problem; we humans haven't been able to generate enough power to access and amplify gravity A. We've done pretty good accessing gravity B, the atoms, with the heaviest element we've found here, uranium, that we've generated to plutonium with the use of a collider at Oak Ridge, Tennessee.''

"The Atom Bomb?'' she said.

"Right. And since then we've been able to create elements through bombarding the uranium as heavy as 111 and still keep them stable. We know that the aliens use a fuel as heavy as element 115 to access gravity A. It's the fuel on the Zeta ships MJ-12 has at Groom Lake, and it's the fuel on the Nefilim ship we have. MJ-12 was about to create their own element 115 in that SuperCollider outside of Dallas until Congress cut off their funding because MJ-12 wouldn't truthfully explain just what it was they wanted it for.

"If we had the power to access gravity A, we could get beyond the dimensional perimeters of the atom and amplify a force that would allow us to access the gravity wave within the electromagnetic fields. With this power we could distort time and space as the aliens do. We wouldn't have to travel a straight line from point A to point B, which would be traveling by light years. We could just program a point in time/space, push the power and be there. Across the universe in a minute.

"That's about it. We have a ship that has the fuel, element 115, the reactors and the gravity amplifiers to access the wave, but we couldn't find the spark that would kick on the reactors. Seems as if it takes the spiritual energy of our creators to do that. We thought David had released his energy, powerful enough to be that spark, but as it turned out, he wasn't.''

"What made you think David was the one?''

"Because of what he was capable of doing, accessing other dimensions, creating the holography with his consciousness.''

"Explain.'' Susan said.

"Well, it works a lot like the ship's power of accessing

the dimensions of gravity A. Think of our spiritual energy being the power to be amplified to access other dimensions beyond our normal three dimensions. Let's say, the dimensions of the time/space consciousness. But the thing that keeps us from accessing our true power is our egos. Once we get our egos out of the way, putting our power-draining earth conscious illusions in their rightful place, then we'll have access to our true spiritual powers. David seemed to have become more than proficient at doing this, as you witnessed. The aliens, just as their ships, have the power, spiritual energy, to access these dimensions. The Nefilim have it, and Enki passed it on to us, although diluted from the maternal side, it's still quite strong. Stronger than our ego wants us to believe.

"I believe the Nefilim, Enki probably, in another of His efforts to prove our worth, channeled the texts of A *Course in Miracles* to help us understand separating our ego from our spiritual energy and get back to our powers; though somewhat limited in their dilution. David, with his demonstrations of accessing other dimensions of consciousness, seemed to have the ability to span this dilution, and almost reaching full power by combining multiple energies.

"The Zetas, as a dying race, are in search of this energy that they are losing through cloning. They've found it in us and are trying to get it back through procreation. But thanks to Enki's DNA block, they haven't succeeded. However, in their experimental processes the Zetas are creating a lot of communicable diseases by destroying our DNA immune systems."

Bryan took the last swallow of his tea. "That's about it," he said. "Simple enough?"

"Whew!" Susan sighed. "You were right, that's pretty heavy." Missy jumped up in her lap. Susan hugged her close and cuddled her soft fur.

"It'll give you some idea of what you're looking at when you see the ship tomorrow."

"I've never had any idea that life was this expansive."

"Under the control of ego illusions, no one does."

"And tomorrow we're going to meet one of these Nefilim gods, one of our creators."

"Possibly. Maybe Enki."

"He must be pretty old."

"There's not much aging beyond gravity B."

She ruffled Missy's fur and looked up at him. "I knew from the from the very first," she said, "that knowing you was going to be a real trip. But, I had no idea." She held Missy up, looked her in the eyes and smoothed her fur and ears back. Missy blinked at her. "Know what, Missy?" she said. "I don't think we're in Texas anymore."

JOHN AND MYRA EXHAUSTED themselves with preparations. They had their car packed before they fell into bed, ready to go at the break of dawn.

Frank and Boyd awoke several times during the early morning hours and paced. They talked about it on their way to pick up the rental cab. Neither's rousing had awakened their wives, and their excuses for their early departures on a Saturday morning were the same; they were going to an air show in Harlingen for the weekend. Both wives had barely managed a sleepy hug, kiss and mumbled well wishes before turning over and going back to their interrupted dreams. Boyd and Frank were home free.

They arrived at the truck rental office ten minutes before the sun and the manager, who eventually checked them out in a lemon-yellow, cab over, diesel rig exactly like the one they had rented the past October.

John and Myra were waiting at the Mall when Frank and Boyd roared by. They waved and pulled in behind the cab. After they passed the Texaco just up 528 from the Mall, the rookie agents, following the General's executive orders not to let John Sherman out of their sight, fell in line at a safe, but secure distance. The passenger agent reported their movement to the General's hotel suite on his cellular phone.

At the oil field road turnoff, the agents fell back and watched the truck and car cross the open field before pulling in themselves and reporting their whereabouts. As they drove slowly over the rough road, keeping the truck and car's dust in sight, they decided the road was a one way in and one way out, and they were in the tunnel.

Carefully watching for a return dust cloud, they crept along the narrowing road, over a hill, through some trees and stopped. The truck and Sherman's car were parked at the side of an old tool shed. The truck was backed up to big open doors and the subjects were bustling around inside with the drivers of the truck. The rookies backed up, pulled off the road, hiding their car behind a thick growth of bushes and made their report. They were told to get in closer and find out what was going on.

On foot, the rookies, with binoculars and cellular phone, sneaked in the high grass around to the other side of the shed and a better view. The subjects, Sherman, Bennett and the two men from the truck, they reported, were in the building clearing tables, boxes, lights, cables, cords and whatever away from around a trailer — they were preparing to hook onto the cab.

"What's on the trailer?" they were asked.

"It's covered with a tarpaulin and roped down," they relayed. "It's a weird shape, flat, peaked and rounded. It hangs over the trailer's width by about five or six feet."

"How tall is it?"

"About twelve, fifteen feet. They're backing the cab into the shed and locking onto the trailer. It's locked on. They're hooking cables and raising the knees. The driver's easing the trailer out through the doors. Its top and sides are just barely clearing."

"Can you tell any better what it is?"

"No. They're attaching WIDE LOAD signs to the front and back. They're talking. Sherman's showing the drivers some papers, maps, maybe. The two guys are getting back in the cab, waving, they're pulling the truck onto the road.'' The rookies had to shout into the phone as the truck roared within twenty feet of their position. ''. . . through the trees, heading back toward the main road. Sherman and Bennett are closing the doors and getting into their car.''

"Stick with them,'' the General ordered, ''And keep trying to see what's on that trailer.''

The agents scurried back to their car and followed the dust trail down the road. Even with the dust cover they kept their distance. Above the field weeds at the junction of the old oil road and FM 1462, they saw the truck and Sherman's car stop.

"They're picking up a trooper escort,'' the rookies reported. ''The trooper's leading the truck west on 1462. Sherman and Bennett are heading back toward Alvin.''

"Stick with the truck,'' they were ordered. ''Report its every move, and let us know the minute you know what's on that trailer.''

GENERAL FULLER CLICKED OFF his cellular phone and dropped it to his side. He stood at the large expanse of windows facing the Gulf, staring blankly down at the Saturday morning activity on the beach front, contemplating, figuring, ''They've got something, twenty feet by fifteen feet, sort of flat, peaked and round, on a trailer, heading west,'' he mused to the glass. He frowned at Rawlins, who shook his head. ''Sherman's heading back to Clear Lake. Why?'' Fuller asked himself. A thought came to him and he raised the phone and punched in a number.

Fuller got an answer. ''What's Rodriguez doing?'' he asked.

"Not much,'' the Delta Force officer reported. ''He and his girlfriend are packing stuff in their van, like they might be going on a trip.''

"What kind of stuff? Luggage?"

"Coolers, deck chairs, blankets," the officer said, "picnic, camping out stuff."

"Get back to me the minute he moves," Fuller ordered and clicked off. He glared at Rawlins. "Think, Walt. Think!" he growled. "They're up to something. What? Damn it! They're not gonna outsmart us, no way!"

"We could stop the truck, see what's on it," Rawlins said.

"Too late. It's out in the open. We can't have any scenes we can't logically explain. Not now. Saturday, on those roads. The locals would be all over us. They're trucking whatever it is someplace, that's where we'll take it." Fuller paced, tapping the cellular against his leg as he thought. "But we might need the Force. Where's that map?"

The third Delta Force officer scrambled up a Texas map from a briefcase and spread it across the conference table.

Fuller and Rawlins leaned over the map. Fuller's finger found FM 1462 and traced it west. His finger dropped down to West Beach, then up to Clear Lake. "All six of them were on the boat," Fuller mused. "Where's Mayfield and that school teacher?"

"Clear Lake." Rawlins said.

"Sherman didn't follow the truck, because he and Bennett are going to pick up Mayfield and the teacher," Fuller mused. His finger traced the freeway back down to West Beach. "They're then going to pick up the other two at the beach . . ." his finger traced the San Luis Pass Road through Surfside and Freeport and up Texas 36 to West Columbia and 1462. ". . . and they're going to meet up with the truck, somewhere out here." He stood, stared at the map and rubbed his chin. "Why?" he muttered. "What's on that truck?"

Rawlins brightened with a thought. "I think we're overlooking the obvious here," he said. He went to a stack of papers on a couch and began rifling, hunting through them. "What is it they're in to?" He finally found what he was looking for, pulled it and studied the printed report. "Space ships, aliens," he muttered, as he came back to the table and handed the report to Fuller. "Same as us."

Fuller looked at the report; printouts of electromagnetic pulse disturbances in the Southeast Texas area for the past six weeks. These reports were funneled back and forth between local scientists on the info highway as a matter of interest in their atmospheric studies. The pulse information always accompanied sightings of atomic powered space craft. MJ-12 had been checking their own worldwide sources against the locals ever since the pulse detectors had been invented.

"Look at the past two weeks," Rawlins pointed out. "There are several extended maximum-gauss and one mega-gauss. Look at the date and time of the mega-gauss." Fuller was looking. "Last night, during the hours Rodriguez and the others were missing."

Fuller's eyes popped open and he stared at Rawlins, both realizing the same answer. "They were in that tool shed," Fuller said. "Revving up an atomic engine! Son-of-a-bitch!" he growled. "They have a fuggin' space ship on that truck!"

"I remembered that report coming in this morning."

"Where the hell'd they get a space ship?" Fuller snorted. His teeth clinched hard on his cigar.

"Maybe they built it."

"Bullshit!" Fuller growled. "With an atomic engine? Come on, Walt! We can't do that even from an original model," Fuller paced and chewed his cigar, "Where're they taking it?" He grabbed his cellular phone and punched in the number of the rookie agents with the truck.

"Somewhere to fly it," Rawlins said. "They tested the engine and now they're taking it somewhere to fly it, away from the city.''

"Fly it? Where?'' Fuller bellowed at his Gulf view and
the ringing phone. He got an answer. "Where are you?''
he asked the answering agent. The answer was, three
hundred yards behind the truck and still on 1462. "Does
that thing on the truck look like it could be a space ship
under that tarp?''

The rookie wondered if the General was serious and
said, "Space ship, sir?''

The rookie's puzzled query made Fuller think. Crap,
those two have never seen a space ship, "Stick with the
Truck,'' Fuller ordered. "Report any direction change, and
whatever you do, don't blow your cover.'' He clicked off
and looked at Rawlins and the Delta Force officer. "Pack
it up,'' he said. "Let's get out to the plane and get a
tactical unit in here to clean this up.''

JOHN AND MYRA HELPED Susan and Bryan load
their overnight gear into John's car. John stowed sleeping
bags and folding chairs and stopped when he saw Susan
holding an electric fan in one hand and a bug zapper in the
other.

"Where you gonna plug those in?'' John asked.

Susan shrugged. "Can we take 'em, just in case we find
a place? Maybe David has one of those cigarette lighter
plugs.''

"We've got some bug spray,'' Myra said.

"I hate that stuff,'' Susan frowned. "It's so messy.''

"We have a yellow light Coleman,'' Myra said. "Maybe
they'll hang around that.''

They found a place for everything identified as a
necessity, Myra's cameras being the tops on her list, piled
into John's car and headed down the freeway to Galveston.

"What did the Barretts say about us bringing the ship
back?'' Bryan asked John.

"They were surprised,'' John said. "I had to tell them

what we were going to do. They thought it was kind of strange, but I think they accepted it. Roland said he could find something for his hired hands to do away for a few days, but after that, he didn't know. Goes into next week, we'll have trouble keeping it a secret.''

It was eleven and after when they rolled into Karen's drive. Karen and David were waiting and they were glad to see that David was no worse for the wear. They quickly transferred the gear from John's car into David's van as neatly as possible. Inside, there were four cushy swivel seats behind the driver and passenger seats. They packed the bench seat and storage space in back and what couldn't fit inside they tied to the rack on top.

David had noticed the change in agents early that morning and wondered why the need. Had MJ-12 gotten on to what they were doing? Could that be why they hadn't taken him before? They knew about the ship? He casually took notice of the road behind the others after they arrived. They were not being followed. It was just he alone and he was about to lead MJ-12 to the ship this time.

"Trying to start that space ship must've really been something," Susan said to Karen and David as they packed the van. "What'd it feel like? I mean, I can't imagine."

David shrugged as he thought. "You could say," he smiled, "it was an experience like no other on Earth."

"You think that God's gonna show up tonight?" Susan asked, looking for what she considered an expert opinion.

"I think He'd better," David said to lashing a rope around the folding lawn furniture atop the van. "If he wants His ship back? Now's the time."

Finally packed and with everyone settled into their chosen seats, David drove to the main beach road and as close the watching agents' car as he could. David noticed that John and Bryan seemed to be oblivious to the agents watching. But David got a good look, as did the agents. Those guys look tough, he thought, no need alarming the others, might as well let it be, what happens, happens.

GENERAL FULLER LISTENED TO his cellular as he gazed blankly out his rear window at the passing landscape along I-45. "Keep on 'em," he said into the phone, clicked it off and looked at Rawlins, riding across from him. They wore their uniforms again, rolling up the freeway in their staff car with the Sergeant Major driver and DF officer in the front seat. "The truck turned south on 36," a pensive Fuller said. "Where'd they get a space ship?"

"Let's look at the facts, as we know them," Rawlins said. "The craft has an atomic engine, they revved it. Obviously, they didn't build it, so it has to be alien. Since it passed through the network without detection, it belongs to those who have access to the time portals. They're trucking it because they can't fly it. Where, we don't know, yet, but away from the city. Who's involved? Four people who know more about our operation than we care to have known. They're a threat to our National Security and qualify for elimination as subversives. Two of them were involved in tagging one of our SDI satellites." Rawlins paused, studying Fuller, thinking that he might realize. Fuller stared, trying to get the point. "Cal," Rawlins continued, "you're so pissed at them for having an alien craft you can't see what they're up to. If they get that craft flying, they're going after the satellite."

Fuller saw the picture and his jaw dropped. "Those sons-of-a-bitches!" he gasped. "Those bastards!" he growled. "I'll kill every fuggin' one of them this time myself!"

Fuller's cellular rang. He answered it, "Yeah?" he hissed, and he listened, this time studying the floor mats. "Stick with 'em," he said, clicked off and looked at Rawlins. "They went to the beach, just like I figured," he said. "Loaded Rodriguez's van with camping, picnic stuff and headed west, toward the truck." Fuller frowned. "Camping stuff? What's that?"

"Hmmm? Camping?" Rawlins mused. "Gimme a minute."

"YOU THINK THIS NEFILIM who flew the ship here is a god?" Susan asked David. She was sitting in the seat behind him.

"Probably one of the gods," David said.

"Not one of the Anunnaki?" Susan asked. "One of His angels, with a message?"

"No, I wouldn't think so," David said to the road in front.

"How long do you think we'll have to wait?" Susan asked.

"Not long," David said. "Maybe no longer than tonight." He was thinking about how fast it would take MJ-12 to be on top of them after the agents following them saw the craft.

"Then you think He's somewhere around here, close?" Susan asked, glancing out the big window beside her chair.

"He probably hasn't been too far from that ship since He's been here. He probably knows exactly where it is right now."

"A Nefilim god wouldn't be hard to spot," Myra said. "Why haven't we seen him?"

"The Nefilim gods have super powers we don't understand," David said. "They can take many forms."

"That's what I thought," Myra said.

At the toll booth atop the San Luis Pass Bridge, David got a good look at the agents' car in the van's side mirrors. They were four cars back, behind a pickup towing a small Chriscraft. The beaches around the pass were crowded with families, fishing, swimming and picnicking. He had been down the road many times and couldn't think of a place he could shake the agents. They looked experienced; there was no way he could lose them with a van full of people.

"What if He's already at the ranch when Boyd and Frank get there," Myra said. "Kicks their butts, jumps in his ship and takes off before we get there?"

They laughed at her visual scenario, but not for long.

"I wouldn't want to be in their shoes," John said. "Wonder if Frank and Boyd have thought about that?"

"What if He takes them for a ride instead?" Susan said.

Myra laughed. "I doubt even a god could put up with their arguing over who gets to drive."

White letters on a green road sign stated they were coming to the cutoff to 288 and Clute. Clute was toward Angleton.

"Let's go on to Freeport," John said. "We'll catch 36 over to West Columbia. I can take over the driving from there. The ranch is only about five, six miles west."

David nodded. "Okay," he said. "What say we stop in West Columbia for supplies and a bite to eat?"

THE GENERALS' STAFF CAR wheeled into the Ellington Field entrance and motored down the main boulevard and through an office park of big name aircraft and air cargo support companies. The once busy Air Force Base was an early victim of military budget cuts, but its long runways and limited flying facilities were turned over to the Texas Air National Guard, NASA and a few cargo lines. The car sped along through the warehouses and out onto the runway apron. A couple of 727s, a DC-3 and several T33s with NASA markings were parked in front of a group of NASA hangars at one end of the field. On a far runway, a group of Guard F-16s were logging weekend hours practicing take-offs, maneuvering exercises over the Gulf and landings.

The staff car screeched to a stop in front of a hanger housing an Air Force jet. Fuller, Rawlins and the DF officer

piled out of the car and were met by the plane's DF crew.
Fuller ordered lunch before he stormed onto his jet. They
were barely inside when his cellular phone rang. He
ordered the DF officer to get the Groom Lake S-4 on the
radio before he answered. He listened, while in the front of
the plane the DF officer, in a headset and mike, was
calling: "Mother Goose, this is Ugly Duckling. Do you
read? Over."

"Stick with 'em," Fuller said into the cellular and
clicked it off. He looked at Rawlins seated across from
him in the plane's command area. "The truck's heading
west again, on 35."

"Ugly Duckling, this is Mother Goose, copy," the radio
squawked.

Fuller went forward and took the headset and mike.
"Mother Goose, this is Papa Bear," he said. "We have a
bone for Grimm to pick up at our house, on a run. We'll
wait on our porch."

"Grimm is on the run, Papa Bear. ETA 2100. Over
and out."

Fuller strolled back down the aisle unbuttoning his
jacket. "Tell 'em to boost the air in here," he ordered out
the door. "We're gonna be here awhile." He tossed his
jacket over a seat, loosened his tie and dropped down into
a plush lounge chair. His face was red and moist and sweat
rings darkened his armpits. He looked at Rawlins, who was
removing his jacket and pulling at his tie. "You figured
out why they're going camping with the space ship, yet?"
he asked.

"Maybe," Rawlins shrugged.

"Try me."

Rawlins rocked in his plush swivel chair while he
summoned his thoughts. "Okay," he said. "What if you
had an alien space craft you couldn't fly?"

Fuller snorted. "Got plenty of those."

"That's right," Rawlins smiled. "And what did we do?

We got the aliens to show us how to fly 'em. Right? And that's what they're going to do.''

"Where're they gonna find an alien? In the boonies?''

Rawlins shrugged and threw up his hands. ''Could be that's where they found the craft,'' he said. ''If there were no bodies, maybe they're thinking the alien, or aliens, are still in the area, looking for their ship?''

Fuller studied him through narrowed eyes. ''That's so far out, Walt,'' he said, ''you just might be right on.''

SIX MILES WEST OF West Columbia Boyd slowed the truck. They passed a road sign that said: OLD OCEAN 2, VAN VLECK 12. Their trooper escort, watching his side mirrors, slowed, too. About two hundred yards on, Boyd and Frank recognized the Barrett ranch entrances. The truck's air brakes squeaked and hissed as they eased into a turn and came to a stop over the culverted bridge that led to the ranch's cattle gate. The highway patrolman circled his bike, parked behind them and approached the cab on foot. Boyd opened his door.

"This it?'' the cop asked, as he pulled papers from his jacket.

Boyd nodded. ''Yeah. Thanks. You were all right.'' Boyd took the papers, signed them and handed them back. Behind them on the road the rookie agents' car passed by.

The cop folded the papers back into his pocket. ''Thanks,'' he smiled. ''You guys be careful, and have a nice day.'' He looked at the load one more time as had walked back to his cycle. ''Cattle tank, eh,'' he said to the overhang and shook his head. Pulling the big gate open, Frank glanced at the law roaring back down the road to West Columbia. Boyd geared the truck and drove through and Frank closed the gate.

Roland Barrett stood on his front porch and waved, flagging the truck and its curious cargo around the house and on down to the barns. Ethel watched from behind a half-opened screen door. Dismayed, but somewhat excited, Roland stepped off his porch, hopped behind the wheel of his pickup and followed.

Boyd stopped the truck just beyond the barns and leaned out the window. Roland pulled up beside them in the settling dust.

"Hey, Roland!" Boyd waved. "How ya doing?"

"Ya gonna put it back in the same place?" Roland shouted over the idling diesel.

"Yeah," Boyd nodded.

"Ya want me to load the stuff on the hay wagon and follow you down?"

"Is it muddy?" Boyd shouted.

"Naw. Dry as a bone," answered Roland.

"Think we can get the truck across the gully?"

"Might give it a try."

"Let's go take a look. Lead the way."

Roland pulled his old pickup around them and headed across the open pasture. Boyd threw the truck into her pulling gears and tried to keep up with the old man. The stack pipe blew a cloud of black smoke. They watched the loose equipment in the back of Roland's truck, a roll of wire, a box of tools, a bucket and a spare tire, bounce up and down and side to side. The big truck rocked and rolled, slowly grinding brush and weeds under its many wheels. Through the rear mirrors and window, Frank watched the ship ride easy straining against her ropes.

Back on the main road, the rookie agents had circled back and were parked on the side of the road, half a mile west of the ranch's entrances. Their binoculars were trained on the two-truck convoy lumbering around the pasture trees and brush and wondering whether or not they could follow onto the ranch without being detected. They had their orders. One dialed the General's phone. He told the General what was transpiring then listened to their new orders, then clicked off and looked at his waiting partner.

"The General says to hide the car and one of us follows the truck on foot. He wants to know exactly where they are and what they're doing."

They looked at the pasture and then at each other.

"These are hundred and sixty dollar shoes, man," one said. "What are those?"

The other looked at his shoes and shrugged. "Crap," he grunted and began rolling up his pant's legs.

ROLAND'S PICK-UP TOPPED the low ridge above the gully and stopped. Boyd pulled up beside him and shifted the diesel into idle. The chopped trees were exactly where they had left them, dead and bare. Frank thought he could see the cable still hanging from the top of the far oak. They got out and shook Roland's hand. Then they sized up the possibility of driving across the dry gully.

"I think we can do it," Boyd said. "We get the truck across the gully, back the trailer up to the trees and slide the ship right off the back, right into the trees where she was."

Roland pointed down the gully. "Right down there's a place where you can go straight down without any problem," he said. "And then you can angle up the other side." He looked at them. "Think you can do that?"

Boyd nodded. "Think so. Let's give her a try."

They climbed back into their trucks and Roland led them carefully through the steps he'd outlined. There were places where the big truck looked as if it might tip over, and they held their breath while it dug in and ground its way to the top of the other side. Boyd circled the truck around the trees and with Frank and Roland as guides backed the trailer, crunching the dead limbs, to the exact spot where they had cut her free.

Boyd and Frank circled the trailer untying ropes. Roland helped and lifted the tarp. "Damnation!" he huffed. "I figured I'd never have anything to do with this son-of-a-bitch again.''

"Well, Mr. Barrett," Frank said, "the way we're figuring it, none of us will have to put up with her much longer."

"Where's that John fella?" Roland asked, glancing across the gully. "Thought I saw another car on the road behind you."

"He's coming," Boyd said. "Along with some others."

"Others?"

"Some other people who got themselves involved," Boyd said.

"Oh, well," Roland said. He studied the ship, as the tarp came off. "How you gonna slide her off the trailer? She looks pretty heavy."

Boyd tossed some of the plywood packing. "Easy," he said. "You take your truck back across the gully. We hook your wench cable to the ship and you drag her off the trailer, into the trees, right where she was. Simple."

"Won't that bang her up?" Roland questioned, squinting under his sweaty old Stetson.

"Nah," Boyd grinned. "You couldn't dent her if you dropped her a mile."

From thick brush a quarter mile west down the gully, the rookie agent watched their activity through his binoculars. The General's suspicions were right on; the thing under the tarp was a shiny little space ship. He'd seen pictures in secret files at Headquarters, and in books, and that was a space ship. He knew a space ship when he saw one, and that was one. Damn! It hit him and he got excited. They have a space ship! This is big stuff. Wait till the General hears about this!

Roland lined his truck across the gully with the trailer and trees. They slacked his wench cable through the tree and hooked it onto a rope sling around the craft. Boyd gave him a go signal and he threw the wench into pulling gear. The cable pulled taut, the craft wobbled and slid into

its old place between the trees. Boyd unhooked the cable
and Roland reeled it in. He and Frank threw everything
back on the truck and drove it back across the gully,
parking it atop the ridge.

"That it?" Roland asked. He wiped a bandanna over
his face, neck and around inside his hat band. They stood
in the shade of a tall oak.

"That's it," Boyd sighed. "Now we wait."

"You fellas ate yet?"

Boyd shook his head. "Nope."

"Well," Roland said. "Let's go back up to the house
and get you somethin' while we wait."

They piled into Roland's truck.

Chapter Twenty-Six:
The Repast

FINDING A NICE SPECIALTY restaurant in East or West Columbia was out of the question. Outside of the fast food drive-throughs, the most popular eating place was a Kountry Kitchen on the outskirts of town.

It was almost two when the van pulled up. The place was nearly empty as the group was shown to a table for six in the non-smoking family section.

After the waitress left with their order, David saw the two Delta Force officers enter, glance at them, sidle up to stools at the front counter and try to blend in. Big pockets on their black fatigue pants sagged under the weight of weapons. A local deputy, picking his teeth at the other end of the counter, gave them a once over and looked the other way as if he knew who they were.

"Look at these people," Susan said. "A laid back Saturday afternoon. They have no idea what's going on around them. My hometown isn't half this size, and I wonder, looking back, just how can I write a book that will help these people realize the truth. Somehow, put it in their words."

"It'll be difficult, for sure," Bryan said.

"I can see me, in a few weeks, going home for my usual summer visit," Susan said, "and telling my mother what I've seen and heard in the past month, and how my world has taken on a new perspective. She'll say I'm crazy, running around with the wrong people like that."

"You never know," Bryan said. "You can't fear giving truth a try. Like your family and friends, and all the people in small and big towns all over the world, you were educated in that beehive fear mentality, everyone controlled by the same principles, good or bad. Somewhere along the line, you acted on your feeling that something just wasn't right, and you took it upon yourself to begin thinking on your own. That feeling was spiritual consciousness. And it was your first move away from the power of your ego illusions. All you needed then was an opportunity to replace those illusions with the truth. When that opportunity was presented, as an independent thinker, you had the spiritual right to choose. You believe everyone should have the right to the truth. Tell her that.''

"That's why we've put so much on the line to see that everyone gets it,'' Myra said. "Take it or leave it.''

"The Zeta Grays control through the fear of not knowing,'' David said. "That's how they've taken over this planet. They've always had the superior power to destroy us with an invasion, but that would have defeated their purpose of propagating their race by integrating with the precious Nefilim genetic heritage we possess, thanks to Enki. And thanks to Enki, whether he realized it at the time, He set a block against them getting it: the chimpanzee/ape Homo erectus DNA. That's why you never hear of the Zetas abducting blacks. They have more of the blocking DNA than any of us.''

John, Bryan and Myra smiled. "I never thought about it,'' John said. "But you're right. Outside of Barney Hill, I don't think we have many cases of black abductees.''

"If they took one,'' David said, "it would be purely by accident. They prefer blue-eyed blonds. Blue eyes for sure.''

They glanced around the table, all had blue eyes except David. And there were three blonds.

"Does that mean, they wouldn't take you?'' Myra asked.

"They would,'' David grinned. "But they prefer blue eyes.''

"Tell us more about this genetic experimenting,'' John said, after the waitress returned with their orders. "Is it what you discovered that got you in trouble with MJ-12?''

David nodded. "Yes,'' he said. "You probably know

that the Zeta Grays have been doing experimental cloning and mind control implanting on this planet for hundreds of thousands of years. The government got involved through MJ-12 back in '54, you know, when they made that deal with them for alien technology.''

"Maybe you guys know," Susan said. "But I don't think I do. Bring me up to date.''

"You know about the little live Zeta that they got from the crashed ship at Socorro," Bryan said.

"You mean, EBE-1, the little robot," Susan said. "Yes.''

"Well, questioning little EBE-1 at Los Alamos," David said, "MJ-12 began to realize they weren't talking *to* it. They were talking *through* it, to its creators, somewhere out there in space. And when John Von Neumman took the transistors out of the ship, EBE-1 quit communicating. When Von Neumman put the transistors back in the ship, EBE-1 transmitted again. EBE-1 was tied into the ship's onboard computers. MJ-12 brought in their top geneticists to do autopsies on the robot bodies, and EBE-1, when he died. MJ-12 wanted to learn the secrets of cloning, with the prospects of creating an army of bio-chemical robots. They soon discovered they didn't possess the technical knowledge to do cloning, but they did discover that the robots had a DNA mind control gene that was like a chip that tied them into the Zeta's lone mind computer-controlled brain waves. And, besides all the Zeta ships and military hardware the mind control implants were one of the things MJ-12 traded for at Edwards in '52.

"Since MJ-12 couldn't clone an army of robots, they decided to implant the mind control chips into the DNA of the soldiers they already had. And they did, with some disastrous results. A company in Viet Nam was implanted with the chips, and when the controllers sent a message to make the soldiers more aggressive, they suddenly began attacking and killing everything in sight, even themselves. They've never been able to return the survivors to normal. They're now quarantined in a Hawaiian jungle still fighting some imagined war. I checked it out.

"Those minor miscalculations didn't stop MJ-12.

Unaware that the Zetas had implanted their mind controls within them, MJ-12 was now a victim of their own greed. The mistake in Philadelphia Harbor and the crashes thereafter were all planned by the Zetas to trick the government leaders into trading alien technology to help conquer communism, for their covert genetic propagating, an alien DNA mismatching that created some devastating diseases. The Zeta Grays are using these diseases and ethnic conflicts to destroy that portion of humanity which is diverse to their plan. It is a desperate plan that will ultimately destroy Earth, as it has on other planets.

"Somehow, the Zeta Grays have to be stopped," David said to no one in particular. "The only way is by exposing them through the power of our truth, the knowing." David glanced around the restaurant. "The world is overflowing with those who are sleepwalking through the trivial illusions of life, completely oblivious to any threat from other dimensions. But we can't let their fear of not wanting, or needing, to know keep us from an initial educated effort."

Susan glanced over her shoulder. "Which one of these sleepwalkers would you start with?" she asked David.

"Oh, no!" Myra gulped. "Please! Don't get him started."

Susan saw their waitress approaching with their check. "Maybe the waitress," she whispered.

They watched, apprehensively, as David smiled up at their waitress. She smiled, slipping their check on the table next to David. "Thank ya'll very much," she said. "Ya'll come back now, ya hear." She'd been playing the role of a country lady-waitress a long time.

Each held their breath as she and David exchanged looks, and relaxed when she escaped, returning to the peace and quiet of a Mediocreville day.

"Here we are," Susan said. "On our way to what might be an audience with one of our extra-terrestrial ancestors, possibly our Creator, so I've been led to believe. Why don't we ask one of these people to go along?"

David grinned. "Without the knowing it's just another space ship," he said. "And all of them know, only the town weirdos see those things. Heaven help them, if they should be so different."

ON HIS JET, GENERAL Fuller listened to the agents' report on his cellular. Near finished take-out meals in molded Styrofoam boxes lay on the table between him and Rawlins. Fuller sipped from a large paper cup before he asked, "What'd it look like? Describe it." Rawlins picked at the . remains of his meal and watched Fuller's expression. Fuller's eyes darted here and there and out the window beside him. "Okay. Look, stay where you are. There'll be a couple of special agents joining up with you. When they do, get back to me."

Fuller clicked off and, still staring out the window, said pensively, "They put the ship in a clump of trees on the side of a ravine." He turned to Rawlins. "What do you make of that?"

Rawlins raised a brow and shrugged. "Don't know. Strange. Could be where they found it. What'd it look like?"

"Round, shiny. Dome, top and bottom," Fuller mused. "About twenty-five across, fifteen to twenty top to bottom. Sounds like a sport model, shuttle craft."

Chapter Twenty-Seven:
The Ravine

ETHEL BARRETT STOOD BY the pickup, staring up at the shiny space craft. This was her first real good look. She'd gotten a glimpse of it when they brought it out of the pasture that day, before they covered it up in the barn. She was afraid of it, afraid of those ugly beings that flew around in those things, stealing and butchering cattle they way they did. And now they were going to stand around and wait for them to come back. What if they did to them what they did to the cattle, she'd asked her husband when he asked her if she wanted to come along. He'd said he was scared, too, but he didn't want to miss seeing those mean little critters. He was loading his twelve- and sixteen-gauge shotguns at the time he was saying it. He'd rolled them up in an old quilt and put them in the pickup behind the seat. That made her feel a little better, but not much.

"Looks almost like the day I found her," Roland said, leaning on his pickup's fender next to Boyd and Frank, "except for the trees." He sucked air through a gap in his teeth.

"You tell anyone about finding her?" Boyd asked.

"Nope," he said. "Nary a soul." He did tell Josh and Scooter down at the feed store, but they never believed him, so that didn't really count. He hadn't heard if they told anyone else, no gossip about him seeing things in his old age.

"Want I should bring in a couple of my cows and stake 'em out down here?"

Frank shook his head. "Naw. Fella flying that ship's not interested in your cows."

"What's he want then?"

"That's what we hope to find out."

"Don't think it's us, do ya?" Ethel asked.

"Don't know," Boyd shrugged. "Maybe."

"PLACE LOOKS DIFFERENT," MYRA said, as they drove through the front gate. "All green, flowers blooming."

"Those are beautiful roses," Susan said. "Reminds me of back home.'

John circled the van around the ranch house. There was no sign of the Barretts or their pickup. Down beyond the barns he found the truck's tracks and followed them into the pastures and through the crushed underbrush.

The van bumped and rolled across the rough pasture, rocking its passengers side to side. Sticks and bushes trampled by the big truck crunched again under the van's tires. A stand of yupon scraped their thorny fingers along one side. Long, deep shadows stretched around them and the low sun played hide and seek in the tall trees. From front to side, they strained to see where they were going.

"I don't see anything," Karen said. "You're sure this is where it is?"

"Just hang on," John said. "We're getting there."

When the trail seemed as if it would never end, the van topped the rise to the gully and they saw the space craft, like a silver pearl riding the gully's purple shadow. Susan gasped. Seeing the ship for the first time suddenly brought its place in her reality into a sharp focused perspective. It was true. She felt a rush of excitement hit her dead-on. If she had doubts before, she didn't now; there was indeed a space craft, and that meant there would probably be an alien, or a god, to deal with.

Susan looked at Bryan, and Myra. She couldn't hide her rapturous wide-eyed amazement. They were grinning, and she grinned, like a five-year-old seeing an incredible gift under the tree on Christmas morning. There really was a Santa Claus.

"What'd ya think?" Bryan said. "Did we tell it like it is, or what?"

"Incredible!" Susan nodded. "She's beautiful."

John eased the van carefully down the embankment into the gully's dry bed. Frank, Boyd and the Barretts awaited by the pickup. The van stopped and all the doors flew open together. Each passenger tumbled out looking up at the space craft, nestled in the trees near the top of the opposite embankment about fifteen feet above their heads.

"Have any trouble?" John asked, coming around the van, greeting the Barretts and congratulating Frank and Boyd on a job well done.

Boyd and Frank shook their heads. "Naw," Boyd said, and glanced at the ship. "Look about like she was?"

"I guess." John shrugged. "I don't think we can hide the fact that we've moved her."

"Think we should open her door then?" Frank asked. John thought about it, glanced at the others. "Thought maybe we might want to go inside once more," Frank added. "You know, while we're waiting."

"Yeah, why not?" John decided.

Frank and Boyd went to open the craft's door.

"Ya'll shore surprised us, bringing that thing back," Roland said. He shook John's hand. "Figured the next time we saw it would be on TV."

"Sorry, Mr. Barrett," John said. "Things didn't work out like we planned."

"These members of your organization?" Roland asked looking past John at the rest off the group.

"Oh, yes." John said. "You remember Bryan and Myra."

"Sure do," Roland said, shaking their hands. "How ya been?"

"And that's Bryan's friend, Susan, and this is Karen and David. This is Mr. Barrett, and his wife . . . "

"Ethel," Roland added, waving his wife up to meet everyone.

"Yes. Ethel," John smiled as the introductions were done.

"Frank and Boyd was tellin' us a pretty wild story while we was waitin' for ya," Roland said, "'bout that thing belongin' to a god from some other planet. Said this god was walkin' 'round here someplace," he glanced at the pastures, "and that's who you gonna be waitin' for, to come back and get his ship."

"That's about the size of it, Mr. Barrett," John said. "You didn't happen to mention finding the ship to anyone, did you?"

"Us? Gosh, no," Roland lied, figuring Scooter and Josh down at the feed store didn't count. "They'd think we was crazy."

"Where's your cattle?" Bryan asked. "I didn't see any when we drove in."

Roland lifted his hat and wiped his brow with his sleeve. "Only got 'bout a hundred head now. Had my brother's boys round 'em up and drive 'em over to his place," he said, nodding in that general direction. "He's 'bout out o' the cattle business, but he's got some good pasture that could stand some grazin'. How long you think it's gonna take this, uh, god fella to come 'round?"

"Don't know," John said. "We'll give it awhile."

"What if He don't come back," Ethel said. "He be gone a long time. What if somethin's happened to him?"

Bryan chuckled. "What's gonna happen to a god?"

Roland shrugged. "Don't know," he said. "Never knew one."

"You haven't seen any strangers, hanging around here since we took the ship, have you?" John asked. "Someone looking like they might be hunting for something?"

Roland and Ethel thought about it and shook their heads. "Nope, can't say as we have," he said. "You figure he might've come back already?"

"Maybe."

"What's he look like?" Roland asked.

"Big guy." John said. "Probably seven, eight feet tall."

"Nope," Roland shook his head and grinned. "Hadn't seen anybody like that. I'da shore remembered it, if I had."

John glanced at his watch. Six-forty. "Well," he sighed, looking around. "Guess we might as well get things set up."

"'Spose so," Roland said. "Do ya think it'd be aw' right if Ethel and I wait with ya? We'd shore like to see this, uh, god fella."

"Sure," John said. "If you're up to it. Don't see why not."

"Would it be askin' too much," Roland said, "if we brought our portable TV down here from the house? Some of our favorite shows're on tonight, and it looks like it might be a while, but if you think it'd scare him off, o' course we . . ."

"No, no, it's okay," John said. "I don't think God would mind. A little TV's no less a desecration than what we've done."

"Another thing."

"Yes?"

Roland glanced at the ship. "Would it be aw' right if we took a look inside that thing?" His smile glowed with hope.

John grinned. "Sure," he said. "I'm sorry I didn't invite you. Come on, we'll give you a guided tour." He looked at the others. "Anyone else?"

They all went.

"DID YOU GET THOSE STRONG beam flashlights?" Fuller asked the DF officer on the other end of his cellular. The answer was, yes. "Okay," he said. "I want each of you to take one of the CIA guys, the flashlights and phones. Get down to that ravine. Set up phones and lights, either side of that ship. Got that? Good. Soon as the unit gets here, we'll be coming down and I want you to bring us in. Call in when you're set." He clicked off, set the phone down, got up and strolled out of the plane. The sky was a deep magenta and orange, the sun far west, above his Blue Beret unit.

Fuller's thoughts were of his circumstances, how he might have avoided all his present problems, just by eliminating John Sherman and Myra Bennett that night when they broke into his S-4 section at Groom Lake. At the time MJ-12's policy of permanently eliminating any unauthorized person or persons caught beyond the restricted perimeters was no longer in force. A new, more humane method had been installed; intense brainwashing, mind control implants, and if that didn't work, threats of social and financial annihilation.

What had saved John and Myra the rigors of expert interrogation that night was Fuller's admiration of their ingenuity and intense persistence in the face of incredible odds.

"They're good, real good," he remembered saying to Walt Rawlins when they discovered John and Myra were on their way onto the site disguised as members of their elite guard. "They want this real bad."

"We can stop them any time, Cal," Rawlins had said.

"No," he had said, as they watched John and Myra's progress on the hi-tech surveillance monitors. MJ-12 was well aware of the Federal Court case in Houston, Betty Cash and Vicky Landrum vs. the United States Government, John Sherman's involvement as an investigator and his need for evidence that the government had alien craft and had something to do with the craft that was seen by Betty and Vicky and from which they received cancerous radiation burns. "Not John Sherman," Fuller had mused. "Sherman's driven by some unconscionable desire. He's survived everything we've ever thrown at him, outside of killing him, and he keeps on coming. He's not one of those oddly curious, he's a professional malcontent. Brainwashing and mind control are useless on his kind. No, he'll never give up until we kill him. And that's the worst thing we could do. He comes up missing, and all of his buddies will know exactly who did it. And he has many, all over the world. They'll come after us with a vengeance. Giving tooth to those Congressional do-gooders and we'll have more trouble than our debunkers can handle. Even the smallest investigation would be detrimental to our purpose. We can't have that. No, sir, not now."

They studied the situation while watching John and Myra's progress on their monitors. They were approaching a check point.

"You know, Walt," Fuller had said, "there's something to be said about, the worst thing that can happen to someone is they get what they most dearly desire. Then have it taken away from them, with the knowledge that possessing it has no meaning of any consequence. That's the only way we'll stop Sherman short of killing him. He wants to get in, see what we have here? Fine. Then we'll give him what he wants.''

Fuller had pulled all the elite guard back and let John and Myra roam free, but not unwatched, through the underground hangers, all the way to the sixth level before he confronted them on a line of alien craft with their rolls of exposed film and video tapes. After relieving them of their cameras, he took them on a tour of Area 51, Dreamland, MJ-12's Above Top Secret S-4 Groom Mountain operations that overlooked Papoose Lake.

Fuller and Rawlins showed them everything; the alien craft, they had over two dozen on line at the time; the alien instructors, there were six, and the technical labs where engineers and scientists studied and copied the finer qualities of alien technology. Everything from the finest computers and lasers to the invisibility components of time travel and parallel universes.

John, Myra and Frank were astounded. They knew MJ-12 was heavily involved, but this — they had no idea.

"That's it, John," Fuller had said at the end of their tour. "Was it anything like you pictured it would be?"

"Exactly, General, and more so," John had said. "What now? Is this where you eliminate us?"

Fuller shook his head and smiled, slyly. "Now you can go home and forget about us. You've been to the mountain and you've seen the fire. You can tell anybody who'll listen to you, but just like before, they'll never believe you, and that'll be worse than death to you. You have no need to come here again, but if you ever do, I promise you, we *will* kill you."

Fuller clinched his jaw and ground his teeth through the tip of his cigar. He spat it on the tarmac outside his jet. He would have rather seen John's head rolling in the runway's dried oil and grit. Taking that craft meant killing all of them, or taking them back to Groom Lake and having the Zetas take them to the Mars underground mines.

Rawlins called from the plane's door. The DF agents were in their positions at the ravine.

"They're camping out in the ravine, by the ship," Fuller repeated into his phone and glanced at Rawlins. "The ship's door is open? Can you see inside?" Anxiously, Fuller and Rawlins stared at each other as they waited. "Good," Fuller smiled. "What do you see inside? A chair? One chair? How big? Large, like for a giant. Hmmm." Fuller mused and exchanged a glance with Rawlins. "Okay. Hold your positions. We'll be in the air within the hour."

Fuller clicked off. He slammed the cellular on the table and glared at Rawlins. "They have a goddammed Nefilim ship!" he growled. "Where the hell'd they get a Nefilim ship!"

After thinking about it, Rawlins said, " Maybe right there on the ranch. Maybe that's what this is all about. They found it, or the rancher found it, called them, they hid it away in that tool shed and were trying to fly it. They couldn't fly it and now they've taken it back. And they're sitting out there, waiting for the Nefilim to come back and show them how to do it."

"Hmmmm," Fuller mused. "You know, Walt, you might have something there." He brightened and grinned. "I'm gonna love adding a Nefilim ship to our collection."

Chapter Twenty-Eight:
The Visitor

THEIR CAMP WAS SET up around the van. The space craft's tarp cover was stretched over the van in front and one side. They had cut poles to support the three corners, making a wide, run-around porch addition. Patio and lawn chairs were unfolded in the vicinity of a card table loaded with boxes and bags of snacks, including a feast of ham and turkey sandwiches and a two-gallon jug of ice tea donated by the Barretts. Yellow light spilled out into the darkness from two buglight lanterns hung on a front and back tent pole. A pale blue light flickered over those who had gathered at the tailgate of the Barrett's pickup watching a TV, hooked up to a spare battery, Roland had brought back from half of the group's potty trip to the house.

"Damn! Did you ever see such big mosquitos?" Susan yelped, as she slapped at a swarm around her legs. She and Karen were hanging her bug zapper on the side tent pole. They had run a line from Roland's battery and the blue light was already making big kills.

Myra sprayed a fog around the tent and truck from an aerosol bug fogger. "I think we're gonna need something stronger for these mutants," she said. She sprayed a final cloud and set the can on the table.

"A big electric fan would be nice, too," Susan said. "This humidity's something else. I'd have brought one if I'd known we'd have a place to plug it in."

"We could all get in the van and turn on the air," David offered, "but I can't guarantee the battery would last."

"Did I hear someone say it would cool off out here at night," asked Karen.

"It will," John said. "Probably drop all the way down to seventy-five, or so."

"Why don't we just think us up a nice luxury motel or something," Susan said, glancing at David. Those around the TV laughed with the canned laughter. David shot her a thin smile. The others tried to ignore her suggestion. She unwrapped a package of cassette tapes and inserted one into her tiny recorder. She clicked it on. "Just a suggestion." she said into its mike screen. She pulled her lawn chair up close, between David, John and Bryan. "I would've had this in the restaurant," she said of her recorder to David, "if I'd known you were gonna have so much to say. Now, there's some questions I have of what you said, about what went on at Los Alamos. Why was it that we couldn't clone like the Zetas?"

David glanced at her and the little recorder in her hand and wondered if she would understand. "It had something to do with the crystalline structures and the size of the brains. The implants wouldn't take in the altered DNA strings," he said. "Something like that."

"Oh," Susan said, not really understanding, but she had it on tape and she would study it later.

"They've been cross-bred so many times," David added, "that they've been experiencing replicative failures in their genetic structures. The cloning process weakens the spiritual energies, the soul, the emotions of ethical values. That is what they want from us, our spiritual energies, the same as they want from their brothers, and our ancestors. They're a dying race. They can't pass on spiritual energies through cloning. It has to be done through the birthing process. They can't find their Nefilim brothers, but they've found a fantastic Nefilim energy pool in us. They tricked MJ-12 into trading us for the powers of their technology. MJ-12 didn't know what they really wanted.''

Myra shot a couple of pictures. The flash bulbs lit up the group and the ship in the background.

"That's why it's so important for us to know our spiritual being," Bryan said. "If we don't know what we must defend, how can we defend it?"

"That Nefilim ship up there," David said to the ship, its inner light flowing through its open door. "Says that their planet, Nebiru, is close, heading this way. I suspect, the Zetas haven't found it because it's in another dimension. But they know it's there and they're setting a trap. The Zetas have given humanity atomic powers, the very thing the Nefilim never wanted us to have, and have used our ego illusions to push us to the brink of a great war. If it happens, the Zetas are hoping the Nefilim will come to our rescue, and that's when they'll have them, and maybe even a greater war.

"If that happens," David went on, "there might be such an atomic implosion that it would create a black hole that only the strongest of souls could pass through. And that would eliminate the weaker Zeta energies.''

They stared, waiting for him to go on. But where was there to go?

"That's what could happen?" Susan asked.

David nodded and shrugged.

"A whole planet in another dimension!" Bryan frowned.

"There are whole universes in other dimensions," David said.

"How do you know all that, what you said?" John asked.

"I figured it out," David said. "Our salvation is in the strength of our knowing.''

In their solemn silence the TV sit com's theme song rolled over them before someone got up and turned it off.

"It's really very simple when you know," David smiled.

Roland yawned and stretched as he led Ethel, Boyd and Frank under the tent porch. "It's 'bout nine," he said. "No sign of Him, eh? Any idea when that fella might show up?"

"Nope," Bryan shrugged. "Your guess is as good as ours."

"A real night owl, eh?"

"Well, we can't say he's on our time," John said. He hoped he wouldn't have to explain space-time to Roland. Roland let it pass — he knew about eastern, central, standard time zones.

"What d'ya figure a god looks like?" Roland asked, rustling in the plastic bags on the table. He came up with a handful of cookies. "Like, maybe, those painted pictures ya see that's in the Bible and churches? Long hair, robes, such as that?"

"Maybe," John said. "We'll have to wait and see." As with the time thing, he didn't want to get into a description of the Nefilim. That would just lead to a very long discussion Roland and Ethel could never relate to. Best they wait until whoever shows up and then it would be much easier.

Roland looked around the table. "Didn't bring no coffee?" he grumbled. "Anybody 'sides me and Ethel want coffee?"

"That'd be nice," Myra piped up.

"Well, we'll go up to the house directly and make some," he said. He put the cookies back in the bag. "Can't eat my sweets without my coffee, no sir. A little sweets before bed lets ya have sweet dreams."

Karen grinned. "That true?"

"My momma told me when I was little," he said, proudly. "Never been bothered with bad dreams since."

"My mother used that one on me, too," Myra grinned.

"So, if you don't know what he looks like," Roland

said, getting back to the god, "how're you gonna know him if he shows up? Ya just gonna take to the first thing that comes down that gully? Might be somethin' ya don't wanna have anythin' to do with, like maybe a wildcat, or a panther."

"Or a snake," Karen added.

"History says like us, only much taller," John said.

"Hmmm," Roland mused. "Ya suppose he'll be walkin' or ridin'?"

"Riding a white horse," David laughed. "With wings."

"Hmmm," Roland mused, eyeing David suspiciously. He had a feeling they were beginning to make sport of his not knowing what they knew. But he wasn't the fool that was sitting out here in the pasture waiting for some god to come walking by, or riding, no siree. "Well, if he is, he probably stole it," he said. "And that don't make him a god." He turned to go. "Well, come on Ethel, let's go get that coffee."

Ethel headed for her side of the truck. Roland stopped to put up the tailgate. "Ya want," he said. "I'll leave ya the TV."

Boyd and Frank waved him off. "No, that's okay," John said. "Take it. But leave us the battery, if you will?"

Roland took the battery and set it on the ground. Taking the TV, he slammed the tailgate. He put the TV in the front seat next to Ethel. "Look," he said, before getting in. "If that god shows up before we get back, give us a holler, will ya? Blow your horn or something."

"We will," John waved. "We have a phone, there, in the van."

Roland slammed his door and started the engine. He cranked it in gear and roared away down the gully and up over the ridge.

"Blow our horn," Frank said to the truck's fading tail-lights. "Right. It's damn near two miles up to that house."

"Sounds carry out here on a still night," John said.

"Maybe some of us should've gone with them," Susan said.

"Any of you get the feeling, they're, just sort of, going along with this?" Myra asked.

Frank and Boyd pulled their chairs under the tent porch and got themselves drinks from the cooler.

"Yeah, I did," Susan said. "I mean, can you blame them? This whole thing is so weird. Look at us, sitting out here in his cow pasture, in the middle of the night, waiting for some alien to come get his space ship. Now, is that strange, or what? They're probably laughing all the way to the house."

"I don't think so," John said. "Roland will never forget the way his cows looked."

"Just look at her," Boyd said to the ship. "From the first time I saw her I've never stopped marveling at her sleek power, the dimensions she must've crossed, the hands and minds who made her. I'd wait forever to meet those geniuses."

"Yes, incredible geniuses," Bryan said thoughtfully. The others looked around to see him slouched in a chair, quietly studying David. "Incredible intelligence, the mysterious miracle makers of ancient histories. Why them and not us? Why you and not us?"

Bryan's statement, question, to David got their attention. Or, was it an accusation? David shifted slightly in his chair, returning Bryan's focused observation with a half smile. Susan settled back into her chair, checked her recorder, clicked it on and sat it on the table between the two. Myra exchanged a glance with John and eased down onto the cooler next to him.

"Things are beginning to make some sense," Bryan continued. "Let's see if I have this right. The Nefilim, Anunnaki, are from a planet in a multi-star system. And if history serves us right, their travels to Earth have been through planets in multi-star systems. Any physcist knows there is an abundance of the strong force in multi-star systems, an abundance of the fourth dimension energy. So wouldn't it seem logical that beings from a multi-star system would have a spiritual energy that could access the fourth dimension? Altering time/space and performing miracles would be common to them, mysteries to beings of a single-star system and its third dimensional reality?''

After a long moment, David returned Bryan's grin. ''Bryan, you're absolutely right,'' he said, and glanced at the ship. ''The power source in that ship works the same as spiritual energy in them, and in us. Knowledge increases its density and through that power we can access other dimensions. We're the same in spirit as the Nefilim gods. It's the knowing that we are that makes the difference. They sent us *The Ten Commandments, Jesus, The Bible, The Earth Chronicles, A Course in Miracles* to help us in our knowing, so we could realize our truth in knowing all our dimensions. As you've said, the knowing is the key.''

They stared across the gully at the space craft with its inviting open door and let the somber realization of what they were doing settle over them. Except for the distant sounds of some night creatures and Roland's truck, it was eerily quiet.

The rumble of Roland's truck had almost faded away when it suddenly began to get louder, as if it was coming back. All of them turned toward the sound, thinking they might see the truck's headlights returning. They didn't, but the roar kept getting louder and louder, with a definite clatter, and a chop. It was an echo and it was coming from the other end of the gully. They all turned at once.

''Choppers!'' Boyd yelled. He'd heard enough of them in Nam to never forget that sound. ''Incoming!'' he added from an old reflex. Flashing running lights came blinking beyond the trees.

''Kill the lights!'' John yelled above the roar.

They scurried, knocking over chairs and tables, pulling

down the lanterns. Dousing the lights, they looked up to
see the flashlight beams from opposite ends of the gully
swinging over them like the main event's opening night.
And the light from the ship's open door held them in its
spotlight.

"What the hell!" John shouted. "What's going on?
Who are those people!"

The unmarked black helicopters, with their searchlights
sweeping the ground, rose over the trees and swung up the
gully right at them.

Generals Fuller and Rawlins rode in the lead gunship
with half a squad of Blue Beret hanging out the open door.
To their rear wing was a second gunship with the DF
officer and the rest of the squad in its open doorway.
Another bigger helicopter hung back, circling above the
trees from where they had come.

Caught like night creatures in headlights, they huddled
under their flapping tent porch, shielding themselves from
the blinding lights, blowing dust, sand and leaves pushing
up the gully ahead of the black marauders. Spotlights, two
beneath each gunship, ran long, stark shadows around them
in the great wind.

Blazing guns clattered from the open door of the lead
gunship as it went by. Bullets kicked deep little pits in the
sand and whizzed through the camp site and pocked the
van. Folding chairs flew in the wake of the roto wash as
their tarp porch blew away. They scrambled for cover
behind and under the van.

Crouched behind a folding table, John risked a squinting
peek as the lead gunship went by. A heavy broadside from
the second gunship ripped his fragile hideaway in half. He
ducked, leaped and rolled under the van with the others.
Behind him, bullets stitched holes across the limp tarp,
riddled the van's side and roof, and blew out its windshield.

"Geezus!" Bryan yelled, as the dust settled around
them. "What the hell! They're trying to kill us! Who is

that?''

"Is anybody hit?'' John shouted. Water from the van's radiator trickled down onto his back.

Miraculously, no one was, just shaken and scared as hell.

Susan cried. "Why am I here? Why am I doing this?''

David thought of the tailing agents. He had brought MJ-12 upon them. He had been expecting them, but never like this.

The gunships circled down the gully and the lead ship slowly descended and set down fifty yards away in the dry bed. Sitting sideways in the gully its rotors barely missed clipping the sides and top. Its blocking position aimed its open doors and guns right in the bewildered faces under the van.

"Who are those people!'' Susan shrieked. "Why are they trying to kill us!''

"Delta Force!'' Boyd blurted.

"No. Blue Berets!'' Frank shouted. "Groom Lake!''

John spit sand. "It's MJ-12. Fuller and his Blue Berets.''

"Fuller?'' Bryan gasped. "How!''

"I don't know how,'' John said, as they watched the second gunship rise up over the first and clatter back up the gully toward them. "But I know what he wants. *Everyone duck!*''

The second gunship roared by, spraying the area with another hail of bullets. The van took several more hits; a side mirror blew off and the windows along that side were shattered. A small arms rocket just missed the van and blew a deep hole in the ridge above them. Sand rained down over and around them. "Oh, God!'' Susan screamed. "They're gonna kill us!''

". . . he wants that ship!'' John finished saying, as he lifted his head.

"He's making it clear he means business,'' Bryan

groaned.

"What're we gonna do?" Myra said. "We don't have any guns. We're sitting ducks!"

"They want the ship?" Susan screeched. "Let 'em have it!"

"It's not that easy," Myra observed.

The second gunship circled the opposite end of the gully and slowly settled onto the bed in a sideways blocking position copying the lead ship. Each end of the gully was now sealed from any possible escape. The heavy cargo helicopter moved around the trees and hung above and beyond the space craft, like a giant mechanical dragon fly eyeing its next meal.

"We're in a crossfire," Bryan said, echoing what was obvious. "They'll walk right in and take us."

"Kill us, you mean," Myra added.

"They could hit the gas tank. Stay here, we die," John said, assessing their situation. "The ship! The ship's our only chance. It's bulletproof! It has lasers!"

"They'll cut us down before we get halfway there!" Boyd said.

Blue Beret units jumped from the helicopter doors at each end of the gully, the Generals at one end, the DF from the other, charging toward the van and each other.

"Those are Blue Berets," Frank groaned. "They don't miss."

"Stay here and we all die," John snapped. "We're between them. Maybe they won't fire at each other! Quick! Roll out and run for the ship! Hurry!"

"Oh, God!" Susan moaned. "I can't believe this! I didn't do anything!

A mass of arms, legs and bodies rolled out from under both sides of the van. Boyd was the first to clear, then Frank. They crouched low as they could and ran. John grabbed Myra's hand as they rolled clear. "No!" she shouted. "Everybody's on their own! Don't stop! Go!"

Guns from both ends of the gully opened up before Boyd got between them. Bullets kicked dirt all around him. Frank was close behind, head down, hopping and zigging. The helicopter spotlights fought for their dancing images.

The others followed like ducks in a shooting gallery. Myra, John, Karen, David, Susan and Bryan, low, leaping and hopping.

"Go! Go! Go!" Bryan hollered. "Don't stop! Keep running!"

Every Beret gun sprayed hot lead, first at them and as they got between them, at their legs and feet. Bullets whizzed around them thick as bees. Sprinting upright and leaping, Myra caught up with Frank. David ran along side of Karen, shielding her from one end. Susan stumbled and did a head over heels roll. Bryan pulled her to her feet on the run and practically drug her. She tried to scream, but she couldn't find the breath.

They hopped, skipped, leaped and clawed up the embankment, onto the ship's ramp and tumbled through its open door. Bullets whined and ricocheted everywhere off the ship. Bryan and Susan dove through the door as Boyd and David quickly pulled it up. Some rounds clipped in over the closing door and rattled around inside the ship. The door eased up and slammed shut.

Dirty, panting and sweating, they lay frightened and exhausted on the ship's floor and against its wall around the chair. Myra huddled in the chair. Outside the automatic weapons fire pelted the ship like rain on a tin roof. And like a dark cloud passing, the rain slacked off until it stopped.

In the silence, their heavy breathing subsided to a collective sigh of relief. One by one, they moved slowly through a process of recovery, testing working parts and searching for bloody wounds. Incredibly, nobody had been hit. Either the Blue Beret had become very bad shots, or they shied away from hitting each other. A third possibility; they were just damn lucky.

Another miracle.

"What now?" Susan asked the inevitable question the others had already asked themselves. "How do we get out of here alive?" She was propped up against the wall between John and Bryan.

"We don't," Bryan said. "Remember me telling you about MJ-12? Well, that's them out there, and they want this ship."

"I don't know how they found out we had it," John said. "I thought we'd been real careful." He got to his feet and felt the edges of the closed door and realized it was closed tight. It hadn't been that closed since the day it accidentally opened.

"Let's give 'em the ship," Susan said.

"We'd still be just as dead," John said. "Did we ever find the switch that opened this thing?"

No one answered. They were stuck.

"They can't get in, we can't get out," John said. "Well, we'll worry about that later. First, let's see if we can get rid of Fuller and his Berets."

Knowing it was risky without their heat suits, Bryan got a boost up from Boyd, reached behind the top of the console and switched on the ship's power. The panels lit up and the viewing screens came on, showing the spotlighted gully, gunship to gunship and the Generals with their squad of Blue Beret directly in front of them, milling around, studying the situation. Behind them, the tall, gapbelly flying crane helicopter settled down into the gully.

John slid into the pilot's chair.

"Those are our soldiers?" Susan asked the screen images.

"True and blue," Bryan said. "Our black budgets at work."

"How can they shoot us! We're Americans, too!"

"They're not," John said. "They're MJ-12 Blue Berets, the infallible Super Race."

On the screens they saw Fuller talking to the crane pilot, giving him instructions that he punctuated with hand motions. Making a claw-like, grabbing sign, he pointed to the top of the space craft. The pilot studied the craft as Fuller's hands made a lifting motion. The pilot nodded and saluted.

"Read that?" John said. "They're going to take the ship, and us in it."

"Damn it!" Myra groaned. "They'll open us like sardines at Groom Lake."

"Yeah, and serve us to the Zetas on crackers," Frank said.

"Oh, God," Susan gasped.

"Take it easy," Bryan said. "We don't know that they've ever eaten a human."

John flipped open the firing button's covers on the chair's arms. "We know the lasers are in the front of the ship, in front of the chair," he said, glancing at the screens. "The chair's pointing in the general direction of the crane. I don't know how to aim these things, but we'll have to take a chance on hitting it. If not, we'll at least let them know we have fire power in here."

"Do it! Before it moves!" Boyd urged.

They stared at the crane chopper on the screen and held their breath. John pushed the buttons. Red laser beams shot from the ship, streamed through the crane chopper's wide cargo gap and zapped David's van beyond. The van exploded in a fire ball and a thick cloud of smoke.

The Generals and Blue Berets fell to the ground, scrambled to their feet in panic and ran for cover.

Horrified, they stared at the burning van on the screen.

"Crap!" John hissed.

"Well, so much for the van," Myra sighed. She looked for David's reaction. She didn't see him. But what she did see behind them shocked her. She gasped, incredulously.

"Give it another shot!" Boyd barked.

Suddenly, a large hand and arm pushed through from behind them and clamped over John's hand and the buttons. A deep voice reverberated through the ship.

"Get ye from my chair, lest thou killest someone!"

Chapter Twenty-Nine:
The Reason

A MAN. A GIANT, MUSCULAR MAN, seven to eight feet tall, masculine, yet ethereal. His skin was an alabaster flesh. His face was exquisite, high cheekbones and piercing cobalt blue eyes framed with shoulder length blond hair, didn't look a day over forty. He wore a glowing white robe trimmed in gold that bore an intricate pattern on its front. John tumbled from the chair. The giant brushed the others aside on his way to the control panels where he quickly pushed switches and buttons. A matching pair of golden serpent armlets glittered from his massive biceps. He whirled and glared at them, not angrily but curiously, then serenely, with the hint of a knowing smile. Everything fell into place when the gold-embroidered serpent entwined flying cross caduceus emblazoned down the front of his robe jumped at them. No doubt about it, He was the Nefilim God, Enki.

They were stunned. Where? How? They slowly eased behind the chair, a buffer to their guilt of taking His ship. Yes, it was His ship and the fact He was back gripped them.

Enki took a small step toward them, and they took a quick, reflexive step backwards. Their frightened, questioning eyes darted between each other and the giant god. Their big question; beyond what was He about to do, was how did He get in? All the things that they had prepared themselves to say vanished in the sudden shock of His reality. Maybe if they had seen Him coming from a distance, up the gully, the realization of His truth might not have been so dramatic. They would have a little more time to fashion their excuses. But they were so overwhelmed with His presence, all excuses went out the window.

"Enki?" John whispered. "Sir . . . Your Majesty?" What? How the hell did you address a god? "We . . . uh, we . . . Lord, help us."

"Where's David?" Myra asked, softly, glancing about the ship's close confines.

The question and the sudden need of a spiritual defense from their enlightened mentor led the others to risk a fleeting glance around. David, indeed, was missing. How?

On the screens behind Enki, Fuller, Rawlins and the Blue Berets crept cautiously from cover and carefully approached the space ship, edging around its suspected field of fire.

Enki saw their concern and glanced at the screens. He reached for a button at the side of the control panel and waited for all the troops to gather below the ship's door before He pushed it. On the screens they saw a blue beam stream from above them, from the ship's dome, and engulf the Generals, the Blue Berets, the DF officers, the rookie agents and the helicopters, freezing them in time, like statues, blue toy soldiers rooted to a war map.

Their outer threat neatly halted, Enki turned back to His awestruck, cowering covey, still mystified in the sudden event. He stood tall and majestic, towering over them, His full height barely a foot from the domed ceiling. Hands behind His back, He studied them, and they studied Him. He stepped toward them, smiling and shaking His head, incredulously. They moved around the chair, keeping it between Him. His presence was overpowering. Looking each in the eyes, He calmed them. *"Be ye not afraid,"* He said, His voice deep, soft and reassuring.

"Where's David?" Karen asked.

Enki, still smiling, shrugged. *"David, my foil,"* He said, His voice celestial, Godly, enochian.

"You were David?" Karen asked, hesitantly.

Enki nodded.

Together, they felt their loss . . . and their gain.

"David was my mask, thou mortal illusion. I needed to walk among thee," the giant God said. *"I found David at his untimely crossing. We struck an arrangement, I take his ego for my limited use, he everlasting life. I am Enki, son of thy Nefilim Father, Anu, from thy tenth solar sister, Nebiru."*

"Enki?" John smiled.

"I am, that I am. The bastard son of Anu."

"Then," John figured, "you'd have to be over five-hundred-thousand years old!"

"Yay, if I be a mere mortal, limited to this dimension," Enki said. *"Ye own creations lack the string of longevity, among other coveted, immortal qualities of dimensionality."*

"Then it was you? The light, the island?" Karen grinned. "Neat. I had a feeling it had to be more than just our knowing. I don't know about the rest of you, but I'm glad to know you." She stuck out her hand to shake His, then embarrassed, pulled it back. Should one shake God's hand? "I've never met a god before, I mean, I met David and he was real nice, but I don't know, is it all right to think of you the same way as we did him, before?"

Enki smiled. *"Thee were not created to worship, only to serve by our law."* He took her hand, shook it and held it.

Hands came around the chair from all directions, and Enki shook each one.

For the first time, Susan realized she still had her little tape recorder strap looped around her wrist, and it was still taping.

"You were with us all along," Susan said. "And you did all those things?"

Enki nodded. *"Nothing thou might do thyself."*

"And, you almost got us killed," she added. "When you could've just zapped those people before . . . "

"Ye were never in danger," Enki said. *"Even unto the Valley of Death."* He glanced at the frozen soldiers on the screens. It was sort of a valley, more of a gully. *"Granted, thy fear of Death is unnatural. Man against man. Man beyond Anu's laws. So foiled a creation without a proper base."* He reached beneath the panel, pushed a switch, the door opened and the ramp went down. The humid night air rushed in around them. *"Come,"* He said, charging them to follow him outside. *"I will show ye thy source of incredible chaos."* He ducked going out the door.

Cautiously, they followed Enki down the ramp in single file.

"Stay beyond the blue light," He warned as they slid down the embankment into the gully.

An eerie, cold blue stillness hung over the crowded gully; a tiny forest of uniformed humanity and war machines with frozen wings. They crept along the outer edge of the blue beam, awestruck by the abstract strangeness of the scene. Enki didn't hesitate, striding boldly into the blueness among the lifelike' figures of Generals and Blue Berets, statues captured in time, like action bronzes in a mall plaza.

They were astounded when they saw Enki insert three fingers of his right hand into Fuller's head behind his left ear. Fuller never flinched. Enki withdrew His fingers and deposited something into the palm of his left hand. Moving on through the blue statues he repeated the operation in Rawlins' head and then in each of the Blue Berets, the DF officers and the rookie agents.

Juggling whatever He had in His hands, Enki returned to the group. *"Zeta slaves,"* He said, and offered them His handful. John cupped his hands under Enki's fist. Fuzzy metal-like gravel, what seemed to be tiny BBs with filament antenna, dropped into John's hands.

"Mind control implants," Enki announced. *"Thou leaders bartered with the Zetas for this technology, unaware that the Zetas were already using these implants to control them. This be thy greatest will to insurrection."*

"Incredible!" John said, as he showed the tiny implants to the others.

"Not so," Enki accused. *"Thou knew of this."*

"True," John admitted. "We'd heard reports, rumors. But we'd never, actually, seen one. Honest."

"Now thou hast."

"The proof we've been looking for," Bryan said.

"Look quickly," Enki warned. *"Each evaporates even as ye speaketh."*

It was true. To their amazement and futile hope for proof the handful of implants was shrinking. In a matter of minutes they would be completely gone.

"'Tis ye atmosphere, and ye touch," Enki said.

"Isn't there anything we can do to save them?" John asked. "We need the evidence."

"Nay," Enki shook his head. *"'Tis the Zetas' design to default detection."*

Boyd took what was left of the implants from John and tried as best he could to examine the vaporizing pieces.

"Was it you I met before?" Karen asked. "In the park?"

"Nay," Enki said. *"T'was my sister, Ninhursag, who proudly glorified thy beauty and thy knowledge. Ye, indeed, are truly a magnificent specimen."*

"Specimen?" Karen said, arching her brow.

"Ye knowest the source of thy creation," Enki smiled. *"Of thy line, thy evolution. T'was Ninhursag's plan of your being, your image. She hast long sought her reward. All of thee hath garnered thy truth in knowing."* Towering over them, his outstretched arms encompassed them in a praising gesture. *"Ye are righteously acceptable beyond*

thy faults.''

"Righteously acceptable?'' Myra said. "What does that mean? We have blue eyes?''

"*'Tis thy purity of inheritance,''* Enki said, proudly. *"A numbering to be raised from the dead.''*

"Raised from the dead?'' Bryan questioned.

"You're talking about the prophecies, right? The Bible, Revelations?'' Susan said.

"Armageddon?'' John added.

"As was the ways of our planets many orbits ago,'' Enki said, *"their paths are destined to cross again. Drought, earthquakes and waters will again cover thy land. Our Father was pleased with my saving of Noah's kin, a most righteous family, and the animals, to start again. Lo, Anu has granted his twelve of the God Council twelve thousand souls each, righteously acceptable as Noah's, to be saved.''*

"And God shall sound a trumpet call, and 144,000 shall rise up from the dead,'' Susan said, paraphrasing the best she could the Biblical predictions from Revelations.

"Thou hath multiplied abundantly,'' Enki gestured. *"Some hath prospered, but many hath forgotten thy Father's words. To find twelve thousand of the knowing is a difficult task, indeed.''*

"Rise up! In space ships!'' John gasped, realizing the true interpretation of Anu's words. "You're going to airlift 144,000 from the coming catastrophe? Is that it? That's why you're here?''

"Yay, if a true number can be found,'' Enki said. He glanced at the blue statues behind him. *"Without a shepherd, his flocks hath gone astray. Zetas hath poisoned thy leaders to wither thy vines and rotted thy harvest with the salt of deceit and fear. They hath a purpose to rule thy home.''*

"They'll die when the waters cover the Earth again, won't they?'' Karen asked.

Enki shrugged and said to the blue troops. *"Many ships they hath, with thy leader's and the lying Zetas."*

"But, only enough ships for themselves," John ventured.

"Yay. 'Tis a devious plan."

"Groom Lake, Los Alamos, Lancaster." John mulled. "That's what it's all about? Their denying the alien alliance; they're planning their own escape! Building their own ships!"

"How low can they get?" Myra said. "Lying. Using our tax dollars to get the heck out of Dodge."

"How long before this crossing?" Bryan asked.

"Ye orbits of twenty plus five."

"That's plenty of time," Karen said. "We can spread the word, the knowing. We can help you, and the others, find your Noahs and fill your quotas."

"Yes!" Myra said. "We can help. You can show them some of those things you showed us."

"Thou dost forget," Enki said. *"T'was tried before. Anu's only begotten son walked the Earth as the knowing of Jesus, challenged to correct past mistakes with the Adams and Eves in the Garden. Religious greed and fears still crucify thy truth. Nay, 'tis better the knowing find fertile ground beyond these weak illusions."*

"The separation in the Garden," Bryan said. "The ego?"

"As thou creator with powers of many DNA strings, as a precaution, thou inheritance was restricted by thy maternal roots to only dual strings. 'Tis a reality I gave the Adams and Eves, pleasures of procreation without the proper powers to control their knowledge and desires. The mistake did bear an abundance of tasteless fruit."

"The only difference between our Creator, you, and us, is in our DNA?" Bryan asked.

"Yay, tis a maternal truth. A miscalculated fault that restricts immortality, and a hinderance to knowing thy pure

universal powers."

"Pure universal powers?" Bryan said. "You mean, your God, your Creator, and in a sense, our God and Creator, many millions of years removed? We could have been gods, so to speak, if it wasn't for our maternal roots?"

"Yay. 'Tis true."

"And the knowing is of that God power within," Karen said.

"The inheritance of our paternal roots, you?"

Enki smiled and nodded. *"'Tis not difficult to conceive thou only salvation. Ye knowing is diminished greatly through this multitude of confused and fearful humanity."*

"Yes, but I'll bet they'll shape up when we tell 'em about the crossing and the coming catastrophe," Susan said.

"Scare the heck out of em," Myra said. "Right?"

"Nay. No fearful one shall be saved," Enki said. *"Only those who know love in life and spiritual power. 'Tis Anu's law. God's golden law."*

"Do unto others as you would have them do unto you," Myra said.

"Love thy neighbor as thyself," Karen added.

"Love's the ticket, eh?" Bryan said.

"Most truly," Enki said, disheartedly. *"Much hath occurred since last we were here. Much hate and fear and violence; the wars. Chaos. Ye now hath atomic weapons, and crude space craft. Anu is justly pleased to decree a cleansing. Only the knowing of thy true love shall save thee in His eyes. Few of ye hath proven me right in bidding ye free choice.*

"Time hath proven my stay good. To a greater number my message is clear. 'Tis a truth, thy knowing of spiritual powers within thee conquers fear and will grant ye life everlasting."

"Does that mean, we make the cut?" Karen asked.

Enki grinned. *"Most truly. But thy test of fine mettle*

is as a disciple, give of thy life to save another." He glanced at the van and studied its smoldering ruin beyond repair. Turning and heading for His ship, He beckoned them follow. *"Come, ye hath much witnessing to do. I shall give thee passage home."*

Enki led them up the ramp. They were proud and happy to be His chosen ones. They did good, He was not angry that they had taken His ship. They took parting glances at the blue soldiers.

"Wait!" John said. "Will we need our heat suits?"

Enki stopped in the doorway as He considered the danger. *"Yay,"* He said, gesturing toward the truck. *"Fetch them."*

The men quickly jumped from the ramp, carefully avoiding the blue beam, and hurried across the gully to get the suits from the truck.

Boyd stopped and turned. "What about the truck?" he asked.

Enki shrugged at his appeal. *"Ye shall return it home."*

"But, I wanted to ride in your ship," Boyd pleaded. "It's all I've ever wanted in life, to fly in one of those babies."

"Another time," Enki waved him off. *"Frank shall assist thee in thy task."*

"But . . . " Frank stuttered before Enki stopped him with a divine glare. God had spoken. There was no reprieve.

"You promise there'll be another time?" Boyd asked as he and Frank backed away.

"Many times," Enki said. *"Ye shall hath thy own ships on Nebiru."*

Somewhat encouraged by Enki's promise, they plodded on, grumbling, passing John and Bryan scurrying back to the ship with an armload of heat suits.

"Sorry about that," John said on hearing the news.

"If we knew how to drive that thing we'd do it."

"It's easy," Boyd said. "We'll show you."

"You have the license," John said. "See ya back home."

With the heat suits glistening in the blue light, John and Bryan bolted up the ramp. At the truck, beyond the frozen blue soldiers, a dejected Boyd and Frank watched the ramp fold into its invisible cut.

Frank climbed into the cab's passenger seat. Boyd walked around the back of the trailer checking for loose material. There was none and he climbed up into the driver's side.

"You think He meant it?" Boyd asked, as they stared across at the ship. "About taking us for a ride later?"

"Hell, I don't know," Frank sighed. "I wasn't gonna argue with Him. No telling what He might have done."

"Sure hope He did," Boyd said. "Man! That's a once in a lifetime ride."

"Come on, let's get out of here," Frank said. "I don't want to be around when He unzaps those Blue Berets."

Boyd started the truck's diesel and threw it into gear. The truck chugged up the gully's ridge above what was left of their camp. The scorched tarp lay in shreds where the van had been.

"Hold it!" Frank said, as they were about to turn from the ridge. "Let's see it take off." Boyd stopped and they waited.

Inside the ship, the group finished zipping up their suits as Enki cleared His lock-up. He stood on the lighted disk in front of the pilot's chair and threw some switches on the panel only His long arms could reach. A ray of bright light from the disk above passed through Him and into the disk below. The ship whined softly and came to life.

"Why didn't it start when we did that with David?" John asked.

"*David's body canceled the charge,*" Enki said. He

settled into His chair. *"Ye bodies are of Earth, diluted to a two string DNA, and ye shall remain of the Earth. Only when thy knowest thy inherent power shall thy venture forth unto other dimensions."*

The whine of the ship faded into a deep, soothing hum. They couldn't feel it, but the view on the screens showed they were moving up above the tree tops.

"Starting the ship would hath given thee little purpose," Enki said. *"Its zero time reference is of this place, and a time portal. My reason for thou returning her straight away."*

Boyd and Frank gaped from under the truck's roof. The ship moved slowly and silently above the tree line. Its blue beam retracted and the Generals and Blue Berets collapsed in their tracks.

The ship circled the area, did a couple of quick zigs and zags and vanished into a fold of time.

"Damn!" Boyd gasped. "Isn't that something? Now you see it, now you don't. Beautiful fold. He can really fly that baby!"

He put the truck in gear and they rumbled on across the pasture trail. Almost to the ranch house they met the Barrett's truck and them with their canister of coffee heading for the gully.

"Where ya'll going?" Roland shouted as he stopped.

"It's all over," Boyd said through his open window. "The god showed up and took His ship."

"He did?" Roland frowned. "Damnation! Why didn't ya'll call us or somethin'?"

"Couldn't. It happened too fast."

"Well, where're the others? They gonna be comin'? We got this coffee . . . "

"No. no need," Boyd said. "The van got smashed, so the god gave 'em a ride back home."

Roland thought about it before he said, "Are you spoofin' us?"

"No, no. It's the truth, God help us, we wouldn't kid you about something like this," Boyd said. "They're gone. You can go see for yourself. But, I wouldn't right now. There's some Air Force people down there that're pretty shook up."

GENERALS FULLER AND RAWLINS roused themselves from their stupor. They felt numb all over and their heads ached. In their daze they painfully surveyed the scene. Blue Berets were picking themselves up and stumbling around in the lights from the helicopters, their big blades again slowly clicking in neutral.

"What happened?" a bewildered Rawlins muttered. "What are we doing here?"

Fuller frowned and rubbed his vacant temples. "I have no idea," he said. "Seems like, I faintly remember something about a space ship."

Rawlins winced. "Yes. Yes. A space ship. Where?"

Fuller's eyes narrowed. "They flew off in that ship," he mumbled. "Why is it I have this need to tell everyone?"

Chapter Thirty:
The Onus

THERE WAS NO WEIGHTLESSNESS within the ship. John and Bryan were not surprised. Having studied the power systems of alien craft John had drawn up after his tour of the Groom Lake fleet, they knew the electromagnetic field and gravity wave were set by the gravity amplifiers and the wave guide terminator. The cabin enclosure had its own pocket of gravitation and they felt very comfortable even in their heat suits. Unless it was in, or under, His robes, Enki wore no protection. Seeing Him conduct the ship's starting charge was enough proof He didn't need any.

Bryan caught a glance and smile from Karen after Enki had transmitted the starting charge. "Does that solve the sparkler mystery?" he had whispered and they shared a private grin.

Enki opened the viewing screens all around the ship's inner walls. The wide strip suddenly appeared as though see-through metal, far surpassing the scope of the best Circlarama theatre.

The sun was behind Earth's blue sphere in the rear screens, and the silvery moon hung in the blackness to their left front. Except for the space junk zooming by around them, there was no sensation of motion, as if they were standing still in time. "We're looking for one with a big flag," John said, as if Enki needed a reminder. The group watched, standing in a semicircle around the back of His *chair.*

"*Yay, 'tis sad thy mixture of fear and technology,*" Enki said, *as the tagged satellite came into view heading in* the opposite direction.

"That one!" Bryan barked. Enki had already put His ship in a tight reverse oblique.

They came alongside the satellite and gave it a thorough inspection. "*We must be careful.*" Enki said. He turned His ship to face the satellite and flipped open the covers over the laser firing buttons. He reached some buttons on the control panel and a skeleton picture of the satellite, showing its working parts, flickered onto a monitor. Enki studied the diagram before firing His lasers. He held the lasers on steady beams as He tilted the ship. The beams moved across the satellite's rear, cutting off it's control section and the flag. The satellite was, now, just so much junk.

"Why not just blast it?" Bryan asked.

"*An atomic explosion-implosion of that size, out here, might cause a black hole,*" Enki said. "*We hath no need for more, nor to visit a neighboring universe.*"

"If we had been able to fly your ship," John mused, "come out here and blasted that satellite, we would have been sucked through the hole."

"*Yay,*" Enki said to the monitor as He clicked it off.

They glanced at each other, shaking their heads, incredulously. Thank goodness for not starting the ship.

"*Ye hath no concept of the universe,*" Enki said, "*as ye hath little knowing of thou connections to its dimensions.*"

"Is there any way we can get them to understand, see, what they're doing?" Myra asked.

"*Expose them for who they be,*" Enki said. "*Take back thy lives, and thy planet. Ye are now armed with much evidence in thou knowing.*"

"Are you kidding?" Susan huffed. "No one's gonna

believe this. Unless, you stay. They'll listen to you. Be our proof.''

"Proof is everywhere," Enki said. *"Its truth hath been twisted much beyond a sudden repent. Yet, there is time."*

"But, but, we have prospered much since you were here last. There's TV, movies, books, newspapers," Myra pointed out. "You could be everywhere, reach everyone in one big sweep. Your message wouldn't be just from a mountain top this time. It could be in the great stadiums. People would come. I know they would."

"Nay." Enki shook His head. *"Doth thy form of crucifixion matter?"*

"Don't take on an earthly body this time," Karen said. "Just be yourself, our Creator, the actual Son of God."

"Yes!" Susan said. "A few lightning bolts thrown in the right places will get their attention. It sure did mine."

Life's experiences, through hundreds of thousands of years, had taught Enki that all His mistakes had been results of His trouble dealing with feminine wiles. He had learned the hard way that a simple no would have kept Him from being a victim. *"Nay, 'tis a late hour,"* He said. He stood, benevolently, towering over them. On the screens behind Him, Earth rose to meet them. *"Thy destiny hath been marked. Only those of the knowing will be numbered 144,000. Those in ego insanity, fear, ignorance and religions will perish. Anu will not waiver."* Business as usual. Cut the partying: lying, cheating, stealing, killing. *"Learn thy lessons from thy history. Ye are greater."*

The space ship settled down over the Gulf waters and sailed quickly and silently to the beach in front of Karen's house, a beach Enki had known many pleasant times with Karen as David.

"This it?" John smiled, sadly. "I was hoping we could talk you into a tour of Mars while we were at it."

"What know ye body of Mars?" Enki said, as He

opened a shaft of blue light to the beach.

"Yeah, I guess not," John said. "Just a pass by would be asking too much?"

Enki shook His head and moved to the shaft of light.

"Yeah, well, I guess this is it," John said, glancing down the shaft at the beach. Enki hugged him, then watched as John disappeared in the blue shaft.

Enki embraced each one over the shaft.

Myra said, "I still want a picture," and slipped away.

"It was good to know you," Susan smiled. "Wish we had more time." She was gone.

"You were all I hoped you'd be. See you." Bryan said, his words fading away in the blueness.

"I will remember our days always," Karen said, as she held Enki. "I will miss you."

"*And I you,*" Enki whispered. "*Ye were indeed a princess lost. I shall watch over thee, and thy shall hath a special place.*"

He removed one of his gold snake armlets, put it on her arm and squeezed it closed.

"What would your wives say?" Karen grinned.

Enki shrugged. "*No more than thee.*"

They kissed and sparks fell all around them. She slipped into the blue and was gone.

The shaft of blue light had released each in a circle on the beach beyond the surf's reach. Dazed, one by one they slowly slipped back into their earth time, picked themselves up, and searched the clear, starry sky. Turning around and around, from horizon to horizon, there was no sign of the space ship. The full moon, only moments before so close, shone back at them from so far away.

"We were just there," an entranced Susan said to the moon. "Now we're here, zip, zip, zoom, just like that." She looked at her recorder hanging from its strap around her wrist. It was still recording. She stopped it and put it into rewind.

Bryan looked at his watch and unzipped his heat suit. "Two thirty," he remarked. He slipped his arms out of his suit.

The others began to discard their suits.

"Anybody see him go?" Myra asked.

"I did," Karen said. "That way." She pointed toward the southwest. "It was so fast. Just a red streak, then nothing."

Seeing her standing there, alone, the others suddenly shared her strange feeling of loss.

"Gone to find his 12,000 knowing souls," Karen added.

"Yeah," John sighed. "I wish him luck."

"He's a god." Susan said. "His judgement is rather thorough and true, wouldn't you say? I don't think He's gonna take any bull from anyone. No half-hearted accepting the miracle."

They were about a hundred yards up the beach from Karen's house. Bryan began wandering in that direction, dragging his suit behind him. Still a bit perturbed, the others followed, stringing out along the beach. Bryan saw Stanley flying toward them. He circled around and floated the stiff breeze above them.

"Yeah, I guess you're right," John said, almost to himself. "We're lucky we had a chance to know the truth. Did anyone hear Him say for sure we're going to have a place in Their rescue?"

No one answered. Perhaps they hadn't heard him. The surf roared and lapped the beach. Except for a scattering of outside lights, the beach houses were dark. Somewhere in the distance a loud burglar alarm rang.

"Twenty, twenty-five years from now," Myra said. "I'll be too old to care if I'm rescued. He should be looking for younger people."

"Old, young," Bryan said. "All anyone needs to know is that their only sin is the mistake of not knowing.

Correct it, and be young forever. I feel ten years younger already."

"Just think," Susan said to the dark beach houses. "Twenty years, all of this will be gone. Everything'll be gone. Cities, homes, cars, money, people . . . everything. All that'll be left will be 144,000 people with nothing but the clothes on their backs, looking down at a ball of water in space. Can you imagine that."

"It happened once," Bryan said. "And they started all over. We'll do it again."

"Well, at least Anu's allowing us more than a boat load this time," Myra said.

Bryan stumbled up the boondock bridge steps. He tossed his suit on the railing and sat down on the top step. Karen did the same and sat down beside him. Susan, Myra and then John, tossed their suits atop the others and slumped wearily on the bottom steps. Exhausted, they quietly stared at the Gulf waves and the stars above. Stanley settled onto the bridge railing behind them and pranced closer.

"He had us all the way," Karen said. 'Getting in, watching, pushing us to our limits, making us experience our reality. He gave us so much to live by. How can we pass it on without Him?"

"We have your tapes," Bryan said.

"I have my tape," Susan said. She held her recorder up an pushed the play button. David's voice in the gully came through loud and clear. "I think it's all on here. The fight and Enki on His ship."

"That's great!" Bryan smiled. "When we find that someone who knows what we're talking about and will risk publishing your book, we'll have the tapes as proof."

"Where's that alarm?" Myra said over her shoulder. "Why doesn't someone turn it off? Robbing and stealing, someone thinks their stuff is worth protecting."

"You think the tapes will be too tough?" Karen said.

"I mean, for anyone not already aware of the knowing?"

"Only egos make the knowing tough," John said. "If they won't let go of the insanity of fears and illusions, and return to the sanity of love, then they don't get saved."

"That's their selection test?" Susan said.

"Yes," Bryan said. "Someone reads the book, listens to the tapes, and says, 'Yes! That's right! I see the truth,' and then starts practicing it. Then I'd say it's pretty clear they will probably make the cut."

The burglar alarm in the distance stopped ringing. "Thank, God," Myra said. The others gave her a look. She shrugged.

"Enki's probably somewhere right now getting set to pull off the same tests He did with us with someone else," Karen said.

"Lucky people," Susan said.

"He'll have to go some if He expects to reach His quota by the time Nebiru gets here," John said.

"There's twelve of Them," Myra said. "Probably working 'round the clock."

"It's obvious that Enki's depending on us to help Him spread Their message," Bryan said. "Why else would He have taken the time?"

"That's the joy in *getting it*," Karen said. "I can't help but want everyone else to know the peace of that love."

"Better be careful there," John said. "So many are just not ready to believe in other dimensions."

"What about those friends who don't, or won't, *get it*?" Susan said. "What can we say when that planet shows up and the waters start rising?"

"We could be one of them," Myra said. "I mean, we could all *get it* and still not be chosen. I mean, with the growing New Thought movement nowadays, I'm sure there will be more than 144,000 who'll *get it*, don't you?"

Everyone quietly thought about that while a dozen

waves rolled onto shore.

"I never knew a god could have so much guilt," Bryan mused.

"I've always wondered why MJ-12 wouldn't admit they were dealing with the aliens," John said. "All those years, killing those involved, covering it up, saying that the public couldn't handle the truth. Maybe they knew about Nebiru coming back, and what's going to happen when it does. I can see why now. Outside the panic, and the storming of Groom Lake, Los Alamos and Lancaster, there would be a worldwide purge of government leaders. Then a futile depression over being too late to do anything. There would be no future, no hope."

"Maybe we shouldn't tell anyone either," Myra said. "I can't say as I relish the thought of starting over."

They noticed a car coming up the beach toward them. As it passed close to some outside lights, they recognized the roof light bar of a police car. It wasn't unusual to see them patrolling the beach at that hour.

"That's the whole point of Enki showing us our knowing," Karen said. "Don't you see? That's why everything happened the way it did, so we would understand. We *got it*. And now we owe our understanding of the knowing to anyone who wants to heal his pain with his power. That's what loving your neighbor's all about. We have to give everyone a shot at knowing, whether they realize their presence of self to believe, or not."

The patrol car rolled to a stop in front of them. The door shield said they were from Pirates' Beach, a village up the road. Karen recognized the heavy set cop in the passenger seat.

"Evening, folks," the cop said. "How're ya'll tonight?"

"Just getting some air, Mike," Karen said, standing and stretching. "Great night, isn't it? What brings you guys down this far?"

"Some people up the beach, some night fishermen, called in," Mike raised a thumb toward the back of the car. "Said they saw a UFO somewhere down this way." He grinned real big and shrugged. "You folks didn't happen to see anything, did ya?"

The five exchanged quizzical glances, smiled and chuckled. The cops chuckled, too.

"Nope," Karen shrugged. "Can't say as we have. When did they say they saw this UFO?"

"About half an hour ago."

"Naw. We were out here before that," John said. "Didn't see any UFO. Did they say what it looked like?"

"Round. Blue light coming outta the bottom."

"No. Nothing like that. Sorry." John said. Myra and Susan covered a giggle.

"Where was that burglar alarm, Mike?" Karen asked, changing the subject and glancing up the beach.

"Charlie Bolivar's", Mike said.

"Charlie's?" Karen gasped. "Somebody broke into Charlie's?! They wouldn't dare!"

"Yeah," Mike said. "The place's a mess. Strange thing is, we couldn't find Charlie. He's disappeared."

"Charlie's gone?" Karen said.

"Yeah. It's not like him at all," Mike said. "His wife said he was there one minute, gone the next. Vanished. We looked all over. Finally had to smash the alarm ourselves."

Karen and Bryan had to stifle a laugh.

"What's so funny?" Mike asked.

"Nothing," Karen said, forcing a straightened face. "Nothing at all. Just a private joke."

"Hmmm," Mike mused, studying them. He couldn't think of anything funny about Charlie being missing. "Ya'll wouldn't happen to know where he is, would you?"

"Nope," Karen said. "Gone's gone."

"Well, you folks have a good evening," Mike said.

"And if you see Charlie, tell him to get home."

"We will," Karen said. "Goodnight."

The patrol car turned around and headed back up the beach. When it was far enough away, Karen looked at Bryan and their repressed laughter gushed out. The others laughed at their laugher, not knowing why, waiting for an explanation.

Karen held up her palm. "All right!" she shouted. Bryan slapped her high five.

Stanley lifted up from his perch and circled above them. He gave out a few squawks that sounded a lot like laughter, too.

"Charlie's getting the ride of his miserable little life," Karen laughed along with Bryan.

REFERENCES

THE BIBLE, Aramaic version.

A COURSE IN MIRACLES, Foundation for Inner Peace, New York, Colman Graphics, 1977.

THE EARTH CHRONICLES, Zecharia Sitchin:
   The Twelfth Planet, New York, Avon Books, 1976.
   The Stairway to Heaven, New York, Avon Books, 1980.
   The Wars of Gods and Men, New York, Avon Books, 1985.
   The Lost Realms, New York, Avon Books, 1990.
   Genesis Revisited, New York, Avon Books, 1990.
   When Time Began, New York, Avon Books, 1993.
   Divine Encounters, New York, Avon Books, 1995

MAJESTIC, Whitley Strieber, New York, Berkley, 1989.
TRANSFORMATION, Whitley Strieber, New York, Avon, 1988. *COMMUNION*, Whitley Strieber, New York, Avon, 1987.

SECRET LIFE, David M. Jacobs, Ph.D, New York, Simon & Schuster, 1992.

THE MONTAUK PROJECT, Preston Nichols with Peter Moon, New York, Sky Books, 1992.

MONTAUK REVISITED, Preston Nichols with Peter Moon, New York, Sky Books, 1993.

THE UNIVERSE AND DR. EINSTEIN, Lincoln Barnett, New York, Bantam, 1968.

A BRIEF HISTORY OF TIME, Stephen W. Hawking, New York, Bantam, 1988.

JOHN VON NEUMANN AND NORBERT WIENER, Steve J. Helms, MIT Massachusetts, 1982.

JFK-THE BOOK OF THE FILM, Oliver Stone & Sklar Zachary, New York, Applause, 1992.

A NATION BETRAYED, James "Bo" Gritz, Nevada, Lazarus, 1988.

EXTRA-TERRESTRIALS AMONG US, George C. Andrews, Georgia, Llewellyn, 1987.
EXTRA-TERRESTRIAL FRIENDS AND FOES, George C. Andrews, Georgia, Illuminet, 1993.

THE GEMSTONE FILE, Jim Keith, Georgia, Illuminet Press, 1992.

THE PHILADELPHIA EXPERIMENT & OTHER UFO CONSPIRACIES, Brad Steiger with Al Bielek, New Jersey, Inner Light, 1990.

ABOVE TOP SECRET, Timothy Good, New York, Morrow, 1988.

THE GULF BREEZE SIGHTINGS, Ed & Frances Walters, New York, Morrow 1990.

AN ALIEN HARVEST, Linda M. Howe, Pioneer, 1989.

MUFON INTERNATIONAL SYMPOSIUM PROCEEDINGS & JOURNAL, Seguin, Texas 1989-95.

DIMENSIONS, CONSCIOUSNESS & NON-LOCALITY, Simon HarveyWilson, Mufon Journal, Seguin, Texas, 1995.

MISSING TIME, Bud Hopkins, New York, Berkeley, 1981.
INTRUDERS, Bud Hopkins, New York, Random, 1987.

EXCALIBER BRIEFING, Thomas Bearden, Strawberry Hill, 1980.

THE PRISM OF LYRA, Lyssa Royal & Keith Priest, Arizona, Royal-Priest, 1989.

VISITORS FROM WITHIN, Lyssa Royal & Keith Priest, Arizona, Royal-Priest, 1992.

Disc: Zeta Sport Craft at Groom Lake S-4, Robert Lazar & Gene Huff, PUL/JFL, Las Vegas, Nevada, 1994.

About the Author:

Al Bates as a NASA astronaut? No. A neat illusion. Separating our illusions from our realities is a gift of the *Knowing*.

During an abduction/contact in December of '82, Al Bates met the Nefilim and was asked to write the story that is THE KNOWING. He is from Louisiana and now lives in Houston.